GORDON R. DICKSON

ENDS

BAEN
BOOKS

ENDS

Copyright © 1988 by Gordon R. Dickson

A Baen Books Original

Baen Publishing Enterprises
260 Fifth Avenue
New York, N.Y. 10001

First printing, October 1988

ISBN: 0-671-69782-X

Cover art by Carl Lundgren

Printed in the United States of America

Distributed by
SIMON & SCHUSTER
1230 Avenue of the Americas
New York, N.Y. 10020

TABLE OF CONTENTS

ONE AGAINST THREE THOUSAND . . .

The shouting of the soldiers had stopped, suddenly. The front line was trying to slow down against the pressure of those behind. The attack was halting as more and more of them checked and stared at the slope.

What was happening there was that the lid of El Conde's private exit from Gebel Nahar was rising. To the Naharese military it must have looked as if some secret weapon was about to unveil itself on the slope—and it would have been this that had caused them to have sudden doubts and dig in their heels.

But of course no such weapon came out. Instead, what emerged was a head wearing a regimental cap, with what looked like a stick tilted back by its right ear . . . and slowly, up onto the level of the ground, and out to face them all came Michael.

He was without weapons. But he was dressed in his full parade regimentals as band officer; and the *gaita gallega* was resting in his arms. He stepped onto the slope and began to march down it toward the Naharese.

The silence was deadly; and into that silence, striking up, came the clear sound of the bagpipe. Clear and strong it came to us; and clearly it reached as well to the now-silent and motionless ranks of the Naharese.

He went forward at a march step, shoulders level, the instrument held securely in his arms; and his playing went before him, throwing its challenge directly into their faces. A single figure marching against three thousand.

Foreword

It is surprising, as I've been telling audiences from platforms for years, how often it is forgotten that the words of a story are really only vehicles for that story, itself. I say this because, in a very real sense, any story is made as much by the reader as by the writer. In fact, in at least one sense, it is not wrong to say that it is made more by the reader than by the writer—since the reader has the final word as to whether the character is likeable, or unlikeable; the scene real, or unreal.

This fact is not so much forgotten as overlooked—not only by readers themselves, but by those who must work to bring the story into print: editors and copyeditors, typesetters; even those who sit in the padded chair of the publisher, himself or herself.

Even by writers, it is forgotten—at least on a conscious level. But no one can succeed in making a publishable and readable story without appreciating the fact on some level.

What I am saying is, first, that it is impossible to

tell a story unless you have one within you to tell. And within you, the story is not in words, but in an invisible, rare and magic stuff spun by the imaginative machinery of the writer.

By the same token, no reader can ever live through the story in the pages before him or her unless he uses his own version of that same imaginative machinery—to turn the words before him back into that same invisible, rare and magical stuff. It takes as much imagination to read as to write. . . .

And when a reader does this, his or her mental fingerprints mark the story forever. That's because no writer—not even the greatest—has the power to *make* you, the reader, see as much as a stray cat. The very most the writer can do is make a signal to you, the reader—by the words into which he has translated his own magical stuff—to reproduce such a cat from the magic of your own magical stuff.

Look at those words, *of your own*, again; because they are the key to all the enjoyment that the art of story-telling has ever been able to achieve for those receiving its product. A story-teller could use a million words to describe that same stray cat and still not succeed in making you see, in your mind, that cat that he, himself, sees as he writes. Because you, the reader, will indeed see a cat, if you take that story into your imaginative machinery—but it won't be the same cat that the writer saw. If you see any cat at all, it will be *your* cat.

Nor will any other reader see the same cat that you see. Another reader will see his own cat—and no other. It will be a cat composed from that person's own life-experiences and his inventive abilities. And all of that person's reactions to the cat he's reading about will be affected by the reactions he or she has had to cats in general, and to particular cats he has known. No matter how strongly the author tries to bend that reaction to some end of his own—people are different, and each of us sees a slightly different cat.

That's why, in the end—and if they only discuss it long enough—no two readers will ever react in exactly the same fashion to the same story. There must be some point of disagreement about it—because each of them has not read the same story as the other. Rather, each read the story that they made for themselves out of the words put before them; and it is the reader who usually determines if the story has, or has not, worked for him.

So it is with the hope that you, who will read this, will find the materials beyond this page and between these covers agreeable to the machinery of your imagination, that I leave you to the stories that follow. From this last word on, you, not I, are the writer of them.

—*Gordon R. Dickson*

Á Outrance

Within the ruined chapel, the full knight
Woke from the coffin of his last-night's bed;
And clashing mailed feet on the broken stones—
Strode to the shattered lintel and looked out.

A fog lay holding all the empty land
A cloak of cloudy and uncertainness,
That hid the earth; in that enfoliate mist
Moved voices wandered from a dream of death.

A warhorse, cropping by the chapel wall,
Raised maul-head, dripping thistles on the stones;
And struck his hooves; and jingled all his gear.
"Peace . . ." said the Knight. "Be still. Today, we rest.

"The mist is hiding all the battlefield.
"The wind whips on the wave-packs of the sea.
"Our foe is bound by this no less than we.
"Rest," said the Knight. "We do not fight today."

The warhorse stamped again. And struck his hooves.
Ringing on cobbled dampness of the stones.
Crying—"Ride! Ride! Ride!" And the Knight mounted him.
Slowly. And rode him slowly out to war.

COMPUTERS DON'T ARGUE

Treasure Book Club
PLEASE DO NOT FOLD, SPINDLE
OR MUTILATE THIS CARD

Mr: Walter A. Child Balance: $4.98
Dear Customer: Enclosed is your latest book
selection. "Kidnapped," by Robert Louis
Stevenson.

> 437 Woodlawn Drive
> Panduk, Michigan
> Nov. 16, 1965

Treasure Book Club
1823 Mandy Street
Chicago, Illinois

Dear Sirs:
  I wrote you recently about the computer
punch card you sent, billing me for "Kim,"
by Rudyard Kipling. I did not open the pack-

age containing it until I had already mailed you my check for the amount on the card. On opening the package, I found the book missing half its pages. I sent it back to you, requesting either another copy or my money back. Instead, you have sent me a copy of "Kidnapped," by Robert Louis Stevenson. Will you please straighten this out?

I hereby return the copy of "Kidnapped."

Sincerely yours,
Walter A. Child

Treasure Book Club
SECOND NOTICE
PLEASE DO NOT FOLD, SPINDLE
OR MUTILATE THIS CARD

Mr: Walter A. Child Balance: $4.98
For "Kidnapped," by Robert Louis Stevenson
(If remittance has been made for the above, please disregard this notice)

437 Woodlawn Drive
Panduk, Michigan
Jan. 21, 1966

Treasure Book Club
1823 Mandy Street
Chicago, Illinois

Dear Sirs:

May I direct your attention to my letter of November 16, 1965? You are still continuing to dun me with computer punch cards for a book I did not order. Whereas, actually, it is your company that owes *me* money.

Sincerely yours,
Walter A. Child

Treasure Book Club
1823 Mandy Street
Chicago, Illinois
Feb. 1, 1966

Mr. Walter A. Child
437 Woodlawn Drive
Panduk, Michigan

Dear Mr. Child:
   We have sent you a number of reminders
concerning an amount owing to us as a result of book purchases you have made from
us. This amount, which is $4.98, is now long
overdue.
   This situation is disappointing to us, particularly since there was no hesitation on our
part in extending you credit at the time
original arrangements for these purchases
were made by you. If we do not receive
payment in full by return mail, we will be
forced to turn the matter over to a collection
agency.

Very truly yours,
Samuel P. Grimes
Collection Mgr.

437 Woodlawn Drive
Panduk, Michigan
Feb. 5, 1966

Dear Mr. Grimes:
   Will you stop sending me punch cards and
form letters and make me some kind of a
direct answer from a human being?
   I don't owe you money. *You* owe me
money. Maybe I should turn your company
over to a collection agency.

Walter A. Child

FEDERAL COLLECTION OUTFIT
88Prince Street
Chicago, Illinois
Feb. 28, 1966

Mr. Walter A. Child
437 Woodlawn Drive
Panduk, Michigan

Dear Mr. Child:
Your account with the Treasure Book Club, of $4.98 plus interest and charges, has been turned over to our agency for collection. The amount due is now $6.83. Please send your check for this amount or we shall be forced to take immediate action.

Jacob N. Harshe
Vice President

FEDERAL COLLECTION OUTFIT
88 Prince Street
Chicago, Illinois
April 8, 1966

Mr. Walter A. Child
437 Woodlawn Drive
Panduk, Michigan

Dear Mr. Child:
You have seen fit to ignore our courteous requests to settle your long overdue account with Treasure Book Club, which is now, with accumulated interest and charges, in the amount of $7.51.
If payment in full is not forthcoming by April 11, 1966, we will be forced to turn the matter over to our attorneys for immediate court action.

Ezekiel B. Harshe
President

MALONEY, MAHONEY,
MACNAMARA and PRUITT
Attorneys

89 Prince Street
Chicago, Illinois
April 29, 1966

Mr. Walter A. Child
437 Woodlawn Drive
Panduk, Michigan

Dear Mr. Child:
   Your indebtedness to the Treasure Book
Club has been referred to us for legal action
to collect.
   This indebtedness is now in the amount of
$10.01. If you will send us this amount so
that we may receive it before May 5, 1966,
the matter may be satisfied. However, if we
do not receive satisfaction in full by that
date, we will take steps to collect through
the courts.
   I am sure you will see the advantage of
avoiding a judgment against you, which as a
matter of record would do lasting harm to
your credit rating.

Very truly yours,
Hagthorpe M. Pruitt, Jr.
Attorney at Law

437 Woodlawn Drive
Panduk, Michigan
May 4, 1966

Mr. Hagthorpe M. Pruitt, Jr.
Maloney, Mahoney, MacNamara and Pruitt
89 Prince Street
Chicago, Illinois

Dear Mr. Pruitt:
   You don't know what a pleasure it is to me in this matter to get a letter from a live human being to whom I can explain the situation.
   This whole matter is silly. I explained it fully in my letters to the Treasure Book Company. But I might as well have been trying to explain to the computer that puts out their punch cards, for all the good it seemed to do. Briefly, what happened was, I ordered a copy of "Kim," by Rudyard Kipling, for $4.98. When I opened the package they sent me, I found the book had only half its pages, but I'd previously mailed a check to pay them for the book.
   I sent the book back to them, asking either for a whole copy or my money back. Instead, they sent me a copy of "Kidnapped," by Robert Louis Stevenson—which I had not ordered; and for which they have been trying to collect from me.
   Meanwhile, I am still waiting for the money back that they owe me for the copy of "Kim" that I didn't get. That's the whole story. Maybe you can help me straighten them out.
Relievedly yours,
Walter A Child
P.S.: I also sent them back their copy of "Kidnapped," as soon as I got it, but it hasn't seemed to help. They have never even acknowledged getting it back.

MALONEY, MAHONEY,
MACNAMARA and PRUITT
Attorneys

89 Prince Street
Chicago, Illinois
May 9, 1966

Mr. Walter A. Child
437 Woodlawn Drive
Panduk, Michigan

Dear Mr. Child:
I am in possession of no information indicating that any item purchased by you from
the Treasure Book Club has been returned.
I would hardly think that, if the case had
been as you stated, the Treasure Book Club
would have retained us to collect the amount
owing from you.
If I do not receive your payment in full
within three days, by May 12, 1966, we will
be forced to take legal action.

Very truly yours,
Hagthorpe M. Pruitt, Jr.

COURT OF MINOR CLAIMS
Chicago, Illinois

Mr. Walter A. Child
437 Woodlawn Drive
Panduk, Michigan

Be informed that a judgment was taken
and entered against you in this court this
day of May 26, 1966, in the amount of $15.66
including court costs.
Payment in satisfaction of this judgment
may be made to this court or to the ad-

judged creditor. In the case of payment being made to the creditor, a release should be obtained from the creditor and filed with this court in order to free you of legal obligation in connection with this judgment.

Under the recent Reciprocal Claims Act, if you are a citizen of a different state, a duplicate claim may be automatically entered and judged against you in your own state so that collection may be made there as well as in the State of Illinois.

COURT OF MINOR CLAIMS
Chicago, Illinois
PLEASE DO NOT FOLD, SPINDLE
OR MUTILATE THIS CARD

Judgment was passed this day of May 27, 1966, under Statute $15.66
Against: Child, Walter A., of 437 Woodlawn Drive, Panduk, Michigan. Pray to enter a duplicate claim for judgment
In: Picayune Court—Panduk, Michigan
For Amount: Statute 941

437 Woodlawn Drive
Panduk, Michigan
May 31, 1966

Samuel P. Grimes
Vice President, Treasure Book Club
1823 Mandy Street
Chicago, Illinois

Grimes:
This business has gone far enough. I've got to come down to Chicago on business of my own tomorrow. I'll see you then and

we'll get this straightened out once and for
all, about who owes what to whom, and how
much!

Yours,
Walter A. Child

From the Desk of the Clerk
Picayune Court

June 1, 1966

Harry:
   The attached computer card from Chicago's Minor Claims Court against A. Walter
has a 1500-series Statute number on it. That
puts it over in Criminal with you, rather
than Civil, with me. So I herewith submit it
for your computer instead of mine. How's
business?

Joe

CRIMINAL RECORDS
Panduk, Michigan
PLEASE DO NOT FOLD, SPINDLE
OR MUTILATE THIS CARD

Convicted: (Child) A. Walter
On: May 26, 1966
Address: 437 Woodlawn Drive
Panduk, Mich.
Crim: Statute: 1566 (Corrected) 1567
Crime: Kidnap
Date: Nov. 16, 1965
Notes: At large. To be picked up at once.

POLICE DEPARTMENT, PANDUK, MICHIGAN. TO
POLICE DEPARTMENT CHICAGO ILLINOIS. CON-
VICTED SUBJECT A. (COMPLETE FIRST NAME UN-

KNOWN) WALTER, SOUGHT HERE IN CONNECTION
REF. YOUR NOTIFICATION OF JUDGMENT FOR KID-
NAP OF CHILD NAMED ROBERT LOUIS STEVEN-
SON, ON NOV. 16, 1965. INFORMATION HERE INDI-
CATES SUBJECT FLED HIS RESIDENCE, AT 437
WOODLAND DRIVE, PANDUK, AND MAY BE AGAIN
IN YOUR AREA.

POSSIBLE CONTACT IN YOUR AREA: THE TREA-
SURE BOOK CLUB, 1823 MANDY STREET, CHI-
CAGO, ILLINOIS. SUBJECT NOT KNOWN TO BE DAN-
GEROUS. PICK UP AND HOLD, ADVISING US OF
CAPTURE . . .

TO POLICE DEPARTMENT, PANDUK, MICHIGAN.
REFERENCE YOUR REQUEST TO PICK UP AND
HOLD A. (COMPLETE FIRST NAME UNKNOWN)
WALTER, WANTED IN PANDUK ON STATUTE 1567,
CRIME OF KIDNAPPING.

SUBJECT ARRESTED AT OFFICES OF TREASURE
BOOK CLUB, OPERATING THERE UNDER ALIAS
WALTER ANTHONY CHILD AND ATTEMPTING TO
COLLECT $4.98 FROM ONE SAMUEL P. GRIMES,
EMPLOYEE OF THAT COMPANY.

DISPOSAL: HOLDING FOR YOUR ADVICE.

POLICE DEPARTMENT PANDUK, MICHIGAN, TO
POLICE DEPARTMENT CHICAGO, ILLINOIS

REF: A. WALTER (ALIAS WALTER ANTHONY CHILD)
SUBJECT WANTED FOR CRIME OF KIDNAP, YOUR
AREA, REF: YOUR COMPUTER PUNCH CARD NOTIFI-
CATION OF JUDGMENT, DATED MAY 27, 1966.
COPY OUR CRIMINAL RECORDS PUNCH CARD HERE-
WITH FORWARDED TO YOUR COMPUTER SECTION.

CRIMINAL RECORDS
Chicago, Illinois
PLEASE DO NOT FOLD, SPINDLE
OR MUTILATE THIS CARD

SUBJECT (CORRECTION—OMITTED RECORD SUP-
PLIED)
APPLICABLE STATUTE NO. 1567

JUDGMENT NO. 456789

TRIAL RECORD: APPARENTLY MISFILED AND UNAVAILABLE

DIRECTION: TO APPEAR FOR SENTENCING BE-FORE JUDGE JOHN ALEXANDER MCDIVOT, COURT-ROOM A, JUNE 9, 1966

From the Desk of
Judge Alexander J. McDivot

June 2, 1966

Dear Tony:

I've got an adjudged criminal coming up before me for sentencing Thursday morning— but the trial transcript is apparently misfiled.

I need some kind of information (Ref: A. Walter—Judgment No. 456789, Criminal). For example, what about the victim of the kidnapping. Was victim harmed?

Jack McDivot

June 3, 1966

Records Search Unit
Re: Ref: Judgment No. 456789—was victim harmed?

Tonio Malagasi
Records Division

June 3, 1966

To: United States Statistics Office
Attn.: Information Section
Subject: Robert Louis Stevenson
Query: Information concerning

Records Search Unit
Criminal Records Division
Police Department
Chicago, Ill.

June 5, 1966

To: Records Search Unit
Criminal Records Division
Police Department
Chicago, Illinois
Subject: Your query re Robert Louis Ste-
venson (File no. 189623)
Action: Subject deceased. Age at death, 44
yrs. Further information requested?

A.K.
Information Section
U. S. Statistics Office

June 6, 1966

To: United States Statistics Office
Attn.: Information Division
Subject: RE: File no. 189623
    No further information required.

Thank you.
Records Search Unit

Criminal Records Division
Police Department
Chicago, Illinois

June 7, 1966

To: Tonio Malagasi
Records Division
Re: Ref: Judgment No. 456789—victim is
dead.

Records Search Unit

June 7, 1966

To: Judge Alexander J. McDivot's Chambers
Dear Jack:
Ref: Judgment No. 456789. The victim in
this kidnap case was apparently slain.

From the strange lack of background information on the killer and his victim, as well as the victim's age, this smells to me like a gangland killing. This for your information. Don't quote me. It seems to me, though, that Stevenson—the victim—has a name that rings a faint bell with me. Possibly, one of the East Coast Mob, since the association comes back to me as something about pirates—possibly New York dockage hijackers—and something about buried loot.

As I say, above is only speculation for your private guidance.

Any time I can help . . .

Best,
Tony Malagasi
Records Division

MICHAEL R. REYNOLDS
Attorney-at-law
49 Water Street
Chicago, Illinois
June 8, 1966

Dear Tim:

Regrets: I can't make the fishing trip. I've been court-appointed here to represent a man about to be sentenced tomorrow on a kidnapping charge.

Ordinarily, I might have tried to beg off, and McDivot, who is doing the sentencing, would probably have turned me loose. But this is the damnedest thing you ever heard of.

The man being sentenced has apparently been not only charged, but adjudged guilty as a result of a comedy of errors too long to go into here. He not only isn't guilty—he's got the best case I ever heard of for damages against one of the larger Book Clubs headquartered here in Chicago. And that's a case I wouldn't mind taking on.

It's inconceivable—but damnably possible, once you stop to think of it in this day and age of machine-made records—that a completely innocent man could be put in this position.

There shouldn't be much to it. I've asked to see McDivot tomorrow before the time for sentencing, and it'll just be a matter of explaining to him. Then I can discuss the damage suit with my freed client at his leisure.

Fishing next weekend?

Yours,
Mike

MICHAEL R. REYNOLDS
Attorney-at-law

49 Water Street
Chicago, Illinois
June 10

Dear Tim:

In haste—

No fishing this coming week either. Sorry.

You won't believe it. My innocent-as-a-lamb-and-I'm-not-kidding client has just been sentenced to death for first-degree murder in connection with the death of his kidnap victim.

Yes, I explained the whole thing to Mc-Divot. And when he explained his situation to me, I nearly fell out of my chair.

It wasn't a matter of my not convincing him. It took less than three minutes to show him that my client should never have been within the walls of the County Jail for a second. But—get this—McDivot couldn't do a thing about it.

The point is, my man had already been

judged guilty according to the computerized records. In the absence of a trial record—of course there never was one (but that's something I'm not free to explain to you now)—the judge has to go by what records are available. And in the case of an adjudged prisoner, McDivot's only legal choice was whether to sentence to life imprisonment, or execution.

The death of the kidnap victim, according to the statute, made the death penalty mandatory. Under the new laws governing length of time for appeal, which has been shortened because of the new system of computerizing records, to force an elimination of unfair delay and mental anguish to those condemned, I have five days in which to file an appeal, and ten to have it acted on.

Needless to say, I am not going to monkey with an appeal. I'm going directly to the Governor for a pardon—after which we will get this farce reversed. McDivot has already written the Governor, also, explaining that his sentence was ridiculous, but that he had no choice. Between the two of us, we ought to have a pardon in short order.

Then, I'll make the fur fly . . .

And we'll get in some fishing.

Best,
Mike

OFFICE OF THE
GOVERNOR OF ILLINOIS

June 17, 1966

Mr. Michael R. Reynolds
49 Water Street
Chicago, Illinois
Dear Mr. Reynolds:

In reply to your query about the request for pardon for Walter A. Child (A. Walter), may I inform you that the Governor is still on his trip with the Midwest Governors Committee, examining the Wall in Berlin. He should be back next Friday.

I will bring your request and letters to his attention the minute he returns.

Very truly yours,
Clara B. Jilks
Secretary to the Governor

June 27, 1966

Michael R. Reynolds
49 Water Street
Chicago, Illinois
Dear Mike:

Where is that pardon?

My execution date is only five days from now!

Walt

June 29, 1966

Walter A. Child (A. Walter)
Cell Block E
Illinois State Penitentiary
Joliet, Illinois
Dear Walt:

The Governor returned, but was called away immediately to the White House in Washington to give his views on interstate sewage.

I am camping on his doorstep and will be on him the moment he arrives here.

Meanwhile, I agree with you about the seriousness of the situation. The warden at the prison there, Mr. Allen Magruder, will bring this letter to you and have a private talk with you. I urge you to listen to what he has to say; and I enclose letters from your family also urging you to listen to Warden Magruder.

Yours,
Mike

June 30, 1966

Michael R. Reynolds
49 Water Street
Chicago, Illinois
Dear Mike: (This letter being smuggled out by Warden Magruder)

As I was talking to Warden Magruder in my cell, here, news was brought to him that the Governor has at last returned for a while to Illinois, and will be in his office early tomorrow morning, Friday. So you will have time to get the pardon signed by him and delivered to the prison in time to stop my execution on Saturday.

Accordingly, I have turned down the Warden's kind offer of a chance to escape; since he told me he could by no means guarantee to have all the guards out of my way when I tried it; and there was a chance of my being killed escaping.

But now everything will straighten itself out. Actually, an experience as fantastic as this had to break down sometime under its own weight.

Best,
Walt

FOR THE SOVEREIGN
STATE OF ILLINOIS
I, Hubert Daniel Willikens, Governor of the State of Illinois, and invested with the authority and powers appertaining thereto,

including the power to pardon those in my
judgment wrongfully convicted or otherwise
deserving of executive mercy, do this day of
July 1, 1966, announce and proclaim that
Walter A. Child (A. Walter), now in custody
as a consequence of erroneous conviction
upon a crime of which he is entirely innocent, is fully and freely pardoned of said
crime. And I do direct the necessary author-
ities having custody of the said Walter A.
Child (A. Walter) in whatever place or places
he may be held, to immediately free, release, and allow unhindered departure to
him . . .

Interdepartmental Routing Service
PLEASE DO NOT FOLD, MUTILATE,
OR SPINDLE THIS CARD
Failure to route Document properly.
To: Governor Hubert Daniel Willikens
Re: Pardon issued to Walter A. Child, July 1,
1966

Dear State Employee:
You have failed to attach your Routing
Number.
PLEASE: Resubmit document with this
card and form 876, explaining your authority
for placing a TOP RUSH category on this
document. Form 876 must be signed by your
Departmental Superior.
RESUBMIT ON: Earliest possible date
ROUTING SERVICE office is open. In this
case, Tuesday, July 5, 1966.
WARNING: Failure to submit form 876
WITH THE SIGNATURE OF YOUR SU-
PERIOR may make you liable to prosecu-
tion for misusing a Service of the State

Government. A warrant may be issued for your arrest.

There are NO exceptions. YOU have been WARNED.

By New Hearth Fires

The last dog on Earth was dying. It was a small, but important, crisis. None other of his kind was known to still exist on any of the other worlds. It was quite probable that there were no others and that with him the race would end. Nothing seemed to be wrong with this dog named Alpha. He was still young and in no way hurt or diseased. But still he was dying.

The curator at this time of the museum world that was Earth was quite concerned about the situation. He had done everything he could with the large, brown and white canine, utilized every device and therapy available at the hospital center in the Adirondack Mountains. But the dog, unlike all the other sick animals brought in from the various parks and exhibit areas of the Earth, responded to none of his efforts. It was not the curator's fault, of course. But still he felt the matter as a sort of failure—that the race of dogs, important as it had been to the past history of man, should terminate during his term of office.

He coded a request to the Galactic Center for the person most likely to be of help to him in this situation, and a few weeks later a well-known historical psychologist Dr. Anium, arrived on Earth, accompanied by his son, a bright twelve-year-old named Geni. The curator was on hand to meet them as they stepped off the transportation platform at the edge of the hospital area.

"Dr. Laee?" said Anius, descending from the platform and offering his hand. He was a tall, brown-haired man in his first hundred years, and his handgrip was firm. "I brought my boy along to give him this chance to look over the home world. He won't be in the way. Geni, this is the curator here, Dr. Laee."

Laee shook hands also with the boy, a slim lad well over two meters in height and showing signs of being another lean, tall individual like his father. Laee, originally from the far side of the galaxy, was from a rather shorter ancestral strain than these Center people, but age had put him past the point of noticing that difference.

"Come along into the hospital," he said.

They strolled up the narrow, resilient walk through the hospital area. The grassy grounds were occupied by a number of different animals, arranged by species, that were currently at the hospital and undergoing treatment. The boy stared in fascination at a whooping crane which was turning around and around in an attempt to get a better look at one of its wings, which had been set for a break and bound in stasis.

"I had no idea there were so many I wouldn't know," he said to the curator.

"The original Earth was very rich in varieties," replied the curator. "One way or another, we have specimens of nearly all, though in many cases we had to breed back for extinct forms."

"How do you keep them separate?" asked Geni,

his gray eyes ranging over the apparently open grounds.

"Tingle barriers separate the groups into small areas," answered Laee. "Remind me to give you a key, when you want to examine the animals more closely."

They reached the entrance to the curator's quarters after seeing a buffalo who had just had his horn amputated, a Kodiak bear with an infected ear, and a large gorilla with a skin rash allergy who sat back in the shadows of his little groves of bushes and watched their passing with sad, intelligent eyes.

"I assume," said the tall Dr. Anius, as they passed into the main lounge of the curator's area, "you could also rebreed the domestic dog from one of your other canine forms if we're completely unsuccessful in saving this specimen?"

"Oh, of course," said Laee. "But naturally, I like to know what his affliction is, so we can stop it if it ever pops up again. And then," he paused, turning his eyes on Anius, "it would be nice to maintain the original line."

They went on into a farther room that was half library, half patio. The bright afternoon spring sun came in through the invisible ceiling and struck warmly upon the patches of grass and flowers. On the white flagstone a furry body lay outstretched, eyes closed and clean limbs stretched out and still, with only the slow rise and fall of the narrow chest to indicate life.

"Is that him?" asked the boy.

"That's him," said the curator. They all three came up and stood over the dog who lifted his eyelids to look at them, then closed the lids again, without stirring.

"Is he helpless?" asked Anius.

"No . . . not helpless," said the curator. "He's weak, mainly from not eating anything to speak of these last few weeks. But he's got energy enough to move around when he wants to. "Alpha" he said, sharply. "Alpha."

The dog opened his eyes again, and half lifted his head. He moved his tail, briefly, and then, as if it were too much of an effort, lay back again. His eyes, however, remained open, watching them. The boy, Geni, stared at those eyes in an odd sort of fascination. They were as brown and liquid as a human's, but they had something different—he thought of it as a clearness or transparency—that he had never noticed before in eyes of any kind.

"If you two don't mind stepping out," said his father, "I'd like to examine him with no one else around to distract him."

The boy and the curator went out together.

"As long as we have to wait," said the curator, "how'd you like to look around the planet a bit?"

"I'd enjoy that," said Geni. "If it's not too much trouble——"

"No trouble at all," said the curator. He led the way to a small platform, sitting by the fireplace in the main lounge, and they both got on. "This job's something of a sinecure, generally."

He set the controls that took them directly to a spot a little ways out from the world where they could see the North American Continent as a whole, and, pointing out various features of historic interest, moved on around the globe.

". . . There are capsules of details on this information back in my library," Laee said, between paragraphs of his talk. "You can pick them out later, if you want. This world, of course, is too crammed with history for anyone to do justice to it on a quick sweep like this, but it's my belief that immediacy is a great virtue. You may get more of the feel of it from this sort of presentation."

"I'm overwhelmed," said the boy. "I am."

"Ah, then, you're a responsive," said Laee. "So few are. Many of the visitors here make a valiant effort—I see them at it—but for all their trouble they achieve no emotional response. And I think they go away thinking that it's all a rather unnecessary expense."

They descended at random and landed on Salisbury plain, in England, within the toothed circle of a reconstructed Stonehenge. The midafternoon July sun struck warmly between the upright blocks as it had for thousands of years, but the heavy shadows were cold.

The boy shivered suddenly, looking about him.

"They were different, weren't they?" he said.

"Anthropologists deny it," said Laee, "that we have changed. But I know what you feel. I feel it myself, sometimes—and particularly on this world."

"Should we go?" asked Geni.

They went on, to see the Louvre and the Forum, and the Taj Mahal and the Angkor Thom and Angkor Vat—and so by way of the Christ of the Andes back to the hospital.

Anius was sitting in the main lounge when they came in, the dog Alpha not far from him, lying stretched out on the rosy tile of the floor with the brown fur of his back turned to the fireplace, as if in disdain at its illusion of a blaze.

"Been seeing the Earth, have you?" he said, smiling up at them as they approached.

"We hit some of the high spots," replied the curator, as he and the boy sat down. "Have you discovered anything about the dog?"

Anius shook his head slowly and looked over at Alpha.

"He's dying because he has no will to live," he answered. "But you know that already. These creatures are strange." He stared at the dog, who returned the gaze without stirring. "Their psychology is baffling."

"But I thought," said the curator, who had turned to the table beside him and was coding for a meal to be served the three of them, "animal psychology was at least as well understood as the human."

"Oh yes, most of them," said Anius. "The monkey and ape family, now"—he smiled suddenly across his lean face—"how we know that bunch! And the wild strains, and the herd animals. But the dog—and to a lesser extent, the cat, and the horse. All of those that had some peculiar partnership in man's history. These, we do not understand." A cart came gliding into the room with the meal upon it and stopped between them. Anius reached out for a tumbler of clear liquid. "Perhaps that's why—they were too close."

"You mean it would be like understanding ourselves?" said Laee. "But we do, don't we?"

"In everything that's pin-downable, we do," said Anius. "But there's more than that, or each one of us wouldn't be an individual, in his own right."

"Father," said the boy, "what were they like—the ones who built Stonehenge?"

Anius laughed and set his glass down.

"You see there?" he said to the curator. "I can't answer that." He turned to his son. "The original Stonehenge, you mean? I can tell you what they looked and talked like and even something of what they thought. But what they felt——"

"That's what I mean," said the boy, eagerly.

His father spread his hands helplessly.

"The science of emotions is no science," he said. "It's an art. Which was why Art developed automatically to express it. Look at what ancient man has done—and you're as close to him as I can come with all I know."

"Yes," said the curator, musingly over a biscuit held in one hand. "I understand that, I think."

"But——" began the boy.

"It's not natural for men to be martyrs and heroes and tyrants," his father continued, as if he had not heard. "But they had them. We can attempt to explain the bad in men of those times by saying these were warped personalities. But how do you explain the good—the better than normal—" he interrupted himself, looking at the curator.

"A code of ethics——" said the curator.

"Does not completely explain it," said Anius. "There was a very good paper written several hundred years back by somebody whose name slips my mind at this moment," he frowned for a second over the effort of remembering, then gave it up, "which attempted to prove that an ethical existence is the most practical one for any intelligent species as a species, from the time that they first begin to show intelligence. But there were flaws in his argument . . . there were flaws. . . ."

He fell silent, and the boy and the curator were both just opening their mouths to speak, thinking he was through, when he looked up and addressed Laee, directly.

"I believe you told me Alpha, here, started his decline from the time he was left alone in the world, so to speak."

"Well, yes," said the curator. "But his symptoms are unique in that. I mean . . . we used to have quite a number of these dogs."

"In a separate area?"

"Yes. We had something like a farm, or a country place, covering several square miles. There was a building, circa 1880s, old reckoning, a barn, some farm animals."

"And some robots in human form, I suppose," said Anius.

"That's right. But they weren't put there for the dogs' benefit," said the curator. "They were just part of the exhibit—as the dogs themselves were, originally."

"And then they started to die off? I mean, the dogs, of course," said Anius.

"The group began to dwindle. Smaller litters were born, the puppies did all right during their growing period, but began to give up, like Alpha, here, and die shortly after maturity. Alpha was one of a litter of two. His sister was born dead, and he and his mother were the last two of the species. When she died——"

"He began to go this way?"

The curator nodded.

"I see," said Anius, thoughtfully, nodding at the glass in his hand. "I see. . . ."

"Father," said Geni, the fresh, tight skin of his brow stretching in a frown, "about these men who *did* build Stonehenge. . . ."

In the following days Dr. Anius gave himself over wholly to the observation and care of the dog. To the curator watching, it all seemed a little marvelous, and he himself felt a touch of humbleness at the thought of having harnessed so much intelligence and erudition, as it were, to such a small and common problem. For a few days Alpha actually seemed to revive under this attention. He occasionally followed Anius around, and even consented to eat several times. But shortly after that it could be seen that he was sinking back into his apathy again.

"Perhaps," Laee suggested, offering the ready-made excuse like a polite host, "it was impossible to begin with. You've been very generous with your time."

"When there's life, there's hope, as that hoary saying goes," objected Anius. They were sitting in the same library-patio, with Alpha stretched out at their feet and apparently dozing. "And the challenge is . . . well, a challenge." He smiled at the curator. "It wouldn't take much imagination to pretend that there's some old magic still at work on this world of yours. You've noticed Geni?"

"He's very interested in the local past," said Laee.

"He's head over heels interested in the local past," said Anius. "But I suppose it's natural at his age."

"That reminds me," said Laee, almost a trifle shyly, "he's dropping by in a few minutes. He wants to ask you something."

Anius raised his head and looked closely at the curator.

"It must be something he suspects I won't approve of," he said dryly, "if he has to send advance warning through you, this way."

"I don't know what he has in mind," said Laee, quickly. And changed the subject.

Some ten minutes later, Geni came into the patio and sat down. His father stared at him. The boy was dressed in an odd, archaic costume consisting of boots, slacks, and jacket.

"I see," said Anius. "You want to play-act some historical role or other? That's your plan."

"Well, yes," said Geni. He shifted, a little uncomfortably on his chair. He had been very sure of himself, but now the words would not come for his argument. He had been out, roaming the face of the Earth by himself, and he had seen the fresh, clean soil black with the dampness of spring and smelled the many odors of the open wind. Something in all this had moved him, but he found that now, facing his father, he had no term for it. "I'd like to try living . . . a little like they used to. And I'd like to take the dog along. It might work for him."

"Fantasy!" said his father, "You realize, you can't go back?"

"Oh, I know that," said Geni quickly. "It'd be play-acting, as you say. But there's something there I'd like to touch."

"The past is the past," said his father. "There's a

certain emotional danger in entertaining the notion that it might be otherwise. Everyone who works in the field of history has to realize that. It's like studying something attractive through a glass which can't be broken. You risk frustration."

"It would be good for the dog," said the boy. "He's not improving, is he? If I took him out and exposed him to nothing but the kind of environment his kind flourished in, then maybe. . . ." He let the sentence hang, watching his father.

"I'm not sure I approve of that, either," said Anius, slowly. "It's rather on the order of tinkering at random with a mechanical device whose principle of operation you do not understand. By accident you may cure its malfunction, but there's an equal or greater chance you may damage it further."

"Alpha's dying," said the boy, "And you aren't saving him. Nobody's saving him. I could try my experiment without him, but I'd rather have him, and it wouldn't hurt to try."

"What do you think?" asked Anius, turning to the curator.

"I've been bitten by Geni's bug many years now." Laee rubbed his short-fingered hands together and smiled wryly. "And I've never got over it. Call me devil's advocate, if you wish. But it might help the dog, at that."

"Has anything like it ever been tried before?" asked Anius.

Laee shook his head.

"Not as far as the records show," he said. "Give the two of them a week or so, why don't you? At the end of that time we should be able to tell about Alpha, one way or another. Of course, I realize it would leave you at loose ends—but now that you're here on Earth, perhaps there's material here in our files or otherwise you may have wanted to examine, a week's worth of it, anyway."

"Much more than that. I'd planned to stay over anyway—" Anius waved his hand, dismissing that element of the problem. "It's just that I feel a certain professional responsibility toward the dog, now . . . well, go ahead, if you want to," he wound up, turning to Geni.

The boy's face lit up.

Early the next morning they left the clinic, Geni, and Alpha. The dog, like all the other animals there, had been restrained by the invisible tingle barriers from straying into areas where he was not wanted to go, and, in spite of the fact that now he, like Geni, wore a key that cut out a barrier as soon as he touched it, he had to be urged to strike out across the grounds, and cringed slightly as he followed the boy at the end of a leash.

"You won't stray off the grounds?" Anius said to Geni, as they left.

"Not if you don't want us to, Father," said the boy, looking up at the man with an expression of slight puzzlement. "It really doesn't matter where we go, as long as we stay out of the clinic itself."

"Fine," said Anius. "Because I'd like to check on the dog from time to time by local scan."

"All right, Father."

They turned and went, walking away through the areas of the sick and injured animals, Alpha's head glancing to right and left at the wild creatures with a wariness, but Geni moving with the unconscious unconcern of a being who knew his science.

Anius and Laee watched them go. The dog, Alpha, trotting at the end of his leash, shied from the Kodiak with the infected ear and sniffed curiously, a second later, at the gorilla with the allergy rash. They moved on, dwindling, and passing at length from sight among a small grove of pines.

"And now," said Anius, turning to the curator, "I'll start my poking through your files."

The files, indeed, turned out to be even far more interesting to an historical psychologist than Anius had expected. They consisted of nothing more—and nothing less—than a great mass of statistics and information about all periods of human history on Earth. Taken item by item, they were as dry as old newsprint, but investigating them was like looking up an item in an encyclopedia, where each page turned over sowed fishhooks for the attention, in the shape of odd and hitherto unknown avenues of knowledge. Anius felt caught, as he had not been caught in decades, by a lust that drew him down these obscure paths and into the wilderness of civilizations long dead and put to rest. The mirage of something not fully understood fled always just a little ways ahead of him, and the more he overtook it in his absorption of facts from the past, the more it drew away from him, and drew him on; until in the end he pursued it headlong, without attempting analysis or self-understanding, like a man in love.

In this occupation he suddenly lost himself, and several days went by as if the time they represented had unexpectedly evaporated. He was startled to find Laee at his elbow one afternoon.

"Eh?" he said, looking up from the screen before him. "What's that?"

"You said you wanted to check on Alpha's condition from time to time," Laee was standing close, with his round face bent a little curiously over him. "You haven't made any attempt, and I just now happened to pick up Geni and the dog on a routine check of the grounds."

"Oh . . . oh, yes," said Anius, getting to his feet. "Where's your scan board?"

"Through here."

Laee led him into a little side room. They looked

over a small ornamental railing into a little area of imaged outdoors, solid enough appearing in its three dimensions to be an actuality. Anius saw his son, still in the archaic jacket and boots, seated cross-legged before an actual wood fire, burning on the grass of an open space surrounded by pine and birch. On the other side of the fire, Alpha lay on his belly, nose between his paws. His eyes were open, but they were not on Geni. They were gazing instead into the almost invisible flames of the fire.

Seeing them there, Anius felt a sudden entirely irrational and new twinge of panic, as if he were watching his son out of reach and drowning in some strange waters.

"Geni!" he called.

"Just a minute," said Laee. The boy had not looked up. The curator adjusted a control and nodded at Anius.

"Geni!" he said again, loudly.

The boy looked up. The dog's ears flicked and stirred, but he did not move. Geni looked over to one side as if he could actually see them, but the gaze of his image went past the two men in the room, the way the gaze of a blind man does.

"Father?" he said.

"It's all right," said Anius more calmly. "I just didn't realize the sound element wasn't on." He took a breath and went on more calmly. "Alpha looks good. How've you been doing?"

"I don't know. I think he's better," said the boy. "We've been moving around the grounds a lot. He's pretty interested in the other animals. He perked up the first day—and he's been eating pretty well until just today."

"Something happen today?" asked the curator.

"No," said Geni, shifting his gaze at the other voice, but still looking past them. "But when I stopped and built the fire here for our midday meal, he didn't seem hungry. And he doesn't seem to want to follow me away from the fire."

"If he shows any obvious signs of physical illness, let me know," said Laee.

"I will," answered Geni. "Father?"

"Yes, Geni?" said Anius.

"Are you keeping occupied all right?"

Anius smiled.

"Yes," he said. "I'm quite busy on some files here. Geni—how far from the clinic are you?"

"About ten kilometers, I imagine," said Geni. "Why?"

"I just wondered. Keep in touch with us, son."

"I will."

"Good-by."

"Good-by, Father."

"Good-by," said Laee.

"Good-by."

Laee touched a control and the scene vanished, leaving a small area of bare, bright yellow floor enclosed by the little railing.

"I've a little more scanning to do," said Laee, looking up at his tall guest. "I won't keep you from your own work."

"Oh, yes . . . yes," said Anius, starting a little. He lifted his hand in a friendly gesture and went out the door of the scan room. But he did not go back to the files. Deep in thought, he wandered through the living quarters of the clinic and out onto the grounds. The afternoon was reddening into its later hours just before sunset and the long shadows lay across his path. Again he felt the whisper of something like a panic, but it sank and mellowed into a sadness, a feeling of regret no deeper than the transience of the passing day. He found himself standing by the area where the gorilla sat and he looked across the distance of a few short meters into its wrinkle-hooded eyes. And the gorilla looked back with a wondering unhappiness that had no language to explain itself, its great and hairy arms crossed on its knees.

"What do you know?" Anius asked it. "What do *you* know?"

And the gorilla blinked and turned its head shyly and painfully away.

Anius sighed and turned back toward the clinic, and the files.

"I hesitate to mention this," said Laee, over lunch two days later, "but have you run across something in the files that disturbs you? It's not my intention to pry, but as curator here——"

"Of course," said Anius. He put down the glass he was holding and shook his head. "There's nothing, except—" he hesitated. "There is nothing, that's just it."

"I'm afraid—" began Laee.

"I know, I'm not being clear," Anius waved a hand in apology. "It's not the files. It's this whole world of yours . . . I'm half prepared to believe it's haunted. It puts questions into my mind."

"For example?" said Laee, encouragingly.

"Do you suppose," said Anius, very slowly, "that something could be lost without its loss being known?"

"Lost from the files?"

"No," said Anius. "Lost to us, by us, as a people, without our knowing it. Do you suppose it would be possible for us to have taken a turning, somewhere along the way—a turning that was maybe right, and maybe wrong—but a turning that put us past the hope of going back to find our original path?"

Laee spread his hands and smiled, with a little shrug.

"No!" said Anius, forcefully. "I mean it as a serious question." Laee frowned at him.

"In that case—" he said, and paused. "No, I still don't understand you."

"There was an old legend on this world, once,"
said Anius, "about the elephants' graveyards."

"I know it," Laee nodded.

"Because the remains of dead elephants were not
found, because of the value of ivory if great boneyards
existed, a theory of a dramatic end for elephants was
invented. Only the truth was that the scavengers,
small and large, in the jungle disposed of all remains.
The true end was not remarkable, not impressive,
but natural and a little dull. Gradually, the dead
elephant disappeared. As if"—Anius hesitated—"he
had never been."

"Come now," said Laee smiling, "the human race
is a long way from the end of its existence—if, indeed, it's going to end at all."

"I think," said Anius, with a slight shiver, "all
things end."

A sudden mellow note, like the sound of a gong,
echoed through the clinic. Both men looked up,
startled, and Laee, frowning in surprise, reached
over and pressed a stud on the table by his chair. A
bright little shimmer sprang into existence in front of
the imitation fire on the hearth of the lounge and
resolved itself into the face of Geni, looking up at
them.

"What is it, Son?" asked Anius, for the boy's face
was strained.

"I'm sorry, Father," said Geni. "But I've lost Alpha. I thought I could find him by myself and not
bother you. But I can't."

"Tell us what happened," said Laee, leaning
forward.

"He ran off yesterday, during the night, I guess,"
said Geni. "He was gone in the morning. I hunted
for him yesterday, and found some tracks this morning crossing a couple of tingle barriers. No other
animal could do that—Alpha's the only one carrying
a key—" the boy broke off. "I think . . . I think the

gorilla got him. You know . . . the one just a little
way from the clinic. I'm at the gorilla's area, now.
But I don't have anything protective with me. I don't
dare go in."

"We'll be right there," said the curator, getting to
his feet.

"Wait where you are, Geni," said Anius, also rising.

"All right, Father. I'm sorry," said the boy. He
broke the connection.

Laee got a paralyzer from his stores and the two
men set out on foot toward the area where the gorilla
was enclosed. It was just a couple of minutes'
walk from the clinic, and as they rounded a little
clump of lilac bushes they saw Geni standing unhappily at the edge of the area, and the gorilla itself
squatting in front of the little grove of bushes that
had been designed to give it the privacy the powerful but shy anthropoid desired.

Geni turned to look at them as the two men approached together, Laee carrying the paralyzer with
a practiced and competent grip.

"I'm sure he's back in there," Geni said, as they
came up. "I can't quite see him now, but I saw him
before."

"Let me call him," said Laee. He stepped up to
the edge of the tingle barrier and raised his voice.
"Alpha!" He waited a second, and then called again.
"*Alpha!*"

There was no immediate response from the shadows of the bushes, but the gorilla, his attention suddenly directed to Laee, all at once recognized the
paralyzer in the curator's hand and threw up one
thick clumsy arm before his face, shrinking back and
away.

Immediately, there was movement in the bushes
and the dog came out. Pushing in front of the huddled gorilla, he stood squarely, facing the men.

"There he is," said Laee, raising the paralyzer.

The gorilla whimpered. Alpha snarled suddenly, and
Anius caught at the curator's arm.

"No!" he said. "Don't."

Laee turned and stared at him. The boy cried out.

"But he's got Alpha!"

"Come along," said Anius, putting a hand on both
of them. "Leave them."

Slowly, the curator lowered the paralyzer. He was
frowning at Anius. Then his frown cleared and he
slowly nodded.

"But," cried the boy again, "he's got Alpha. He's
got our dog."

Anius put his long arm around his son's shoulders
and turned him about. And the three of them walked
away, toward the silver dome of the clinic, which
from where they were seemed to shimmer in the
noon sun like a bright bubble, Earth-tethered there
for only a little time and against its will.

"No, Son," he said, gently. "Not our dog. He's not
our dog any more."

Ancient, My Enemy

They stopped at the edge of the mountains eight hours after they had left the hotel. The day was only a dim paling of the sky above the ragged skyline of rock to the east when they set up their shelter in a little level spot—a sort of nest among the granitic cliffs, ranging from fifty to three hundred meters high, surrounding them.

With the approach of dawn the Udbahr natives trailing them had already begun to seek their own shelters, those cracks in the rock into which they would retreat until the relentless day had come and gone again and the light of the nearer moon called them out. Already holed up high among the rocks, some of the males had begun to sing.

"What's he saying? What do the words mean?" demanded the girl graduate student, fascinated. Her name was Willy Fairchild and in the fading light of the nearer moon she showed tall and slim, with short whitish-blond hair around a thin-boned face.

43

Kiev Archad shrugged. He listened a moment. He translated:

> *You desert me now, female*
> *Because I am crippled,*
> *And yet all my fault was*
> *That I did not lack courage.*
> *Therefore I will go now to the*
>   *high rocks to die,*
> *And another will take you.*

Kiev stopped translating.

"Go on," said Willy. The song was still mournfully falling upon them from the rocks above.

"There isn't any more," said Kiev. "He just keeps singing it over and over again. He'll go on singing until it's time to seal his hole and keep the heat from drying him up."

"Oh," said Willy. "Is he really crippled, do you think?"

Kiev shrugged again.

"I doubt it," he said. "If he were really hurt he'd be keeping quiet, so none of the other males could find him. As it is, he's probably just hoping to lure another one of them close—so that he can kill himself a full meal before the sun rises."

She gasped.

He looked at her. "Sorry," he said. "If you weren't printed with the language, maybe you weren't printed with the general info—"

"Like the fact they're cannibals? Of course I was," she said. "It doesn't disturb me at all. Cannibalism is perfectly reasonable in an environment like this where the only other protein available is rock rats—and everything else, except humans, is carbohydrates."

She glanced at one of the several moonplants growing like outsize mushrooms from the rocky rubble of the surface beside the shelter's silver walls. They had already pulled their petals into the protection of horny overhoods. But they had not yet retreated into the ground.

"After all," she said into his silence, "my field's anthropopathic history. People who disturb easily just don't take that up for a study. There were a number of protein-poor areas back on Earth and so-called primitive local people became practical cannibals out of necessity."

"Oh," said Kiev. He wriggled his wide shoulders briefly against the short pre-dawn chill. "We'd better be getting inside and settled. You'll need as much rest as you can get. We'll have to strike the shelter so as to start our drive at sunset."

"Sunset?" She frowned. "It'll still be terribly hot, won't it? What drive?"

He turned sharply to look at her.

"I thought—if you knew about their eating habits—"

"No," she said, interested. "No one said anything to me about drives."

"We've been picking up a gang of them ever since we left the hotel," he said. "And we're protein, too, just as you say. Or at least, enough like their native protein for them to hope to eat us. Sooner or later, if there get to be enough of them, they'll attack—if we don't drive them first."

"Oh, I see. You scare them off before they can start something."

"Something like that—yes." He turned, ran his finger down the closure of the shelter and threw back the flap. "That's why Wadjik and Shant came this far with us—so we could have four men for the drive. Come on, we've got to get inside."

She went past him into the shelter.

Inside, Johnson and the other prospecting team of Wadjik and Shant—who would split with them next evening—were already cozy. Johnson was hunched

in his thermal sleeping bag, reading. Wadjik and
Shant were at a card table playing bluet. Johnson
turned his dark face to Kiev and Willy as they came
in.

He said, "I laid your bags out for you—beyond the
stores."

"Regular nursemaid," said Wadjik without looking
up from his cards.

"Wad," said Johnson, quietly. "You and Shant can
shelter up separately if you want." His bare arms and
chest swelled with muscle above the partly open slit
of his thermal bag. He was not as big as Wadjik or
Kiev but he was the oldest and knew the mountains
better than any of them.

"Two more cards," said Wadjik looking to Shant.

The gray-headed man dealt.

Kiev led the way around the card table. Two unrolled thermal bags occupied the floor space next to
the entrance to the lavatory partition that gave privacy to the shelter's built-in chemical toilet. Kiev
gave the one nearest to the partition to Willy and
unrolled the other next to the pile of stores.

The pile was really not much as a shelter divider.
By merely lifting himself on one elbow, once he was
in his bag, Kiev was able to see the other three bags
and Johnson, reading. The card players, sitting up at
their table, could look down on both Kiev and Willy—
but, of course, once it really started to heat up, they
would be in their sacks too.

Kiev undressed within his thermal bag, handing
his clothes out as he took them off and keeping his
back turned to the girl. When at last he turned to
her he saw that, while she was also in her bag, she
still wore a sort of light blouse or skivvy shirt—he
had no idea what the proper name for it was.

"That's all right for now," he said, nodding at the
blouse. "But later on you'll be wanting to get completely down into the bag for coolness, anyhow, so it

won't matter for looks. And any kind of cloth between you and the bag's inner surface cuts its efficiency almost in half."

"I don't see why," she answered stiffly.

"They didn't tell you that either?" he asked. "Part
of the main idea behind using the thermal bag is that
we don't have to carry too heavy an air-conditioning
unit. If you take heat from anything, even a human
body, you've got to pump it somewhere else. That's
what an air-conditioning unit does. But these bags
are stuffed between the walls with a chemical heat-
absorbent— "

He went on, trying to explain to her that the bag
could soak up the heat from her naked body over a
fourteen-hour period without getting so full of heat it
lost its cooling powers. But the lining of the bag was
built to operate in direct contact with the human
skin. Anything like cloth in between caused a build-up
of stored heat that would overload the bag before the
fourteen hours until cool-off was over. It was not just
a matter of comfort—she would be risking heat pros-
tration and even death.

She listened stiffly. He did not know if he had
convinced her or not. But he got the feeling that
when the time finally came she would get rid of the
garment. He lay back in his own bag, closed his
eyes and tried to get some sleep. In another four
hours sleep would be almost impossible even in
the bags.

Wadjik and Shant were fools with their cards. A
man could tough out a drive with only a couple of
hours of sleep; but what if some accident during the
next shelter stop kept him from getting any sleep at
all? He could be half-dead with heat and exhaustion
by the following cool-off, his judgment gone and his
reflexes shot. One little bit of bad luck could finish
him off. Characters like Johnson had survived in the

mountains all these years by always keeping in shape. After four trips into the grounds Kiev had made up his mind to do the same thing.

He slept. The heat woke him.

He found he had instinctively slid down into his bag and sealed it up to the neck without coming fully awake. Opening his eyes now, feeling the blasting dryness and quivering heat of the air against his already parched face, he first pulled his head down completely into the bag and took a deep breath. The hot air from above, pulled momentarily into the bag, cooled on his dust-dry throat and mouth. He worked some saliva into existence, swallowed several times and then, sitting up, pushed his head and one arm out of the bag. He found his salve and began to grease his face and neck.

He glanced over at Willy as he worked. She was lying muffled in her thermal bag, watching him, her features shining with salve.

"You take that shirt off?" he asked.

She nodded briefly. He looked over past the deserted card table at the three other thermal bags. Johnson, encased to his nose, slept with the ease of an old prospector, his upper face placidly shining with salve. Shant was out of sight in his bag—all but his close-cut cap of gray hair. Wadjik was propped up against a case from the stores, his heavy-boned face under its uncombed black hair absent-eyed, staring at and through Kiev.

"Wad," said Kiev, "better get Shanny up out of that. He'll overload his sack in five hours if he goes to sleep breathing down there like that."

Wadjik's eyes focused. He grinned unpleasantly and rolled over on his side. He bent in the middle and kicked the foot of his thermal bag hard against the side of Shant's. Shant's head popped into sight.

"You go to sleep down there," Wad snarled, "and you won't live until sunset."

"Oh—sure, Wad. Sorry," Shant said, quickly.

A short silence fell. Wadjik had gone back to staring through unfocused eyes. Johnson woke but the only sign he gave was the raising of his eyelids. He did not move in his bag. Around them all, now, the heat was becoming a living thing—an invisible but sentient presence, a demon inside the shelter who could be felt growing stronger almost by the second. The shelter's little air-conditioner hummed, keeping the air about them moving and just below unbreathable temperature.

"Kiev," said Wadjik, suddenly. "Was that old Hehog you and Willy were listening to out there, just before dawn?"

"Yes," said Kiev.

"This time we'll get him."

"Maybe," said Kiev.

"No maybe. I mean it, man."

"We'll see," said Kiev.

A movement came beside Kiev. Willy sat up in her bag.

"Mr. Wadjik—"

"Joe. I told you—Joe."

Wadjik grinned at her.

"All right. Joe. Do you mean you don't know which Udbahr male that was—the one who was singing? Don't you know why I'm going to these prospecting grounds of yours? Don't you know about the remains of a city there built by these same Udbahrs?"

"Sure, I've seen it. What of it?"

"I'm telling you what of it! They had a high level of civilization once—or at least a higher level than now. But that doesn't mean anything to you—"

"They degenerated. That's what it means to me. They're cannibal degenerates. And you want me to treat them like human beings—"

"I want you to treat them like intelligent beings—which they are. Even an uneducated, brutal, stupid man like you ought to understand—"

"Listen to who's talking. The kid historian speaks. I thought you were still in school, writing a thesis. You didn't tell me you'd been at this for years—"

"I may be only a graduate student but I've learned a few things you never did—"

Looking past Wadjik's heat-reddened face, flaming under its salve, Kiev saw the upper part of Johnson's countenance beyond. Johnson seemed to be calmly listening. There was nothing to do, Kiev knew, but listen. It was the heat—the sickening intoxication of the deadly heat in the shelter—that was making the argument. When the heat reached its most relentless intensity only the instinct keeping men in their thermal bags stopped them from killing each other.

Wadjik finally broke off the argument by drawing down into his bag and rolling across the floor of the shelter to the lavatory door. He pressed the bottom latch through his bag, opened the door, rolled inside and shut himself off from the rest of the room. Willy fell silent.

Kiev looked sideways at her.

"It's no use," he whispered to her. "Save your energy."

She turned and glared at him.

"And I thought you were different!" she spat and slid down, head and all, into her bag.

Kiev backed into his own cocoon. Fueled by the feverishness induced by the heat, his mind ran on. They were all a little crazy, he thought, all who had taken up prospecting. Crazy or they had something to hide in their pasts that would keep them from ever leaving this planet.

But a man who was clean elsewhere could become rich in five years if he kept his head—and his health—both on the trips and back in civilization. On Kiev's

first trip into the mountains, two years ago, he had
not known what he was after. Just a lot of money, he
had thought, to blow back at the hotels. But now he
knew better. He was going to take it cool and calm,
like Johnson—who could never leave the planet.

Kiev meant to keep his own backtrail clear. And
he would leave when the time came with enough to
buy him citizenship and a good business franchise
back on one of the Old Worlds. He had his picture of
the future clear in his mind. A modern home on a
settled world, a steady, good income. Status. A family.

He had seen enough of the wild edges of civilization. Leave the rest of it to the new kids coming out.
He was still young but he could look ahead and see
thirty up there waiting for him.

His thoughts rambled on through the deadly hours
as his body temperature was driven slowly upward
by the heat. In the end his mind rambled and staggered. He awoke suddenly.

He had passed from near-delirium into sleep without realizing it. The deadly heat of mid-afternoon
had broken toward cool-off and with the first few
degrees of relief within the shelter he, like all the
rest, had dropped immediately into exhausted slum-
ber. By now—he glanced at the wristwatch on the
left sleeve of his outergear—the hour was nearly
sunset.

He looked about the shelter. Willy, Shant, Wadjik,
Johnson were still sleeping.

"Hey," he croaked at them, speaking above a whisper for the first time in hours. "Time for the drive.
Up and at 'em."

In forty-five minutes they were all dressed, fed
and outside, with the shelter folded and packed,
along with the other equipment, on grav-sleds ready
to travel. Wadjik and Shant took off to the north,
towing their own grav-sled. Kiev and Johnson were
left with their sled and the girl. They looked at her

thoughtfully. The sun was already down below the peaks to the west. But three-quarters of the sky above them was still white with a glare too bright to look at directly and the heat, even with outersuit and helmet sealed, made every movement a new cause for perspiration. The climate units of the suits whined with their effort to keep the occupants dry and cool.

"I'm not going to join you," Willy snapped. "I won't be a party to any killing of the natives."

"We can't leave you behind," Kiev answered. "Unless you can handle a gun—and will use it. If any of the males break away from the drive they'll double back, and you'd make an easy meal."

Inside the transparent helmet her face was pale even in the heat.

"You can stick with the grav-sled," said Kiev. "You don't have to join the drive. Just keep up."

She did not look at him or speak. She was not going to give him the satisfaction of an answer, he thought.

"Move out, then," said Johnson.

They began to climb the cliffs toward the brightness in the sky, the grav-sled trailing behind them on slave circuit, its load piled high. Willy, looking small in her suit, trudged behind it. Under the crown of the cliffs they turned about, deployed to cover both sides of the clearing below and began their drive.

They worked forward, each man firing into every rock niche or cranny that might have an Udbahr sealed up within it. Deep, booming sounds—made by the air and moisture within each cranny exploding outward—began to echo between the cliffs. Soon a shout came over Kiev's suit intercom in Johnson's deep voice.

"One running! One running! Eleven o'clock, sixty meters, down in the cleft there."

Kiev jerked his gaze ahead and caught a glimpse of

an adult-sized, humanlike, brown figure with a greenishly naked, round skull and large tarsierlike eyes, vanishing up a narrow cut.

"No clothing," called Kiev over the intercom. "Must be a female, or a young male."

"Or maybe old Hehog playing it incognito—" Johnson began but was interrupted.

"One running! One running!" bellowed Wadjik's voice distantly over the intercom. "Two o'clock, near clifftop."

"One running! Deep in the pass there at three o'clock!" chimed in Johnson, again. "Keep them moving!"

The sounds of the blasting attack now were routing out Udbahrs who had denned up for the day. Most were females or young, innocent of either clothing or weapons. But here and there was a heavier, male figure, running with spear or throwing-stick in hand and wearing anything from a rope of twisted rock vines or rat furs around his waist to some tattered article of clothing, stolen, scavenged—or just possibly taken as a war prize—from the dead body of a human prospector.

The males were slowed by their insistence on herding the females and the young ahead of them. They always did this, even though nearly all prospectors made it a point to kill only the grown males—the warriors who were liable to attack if left alive. The pattern was old, familiar—one of the things that made most prospectors swear the Udbahrs had to be animal rather than intelligent. The females and young were gathering into a herd as they ran, joining up beyond the screen of the males following them. When the herd was complete—when all who should be in it had been accounted for—the males would choose their ground, stop and turn to fight and hold up the pursuers while the females and young escaped.

*   *   *

They always reacted the same way, no matter whether the tactic were favorable or not in the terrain where they were being driven, Kiev thought suddenly. Everything the Udbahrs did was by rote. And strange to creatures who reasoned like men. No matter what Willy said, it was hard to think of them as any kind of people—let alone people with whom you could become involved. For example, if he, Johnson, Shant and Wadjik quit driving the natives now and pulled back, the Udbahr males would immediately turn around and start trying to kill each other. It was only when they were being driven or were joining for an attack on prospectors that the males had ever been known to cooperate.

So, as it always went, it went this sunset hour on the Udbahr Planet. By the time the last light of the day star was beginning to evaporate from the western sky and the great ghostly circle of the nearer moon was beginning to be visible against a more reasonably lighted sky, some half dozen of the Udbahr males disappeared suddenly among the boulders and rocks at the mouth of a pass down which the herd of females and young were vanishing.

"Hold up," Johnson gasped over the intercom. "Hold it up. They've forted. Stop and breathe."

Kiev checked his weary legs and collapsed into sitting position on a boulder, panting. His body was damp all over in spite of the efforts of his suit to keep him dry. His head rang with a headache induced by exhaustion and the heat.

The Udbahr males hidden among the rocks near the mouth of the pass began to sing their individual songs of defiance.

Kiev's breathing eased. His headache receded to a dull ache and finally disappeared. The last of the daylight was all but gone from the sky behind them. The nearer moon, twice as large as the single moon of Earth by which all moons were measured, was sharply outlined, bright in the sky, illuminating the scene with a sort of continuing twilight.

"What're you waiting for?" Willy's voice said dully in his earphones. "Why don't you go and kill them?"

He turned to look for her and was astonished to find her, with the grav-sled, almost beside him. She had sat down on the ground, her back bowed as if in deep discouragement, her face turned away and hidden from him within the transparent helmet.

"They'll come to us," he muttered without thinking.

Suddenly she curled up completely into a huddled ball of silver outerwear suit and crystalline helmet. The sheer, unutterable anguish of her pose squeezed at his throat.

He dropped down to his knees beside her and put his arms around her. She did not respond.

"You don't understand—" he said. And then he had the sense to tongue off the interphone and speak to her directly and privately through the closeness of their helmets, alone. "You don't understand."

"I do understand. You like to do this. You like it."

Her voice was muffled, dead.

His heart turned over at the sound of it and suddenly, unexpectedly, he realized that he had somehow managed to fall in love with her. He felt sick inside. It was all wrong—all messed up. He had meant to go looking for a woman—but eventually, after he'd made his stake and gone back to some civilized world. He had not planned anything like this involvement with a girl he had known only five days and who had all sorts of wild notions about how things should be. He did not know what to do except kneel there, holding her.

"If you don't like it why do you do it?" her voice said. "If you really don't like it—then don't do it. Now. Let these go."

"I can't," he said.

The singing broke off suddenly in a concerted

howl from the Udbahr males, mingled with a triumphant cry over the intercom from Wadjik.

"Got one." And then: "Look out. Stones."

Kiev jerked into the shelter of a boulder, dragging Willy with him. Two rocks, each about half the size of his fist, dug up the ground where they had crouched together.

"You see?"

He pushed her roughly from him and drew his sidearm. Leaning around the boulder, he searched the rocks of this slope below the pass, watching the vernier needle of the heat-indicator slide back and forth on the weapon's barrel. It jumped suddenly and he stopped moving.

He peered into the gun's rear sights, thumbing the near lens to telescopic. He held his aim on the warm location, studying the small area framed in the sight screen. Suddenly he made it out—a tiny patch of brown between a larger boulder and a bit of upright, broken rock.

He aimed carefully.

"Don't do it."

He jerked involuntarily, sending his beam wide of the mark at the sound of her voice. A patch of bare gravel boomed and flew. The bit of brown color disappeared from between the rocks. He leaned the front of his helmet wearily against the near side of the boulder before him.

"Damn you," he said helplessly. "What are you doing to me?"

"I'm trying to save you," she said fiercely, "from being a murderer."

Another stone hit the top of the boulder behind which they hid and caromed off their heads.

"How about saving me from that?" he said emptily. "Don't you understand? If we don't kill them they'll try to kill us—"

"I don't believe it." She, too, had shut off her

intercom. Her voice came to him distantly through two thicknesses of transparent material. "Have you ever tried? Has anyone ever tried?

Another sudden volley of stones was followed by more dull explosions as the heat of the human weapons found and destroyed live targets. Shant and Wadjik were howling in triumph and shooting steadily.

"We got five—they're on the run." Shant whooped. "Kiev! Johnson! They're on the run."

The explosions ceased. Kiev peered cautiously around his boulder, stood up slowly. Wadjik, Shant, and Johnson had risen from positions in a semicircle facing the distant pass.

"Any get away?" Johnson was asking.

"One, maybe two—" Shant cut himself short. "Look out—duck. Twelve o'clock, fifty meters."

At once Kiev was again down behind his boulder. He dragged down Willy, tongued on his intercom.

"What is it?"

"That chunk of feldspar about a meter high—"

Kiev looked down the slope until his eyes found the rock. A glint that came and went behind and above it, winking in the waxing light of the nearer moon that now seemed as bright as a dull, cloudy day back on Earth. The flash came and went, came and went.

Kiev recognized it presently as a reflection from the top curve of a transparent helmet bobbing back and forth like the head of someone dancing just behind the boulder. A male Udgahr's voice began to sing behind the rock.

> *Man with a head-and-a-half,*
> *come and get your half-head.*
> *Man with a head-and-a-half*
> *Come so I can kill you.*
> *Ancient, my enemy.*
> *Ancient, my enemy—*

"Hehog," snapped Johnson's voice over the helmet intercom.

Silence held for a minute. Then Wadjik's voice came thinly through the phones.

"What are you waiting for, Kiev?"

Kiev said nothing. The transparent curve of the helmet top rose again, bobbed and danced behind the boulder. It danced higher. Within it now was a bald, round, greenish skull with reddish, staring tarsier eyes and—finally revealed—the lipless gash of a fixedly grinning mouth.

"What is it? What's Wadjik mean?" Willy asked.

Her voice rang loud in Kiev's helmet phones. She had reactivated her intercom.

"It's Hehog down there," Kiev said between stiff jaws. "That's my helmet he's wearing. He's had it ever since he took it off me my first trip into the mountains."

"Took it off you?"

"I was new. I'd never been on a drive before," muttered Kiev. "I got hit in the chest by a stone, had the wind knocked out of me. Next thing I knew Hehog was lifting off my helmet. My partners came up shooting and drove him off."

"What about it, Kiev?" The voice was Johnson's. "Do you want us to spread out and get behind him? Or you want to go down and get the helmet by yourself?"

Kiev grunted under his breath, took his sidearm into his left hand and flexed the cramped fingers of his right. They had been squeezing the gunbutt as if to mash it out of all recognizable shape.

"I'm going alone," he said over the intercom. "Stay back."

He got his heels under him and was ready to rise when he was unexpectedly yanked backward to the gravel. Willy had pulled him down.

"You're not going."

He tongued off his intercom, turned and jerked her hand loose from his suit.

"You don't understand," he shouted at her through his helmet. "That's the trouble with you. You don't understand a damn thing."

He pushed her from him, rose and dived for the protection of a boulder four meters down the slope in front of him and a couple of meters to his right.

A flicker of movement came from below as he moved—the upward leap of a throwing-stick behind the rock where Hehog hid. Kiev glimpsed something dark racing through the air toward him. A rock fragment struck and burst on the boulderface, spraying him with stone chips and splinters.

Reckless now, he threw himself toward the next bit of rocky cover farther down the slope. His foot caught on a stony outcropping in the shale. He tripped and rolled, tumbling helplessly to a stop beside the very boulder behind which Hehog crouched, throwing-stick in one hand, stone-tipped spear in the other.

Kiev sprawled on his back. He stared helplessly up into the great eyes and humorlessly grinning mouth looming over him inside the other helmet less than an arm's length away. The spear twitched in the brown hand—but that was all.

Hehog stared into Kiev's eyes. Kiev was aware of Willy and the others shouting through his helmet phones. A couple of shots blasted grooves into the boulder-top above his head. And with a sudden, wordless cry Hehog bounded to his feet and dodged away among the boulders toward the pass.

Kiev climbed to his feet, shaking inside. He awoke to the fact that he was still holding his sidearm. A bitter understanding broke upon him with the hard, unsparing clarity of an Udbahr Planet dawn.

He could have shot Hehog at point-blank range during the moment he had spent staring frozenly at the spear in Hehog's hand and at the great-eyed, grinning head within the helmet. Hehog had to have seen the gun. And that would have been why he had not tried to throw the spear.

Kiev cursed blackly. He was still cursing when the others slid down the loose rock of the slope to surround him.

"What happened?" demanded Shant.

"He—" Kiev discovered that his intercom was still off. He tongued it on. "He got away."

"We know he got away," said Wadjik. "What we want to know is how come?"

"You saw," Kiev snapped. "I fell. He had me. You scared him off."

"He had you? I thought you had him, damn it!"

"All right, he's gone," Johnson said. "That's the main thing. Leave the other bodies for whoever wants to eat them. We've had a good drive. We'll split up now." He looked at Wadjik and Shant. "See you back in civilization."

Wadjik cursed cheerfully.

"Team with the heaviest load buys the drinks," he said. "Come on, Shanny."

The two of them turned away, dragging their loaded grav-sled through the air behind them.

Kiev, Willy and Johnson reached Dead City a good two hours before dawn. They had time to pick out one of the empty, windowless houses, half-cave, half-building, to use as permanent headquarters. Tomorrow night they would cut stone to fill the open doorway but for today the shelter, fitted double-thick into the opening, would do well enough.

No singing came from the surrounding cliffs. Johnson crawled in. Kiev lingered to speak to Willy.

"You don't have to worry." The words were not what he had planned to say. "The Udbahrs are scared of this place."

"I know." She did not look at him. "Of course. I know more about this city and the Udbahrs than even Mr. Johnson does. There's a taboo on this place for them."

"Yes." Kiev looked down at his gloved right hand and spread the fingers, still feeling the hard butt of his sidearm clamped inside them. "About earlier tonight, with Hehog—"

"It's all right," she said softly, looking unexpectedly up at him. Her intercom was off and her voice came to him through her helmet. In the combination of the low-angled moonlight and the first horizon glow of the dawn, her face seemed luminescent. "I know you did it for me—after all."

He stared at her.

"Did what?"

She still spoke softly: "I know why you let that Udbahr male live. It was because of what I'd said, wasn't it? But you need to be ashamed of nothing. You simply haven't gone bad inside, like the others. Don't worry—I won't tell anyone."

She took his arm gently with both hands and lifted her head as if—had they been unhelmeted—she might have kissed his cheek. Then she turned and disappeared into the cave.

He followed her after some moments. A small filter panel in the shelter had let a little of the terrible daylight through for illumination. Here artificial lighting had to be on. Kiev saw by it that she had piled stores and opened some of her own gear to set up a four-foot wall that gave her individual privacy.

He laid out his own thermal bag. The heat was quite bearable behind the insulation of the thick-walled building as the day began. Kiev fell into a deep, exhausted sleep that seemed completely dreamless.

He awoke without warning. Instantly alert, he rose to an elbow.

The light was turned down. He heard no sound from Willy. Johnson snored.

Kiev remained stiffly propped on one elbow. A feeling of danger prickled his skin. He found his ears were straining for some noise that did not belong here.

He listened.

For a long moment he heard only the snoring and beyond it silence. Then he heard what had awakened him. It came again, like the voice of some imprisoned spirit—not from beyond the wall but from under the stone floor on which he lay.

> *Man with a head-and-a-half,*
> *come and get your half-head.*
> *Man with a head-and-a-half,*
> *Come, so I can kill you.*
> *Ancient, my enemy.*
> *Ancient, my enemy*

The singing broke off suddenly. Kiev jerked bolt upright and the thermal bag fell down around his waist. Suddenly more loudly through the rock, and nearer, the voice echoed in the dim interior of the stone building:

> *Only for ourselves is the killing*
> *of each other!*
> *Man with a head-and-a-half,*
> *come and get your half-head.*
> *Man with a head-and-a-half . . .*

The singing continued. Fury uprushed like vomit in Kiev. He swore, tearing off his thermal bag and pawing through his piled outerwear. His fingers closed on the butt of the weapon. He jerked it clear, aimed it at the section of floor from which the singing was coming and pressed the trigger.

Light, heat and thunder shredded the sleeping quiet of the dimly lit room. Kiev held the beam steady, a hotter rage inside him than he could express with the rock-rending gun. He felt his arm seized. The sidearm was torn from his grip. He whirled to find Johnson holding the weapon out of reach.

"Give me that," Kiev said thickly.

"Wake up," Johnson said, low-voiced. "What's got into you?"

"Didn't you hear?" Kiev shouted at him. "That was Hehog—Hehog! Down there!"

He pointed at the hole with its melted sides, half a meter deep into the floor of the building.

"I heard," said Johnson. "It was Hehog, all right. There must be tunnels under some of these buildings."

Willy chimed in.

"But Udbahrs don't—"

Kiev and Johnson turned to see her staring at them over the top of her barricade. Kiev became suddenly conscious that, like Johnson, he was completely without clothes.

Willy's face disappeared abruptly. Kiev turned back to look at the hole his gun had burned in the stone. It showed no breakthrough into further darkness at the bottom.

"All right," he said shakily. "I'm sorry. I woke up hearing him and just jumped—that's all. We can shift to another building tomorrow. And sound for tunnels before we move in."

Johnson turned and returned to his thermal bag. Kiev resumed his cocoon. He lay on his back, hands behind his head, staring up at the shadowy ceiling.

. . . Ancient, my enemy . . . ancient, my enemy . . .

The memory of Hehog's chant continued to run through his head.

You and me, Hehog. I'll show you, Udbahr. . . .

After some time he fell asleep.

*   *   *

They moved camp the next night, as soon as the sun was down. Kiev and Johnson quarried large chunks of rock from the wall of an adjoining building, melted them into place to fill up the new door opening, except for the entrance unit, which was set up double as a heat lock and fitted into place.

Now the shelter air-conditioner could keep the whole interior of the new building comfortable all day long. The night was half over by the time they finished.

Kiev and Johnson had some four hours left to trek to their prospecting area. The gold ore deposits in the neighborhood of Dead City were almost always in pipes and easily worked out in a few days by men with the proper equipment.

Kiev hesitated.

"I'll stay," he said. "With Hehog around, someone's got to stay with Miss Fairchild."

Johnson regarded him thoughtfully.

"You're right. If we leave her here alone Hehog's sure to get her. And who would sell us gear for our next trip if word got out about how we left her to be killed?" He hesitated. "Tell you what—we'll draw straws."

Kiev said, "I'll stay. Drop back in a week. I'll tell you then if I need you to take over."

Johnson nodded. He turned away and began his packing—food, weapons, equipment, a water drill for tapping the moonflower root systems. Also, a breathing membrane for sealing the caves they would be denning up in by day. Kiev, squatting, making a final check of the seal around the entrance, saw a shadow fall across a seam he was examining.

He stood up, turned and saw Willy down the street, taking solidographs of one of the buildings. Johnson stood just behind him, equipment already on his backpack.

"We haven't had a chance to talk," Johnson said.

"No."

"Let me say now what I've wanted to say. Why don't you pack up and go back—and take the girl with you?"

"I've got my stake to make out here—like everybody else."

"You know there's more to the situation. Hehog's changed everything. Also, there's the girl—we both know what I mean. And there's something else—something I don't think you're aware of."

"What?"

"You've heard how sometimes the males—if they've just fed so they aren't hungry and there's only one of them around—will come into your camp and sit down to talk?"

Kiev frowned at him.

"I've heard of it," he said. "It's never happened to me."

"It's happened to me," said Johnson. "They ask you things that'd surprise you. Surprise you what they tell you, too. You know why Hehog's broken taboo and come right into Dead City?"

"Do you?"

Johnson nodded.

"There's a thing the Udbahrs believe in," Johnson said. "They figure that when they eat someone they eat his soul, too."

"Sure," said Kiev. "And that soul stays inside them until they're killed. Then, when they die, if no one else eats them right away, all the souls of all the bodies they've eaten in their lives fly loose and take over the bodies of pups too young to have strong souls of their own."

Johnson nodded. He tilted his head at the distant figure of Willy.

"You've been learning from her," he said.

"Her? As a matter of fact, I have," said Kiev. "But

you were the one told me about Udbahr cannibalism—a year or more ago."

"Did I?" Johnson looked at him. "Did I tell you about Ancient Enemies?"

Kiev shook his head.

"Once in a while a couple of males get a real feud going. It's not an ordinary hate. It's almost a noble thing—if you follow me. And from then on the feud never stops, no matter how many times they both die. Every time one is killed and born again—when he grows up it's his turn to kill the other one. The next time the roles are reversed. You follow me?"

Kiev frowned.

"No."

"Figure both souls live forever through any number of bodies. They take turns killing each other physically." Johnson looked strangely at Kiev. "The only thing is that no soul ever remembers from one body to the next—they never know whose turn it is to be killed and which one's to be the killer. So they just keep running into each other until the soul of one of them tells him, 'Go!' Then he kills the other and goes off to wait to die."

Johnson stopped speaking. Kiev stared.

"You mean Hehog thinks he and I—he thinks we're these Ancient Enemies?"

"Night before last," said Johnson, "you and he were face to face, both armed—and neither one of you killed the other. Yesterday—while we were denned up—he showed up here in the Dead City where it's taboo for him to be. Being Ancient Enemies is the only thing that'd set him free of a taboo like that. What do you think?"

Kiev turned for a second look down the street at Willy.

"Hehog's not going to leave you alone if I'm right," said Johnson. "And he's smart. He might even get away with killing one or two of us so he could stay close to you. And the easiest one for him to kill would be that girl. And it's true what I said. We lose a human woman out here and no supplier's going to touch us with a ten-foot pole."

"Yeah," said Kiev.

"I'm not afraid of Hehog, myself. But I've got no place else to go. I plan to die out here some day—but not yet for a few trips. Take the girl and head back. Give up the mountains while you still can. Kiev—I mean it."

"You can't make us leave," Kiev said slowly.

"No," said Johnson. His face looked old and dark as weather-stained oak. "But you keep that girl here and Hehog'll get her. She doesn't know anything but books and she doesn't understand someone like Hehog. She doesn't even understand us." He took a step back. "So long, partner," he said. "See you in three nights—maybe."

He turned and walked away slowly, leaning forward against the weight of the pack, until he was lost among the rocks of the western cliffs.

Kiev turned and saw the small shape of Willy even farther down the street, still taking pictures.

He continued to think for the next two days and nights, which were quiet. He spent most of his time studying the aerial maps of areas near Dead City he had planned to work during this trip. Actually he was getting his ideas in order for explanation to Willy, who seemed to be having the time of her life. She was measuring and photographing Dead City inch by inch, as excited over it as if it were one large Christmas present. She had changed toward him, too, teasing him and doing for him, by turns.

Hehog did not sing from underground in the new building.

On the third night Kiev invited himself along on her work with the City.

He realized now that what Johnson had told him was true. Johnson's words had been the final shove he had needed to make up his mind. The fact that he and Willy had met less than a week ago meant nothing. Out here things were different.

He had worried about how he would bring up the subject of his future—and hers. But it turned out that he had no need to bring it up. It was already there. Almost before he knew it they were talking as if certain things were understood and taken for granted.

He said, "I've got at least five more trips to make to get the stake I need for a move back to the Old Worlds. You'd have to wait."

"But you don't need to keep coming back here," she said. "I know how you can make the rest of the money you need without even one more trip. I know because a publishing company talked to me about doing something like it. There's a steady market for information about humanoids like the Udbahrs. Books, lectures. Acting as industrial and economic consultant—"

He stared at her.

"I couldn't do anything like that," he said. "I'm no good with words and theories—"

"You don't have to be. All you have to do is tell what you've seen and done on these trips of yours. You'll collect enough on advance bookings alone for us to go back to any Old World you want—after I get my doctorate, of course—and settle down there. Don't forget I've got my work, too. I'll be teaching." She stared at him eagerly. "And think of what you'll be achieving. Intelligent natives are being killed off or exploited on new worlds like this one simply because there's no local concern over them and because our civilization hasn't understood them enough to make the necessary concessions for them to accept it. You could be the one to get the ball rolling that could

save the Udbahrs from being hunted down and killed
off—"

"By people like me, you mean," he said, a little
sourly.

"Not you. You haven't yet been infected with the
sort of killing lust Wadjik and Shant—and even
Johnson—have."

"It isn't a lust. Out here you have to kill the
Udbahrs to keep them from killing you."

She looked at him sharply.

"Yes—if you're a savage," she said. "As the Udbahrs
are savages. I couldn't love an Udbahr. I could only
love a man who was civilized—able to keep the
savage part inside him chained up. That Ancient
Enemy business Hehog sang at you—that's the way a
savage thinks. I don't expect you not to have the
psychological capacity to lust for killing—but if you're
a healthy-minded man you can keep that sort of
Ancient Enemy locked up inside you. You don't have
to let him take you over."

He opened his mouth to make one more stubborn
effort to explain himself to her, then closed it again
rather helplessly. He found a certain uncomfortable
rightness in part of what she was saying. Although
from that rightness she went off into left field somewhere to an area where he was sure she was wrong.
While he groped for words to express himself the
still air around him was suddenly torn by the sound
of a gun-bolt explosion.

He found himself running toward the building they
had set up as their headquarters, sidearm in his
hand, the sound of Willy's voice and footsteps following him. The distance was not great and he did not
slow down for her. Better if he made it first—or if
she did not come at all until he knew what had
happened.

He rounded the corner of the building and saw the
shelter entrance hanging in blackened tatters. He

dove past it. By some miracle the light was still
burning against the ceiling but the interior it illuminated was a scene of wreckage. Concussion and heat
from the bolt had torn apart or scorched everything
in the place.

With a wild coldness inside him, he pawed swiftly
through the rubble for whatever was usable. Two
thermal sleeping bags were still in working condition, though their outer covering was charred in
spots and stinking of burned plastic. Food containers
were ripped open and their contents destroyed. The
water drill was workable and most of one air membrane was untouched.

"What happened? Who did it? Kiev—"

He awoke to the fact that Willy was with him
again, literally pulling at him to get his attention. He
came erect wearily.

"I don't know," he said, dully. "Maybe some prospector has gone out of his head entirely. Or—"

He hesitated.

"Or what?"

He looked at her.

"Or an Udbahr male has gotten hold of the gun of
a dead prospector."

Her face thinned and whitened under the light of
the overhead lamp.

"A dead—"

She did not finish.

"That's right," he said. "One of our people, it
could be—Wadjik, Shant or Johnson."

"How could a savage who knows only sticks and
stones kill an experienced, armed man?"

Willy sounded outraged.

"All sorts of animals kill people." He felt sick
inside, hating himself for not having set up at least a
trigger wire to guard the building area. "We've got

to get out of here. We can't spend another night in a building, anyway, without a shelter entrance."

"Where'll we go?"

"We'll head toward Johnson," Kiev said. "He isn't digging so far away that we shouldn't be able to make it before dawn—if he isn't dead."

They started out on the bearing Johnson had taken and soon left the city behind them. Fully risen moonflowers—some of them giants over three meters high—surrounded them. They were lost in a forest of strange, pale beauty, where by day there would only be the bare, heat-blasted mountainside.

"Aren't we likely to pass him and not even see him?" asked Willy.

"No," Kiev said absently. "He'll be following contours at a constant elevation. So are we. When he gets close enough, we'll hear static in our earphones."

He did not again mention the possibility of Johnson's being dead—partly because he wanted to be easy on himself.

They tramped on in silence. Kiev's mind was busy among the number of problems opened up by their present situation. After about an hour he heard the hiss of interference in his helmet phones that signaled the approach of another transmitting unit.

He stopped so suddenly that Willy bumped into him. He rotated his helmet slowly, listening for the maximum noise. When he found it, he spoke.

"Johnson? Johnson, can you hear me?"

"Thought it was you, Kiev." Johnson's voice came distorted and weakened by rocky distance. "The girl with you? What's up?"

"Somebody fired a gun into our building," said Kiev. "I scraped together a sort of maintenance kit out of what was left—but I'm carrying all the salvage."

"I see." Johnson did not waste breath on speculation. "Stop where you are and wait for me. We better head back toward Wad's and Shanny's diggings as soon as we're together. No point your burning energy trying to meet me halfway."

"Right."

Kiev loosened his pack and sat down with his back to the trunk of a moonflower. Willy sat beside him. She said nothing and, busy with his own thoughts still, he hardly noticed her silence.

By the time Johnson found them Kiev had already worked out the new compass heading from their present location to the diggings where Wadjik and Shant had planned to work. A little over three hours of the night remained.

"Do you think we can make it before dawn?" Kiev asked as the three of them started out on the new heading. "You've been through that area before, haven't you?"

Johnson nodded.

"I don't know," he said. "It'll be faster going once the moonflowers are down." He looked at Willy. "We'll be pushing on as fast as we can. Think you can keep up?"

"Yes," she said without looking at him. Her voice was dull.

"Good. If you start really to give out, though, speak up. Don't overdo it to the point where we have to carry you. All right?"

"Yes."

They continued their march. Soon the moonflowers had drawn in their petals until they were hardly visible under the hoods and begun their retreat into the ground. The men were now able to see, across the tops of the hoods, the general shape of the terrain and pick the most direct route from contour point to contour point. Willy walked between them. The moonflower hoods still stood above her head—tall as she was for a woman—but did not seem to bother her. She looked at nothing.

Johnson glanced at Kiev across the top of her helmet, and tongued off his helmet phones. He let her walk slightly ahead, then leaned toward Kiev until their helmets touched.

"I told you," Johnson said softly through the helmet contact. "She didn't understand or believe. We were something out of books to her—so were the Udbahrs. Now she's trying hard to keep on not believing. You see why I told you yesterday to get her out of here?"

Kiev said nothing.

Johnson pulled back his helmet, tongued his intercom back on, kept walking.

After a while the sky began to whiten ominously. The nearer moon was low and paling on the horizon behind. Johnson halted. Kiev and Willy also stopped.

"It's no good," said Johnson, over the intercom to Kiev. "We're going to have to take time to find a hole to crawl into before day. We're going to have to quit now and wait for night."

Kiev nodded.

"A hole?" echoed Willy.

Kiev looked at Johnson. Johnson shrugged. The message of the shrug was clear—there were no caves in this area. But they hunted until Johnson called a halt.

"This will have to do."

He pointed to a crack in a rock face. He and Kiev attacked the crack with mining tools and their guns.

Twenty minutes' work hollowed out a burrow three meters in circular diameter, with an entrance two feet square. Above the entrance the crack had been sealed with melted rock. The trio crawled inside and fitted the breathing membrane in place against the opening.

Kiev waited until all were undressed and in their thermal bags before setting the light he had saved from the building in place against the rocky ceiling.

The cramped closeness of their enclosure came to solid life around them. The den was beginning to heat up.

The place had no air-conditioning unit—the shelter had been a palace by comparison. Even Kiev had to struggle against the intoxicating effect of the heat and the claustrophobic panic of the enclosed space. Willy went out of her head before noon. Kiev and Johnson had to hold her in her thermal bag. Shortly after that she went into snycope and stayed unconscious until cool-off.

Haggard with exhaustion, Kiev leaned on one elbow above her, staring down into her face, now smoothed out into natural sleep. Teetering on the verge of irresistible unconsciousness himself, he felt in him the strange clearheadedness of utter weariness. She had been right, he thought, about that primitive part in him and all men—the Ancient Enemy. The prospectors did not so much fight the Udbahr males out here as something in themselves that corresponded to its equivalent in the Udbahrs. The lust for killing. A lust that could get you to the point where you no longer cared if you were killed yourself.

Kiev never finished the thought. When he opened his eyes the membrane was down from the entrance and outside was the cool and blessed moonlight.

He crawled out to find Willy and Johnson already packing gear.

"Got to move, Kiev," said Johnson, seeing him. "If Wad and Shanny are alive and headed home we want to take out after them as soon as possible. One long night's walk can put us back at the hotel."

"The hell you say." Kiev was astonished. "They didn't come all the way out with us and then cut that far back to find a digging area."

"No," Johnson said, "but from here we can hit a

different pass through the border range. Going back that way makes the hypotenuse of a right triangle. Coming out we would have dog-legged it to reach this point like doing the triangle's other two sides. You understand?"

Within half an hour they were on their way. And within an hour, as they were coming around a high spire of rock, Johnson put out his arm and stopped.

"Wait here, Willy," Johnson said. "Come on, Kiev."

The two men rounded the rock and stopped, staring down into a small open area. They saw the scattered remains of working equipment and of Wadjik and Shant. At least one day under the open sun had mummified their bodies. Wadjik lay on his back with the broken shaft of a spear through his chest. But Shant had been pegged out and left to die.

Their outerwear and guns were gone.

"I thought I saw sign of at least half a dozen males back there," Johnson said. "Hehog, all right—with help. He must be swinging some real clout with the other males to have kept them from eating these two right away." He glanced hard at Kiev. "And all for you."

Kiev stared.

"Me? You mean Hehog tied Shanny up and left him like that on purpose—just so I could come along and see it?"

"You begin to see what Ancient Enemy means?" he responded. "We're in trouble, Kiev. Two guns missing and one of the local males grown into a real hoodoo. We'll get moving for civilization right now."

"You're going to bury them first," Willy said.

The men swung around. She was standing just behind them, looking at them. Her gaze dropped, fixed on the bodies below. For a second Kiev thought that the sight had sent her completely out of her mind. Then he saw that her eyes were clear and sane.

Johnson said, "We haven't time—and, anyway, the Udbahrs would come back to dig them up again when they were hungry enough."

"He's right, Willy," said Kiev. "We've got to go—fast." He thought of something else and swung back to Johnson. "That pass you talked about—they'll be laying for us there, Hehog and the other males he's got together. It's the straightest route home, you say, and they know prospectors always head straight out of the mountains when they get into trouble."

Johnson shook his head.

"Don't think so," he said. "You're his Ancient Enemy, looking for that one spot where you and he come face to face and one of you gets the word to kill the other. He'll be right around this area, waiting for us to start hunting for him. If we move fast we've got as good a chance as anyone ever had to get out of these mountains alive."

Johnson set a hard pace. Several times—before the nearer moon was high in the sky and the moonflowers were stretching to full bloom—Willy tripped and would have gone down if Kiev had not caught her. But she did not complain. In fact, she said nothing at all. Shortly after midnight, they broke out from under the umbrellas of a clump of moonflower petals and found themselves in the pass Johnson had talked about.

"We made it," said Johnson, stopping. Kiev also stopped. Willy, stumbling with weariness, blundered into him. She clung to him like a child—and at that moment a thin, bright beam came from among the trunks of the moonflowers behind them.

The side of Johnson's outerwear burst in dazzle and smoke.

Johnson lunged forward. Kiev and Willy ran behind him. Three more bright beams flickered around them as they lurched over the lip of the pass, took half a dozen long, staggering, tripping strides down the far side and dived to shelter behind some waist-high chunks of granite.

Male Udbahr voices began to sing on the far side of the pass.

Johnson coughed. Kiev looked at him and Johnson quickly turned his helmet away, so that the face plate was hidden.

"Move out," Johnson said, in a thick voice, like that of a man with a frog in his throat.

"Are you crazy?"

Kiev had his sidearm out. He sighted around the granite boulder before him and sent a beam high into the rock wall beyond the lip of the pass, on the other side. The rock boomed loudly and flew in fragments. The singing stopped. After a moment it started again.

"I can't help you now," Johnson said, still keeping his face turned away. "Move out, I tell you."

"You think I'm going to leave you?"

Kiev sent off another bolt into the rock face beyond the lip of the pass. This time the singing hardly paused.

"Don't waste your charges," Johnson said hoarsely. "Get out. An hour puts you—hotel."

He had to stop in mid-sentence to cough.

"Forget it, partner," said Kiev. "With my gun and yours I can hold that pass until morning. They can't come through."

Johnson gave an ugly laugh.

"What partner?" he asked. "This partnership's dissolved. And what'll you do when dawn comes? Cook? You're still a good hour's trek from the hotel."

Kiev became aware that Willy was tugging at his arm. She motioned with her head for him to follow her. He did. She slid back down among the rocks until they were a good four meters from where Johnson lay, head toward the pass.

Willy tongued off her intercom and touched her helmet to his.

"He's dying," she said to him through the helmets.

"All right."

Kiev stared at her as if she were Hehog himself.

"You couldn't get him to the hotel in time to save his life even if there weren't any Udbahrs behind us. And we'll never make the hotel unless he stays there and keeps them from following us."

"So?"

She took hold of his shoulders and tried to shake him but he was too heavy and too unmoving with purpose.

"Be sensible." She was almost crying. "Don't you see it's something he wants to do? He wants to save us—"

Kiev stared at her stonily.

"Shanny's dead," Kiev said. "Wad's dead. You want me to leave Johnson?"

She did begin to cry at that, the tears running down her pale face inside her helmet.

"All right, hate me," she said. "Why shouldn't I want to live? This is all your fault—not mine. I didn't kill your partners. I didn't make Hehog your special enemy. All I did was love you. If you were back there I wouldn't leave you, either. But that wouldn't make my staying sensible."

"Go on if you want," he said coldly.

"You know I can't find the hotel by myself!" she said. "You know I'm not going to leave you. Maybe you've got a right to kill yourself—maybe you've even got a right to kill me. But have you got the right to kill me for something that's got nothing to do with me?"

He closed his eyes against the sight of her face. After seconds he opened his eyes, looked away from her, and began to crawl back up the slope until he once more lay beside Johnson.

"It's Willy," he said, not looking at the other man.

"Sure. That's right," said Johnson hoarsely.

A flicker of dark movement came from one side of the pass, and his gun spat. The pass was clear of pursuers again.

"Damn you both," Kiev said, emptily.

"Sure, boy," said Johnson. "Don't waste time, huh?"

Kiev lay where he was. The nearer moon was descending in the sky a little above and to the right of the pass.

"I'll leave my gun," Kiev said at last.

"Don't need it," Johnson said.

Kiev reached out and took Johnson's gloved hand in his own. Through the fabric the return pressure of the other man's grip was light and feeble.

"Get out," said Johnson. "I told you I figured on ending out here."

"You told me not for some trips yet."

"Changed my mind." Johnson let go of Kiev's hand and closed his eyes. His voice was not much more than a whisper. "I think instead I'll make it this trip."

He did not say any more. After a long minute Kiev spoke to him again.

"Johnson—"

Johnson did not answer. Only the gun in his hand spat light briefly into the wall of the pass. Kiev stared a second longer, then turned and went sliding down the hill to where Willy crouched.

"We go fast," said Kiev.

They went away without looking back. Twice they heard the sound of a gun behind them. Then intervening rocks cut off whatever else they might have heard. They walked without pausing. After about an hour Willy began to stumble with exhaustion and

clung to him. Kiev put his arm around her; they
hobbled along together, leaning into the pitch of the
upslopes, sliding in the loose rock of downslopes.

The moon was low on the stony horizon behind
them. Ahead came the first whitening in the sky that
said dawn was less than two hours away. Willy staggered and leaned more heavily upon Kiev. Looking
down at her face through the double transparencies
of both helmets, Kiev saw that she was stumbling
along with her eyes tightly closed, her face hardened
into a colorless mask of effort. A strand of hair had
fallen forward over one closed eye and his heart
lurched at the sight of it.

Not from the first had he ever thought of her as
beautiful. Now, gaunt with effort, hair disarrayed,
she was less so than ever—and yet he had never
loved and wanted her more. It was because of the
mountains, he thought. And Hehog, Wad, Shanny—
and Johnson. Each time he had paid out one of them
for her, the worth of her had gone up that much.
Now she was equal to the total of all of them together.

She stumbled again, almost lost her footing. A
wordless little sound was jolted out from between
her clenched teeth, though her eyes stayed closed.

"Walk," he said savagely, jerking her upright and
onward. "Keep walking." They were on the Track,
now, the curving trail that all the prospectors took
out of the valley of the Border Hotel. "Keep walking," he muttered to her. "Just around the curve
there—"

A bolt from a gun behind them boomed suddenly
against the cliff-base to their right. Rock chips rained
down Willy's knees. She lurched toward the shelter
of the nearest boulder.

He jerked her upright.

"Run for it. Run—"

Jolting, stumbling, they ran while bolts from the
gun boomed.

"They can't shoot worth—" Kiev muttered through his teeth.

He stopped talking. Because at that moment they rounded a curve and saw the sprawling concrete shape of the Border Hotel and its grounds—and saw Hehog, holding a sidearm, stepping out from behind a rock twenty feet ahead.

In that instant time itself seemed to hesitate. Kiev's weary legs had checked at his sight of Hehog. He started forward again at a walk, half-carrying Willy. Her eyes were still closed.

He thought, she doesn't see Hehog.

He marched on. Hehog brought up the gun, aimed it—but he, too, seemed caught in the suspension of time. He wore the helmet he had taken from Kiev two years before and now he also wore the white jacket of Shant's outerwear suit—which almost fit him. He stood waiting, one sidearm in a jacket pocket, one in his hand, aimed.

Kiev stumped toward him, bringing Willy. Kiev's eyes were on the bulging eyes of Hehog. Their gazes locked. The only sound was the noise of Kiev's boots scuffing the rock underfoot. From the hotel in the valley below, no sound. From the other Udbahr males that had been firing at them from behind, no sound.

Kiev marched on, Hehog growing before him. The great eyes danced in Kiev's vision. There was a wild emptiness in Kiev now, an insane certainty. He did not move aside to avoid Hehog. They were ten feet apart—they were five—they would collide—

Hehog stepped back. Without shifting the line of his advance an inch, without moving his eyes to follow Hehog, Kiev marched past him. The trail to the hotel sloped suddenly more sharply under Kiev's feet and now he looked only at what was manmade. All the Udbahrs were behind him. And behind him he heard Hehog beginning to sing softly.

Man with a head-and-a-half,
come and get your half-head.
Man with a head-and-a-half,
Come, so I can kill you . . .

The song faded behind him until his stumbling feet carried him in through the great airdoor of the hotel and all things ended at once.

He was nearly four days recovering and three days after that sitting around the Border Hotel, making plans for the future with Willy. They had adjoining rooms, each with a balcony looking out to the dawnrise side of the hotel. Heavy filterglass doors shut out the sunlight and protected the rooms' air-conditioned interiors during the daytime. Kiev had agreed to go back to the Old Worlds with Willy, to get married and write and tell what he knew. There was nothing wrong with making a living any way you could back on the Old Worlds, even if it meant writing and lecturing. Only once did Willy bring up the subject of the mountains.

"Why did Hehog let us pass?" she asked.

He stared at her.

"I thought that your eyes were closed."

"I opened them when you halted. I closed them when I saw him. I thought it was all over then—and that he was going to kill us both. But you started walking and he let us pass. Why?"

Kiev looked down at the thick brown carpet.

"Hehog's never going to get the message," he said to the carpet.

"What?"

"Ancient Enemies—Johnson told me. Hehog thinks he and I are something special to each other with this Ancient Enemies business. We're doomed to have one of us kill the other. We're supposed to keep coming together until one of us gets the message to kill. Then the other just lets it happen. Because he's doomed—there's nothing he can do about it."

He stopped talking. For a minute she said nothing, either, as if she was waiting for him to go on explaining.

"Hehog didn't get the message when we walked past him?" she asked, at last. "Is that it?"

"He'll never get the message," said Kiev dully. "He had two clear chances at me and he didn't do anything. It means he thinks he's the one who's doomed. He's waiting to die—for me to kill him."

"To kill him? Why would he want you to kill him?"

Kiev shrugged.

"Answer me."

"How do I know?" Kiev said exhaustedly. "Maybe he's getting old. Maybe he thinks its just time for him to die—maybe his mate's dead."

There was momentary, somehow ugly silence. Then Willy spoke again.

"Kiev."

"What?"

"Look up here," she said, sharply. "I want you to look at me."

He raised his gaze slowly from the thick carpet and saw her face as stiffly fixed as it had been in the helmet on the last long kilometer to the hotel.

"Listen to me, Kiev," she said. "I love you and I want to live with you more than anything else for the rest of my life—and I'll do anything for you I can do. But there's one thing I can't do. I just can't."

He frowned at her, uneasy and restless.

"I can't help it," she said. "I thought we were getting away from it here and that it wouldn't matter. But it does. If I can feel it there in you I go dead inside—I just can't love you any more. That's all there is to it."

"What?" he asked.

Her hands made themselves into ineffective small fists in her lap, then uncurled and lay limp.

"There are so many things I love about you," she said emptily, "I thought I could ignore this one thing. But I can't think so any more. Not since we saw those two dead men—and not since the walk back here. Our love is just never going to work if you still want—want to kill. Do you understand? If you're still wanting to kill it just won't work out for us. Do you understand, Kiev?"

The bottom seemed to fall out of his stomach. He was abruptly sick.

"I told you that's all over!" he shouted furiously at her. "I don't want to kill anything!"

"You don't have to promise." She rose to her feet, her face still tight. "It doesn't matter if you promise. It only matters if you're telling the truth."

She turned and walked to the door of his hotel room.

"It's almost dawn," she said. "I'm going down to see if the authorization for our spaceship tickets has come through for today's flight—before the sun shuts off communications. I'll be back in half an hour."

She went out. The door made no noise closing behind her.

He turned and flopped on the bed, stared up at the ceiling. Everything was wonderful—or was it? He tried to think about the future in safety of the Old Worlds but his mind would not focus. After a bit he rose and walked out to the balcony.

Before him stood the ramparts of the cliffs. On the balcony was an observation scope. He bent over it and fiddled with its controls until the boulders a kilometer away seemed to hang a dozen meters in front of him.

He turned the sound pick-up on.

It was nearly time for the Udbahrs to be hunting

their dens for the day but he heard no singing. He panned the scope, searching the rocks. There it came—a faint wisp of melody.

He searched the rock. The stone blurred before him. He lost then found the song again and closed in on it until the image in the screen of the scope locked on the figure of a male Udbahr standing deep between two tall boulders—an Udbahr wearing a transparent helmet and white jacket, with a sidearm in his hand.

The song came suddenly loud and clear.

> *Ancient, my enemy. Ancient,*
> *my enemy.*
> *No one but ourselves has the*
> *killing of each other . . .*
> *Man with a head-and-a-half,*
> *come and get your half-head.*
> *Man with a head-and-a-half*

Kiev stepped back from the scope. His head pounded suddenly. His stomach knotted. His throat ached. A fever blazed through him and his skin felt dry, dusty. He turned and strode across the room to his bag. He plowed through it, throwing new shoes, pants and shirts aside.

His hand closed on the last hard item at the bottom. His gun. He jerked out the weapon, snatched up the long barrel for distance shooting and was snapping it into position on the gun even as he was striding toward the balcony.

He applied the magnetic clamp of the gun butt to the scope and thumbed up the near lens of the telescope sight. The red cross-hairs wavered, searched, found Hehog. It was a long shot. The lenses of the sight held level on the Udbahr in a straight line; but below them, on their gimbals, the barrel of the automatically sighting weapon was angled so that it seemed to point clear over the cliffs at the day that was coming. Kiev's dry and shaking fingers curled around the butt. His forefinger reached toward the firing button and instantly all the shaking was over.

His grip was steady. His blood was ice but the fever still burned in his brain. As clearly as a vision before him, he saw the mummified figures of Wadjik and Shant—and Johnson as he had last seen the older man.

Kiev pressed the firing button.

From the cliffside came the sound of a distant explosion. A puff of rockdust plumed toward the whitening sky. A rising murmur, a mounting buzz of voices began beyond the walls of his room. People began to appear on the surrounding balconies.

Kiev faded back two steps, silent as a thief. Hidden in the shadows of the balcony he could still see what the others could not.

Hehog lay beside one of the two boulders between which he had been standing. A blackish stain was spreading on the right side of his white jacket and the sidearm had fallen from his grip.

He was plainly dying. But he was not yet dead. He began to sing again.

> *Man with a head-and-a-half*
> *. . . come and get your . . .*
> *half-head.*
> *Man with a head-and-a . . .*

Through the pick-up of the scope Kiev, frozen in the shadows, could hear the Udbahr's voice weakening. Then the door to the room slammed open behind him.

"Kiev, did you hear it? Someone shot from the Hotel—"

Willy's voice broke off.

He turned and saw her just inside the door. She

was gazing past him at the scope with its picture of Hehog and the sound of Hehog's weakening song coming from it. She stared at it. Then, slowly, as if she was being forced against her will, her eyes shifted until they met his.

All the feeling in him that the sight of Hehog had triggered into life went out of him with a rush, leaving him empty as a disemboweled man.

"Willy—"

He took a step toward her. Her face twitched as if with a sudden, sharp, unbearable pain and her hand came up reflexively as if to push him away, though they were still more than half a room apart.

Her throat worked but she made no sound. She struggled for an instant, then shook her head briefly. Still holding up her hand as if to fend him off, she backed away from him. The door opened behind her and let her out.

The door closed, leaving him alone. He swung slowly back to face the scope. Hehog still lay framed in the lens and above that image the ominous light of day was fast whitening the sky.

Hehog was still feebly singing; but the song had changed. Now it was the song Willy had asked Kiev to translate when she had first heard an Udbahr male. Kiev turned and flung himself facedown on the bed, his arms over his head to shut out the sound. But the song came through to him.

> You desert me now, female,
> Because I am crippled.
> And yet, all my fault was
> That I did not lack courage.
> Therefore I will go now to the
> high rocks to die.
> And another will take you . . .

The slow rumble of the heavy, opaque, thermal glass, sliding automatically across the entrance to the balcony, silenced the song in Kiev's ears. Beyond the dark glass the sun of day broke at last over the rim of the cliffs and sent its fierce light slanting down. There was no mercy in that relentless light and all living things who did not hide before it died.

Turnabout

Paul Barstow was saying,
"And this is the gadget . . ."

His square bright face under its close-cropped blond
hair was animated. He seemed on the verge of reaching up to hook a finger in the lapel buttonhole of Jack
Hendrix's sportcoat to pull the taller man down into
a position where he could shout into his ear.

"You aren't listening!" he protested now. "Buddy!
Jack! Pay some attention. Or has that crumby teaching
job got you to the point where money doesn't mean
anything to you any more?"

Jack Hendrix's long, heavy-boned face almost
blushed.

"I'm listening," he said.

He hadn't been, of course. This was merely one
more piece of evidence to add to the mounting pile
of proof that he was totally incapable of doing anything right. He had been mooning instead over Eva
Guen, whom he had lost some months back. But
they had passed her in the corridor on their way to

89

this small, hidden workroom, and something in the way she had looked at him had set him spinning again. Peculiarly, there had been what Jack could have sworn was a hurt look in her eyes, in that brief moment that they looked at each other in passing. Why there should be a hurt look in *her* eyes, Jack could not understand. She was the one who had left him to come to work for Paul—and very sensibly, too, he told himself, self-righteously, but with the same old twinge of unhappiness.

Eva had been his graduate teaching assistant at the University where he taught physics. She was tall and quiet-faced, with startling wide blue eyes under soft blonde hair. Quite naturally, he had fallen in love with her. And it was then the trouble started.

For from the moment Jack was forced to admit to himself that he was in love, he had to take an unbiased look at his chances of doing something about it. And that look was crushing in its effect. For in the process of assembling Jack Hendrix, a somewhat devastating oversight had occurred. Whatever minor god had been in the supervisory position that day had carefully mixed strength with intelligence, added just a pinch of genius and a sort of ugly-handsome good looks, but had totally forgotten at the last moment to install a governor on Jack's imagination. The result was that Jack was a dreamer.

And the result of that was that he, with three degrees to his name, and a couple of honoraries of various sorts lying around, continued to vegetate in his teaching job, while Paul, in his typical hyperthyroid fashion, was already managing his own commercial research labs. Not that the comparison was strictly fair. Paul had always been more promoter than physicist. And Eva had gone out of Jack's life to a better job with Paul's outfit.

Not that that had anything to do with his accepting

Paul's offer of a job as consultant on a little problem he claimed to have on hand at the moment.

"I'm listening," said Jack.

"Praise Allah," said Paul. "No one knows about this but you and me. It's top secret. *My* top secret."

Women, of course, thought Jack, were naturally secretive. They looked at you with unfathomable blue eyes and waited for you to make the proper move. But how could you make the proper move if you didn't know what they were thinking? That was why he had never gotten around to telling Eva how he felt about her. And then one day she was gone. He didn't blame her, even if without warning it had exploded—

"—Exploded?" stammered Jack, guiltily. "Well, er—when did that happen?"

"Are you sure you've been listening?" said Paul, suspiciously. "I just told you. A couple of weeks back." He went on to explain the circumstances while Jack listened with one ear, the image of Eva flickering like a candle luring his moth-like powers of attention in the back of his mind.

He forced himself to concentrate.

"But what happened to the man you had working on it?" he asked. "And what is it, anyway? You still haven't told me that."

"You mean Reppleman?" said Paul, quickly. "He had a nervous breakdown at the time of the explosion. Got a complete block on the whole thing, and now, they've got him in a nursing home."

A flicker of genuine interest stirred for the first time in Jack.

"Oh?" he said. "How come?"

"Well, that's the thing," said Paul. "I'm going to trust you, Jack. I've got something here that's worth more money than there is in the world today; and I'm willing to give you a slice of it if you can work this thing out for me. But we've got to have secrecy.

"Right at this moment, you and I are the only ones who even know this room has been entered since the explosion. I rebuilt the generator myself from Reppleman's records. And nobody, but you and I, knows we're back here today. The rooms at the back of the building here are all storerooms except this one."

"Generator?" said Jack, for a second momentary instant distracted from the lorelei mental image of Eva.

"A generator," said Paul, slowly and impressively, "of an impenetrable, planar field of force. Come over here."

The image of Eva went out as abruptly as if someone had dropped a candle-snuffer over it. Jack blinked and followed Paul, as he led him up to the equipment in question.

The small room which housed it was right at the bleak northern end of the labs and terminated one narrow wing of the building. It was L-shaped, with the generator in question tucked away in the narrow recess of the foot of the L. The length of the long part of the L, at right angles to this, was strewn with odds and ends of tools and equipment piled on two long benches fastened to the wall. Along the end away from the recess was the door that gave entrance to the room; and just to the left of this as you entered, at the end of the long part of the L, was the room's only window, open at the moment to the summer breeze and the gravel expanse of the parking lot behind the labs.

His mind for once wholly concentrating on the subject at hand, Jack followed Paul into the narrow cubbyhole that was the recess and listened to the other man's explanation of what was before him. It was not true that Jack could not focus on a problem. It was merely that a thing to hold his attention must first arouse his interest. Once it had, he dealt with it with almost fantastic effectiveness.

"You see," Paul was explaining, "it's a very simple sort of circuit. It's easy enough to produce it. The question is to handle it, after you've produced it. The initial power to run it comes from this storage battery hookup. That's all we need."

"Then what's the catch?" asked Jack, his nose half-buried in the creation's innards.

"The trouble is that once it's turned on, there seems to be a sort of feedback effect. Well, no, that isn't quite right. What it seems to do once it's turned on is tap some other source of power that's too much for it. It overloads and you get the explosion."

"But while it's on you have a plane of force?"

"That's right."

"How long?" demanded Jack, his long fingers poking in the wiring.

"You mean from establishment of the field to explosion?" replied Paul. "About half a minute, as far as I can figure from Reppleman's notes and what I could reconstruct about what happened the day it blew up on him."

"You haven't tried it since you rebuilt it?" asked Jack.

"Do I look crazy?" demanded Paul. He put his hand on Jack's arm. "Listen buddy, remember me? The boy with the crib notes up his sleeve at exams?"

Half-lost in the machine before him as he was, Jack felt a sudden little stir of warning. Paul was anything but stupid; and when he went into his dumb-bunny act, there was usually a joker somewhere in the deck. But before he could concentrate on the sudden small danger signal he ran across something that drove it out of his mind.

"What's this?" he demanded, pouncing on a part of the apparatus.

"Oh, that," said Paul. "Just a notion of my own. Obvious answer. A timer setup. You set it, say, to turn the field on for perhaps a ten-thousandth

of a second, then turn it off again. I'll let you play
with it."

Jack frowned.

"Where are the notes?" he asked. "I'd like to see
just what—Reppleman, you said his name was?—had
written down."

Paul grinned and shook his head.

"Not so fast. First I want an answer from you on
whether you think you can tame this baby for me or
not."

"But how can I tell without the background?" protested Jack.

"Won't cost you a cent to say no," replied Paul.
"Don't look at me like that, Jack. Sure, I know I'm
handing you a pig in a poke. But this thing is too big
to take chances with. Do you want it or don't you?"

Jack hesitated. He was strongly tempted to tell
Paul to take a running nosedive into the nearest lake,
and walk out. Then he remembered the long life of
financial ineptitude that had climaxed itself with losing Eva; and his good resolutions to mend his
scatterbrained ways.

"All right," he said. "I'll have a shot at it, anyhow."

"Good boy," said Paul. He patted Jack's arm, in a
way which was somehow reminiscent of approving a
large, shaggy dog. "I'll be in my office. You know
where that is. If you want anything, just hustle me
up."

He gave Jack's shoulder a final slap and strode out.

Left alone, Jack sat down on one of the long
workbenches, filled his pipe and considered the problem. The situation was peculiar to say the least.
Paul's odd insistence on secrecy; and Eva's strange
look when she had passed him in the corridor. And
this story about the man who had developed the
generator. Typically, it did not occur to him to doubt
the generator. Jack was one of those men who have

entertained the impossible in their minds so often that there is little reality can do to surprise them.

So it blew up did it? Jack puffed on his pipe and stared at the generator. But—hold on a minute—if it blew up and when it blew up it sent a man named Reppleman to a rest home, could it have blown up more than once? And if it had blown up only once it must have been turned on only once, and if that was the case, how did Paul know that it had produced a plane of force? Of course he had probably known the theory Reppleman was working on. And what was his purpose in keeping that theory a secret from Jack?

In fact, if the dingus worked, how did it work? Jack returned to the mass of equipment and wiring and began to prowl through it. After a while he stopped and scowled. Nine-tenths of the junk in the setup was mere window-dressing. The only thing about it that could possibly have any effect or function was an oddly wound coil of ordinary silver wire upon a core of some strange-looking silvery metal. Jack tapped this latter with a fingernail and it rang with a faint, light-sounding chime.

By the time this point was reached his interest had been captured. On a hunch he disconnected everything but the coil on its peculiar core. He disconnected the timer Paul had attached to the apparatus, hesitated a second, then made contact by crossing the two lead-in wires.

Nothing happened.

He disconnected the wires and sat back to think.

After a moment, he reached out and felt the winding on the coil. It was metal-cool—air temperature. On second thought, he connected the timer and set it to allow a warm-up period of fifteen seconds. At the end of that time the timer should activate the coil for the period of a ten-thousandth of a second.

Nothing happened.

Jack chewed the stem of his pipe. Once more he disconnected and felt the winding. It was faintly warm—but barely so.

Now let me see, said Jack to himself. We run two sorts of power through this thing. One, low power and steady. To warm it up? That's what I assumed, but there's no indication of it. On the other hand this timer is definitely set to give a sudden short pulse of relatively high current. I tried the high current direct. No result. I tried a short period of low current. What's next?

After he had smoked another pipeful of tobacco, all that occurred to him was to lengthen the warmup period. Let's do it right, he said to himself. Let's give it a good five minutes.

He turned it on once more and set the timer for another ten-thousandths of a second jolt at the end of five minutes of low power. It occurred to him that the two upright metal poles, about two feet in length, between which the field was supposed to be generated, might be too close to the coil, and he moved them out to the full length of their wiring, so that they were now actually in the long part of the room. He glanced at the timer. Almost four minutes yet to go.

He wandered down the long part of the room and stood gazing out the window. There was his car, sitting beside the row of others on the gravel of the parking lot. And there, farther down the row was Eva's. They were the two oldest cars on the lot. You'd almost think we had the same taste in automobiles, thought Jack, a trifle wistfully. Neither of them is worth much—

Abruptly, without warning, his traitorous imagination slipped its restraints and began to build a picture of Eva coming out on to the lot, seeing his old car not very distant from hers, and being overwhelmed by a flood of memories. He pictured her coming out the back entrance of the building as he stood here watching. She would walk across the lot with her smooth, lithe stride, toward her own old grey, four-door sedan. But partway there, her steps would falter as she caught sight of his equally ancient blue business coupe. She would not, of course, say anything, but she would stand there; and he, seizing the moment, would step from this window down onto the gravel only a few feet below and approach her.

The sound of his footsteps crunching the loose rock would warn her of his coming; and she would turn to look at him. She would neither move nor speak, but stand waiting as he came up to her and then—

He was just opening his mouth to speak to her in imagination, when unexpectedly from behing Jack there came the sound of a soft, insidious click . . .

For a moment he thought nothing had happened. The parking lot lay unchanged before him in the sunlight with its row of cars and the sky blue above them dotted with distant clouds. And then he tried to turn around and found he could not, with the slight movement of his effort the scene before him dissolved into a grey field streaked here and there by lines of various colors.

He froze, suddenly, and the scene came back to normal. He reached out to grab hold of the edge of the window to steady himself; but with his first movement he was plunged into greyness and his hands caught nothing. Once more he steeled himself into immobility, and for a moment he hung on the edge of panic. What had happened?

Slowly, he forced his mind back into control of his body and its emotions. Steady, he told himself, steady. Think it through.

As calmness returned he became suddenly and icily aware of two things. The first was that everything within his field of vision appeared somehow artifically frozen into immobility. Just what gave him this impression he was not able to understand. Part of it was the air. A small breeze had been bathing him as he stood in front of the open window. Now, there was nothing. The atmosphere around him was like intangible glass.

The second thing was the discovery that he was no longer standing with his feet on the floor, but lying crosswise athwart the window, in mid-air, at about the former level of his waist.

For a moment he was astounded that he had not realized this immediately. And then reasons began to appear to him. The first of these was the sudden realization that gravity appeared to have altered respective to his position. He felt not at all as if he were lying on his side, but as if he had remained quite normally upright. And another discovery following immediately on the heels of this was the sudden perception that while his body seemed to have moved, his point of view had not. He still looked out at the parking lot from the angle of vision of a man with both feet normally planted on the floor.

All of these, of course, were things that held true only as long as he remained perfectly still. The moment he attempted to move all his senses failed him and he seemed to swim in a grey mist. The conclusion was a very obvious one. Somehow, the generator had worked to produce its plane of force. And somehow he was caught in it.

The explosion should come at any moment now.

For one hideous moment he suffered death in imagination. Then reason returned to point out that the half minute Paul had mentioned as the time limit had undoubtedly been passed already. Still, it was a little while before he could completely fight off the

tension of his body, bracing itself in expectation of
the rending force that could strike at him from behind.

In the end it was his imagination that saved him.
For long habit had made it independent of the rest of
him; and its first move, once the facts of the matter
had been grasped and the immediate danger of explosion discounted, was to draw him a very clear and
somewhat ridiculous mental picture of himself as he
must appear to anyone who might enter the room,
floating broadside as he was, in thin air. It reminded
him suddenly that positions were no respecters of
persons; and he remembered almost in the same
instant of what the White Knight had had to say to
Alice on the subject after resting head-downward in
a ditch. And so, by way of the ludicrous, he scrambled back onto the firm ground of his everyday sanity.

He was caught in a force field. Very well. And
what could he do about it? The obvious answer was
to turn around, go back to the generator and turn it
off. And the one flaw in this plan was that he couldn't
apparently, for some reason, make the turn.

On the other hand, he was able to make some
movements. He experimented, waving first an arm
and then a leg, cautiously. Barring the fact that the
slightest motion caused the room to appear a night-
mare of streaks and lines in a grey field, there was
nothing unusual about the effects of these motions.
The room? He became suddenly aware that he seemed
to have rotated around a center-point somewhere in
the region of his belt buckle. He was now no longer
looking out the window, but turned at a slight angle
toward the bench on what had been the wall at his
right hand. Filled with sudden hope, he closed his
eyes firmly and took what should have been a long
stride forward and up. When he opened them again
he was staring back into the room, down the long
length of the L.

For a long moment he hung, carefully motionless,

considering the implications of what he had just done. It seemed apparent, he thought, that what he had actually accomplished was to turn himself about the way a paper figure would be turned on a turntable— the difference between this and ordinary methods being that as he was now facing in the opposite direction, his head was now where his feet had been and vice versa. Or, to orient more exactly by existing landmarks, where the force field had flipped him into position with his head toward the right wall, his rotation had changed him so that now his head was toward the opposite wall, the one originally on his left.

Conclusion?

Jack winced. The field itself appeared to be a two-dimensional phenomenon; and he, himself, caught up in it, to be restricted to two-dimensional movement. For a second the thrill of panic came back, and he was forced to fight for a moment before he could go back to looking at the situation sensibly and calmly.

The field appeared to be on a level with his waist as it had been when he had been standing normally upright. That was, in effect, level with the tops of the upright rods that had been supposed to generate the field between them. Hah!—*between* them, thought Jack, bitterly—and a few inches above the level of the benches. As he looked down the length of the room he noticed that whatever had touched the plane of the field at any point seemed to have been, like himself, caught up in it. He noticed a hammer and a soldering iron, both of which had been hanging from hooks on the left wall, now floating stiffly at right angles to it. Furthermore, there seemed to have been some sort of polarity involved. In both cases the end which had been upright was at the left and the down end out at the right—that was, of course, from his present point of view—and corresponded exactly with the fact that his own head had gone to the right, and his feet to the left.

But that was enough observing. The thing to do now was to get to the generator and turn it off before something else happened. Jack closed his eyes and made three quick steps, right foot first left foot following, toe to heel. When he opened them again he was mildly surprised to discover that he was still a little short of the end of the room, but a couple more steps solved that problem. He rotated himself through a ninety degree arc and stepped *up* into the narrow alcove that housed the generator and the timer on a bench at its far end.

He banged his head on the wall and blinked with the shock of it. He opened his eyes and looked down at the generator.

With a sudden, sickening sense of shock, he realized that it was below him, and therefore outside of the plane of the field. His desperation was strong enough to make him reach for it, anyway, and to his surprise it seemed almost to flow upward to reach his fingers and his fingertips pushed against a short length of wire, which bent before them.

As they did so, there was a sudden flare of red light from the coil and he snatched his fingers away as he noticed that that part of the generator was apparently red hot, glowing into incandescence. The whole apparatus, in fact, seemed to quiver on the point of exploding into flame. Curiously, however, there was no sensation of heat emanating from the coil; and what was apparently a wisp of smoke, rising above the generator and out of the field, seemed frozen in midair.

Cautiously Jack retreated slightly from the generator. Two things were immediately apparent. One, that the generator was evidently a part of the field, and reachable, even though it had not been in the original plane as he had. Two, that he had better be careful how he went about shutting it off. It struck him somewhat belatedly that Reppleman's explosion had probably occurred through mishandling the generator when it was in its present state.

No, the way to turn the generator off was the way it had been turned on—through the timer. He looked at the portion of the generator and bench that lay below him but did not see the timer. Then he remembered that this was the left side of the bench at the alcove's extremity and that the timer was at the right. Carefully he rotated to the right as far as the narrow width of the alcove would allow him and out of the corner of his eye, caught a glimpse of the timer on the bench far to the right. The position was an awkward one, but he was in no mood to consider comfort. It might be interesting for a while to be the two-dimensional inmate of a single plane, but the novelty wore off quickly. He pushed his head into the right hand corner of the alcove and started to reach back past his hip to the timer.

It was impossible.

For a moment he hung still, stunned. Then as the truth penetrated, he had to restrain an urge to burst into hysterical laughter. Of course, being two-dimensional he could not move the line of his hand past the line of his body, any more than a normal three-dimensional person in a three-dimensional world can lie on his side on a flat floor and duplicate such an action without moving either floor or body. As long as he remained an inhabitant of the force field, he would never be able to reach behind his back. Around his feet or around the top of his head, yes, but behind his back—never.

For a moment he yielded again to panic and scrabbled around to find a position from which he could reach the timer, but the alcove was too small to allow him his necessary two-dimensional turning radius.

He stopped finally, and common sense came to his aid.

Of course, the thing to do was to back out where there was room and turn around, so that he could come in facing in the other direction.

He moved back out into the long part of the room, mentally berating himself for having lost his head. He closed his eyes and rotated. He was getting quite used to this business of blinding himself while moving and made a mental note that eventually he must get around to keeping his eyes open just to get a clearer picture of what happened, when he did move. Reversed, he stepped back *up* into the alcove.

He opened his eyes to find himself not in the alcove but against the wall of the long room opposite the alcove. For a moment he stared in puzzlement, then understanding came.

"Of course," he said. "I'm reversed. I'll have to step *down*."

He did so. Two steps down took him into the alcove. He opened his eyes to find himself finally facing the corner which housed the timer—*but his feet were the parts of him next to it, and his head and hands were away from it.*

This is ridiculous! he thought. One way it's behind my back and the other way it's down by my feet. He crouched down, trying to squeeze himself into the corner close enough so that he could reach the timer. But it was no use. The alcove was too narrow to allow him to put his feet in the opposite corner and lean far enough over so that his hands could manipulate the timer. The sort of person who can bend over and put both hands flat on the floor could have done it easily, but Jack, like most males of more or less sedentary occupation, was not in that kind of shape. He tried kneeling, squeezing himself as tightly into the right hand corner as he could. But here the earlier prohibition of his two-dimensional existence came again into effect and he was blocked by his own knees. Not only did he have to reach around them, but they blocked off his view of the timer.

In a cold sweat, he finally gave up and backed out into the relatively open space of the long part of the room. It was fantastic. There was the timer directly in front of him. A touch of the finger would shut it off, for he could see its pointer frozen on the mark where it had turned the generator on. And it was a part of the field like the generator wire he had touched, so presumably he could move it. Yet, because of the restrictions of two-dimensional space, it was out of his reach.

To Jack, a born and native three-dimensioner, it seemed grossly unfair; and for one of the few times in his life he blew up.

After having cursed out force-fields, force-field inventors, all known physical laws, the generator, Paul, and himself for being a damn fool and daydreaming when he should have been watching the timer, he found himself feeling somewhat better. From being excited, he suffered a reaction to calmness. Let's look at this sensibly, he told himself.

He reminded himself that he'd been acting like a wild animal caught in a trap, rather than a thinking man. The thing to do was to make an effort to understand what it was that had hold of him rather than just fighting it blindly. If he could not reach the timer, he could not reach the timer. What other possibilities were there?

One—somebody, say perhaps Paul, would eventually come in and perhaps he could turn the timer off. Jack shook his head. No, whoever stepped through the door of the room would probably be caught up in the field the way he had been. If indeed the field was limited only to the room and did not extend beyond its walls already. Jack brightened. If the field was bounded by the room, then all he had to do was get out of it—

Painfully he maneuvered himself around until he was facing the door. The doorknob was below the field, but he had hopes of hooking his fingers onto the door's loose edge and pulling it open. It was a hope that was doomed to disappointment. Jack discovered that in two dimensions you could push, with fingertips, but not grab. The door, presumably because it was hinged to the walls outside the scope of the field, was strictly immovable.

It appeared to be a rule that whatever was loose and touched by the field was picked up by it, but whatever was attached to anything else beyond the limits of the field was not. It did not strictly make sense, because where do you draw the line of attachment? His body was attached to his limbs and his limbs had been outside the field. A matter of relative mass?

Concluding this to be an unrewarding field for speculation, Jack returned to the matter of field size, and at that moment it suddenly dawned on him that all this time the window at the end of the room had been open. If he could get out through that and beyond the limits of the field—

The wish was father to the act. Hardly had the thought occurred to him before he was jockeying for position in line with the window. He got it—back in the same position in which he had first found himself when the field caught him up—and simply walked out, presenting the unusual spectacle of a man strolling through mid-air while lying on his right side. It was all so easy that for the first time he found cause to wonder about the fact that the walking motion enabled him to progress when he was apparently doing nothing more than flailing the empty air. He experimented a little and discovered that he had the sensation of pressing back against something whenever he moved. Apparently the field had some kind of substance of its own, or a type of tension that reacted like an elastic skin when pressed longitudinally.

As soon as he was free of the building he rotated abruptly and *walked* sideways alongside it. His hope was that the field would be cut off by any solid obstacle. He traveled for some little distance before he admitted to himself that this hope was vain. Cheerfully, the field continued to buoy him up and imprison him, even when he reached the street in front of the labs.

The street was unusually silent and deserted. For a moment he considered waiting until somebody came by to help. But his natural shyness and sensitivity to embarrassment overcame the idea, and he turned back to cruise once more along the side of the building, peering in the windows with the hope of locating Paul himself, or at least someone connected with the labs.

The windows on the back and the side he had been down were all closed and the door had taught him that there was no use dealing with any three-dimensional object unless it was, like him, caught up in the field. He crossed past his own open window and started down the far side of the building.

Here there were several open windows, but they all gave on empty offices. But toward the front he came to one through which he could glimpse figures, at the far end. Without hesitation, he closed his eyes and stepped through the opening.

When he opened his eyes inside the room, he was astonished to see a tableau that was more than even his overactive imagination had ever conceived. Before him were Paul and Eva. They stood facing each other in a small room that seemed to be a sort of combination office and laboratory. Paul was leaning forward and his hand was on the smock-sleeved arm of Eva, who was pulling away from him.

For a moment the implications of the scene did not penetrate. When they did, Jack went skidding through the air toward the two figures, too angry even to remember to close his eyes.

When the grey field winked away to reveal the room in its proper dimensions again, he found himself floating in mid-air beside and a little above them. This room was evidently lower than the one from which he had started; and he glared down at the top of Paul's stubbled head and cut loose.

It was a fine exhibition of sizzling language, punctuated by flashes of streaky greyness, when in his excitement he forgot himself and moved or jerked his head. But when at last he began to run down, he was somewhat astonished to discover that neither of the people below had moved or shown any reaction to his presence. They had not even looked up.

In fact, Paul was still clutching Eva's arm and Eva was still leaning backward. They had not moved at all.

An awful suspicion struck Jack with the impact of a solid fist to the pit of the stomach. He had assumed until now that the timer had somehow stuck at the position in which it activated the generator, that no explosion had taken place because he had been careful after that first crimson flare not to monkey with the working parts of the generator. It had not occurred to him that the field in restricting him to two dimensions might *really* have restricted him to two dimensions.

Frantically he rotated until he was able to spot a large electric wall clock above the door of the room. Its hands were frozen at twelve minutes after two, and the long sweep-second hand stood motionless a little beyond the figure 12. He rotated back to where he could view the two people below. On the thick

wrist above the hand that held Eva's arm was a large
gold wristwatch, and this also stood with its hands
immovably at twelve minutes after two. Jack was
caught, not merely in a single plane, but in a single
instant of time.

Up until now he had not really despaired. Always
in the back of his mind had been the notion that
even if he failed completely, sooner or later someone
would come to his rescue.

Now he realized that no rescue was possible.

Somehow he survived that realization. Possibly
because he was the kind of man who does survive,
the sort of person who by birth and training has been
educated to disbelieve in failure. It was just not in
him to accept the fact that he was hopelessly trapped.
And particularly in support of this was the discovery
he had just made about Paul and Eva.

He looked down at them with a sort of bleak
clarity of understanding that he had never succeeded
in obtaining before. He realized now that he had
been—for all effective purposes—blind while Eva
had been working with him at the University.

He had introduced Paul to Eva himself some six
months back when the other man had dropped by to
see him on one of his occasional forays into the
academic area in search of likely hired help. Jack had
not considered the introduction important. It had
not occurred to him that Paul would find Eva the
sort of woman he would want. In fact if anyone had
asked him about such a combination, he would have
thought it rather funny. The two, by his standards,
were opposite as the poles—Eva, with her cool depths,
and Paul with his violent surface huckstering. It had
not aroused Jack's suspicion that Paul should visit
frequently during the months that followed, and that
his visits should stop with Eva leaving the U.

No, Jack had been blind to the possibility of anyone else wanting Eva but himself, obsessed by the battle with his inner shyness that twiddled its thumbs and hoped vainly for a fortuitous set of circumstances that would do his wooing for him. Paul might not have the inner strength that had just brought Jack through where poor Reppleman had foundered, but he had push, and guts enough in his own way. While Jack dreamed, he had carried off Eva; and now, at this late date Jack was finally waking up to the fact that where the mating instinct is concerned we are still close enough to our animal forebears to have to fight for our partners on occasion.

He swung around and made his way once more out of the room. He needed space to think.

Once more in the bright sunlight outside, in the eternal out-of-doors of twelve minutes after two on a warm June afternoon, he continued his survey of the situation he was in. But he returned to it with the cold, dispassionate viewpoint of the trained mind. He marshalled the facts he had learned about his situation and considered them. They amounted to the following:

He was involuntarily imprisoned in what appeared to be a plane of two dimensions only and of unknown extent.

He was kept prisoner by a device operating at this moment.

The natural restrictions of movement in two dimensions, plus a matter of his original position in the plane, prevented him from reaching the means by which he could shut off the device.

Problem: How to shut off the device?

He returned to the room housing the generator and examined it. He studied the objects that, like himself, had been caught up in the field. He could not grasp any of them, but he could push them around within the limits of the field. It would, he thought, probably be quite possible to push the hammer, say, into the core of the generator and short it out. Also, probably quite fatal, if Paul had been telling the truth about the explosion. Reppleman had probably done some such thing. But he was in a rest home now with, again according to Paul, a complete block on the whole business. Still, the hammer possibility might be considered as a last-ditch measure.

"I have only begun to fight," quoted Jack softly to himself.

He studied the two upright rods from the top ends of which the field was generated. A thought occurred to him and he measured the distance between them (about three feet as nearly as he could estimate by eye) and the length of the room to the window in front of which he had been standing. He remembered that it had taken him more steps than he had expected to reach the generator from the window. He checked this and discovered that the first step back from the window was about the length of his normal stride, but that the second was only slightly more than half that, and the third diminished in proportion.

He returned to the window, went through it to the outside, and checked his stride in the opposite direction. His first step out from the window in a direct line away from the rods of the generator was not quite double his normal stride. With the next it doubled again, and half a dozen steps saw him sweeping over the countryside with giant's steps.

On impulse he closed his eyes and continued outward. After a few more steps he stopped and opened his eyes to look. Earth lay like an enormous, white-flecked disc below him. Space was around him. For a second, instinctively, he tried to gasp for air, then realized with a start that he was not breathing, nor had he been breathing for some time. Such things, evidently, were unnecessary in two dimensions.

He looked back down at Earth then ahead into space. Reppleman had gone mad at the end and wrecked the generator. But Reppleman was Reppleman; and he was—Jack. Moreover he had a score to settle back in his normal world. And he had every intention of getting back to settle it.

How far, he thought, had Reppleman wandered, before he had come back to destroy the thing that held him? The thought was morbid and he shook it from him. Firmly he faced away from the world and strode outward. For a moment he twinkled like a dot among the stars. And then he was gone, stepping into enormous distances with ever-increasing stride.

Jack closed the door of the little workroom behind him and turned left in the corridor outside. He went down the corridor, counting doors. At best it would have to be a guess, but if his estimate was right the room he wanted should be—

This one.

He pushed open the door and stepped in, interrupting two people in the midst of an angry argument. For a moment they stood frozen, interrupted and staring at him, and then Eva literally flew into his arms, while Paul's astonishment faded to a bitter smile and he sat down on a corner of the desk beside him and crossed his arms.

"Oh, Jack!" choked Eva. "Jack!"

Jack folded her in his long arms almost automatically, with a feeling of bewilderment that gradually gave way to one of pleasure. He had never seen the calm, self-contained Eva moved like this before; and the corresponding role it demanded of him was rather attractive. He felt sort of contented and self-righteous; and at the same time as if he ought to do something dramatic, like, say, picking up Paul and breaking him in half, or some such thing.

At that, however, it was Paul who got in the first punch.

"She's worried about you," he said, dryly, jerking a thumb at Eva.

"You are?" demanded Jack, looking down at her.

"Oh Jack!" said Eva. "You mustn't do it. You don't know how dangerous it is!"

"What is?" asked Jack, becoming bewildered again.

"The field," put in Paul, as dryly as before.

"Oh that," said Jack. "Well—"

"You don't know what it's like," interrupted Eva. "I was here when they took Max Reppleman out after the explosion. Jack—"

"Never mind that," said Jack, strongly. "Paul said you were worried about me."

"Jack, please listen. That whole business is dangerous—"

"You wouldn't be worried about me unless you were—well, worried about me," said Jack stubbornly. His blood was up now. He had almost lost this girl once to Paul through hesitation and delay. "Eva—" He tightened his grasp on her—"I love you."

"Jack, will you lis—" Eva stopped suddenly. Color flooded her face. She stared up at him in shocked speechlessness.

"Eva," said Jack, quickly, taking advantage of this golden opportunity and talking fast. "Eva, I fell in love with you back at the University, only I was always looking for the right chance to tell you and I didn't get around to it because I was afraid of making some mistake and losing you. And when you left and went to work for Paul I gave up, but I've changed my mind. Eva, will you marry me right now, today?"

Eva tried to speak a couple of times but no sound came out.

"The whirlwind lover," said Paul somewhere in the background.

"Well?" demanded Jack.

"Jack, I—" trembled Eva.

"Never mind," said Jack, breaking in on her. "Because I won't take no for an answer. Do you hear me?" He paused for a second to be astonished at his own words. "You're going to marry me right away."

"Ye gods!" said Paul. He might have saved his breath. Neither one of the other two was paying attention to him.

Jack let her go, and looked at Paul.

"Paul—" he said.

"Yes *sir!*" responded Paul, getting up from the desk and popping exaggeratedly to attention.

Jack looked at him with the jaundiced eye of a conquering general for his defeated rival. Though temporarily vanquished, this man was still potentially dangerous. Proceed with plan B? asked the front part of his mind. Proceed with plan B, responded the back of his mind.

"Paul," he said. "I've got the answers for you on the field."

Paul's ironic pose slowly relaxed. A wary, calculating look came into his eye.

"What?" he said.

"I'll show you," Jack said. "Come on with me. You too, Eva."

And he turned on one heel and led the way out of the room.

"You see," said Jack, "you were wrong in your picture of what the generator does." They were all three standing in the little L-shaped room and Jack had just told them what had happened to him. "It doesn't produce a field at all. What it does is affect certain types of objects close to it so that they become restricted to a certain limited two-dimensional plane in a single moment of time. The generator itself tries to exist both in this and in normal space at the same time, with the result that it blows up—

what you might call a paradox explosion—not after some seconds, but immediately. Of course, this doesn't affect what's been caught up in the single moment-and-plane, because for them that single instant is eternity."

"But it didn't blow up on you," said Paul.

"I turned it off before it had a chance to," replied Jack, a little grimly.

"Now wait," said Paul. "Wait. You just finished telling us you couldn't reach the timer switch because of your position which was essentially unchangeable in two-dimensional space. How did you turn it off? In fact, how did you ever get back?"

Jack smiled coolly.

"What happens to a plane in curved space?"

Paul frowned.

"I don't get it," he said.

"It curves, of course," answered Jack. "And where it's dependent upon something like the generator, it curves back eventually to it."

Paul's eyes narrowed.

"Well—" he hesitated. "What good did knowing that do you, though? You could walk clear around the circle and still not change your position so as to reach the timer switch."

"Ah yes," said Jack. "If it was just a simple circle. But it was a Moebius strip."

"Now wait—" cried Paul.

"You wait," said Jack. "How many points determine a plane?"

"Three."

Jack turned and walked down the length of the room to where the two upright rods still stood connected to the generator. He touched their tips.

"And how many points do we have here?"

Paul looked bewildered.

"Two," he said. "But—"

"Then where's the third point we need? As a matter of fact you're standing right at it."

Paul started in spite of himself and moved slightly aside.

"What do you mean?" he asked.

"The third point," said Jack, "is the focal point of the two lines of force emanating from the two rod tips. They converge right in the middle of the window at the far end of the room there."

"But I still don't see!" said Paul.

"You will," said Jack. He turned and stepped into the alcove. There was a moment's silence, then the sound of tearing paper and he stepped back out holding a long thin strip of newspaper. He walked back to Paul.

"Let's see your thumb and forefinger," he said. "Now look here. This one end of the strip for the length of about an inch we'll say is the part of the plane in this room that's determined by the three points, the two rod tips and the focal point of their lines of force. Hold that."

He transferred one end of the strip to Paul's fingers. Paul held it pinched between thumb and forefinger and watched.

"Now," went on Jack, demonstrating, "the plane goes out like this and around like this and back like this in a big loop and the end approaches the generator between your fingers again. It comes in here and the last inch of it goes back between your fingers, and there you are, reversed and ready to shut off your timer."

"Wait," said Paul, now holding the two ends pinched between his fingers together and the big loop of paper strip drooping in mid-air. "Why does the end come back in the same place? Why doesn't it just circle around behind and touch ends?"

"For two reasons," answered Jack. "The plane must end where it began. Right?"

"Yes."

"*But*," said Jack. "To remain the same plane it must have the same three points in common. And the plane takes its position from the focal point, not the two rod tips. The result is what you've got in your hand there, a loop with a little double tag end."

"But I don't—well, never mind," said Paul. "The important thing is that this is still a straight loop, with no twist in it at all. You could never get reversed on this. This is no Moebius."

"Think again," said Jack. "With that tag end it is." He turned to Eva. "Come on, Eva. We'll leave Paul to figure this out while you and I go get our own affairs taken care of." He took her hand and opened the door.

"Hey!" cried Paul. "You can't—"

"Oh yes, I can," said Jack, turning in the open doorway. "I've answered all your questions. Just take an imaginary little two-dimensional figure and run him around that strip of newspaper. You'll see."

And he led Eva out the door, closing it behind them. Once in the corridor, however, he took her shoulders in his two big hands and backed her against the wall.

"Tell me," he said. "Just why did you quit me at the U. and come down here?"

Eva looked guilty.

"He—Paul said—"

"What did he say?"

"He said," hesitated Eva, "you'd always told him you never intended to marry anyone." A small note of defiance came into her voice. "What was I going to do? Every day I'd come to work and you'd be there, and you never said anything—" she broke off suddenly, eyeing him curiously. "Why did you ask me that now, Jack?"

"Because," said Jack. "For a minute I was tempted to save Paul a walk—a long, long walk."

She stared up at him.

"I don't understand."

He smiled and took her hand.

"Some day," he said tenderly, "some day when we are very old and married and well supplied with grandchildren, I'll tell you all about it. Okay?"

She was too much in love with him to protest—then.

"Okay," she smiled back.

They went down the corridor toward the door leading out to the parking lot behind the labs.

In the room Paul stood frowning at the strip of paper in his hand. It didn't seem possible, but it was. He had just finished walking, in imagination, a little two-dimensional man all the way around the strip; and, sure enough, he had ended up facing in the opposite direction. It was simple enough. But it wasn't a Moebius. Or was it? If the two ends were one end—

Outside on the parking lot he heard the roar of a motor; and he looked up to see a battered old blue business coupe make its turn on the gravel expanse and head out the driveway. As it passed it stopped; and Jack stuck his head out the car window to shout something to him. Paul stepped to the window.

"What?" he yelled.

Jack's words came indistinctly to him over the distance and the racket of the ancient motor.

"—I said—stay right where you are—"

"What?" roared Paul.

But Jack had pulled in his head and the car pulled ahead out the driveway and into the street. Paul watched it merge with the traffic and get lost in the distance.

What had Jack said? Stay right where you are? *Why* should he stay right where he was?

Suddenly he felt the unexpected cold squeeze of suspicion. It couldn't be that Jack would—

—Behind him and from the direction of the timer came the sound of a soft, insidious *click*.

An Honorable Death

From the arboretum at the far end of the patio to
the landing stage of the transporter itself, the whole
household was at sixes and sevens over the business
of preparing the party for the celebration. As usual,
Carter was having to oversee everything himself,
otherwise it would not have gone right; and this was
all the harder in that, of late, his enthusiasms seemed
to have run down somewhat. He was conscious of a
vague distaste for life as he found it, and the immi-
nent approach of middle age, seeking him out even
in the quiet backwater of this small, suburban planet?
Whatever it was, things were moving even more slowly
than usual this year. He had not even had time to
get into his costume of a full dress suit (19th-20th
cent.) with tails, which he had chosen as not too
dramatic, and yet kinder than most dress-ups to his
tall, rather awkward figure—when the chime sounded,
announcing the first arrival.

Dropping the suit on his bed, he went out, cutting across the patio toward the gathering room,

where the landing stage of the transporter was—and almost ran headlong into one of the original native inhabitants of the planet, standing like a lean and bluish post with absolute rigidity in the center of the pretty little flagstone path.

"What are you doing here?" cried Carter?

The narrow, indigo, horselike face leaned confidentially down toward Carter's own. And then Carter recognized the great mass of apple blossoms, like a swarming of creamy-winged moths, held to the inky chest.

"Oh—" began Carter, on a note of fury. Then he threw up his hands and took the mass of branches. Peering around the immovable alien and wincing, he got a glimpse of his imported apple tree. But it was not as badly violated as he had feared. "Thank you. Thank you," he said, and waved the native out of the way.

But the native remained. Carter stared—then saw that in addition to the apple blossoms the thin and hairless creature, though no more dressed than his kind ever were, had in this instance contrived belts, garlands, and bracelets of native flowers for himself. The colors and patterns would be arranged to convey some special meaning—they always did. But right at the moment Carter was too annoyed and entirely too rushed to figure them out, though he did think it a little unusual the native should be holding a slim shaft of dark wood with a fire-hardened point. Hunting was most expressly forbidden to the natives.

"Now what?" said Carter. The native (a local chief, Carter suddenly recognized) lifted the spear and unexpectedly made several slow, stately hops, with his long legs flicking up and down above the scrubbed white of the flagstones—like an Earthly crane at its mating. "Oh, now, don't tell me you want to dance!"

The native chief ceased his movements and went back to being a post again, staring out over Carter's head as if at some horizon, lost and invisible beyond the irridescences of Carter's dwelling walls. Carter groaned, pondered, and glanced anxiously ahead toward the gathering room, from which he could now hear the voice of Ona, already greeting the first guest with female twitters.

"All right," he told the chief. "All right—this once. But only because it's Escape Day Anniversary. And you'll have to wait until after dinner."

The native stepped aside and became rigid again. Carter hurried past into the gathering room, clutching the apple blossoms. His wife was talking to a short, brown-bearded man with an ivory-tinted guitar hanging by a broad, tan band over one red-and-white, checked-shirted shoulder.

"Ramy!" called Carter, hurrying up to them. The landing stage of the transporter, standing in the middle of the room, chimed again. "Oh, take these will you, dear?" He thrust the apple blossoms into Ona's plump, bare arms. "The chief. In honor of the day. You know how they are—and I had to promise he could dance after dinner." She stared, her soft, pale face upturned to him. "I couldn't help it."

He turned and hurried into the landing stage, from the small round platform of which were now stepping down a short, academic, elderly man with wispy gray hair and a rather fat, button-nosed woman of the same age, both wearing the ancient Ionian chiton as their costume. Carter had warned Ona against wearing a chiton, for the very reason that these two might show up in the same dress. He allowed himself a small twinge of satisfaction at the thought of her ballroom gown as he went hastily now to greet them.

"Doctor!" he said. "Lidi! Here you are!" He shook hands with the doctor. "Happy Escape Day to both of you."

"I was sure we'd be late," said Lidi, holding firmly

to the folds of her chiton with both hands. "The public terminal on Arcturus Five was so crowded. And the doctor won't hurry no matter what I say—" She looked over at her husband, but he, busy greeting Ona, ignored her.

The chime sounded again and two women, quite obviously sisters in spite of the fact that they were wearing dissimilar costumes, appeared on the platform. One was dressed in a perfectly ordinary everyday kilt and tunic—no costume at all. The other wore a close, unidentifiable sort of suit of some gray material and made straight for Carter.

"Cart!" she cried, taking one of his hands in both of her own and pumping it heartily. "Happy Escape Day." She beamed at him from a somewhat plain, strong-featured face, sharply made up. "Ani and I—" She looked around for her sister and saw the kilt and tunic already drifting in rather dreamlike and unconscious fashion toward the perambulating bar at the far end of the room. "I," she corrected herself hastily, "couldn't wait to get here. Who else is coming?"

"Just what you see, Totsa," said Carter, indicating those present with a wide-flung hand. "We thought a small party this year—a little, quiet gathering—"

"So nice! And what do you think of my costume?" she revolved slowly for his appraisal.

"Why—good, very good."

"Now!" Totsa came back to face him. "You can't guess what it is at all."

"Of course I can," said Carter heartily.

"Well, then, what is it?"

"Oh, well, perhaps I won't tell you, then," said Carter.

A small head with wispy gray hair intruded into the circle of their conversation. "An artistic rendering of the space suitings worn by those two intrepid pioneers who this day, four hundred and twenty years ago, burst free in their tiny ship from the iron grip of Earth's prisoning gravitation?"

Totsa shouted in triumph. "I knew you'd know, Doctor! Trust a philosophical researcher to catch on. Carter hadn't the slightest notion. Not an inkling!"

"A host is a host is a host," said Carter. "Excuse me, I've got to get into my own costume."

He went out again and back across the patio. The outer air felt pleasantly cool on his warm face. He hoped that the implications of his last remark—that he had merely been being polite in pretending to be baffled by the significance of her costume—had got across to Totsa, but probably it had not. She would interpret it as an attempt to cover up his failure to recognize her costume by being cryptic. The rapier was wasted on the thick hide of such a woman. And to think he once . . . you had to use a club. And the worst of it was, he had grasped the meaning of her costume immediately. He had merely been being playful in refusing to admit it. . . .

The native chief was still standing unmoved where Carter had left him, still waiting for his moment.

"Get out of the way, can't you?" said Carter irritably, as he shouldered by.

The chief retreated one long ostrichlike step until he stood half-obscured in the shadow of a trellis of roses. Carter went on into the bedroom.

His suit was laid out for him and he climbed into the clumsy garments, his mind busy on the schedule of the evening ahead. The local star that served as this planet's sun (one of the Pleiades, Asterope) would be down in an hour and a half, but the luminosity of the interstellar space in this galactic region made the sky bright for hours after a setting, and the fireworks could not possibly go on until that died down.

Carter had designed the set piece of the finale himself—a vintage space rocket curving up from a representation of the Earth, into a firmament of stars, and changing into a star itself as it dwindled. It would be unthinkable to waste this against a broad band of glowing rarefied matter just above the western horizon.

Accordingly, there was really no choice about the schedule. At least five hours before the thought of fireworks could be entertained. Carter, hooking his tie into place around his neck before a section of his bedroom wall set on reflection, computed in his head. The cocktail session now starting would be good for two and a half, possibly three hours. He dared not stretch it out any longer than that or Ani would be sure to get drunk. As it was, it would be bad enough with a full cocktail session and wine with the dinner. But perhaps Totsa could keep her under control. At any rate—three, and an hour and a half for dinner. No matter how it was figured, there would be half an hour or more to fill in there.

Well—Carter worked his way into his dress coat—he could make his usual small speech in honor of the occasion. And—oh, yes, of course, there was the chief. The native dances were actually meaningless, boring things, but then he was the inquiring type of mind. Still, the others might find it funny enough, or interesting for a single performance.

Buttoning up his coat, he went back out across the patio, feeling more kindly toward the native than he had since the moment of his first appearance. Passing him this time, Carter thought to stop and ask, "Would you like something to eat?"

Remote, shiny, mottled by the shadow of the rose leaves, the native neither moved nor answered, and Carter hurried on with a distinct feeling of relief. He had always made it a point to keep some native food on hand for just such an emergency as this—after all, they got hungry, too. But it was a definite godsend not to have to stop now, when he was so busy, and see the stuff properly prepared and provided for this uninvited and unexpected guest.

The humans had all moved out of the gathering room by the time he reached it and into the main lounge with its more complete bar and mobile chairs. On entering, he saw that they had already split up into three different and, in a way, inevitable groups. His wife and the doctor's were at gossip in a corner; Ramy was playing his guitar and singing in a low, not unpleasant, though hoarse voice to Ani, who sat drink in hand, gazing past him with a half-smile into the changing colors of the wall behind him. Totsa and the doctor were in a discussion at the bar. Carter joined them.

"—and I'm quite prepared to believe it," the doctor was saying in his gentle, precise tones as Carter came up. "Well, very good, Cart." He nodded at Carter's costume.

"You think so?" said Carter, feeling his face warm pleasantly. "Awkward get-up, but—I don't know, it just struck me this year." He punched for a lime brandy and watched with pleasure as the bar disgorged the brimming glass by his waiting hand.

"You look armored in it, Cart," Totsa said.

"Thrice-armed is he—" Carter acknowledged the compliment and sipped on his glass. He glanced at the doctor to see if the quotation had registered, but the doctor was already leaning over to receive a refill in his own glass.

"Have you any idea what this man's been telling me?" demanded Totsa, swiveling toward Carter. "He insists we're doomed. Literally doomed!"

"I've no doubt we are—" began Carter. But before he could expand on this agreement with the explanation that he meant in the larger sense, she was foaming over him in a tidal wave of conversation.

"Well, I don't pretend to be unobjective about it.

After all, who are we to survive? But really—how ridiculous! And you back him up just like that, blindly, without the slightest notion of what he's been talking about!"

"A theory only, Totsa," said the doctor, quite unruffled.

"I wouldn't honor it by even calling it a theory!"

"Perhaps," said Carter, sipping on his lime brandy, "if I knew a little more about what you two were—"

"The point," said the doctor, turning a little, politely, toward Carter, "has to do with the question of why, on all these worlds we've taken over, we've found no other race comparable to our own. We may," he smiled, "of course be unique in the universe. But this theory supposes that any contact between races of differing intelligences must inevitably result in the death of the inferior race. Consequently, if we met our superiors—" He gave a graceful wave of his hand.

"I imagine it could," said Carter.

"Ridiculous!" said Totsa. "As if we couldn't just avoid contact altogether if we wanted to!"

"That's a point," said Carter. "I imagine negotiations—"

"We," said Totsa, "who burst the bonds of our Earthly home, who have spread out among the stars in a scant four hundred years, are hardly the type to turn up our toes and just die!"

"It's all based on an assumption, Cart"—the doctor put his glass down on the bar and clasped his small hands before him—"that the racial will to live is dependent upon what might be called a certain amount of emotional self-respect. A race of lesser intelligence or scientific ability could hardly be a threat to us. But a greater race, the theory goes, must inevitably generate a sort of death-wish in all of us. We're too used to being top dog. We must conquer or—"

"Absolutely nonsense!" said Totsa.

"Well, now, you can't just condemn the idea off hand like that," Carter said. "Naturally, I can't imagine a human like myself ever giving up, either. We're too hard, too wolfish, too much the last-ditch fighters. But I imagine a theory like this might well hold true for other, lesser races." He cleared his throat. "For example, I've had quite a bit of contact since we came here with the natives which were the dominant life-form on this world in its natural state—"

"Oh, natives!" snapped Totsa scornfully.

"You might be surprised, Totsa!" said Carter, heating up a little. An inspiration took hold of him. "And, in fact, I've arranged for you to do just that. I've invited the local native chief to dance for us after dinner. You might just find it very illuminating."

"Illuminating? How?" pounced Totsa.

"That," said Carter, putting his glass down on the bar with a very slight flourish, "I'll leave you to find out for yourself. And now, if you don't mind, I'm going to have to make my hostly rounds of the other guests."

He walked away, glowing with a different kind of inner warmth. He was smiling as he came up to Ramy, who was still singing ballads and playing his guitar for Totsa's sister.

"Excellent," Carter said, clapping his hands briefly and sitting down with them as the song ended. "What was that?"

"Richard the Lion-heart wrote it," said Ramy hoarsely. He turned to the woman. "Another drink, Ani?"

Carter tried to signal the balladeer with his eyes, but Ramy had already pressed the buttons on the table beside their chairs, and a little moto unit from the bar was already on its way to them with the drinks emerging from its interior. Carter sighed in-

audibly and leaned back in his chair. He could warn
Totsa to keep an eye on Ani a little later.

He accepted another drink himself. The sound of
voices in the room was rising as more alcohol was
consumed. The only quiet one was Ani. She sat,
engaged in the singleminded business of imbibing,
and listened to the conversation between Ramy and
himself, as if she was—thought Carter suddenly—
perhaps one step removed, beyond some glasslike
wall, where the real sound and movement of life
came muted, if at all. The poetry of this flash of
insight—for Carter could think of no other way to
describe it—operated so strongly upon his emotions
that he completely lost the thread of what Ramy was
saying and was reduced to noncommittal noises by
way of comment.

I should take up my writing again, he thought to
himself.

As soon as a convenient opportunity presented
itself, he excused himself and got up. He went over
to the corner where the women were talking.

"—Earth," Lidi was saying, "the doctor and I will
never forget it. Oh, Cart—" She twisted around to
him as he sat down in a chair opposite. "You must
take this girl to Earth sometime. Really."

"Do you think she's the back-to-nature type?" said
Carter, with a smile.

"No, stop it!" Lidi turned back to Ona. "Make him
take you!"

"I've mentioned it to him. Several times," said
Ona, putting down the glass in her hand with a
helpless gesture on the end table beside her.

"Well, you know what they say," smiled Carter.
"Everyone talks about Earth but nobody ever goes
there any more."

"The doctor and I went. And it was memorable.
It's not what you see, of course, but the insight you

bring to it. I'm only five generations removed from people living right there on the North American continent. And the doctor had cousins in Turkey when he was a boy. Say what you like, the true stock thins out as generation succeeds generation away from the home world."

"And it's not the expense any more," put in Ona. "Everyone's rich nowadays."

"Rich! What an uncomfortable word!" said Lidi. "You should say capable, dear. Remember, our riches are merely the product of our science, which is the fruit of our own capabilities."

"Oh, you know what I mean!" said Ona. "The point is, Cart won't go. He just won't."

"I'm a simple man," Carter said. "I have my writing, my music, my horticulture, right here. I feel no urge to roam—" he stood up—"except to the kitchen right now, to check on the caterers. If you'll excuse me—"

"But you haven't given your wife an answer about taking her to Earth one of these days!" cried Lidi.

"Oh, we'll go, we'll go," said Carter, walking off with a good-humored wave of his hand.

As he walked through the west sunroom to the dining area and the kitchen (homey word!) beyond, his cheerfulness dwindled somewhat. It was always a ticklish job handling the caterers, now that they were all artists doing the work for the love of it and not to be controlled by the price they were paid. Carter would have liked to wash his hands of that end of the party altogether and just leave them to operate on their own. But what if he failed to check and then something went wrong? It was his own artistic conscience operating, he thought, that would not give him any rest.

The dining room was already set up in classic style with long table and individual chairs. He passed the gleam of its tableware and went on through the light-screen into the kitchen area. The master caterer was just in the process of directing his two apprentices to set up the heating tray on which the whole roast boar, papered and gilded, would be kept warm in the centerpiece position on the table during the meal. He did not see Carter enter; and Carter himself stopped to admire, with a sigh of relief, the boar itself. It was a master-work of the carver's art and had been built up so skillfully from its component chunks of meat that no one could have suspected it was not the actual animal itself.

Looking up at this moment, the caterer caught sight of him and came over to see what he wanted. Carter advanced a few small, tentative suggestions, but the response was so artificially polite that after a short while Carter was glad to leave him to his work.

Carter wandered back through the house without returning directly to the lounge. With the change of the mood that the encounter with the caterer had engendered, his earlier feelings of distaste with life—a sort of melancholy—had come over him. He thought of the people he had invited almost with disgust. Twenty years ago, he would not have thought himself capable of belonging to such a crowd. Where were the great friends, the true friends, that as a youngster he had intended to acquire? Not that it was the fault of those in the lounge. They could not help being what they were. It was the fault of the times, which made life too easy for everybody; and—yes, he would be honest—his own fault, too.

His wanderings had brought him back to the patio. He remembered the chief and peered through the light dusk at the trellis, under the light arch of which the native stood.

Beyond, the house was between the semi-enclosed patio and the fading band of brilliance in the west. Deep shadow lay upon the trellis itself and the na-

tive under it. He was almost obscured by it, but a
darkly pale, vertical line of reflection from his upright spear showed that he had made no move. A
gush of emotion burst within Carter. He took a single step toward the chief, with the abrupt, spontane-
ous urge to thank him for coming and offering to
dance. But at that moment, through the open doorway of his bedroom, sounded the small metallic chimes
of his bedside clock announcing the twenty-first hour,
and he turned hastily and crossed through the gathering room, into the lounge.

"Hors d'oeuvres! Hors d'oeuvres!" he called cheerfully, flinging the lounge door wide. "Hors d'oeuvres,
everybody! Time to come and get it!"

Dinner could not go off otherwise than well. Everyone was half-tight and hungry. Everyone was talk-
ative. Even Ani had thrown off her habitual introver-
sion and was smiling and nodding, quite soberly,
anyone would swear. She was listening to Ona and
Lidi talking about Lidi's grown-up son when he had
been a baby. The doctor was in high spirits, and
Ramy, having gotten his guitar-playing out of his
system earlier with Ani, was ready to be companion-
able. By the time they had finished the rum-and-
butter pie, everyone was in a good mood, and even
the caterer, peering through a momentary transparency of the kitchen wall, exchanged a beam with
Carter.

Carter glanced at his watch. Only twenty minutes
more! The time had happily flown, and, far from
having to fill it in, he would have to cut his own
speech a little short. If it were not for the fact that he
had already announced it, he would have eliminated
the chief's dance—no, that would not have done,
either. He had always made a point of getting along
with the natives of this world. "It's their home, too,
after all," he had always said.

He tinkled on a wine glass with a spoon and rose to his feet.

Faces turned toward him and conversation came to a reluctant halt around the table. He smiled at his assembled guests.

"As you know," said Carter, "it has always been my custom at these little gatherings—and old customs are the best—to say a few—" he held up a disarming hand— "a very few words. Tonight I will be even briefer than usual." He stopped and took a sip of water from the glass before him.

"On this present occasion, the quadricentennial of our great race's Escape into the limitless bonds of the universe, I am reminded of the far road we have come; and the far road—undoubtedly—we have yet to go. I am thinking at the moment," he smiled, to indicate that what he was about to say was merely said in good fellowship, "of a new theory expressed by our good doctor here tonight. This theory postulates that when a lesser race meets a greater, the lesser must inevitably go to the wall. And that, since it is pretty generally accepted that the laws of chance ensure our race eventually meeting its superior, we must inevitably and eventually go to the wall."

He paused and warmed them again with the tolerance of his smile.

"May I say nonsense!

"Now, let no one retort that I am merely taking refuge in the blind attitude that reacts with the cry, 'It can't happen to us.' Let me say I believe it could happen to us, but it won't. And why not? I will answer that with one word. Civilization.

"These overmen—if indeed they ever show up— must, even as we, be civilized. Civilized. Think of what that word means! Look at the seven of us here. Are we not educated, kindly, sympathetic people? And how do we treat the races inferior to us that we have run across?

"I'm going to let you answer these questions for yourselves, because I now invite you to the patio for cognac and coffee—and to see one of the natives of this planet, who has expressed a desire to dance for you. Look at him as he dances, observe him, consider what human gentleness and consideration are involved in the gesture that included him in this great festival of ours." Carter paused. "And consider one other great statement that has echoed down the corridors of time—As ye have done to others, so shall ye be done by!"

Carter sat down, flushed and glowing, to applause, then rose immediately to precede his guests, who were getting up to stream toward the patio. Walking rapidly, he outdistanced them as they passed the gathering room.

For a second, as he burst out through the patio doorway, his eyes were befuddled by the sudden darkness. Then his vision cleared as the others came through the doorway behind him and he was able to make out the inky shadow of the chief, still barely visible under the trellis.

Leaving Ona to superintend the seating arrangements in the central courtyard of the patio, he hurried toward the trellis. The native was there waiting for him.

"Now," said Carter, a little breathlessly, "it must be a short dance, a very short dance."

The chief lowered his long, narrow head, looking down at Carter with what seemed to be an aloofness, a sad dignity, and suddenly Carter felt uncomfortable.

"Um—well," he muttered, "you don't have to cut it too short."

Carter turned and went back to the guests. Under Ona's direction, they had seated themselves in a small semicircle of chairs, with snifter glasses and coffee cups. A chair had been left for Carter in the middle. He took it and accepted a glass of cognac from his wife.

"Now?" asked Totsa, leaning toward him.

"Yes—yes, here he comes," said Carter, and directed their attention toward the trellis.

The lights had been turned up around the edge of the courtyard, and as the chief advanced unto them from the darkness, he seemed to step all at once out of a wall of night.

"My," said Lidi, a little behind and to the left of Carter, "isn't he big!"

"Tall, rather," said the doctor, and coughed dryly at her side.

The chief came on into the center of the lighted courtyard. He carried his spear upright in one hand before him, the arm half-bent at the elbow and half-extended, advancing with exaggeratedly long steps and on tiptoe—in a manner unfortunately almost exactly reminiscent of the classical husband sneaking home late at night. There was a sudden titter from Totsa, behind Carter. Carter flushed.

Arrived in the center of the patio before them, the chief halted, probed at the empty air with his spear in several directions, and began to shuffle about with his head bent toward the ground.

Behind Carter, Ramy said something in a low voice. There was a strangled chuckle and the strings of the guitar plinked quietly on several idle notes.

"Please," said Carter, without turning his head.

There was a pause, some more indistinguishable murmuring from Ramy, followed again by his low, hoarse, and smothered chuckle.

"Perhaps—" said Carter, raising his voice slightly, "perhaps I ought to translate the dance as he does it. All these dances are stories acted out. This one is apparently called "An Honorable Death.' "

*   *   *

He paused to clear his throat. No one said anything. Out in the center of the patio, the chief was standing crouched, peering to right and left, his neck craned like a chicken's.

"You see him now on the trail," Carter went on. "The silver-colored flowers on his right arm denote the fact that it is a story of death that he is dancing. The fact that they are below the elbow indicates it is an honorable, rather than dishonorable, death. But that fact that he wears nothing at all on the other arm below the elbow tells us this is the full and only story of the dance."

Carter found himself forced to clear his throat again. He took a sip from his snifter glass.

"As I say," he continued, "we see him now on the trail, alone."

The chief had now begun to take several cautious steps forward, and then alternate ones in retreat, with some evidence of tension and excitement. "He is happy at the moment because he is on the track of a large herd of local game. Watch the slope of his spear as he holds it in his hand. The more it approaches the vertical, the happier he is feeling—"

Ramy murmured again and his coarse chuckle rasped on Carter's ears. It was echoed by a giggle from Totsa and even a small, dry bark of a laugh from the doctor.

"—the happier he is feeling," repeated Carter loudly. "Except that, paradoxically, the line of the absolute vertical represents the deepest tragedy and sorrow. In a little paper I did on the symbolism behind these dance movements, I advanced the theory that when a native strikes up with his spear from the absolute vertical position, it is because some carnivore too large for him to handle has already downed him. He's a dead man."

The chief had gone into a flurry of movement.

"Ah," said Carter, on a note of satisfaction. The others were quiet now. He let his voice roll out a little. "He has made his kill. He hastens home with it. He is very happy. Why shouldn't he be? He is successful, young, strong. His mate, his progeny, his home await him. Even now it comes into sight."

The chief froze. His spear point dropped.

"But what is this?" cried Carter, straightening up dramatically in his chair. "What has happened? He sees a stranger in the doorway. It is the Man of Seven Spears who—this is a superstition, of course—" Carter interrupted himself— "who has, in addition to his own spear, six other magic spears which will fly from him on command and kill anything that stands in his way. What is this unconquerable being doing inside the entrance to the chief's home without being invited?"

The wooden spear point dropped abruptly, almost to the ground.

"The Man of Seven Spears tells him," said Carter. "He, the Man of Seven Spears, has chosen to desire the flowers about our chief's house. Therefore he has taken the house, killing all within it—the mate and the little ones—that their touch may be cleansed from flowers that are his. Everything is now his."

The soft, tumbling sound of liquid being poured filled in the second of Carter's pause.

"Not too much—" whispered someone.

"What can our chief do?" said Carter sharply. The chief was standing rigid with his head bent forward and his forehead pressed against the perfectly vertical shaft of his spear, now held upright before him. "He is sick—we would say he is weeping, in human terms. All that meant anything to him is now gone. He cannot even revenge himself on the Man of Seven Spears, whose magic weapons make him invincible."

Carter, moved by the pathos in his own voice, felt his throat tighten on the last words.

"Ona, dear, do you have an antacid tablet?" the doctor's wife whispered behind him.

"He stands where he has stopped!" cried Carter fiercely. "He has no place else to go. The Man of Seven Spears ignores him, playing with the flowers. For eventually, without moving, without food or drink, he will collapse and die, as all of the Man of Seven Spears' enemies have died. For one, two, three days he stands there in his sorrow; and late on the third day the plan for revenge he has longed for comes to him. He cannot conquer his enemy—but he can eternally shame him, so that the Man of Seven Spears, in his turn, will be forced to die.

"He goes into the house." The chief was moving again. "The Man of Seven Spears sees him enter, but pays no attention to him, for he is beneath notice. And it's a good thing for our chief this is so—or else the Man of Seven Spears would call upon all his magic weapons and kill him on the spot. But he his playing with his new flowers and pays no attention.

"Carrying his single spear," went on Carter, "the chief goes in to the heart of his house. Each house has a heart, which is the most important place in it. For if the heart is destroyed, the house dies, and all within it. Having come to the heart of the house, which is before its hearth fire, the chief places his spear butt down on the ground and holds it upright in the position of greatest grief. He stands there pridefully. We can imagine the Man of Seven Spears, suddenly realizing the shame to be put upon him, rushing wildly to interfere. But he and all of his seven spears are too slow. The chief leaps into the air—"

Carter checked himself. The chief was still standing with his forehead pressed against the spear shaft.

"He leaps into the air," repeated Carter, a little louder.

And at that moment the native did bound upward, his long legs flailing, to an astonishing height. For a second he seemed to float above the tip of his spear still grasping it—and then he descended like some great, dark, stricken bird, heavily upon the patio. The thin shaft trembled and shook, upright, above his fallen figure.

Multiple screams exploded and the whole company was on its feet. But the chief, slowly rising, gravely removed the spear from between the arm and side in which he had cleverly caught it while falling; and, taking it in his other hand, he stalked off into the shadows toward the house.

A babble of talk burst out behind Carter. Over all the other voices, Lidi's rose like a half-choked fountain.

"—absolutely! Heart failure! I never was so upset in my life—"

"Cart!" said Ona bitterly.

"Well, Cart," spoke Totsa triumphantly in his ear. "What's the application of all this to what you told me earlier?"

Carter, who had been sitting stunned, exploded roughly out of his chair.

"Oh, don't be such a fool!" He jerked himself away from them into the tree-bound shadows beyond the patio.

Behind him—after some few minutes—the voices lowered to a less excited level, and then he heard a woman's footsteps approaching him in the dark.

"Cart!" said his wife's voice hesitantly.

"What?" asked Carter, not moving.

"Aren't you coming back?"

"In a while."

There was a pause.

"Cart?"

"What?"

"Don't you think—"

"No, I don't think!" snarled Carter. "She can go to bloody hell!"

"But you can't just call her a fool—"

"She is a fool! They're all fools—every one of them! I'm a fool, too, but I'm not a stupid damn bloody fool like all of them!"

"Just because of some silly native dance!" said Ona, almost crying.

"Silly?" said Carter. "At least it's something. He's got a dance to do. That's more than the rest of them in there have. And it just so happens that dance is pretty important to him. You'd think they might like to learn something about that, instead of sitting back making their stupid jokes!"

His little explosion went off into the darkness and fell unanswered.

"Please come back, Cart," Ona said, after a long moment.

"At least he has something," said Carter. "At least there's that for him."

"I just can't face them if you don't come back."

"All right, goddammit," said Carter. "I'll go back."

They returned in grim fashion to the patio. The chair tables had been cleared and rearranged in a small circle. Ramy was singing a song and they were all listening politely.

"Well, Cart, sit down here!" invited the doctor heartily as Carter and Ona came up, indicating the chair between himself and Totsa. Carter dropped into it.

"This is one of those old sea ballads, Cart," said Totsa.

"Oh!" asked Carter, clearing his throat. "Is it?"

He sat back, punched for a drink and listened to the song. It echoed out heartily over the patio with its refrain of "Haul away, Joe!" but he could not bring himself to like it.

Ramy ended and began another song. Lidi, her old self again, excused herself a moment and trotted back into the house.

"Are you really thinking of taking a trip Earthside—" the doctor began, leaning confidentially toward Carter—and was cut short by an ear-splitting scream from within the house.

Ramy broke off his singing. The screams continued and all of them scrambled to their feet and went crowding toward the house.

They saw Lidi—just outside the dark entrance to the gathering room—small, fat and stiffly standing, and screaming again and again, with her head thrown back. Almost at her feet lay the chief, with the slim shaft of the spear sticking up from his body. Only, this time, it was actually through him.

The rest flooded around Lidi and she was led away, still screaming, by the doctor. Everyone else gathered in horrified fascination about the native corpse. The head was twisted on one side and Carter could just see one dead eye staring up, it seemed, at him alone, with a gleam of sly and savage triumph.

"Horrible!" breathed Totsa, her lips parted. "Horrible!"

But Carter was still staring at that dead eye. Possibly, the thought came to him, the horrendous happenings of the day had sandpapered his perceptions to an unusually suspicious awareness. But just possibly . . .

Quietly, and without attracting undue attention from the others, he slipped past the group and into the dimness of the gathering room, where the lights had been turned off. Easing quietly along the wall until he came to the windows overlooking the patio, he peered out through them.

*   *   *

A considerable number of the inky natives were emerging from the greenery of the garden and the orchard beyond and approaching the house. A long, slim, fire-hardened spear gleamed in the hand of each. It occurred to Carter like a blow that they had probably moved into position surrounding the house while the humans' attention was all focused on the dancing of their chief.

His mind clicking at a rate that surprised even him, Carter withdrew noiselessly from the window and turned about. Behind him was the transporter, bulky in the dimness. As silently as the natives outside, he stole across the floor and mounted onto its platform. The transporter could move him to anywhere in the civilized area of the Galaxy at a second's notice. And one of the possible destinations was the emergency room of Police Headquarters on Earth itself. Return, with armed men, could be equally instantaneous. Much better this way, thought Carter with a clarity he had never in his life experienced before; much better than giving the alarm to the people within, who would undoubtedly panic and cause a confusion that could get them all killed.

Quietly, operating by feel in the darkness, Carter set the controls for Police Headquarters. He pressed the Send button.

Nothing happened.

He stared at the machine in the impalpable darkness. A darker spot upon the thin lacquered panel that covered its front and matched it to the room's decor caught his eye. He bent down to investigate.

It was a hole. Something like a ritual thrust of a fire-hardened wooden spear appeared to have gone through the panel and into the vitals of the transporter. The machine's delicate mechanism was shattered and broken and pierced.

Lost Dorsai

PART ONE

I am Corunna El Man.

I brought the little courier vessel down at last at
the spaceport of Nahar City on Ceta, the large world
around Tau Ceti. I had made it from the Dorsai in
six phase shifts to transport, to the stronghold of
Gebel Nahar, our Amanda Morgan—she whom they
call the Second Amanda.

Normally I am far too senior in rank to act as a
courier pilot. But the situation at Gebel Nahar required a contracts expert at Nahar more swiftly than
one could safely be gotten there.

The risks I had taken had not seemed to bother
Amanda. That was not surprising, since she was
Dorsai. But neither did she talk to me much on the
trip; and that was a thing that had come to be, with
me, a little unusual.

For things had been different for me after Baunpore.

In the massacre there following the siege, when the North Freilanders finally overran the town, they cut up my face for the revenge of it; and they killed Else, for no other reason than that she was my wife. There was nothing left of her then but incandescent gas, and since there could be nothing to come back to, nor any place where she could be remembered, I rejected surgery and chose to wear my scars as a memorial to her.

It was a decision I never regretted. But it was true that with those scars came an alteration in the way other people reacted to me. With some I found that I became almost invisible. But nearly all seemed to relax their natural impulse to keep private their personal secrets and concerns. It was as if I was like a burnt-out candle in the dark room of their inner selves—a lightless, but safe, companion whose presence reassured them that their privacy was still unbreached. I doubt that Amanda and those I was to meet on this trip to Gebel Nahar would have talked to me as freely as they later did, if I had met them back in the days when I had Else, alive.

The Gebel Nahar is a mountain fortress; and for military reasons Nahar City, near it, has a spaceport capable of handling deep-space ships.

The main lobby of the terminal was small, but high-ceilinged and airy with bright, enormous heavily-framed paintings on all the walls. We stood in the middle of all this: no one looked directly at us, although neither I with my scars, nor Amanda were easy to ignore.

I went over to check with the message desk and found nothing there for us. Coming back, I had to hunt for Amanda, who had stepped away from where I had left her.

"El Man—" her voice said without warning, behind me. "Look!"

Her tone had warned me, even as I turned. I

caught sight of her and the painting she was looking at, all in the same moment. It was high up on one of the walls; and she stood just below it, gazing up.

Sunlight through the transparent front wall of the terminal flooded her and the picture, alike. She was in all the natural colors of life—as Else had been— tall, slim, in light blue cloth jacket and short cream-colored skirt, with white-blond hair and that incredible youthfulness that her namesake ancestor, the First Amanda, had also owned. In contrast, the painting was rich in garish pigments, gold leaf and alazarin crimson, the human figures it depicted caught in exaggerated, melodramatic attitudes.

Leto de muerte, the large brass plate below it read. *Hero's Death-Couch*, as the title would roughly translate from the bastard, archaic Spanish spoken by the Naharese. It showed a great, golden bed set out on an open plain in the aftermath of the battle. All about were corpses and bandaged officers standing in gilt-encrusted uniforms. The living surrounded the bed and its occupant, the dead Hero, who, power-fully muscled yet emaciated, hideously wounded and stripped to the waist, lay upon a thick pile of velvet cloaks, jewelled weapons, marvellously-wrought tap-estries and golden utensils, all of which covered the bed.

The body lay on its back, chin pointing at the sky, face gaunt with the agony of death, still firmly hold-ing by one large hand to its naked chest, the hilt of an oversized and ornate sword, its massive blade darkened with blood. The wounded officers standing about and gazing at the corpse were posed in dra-matic attitudes. In the foreground, on the earth be-side the bed, a single ordinary soldier in battle-torn uniform, dying, stretched forth one arm in tribute to the dead man.

Amanda looked at me. She did not say anything. In order to live, for two hundred years we on the

Dorsai have exported the only commodity we owned—
the lives of our generations—to be spent in wars for
others' causes. We live with real war; and to those
who do that, a painting like this one was close to
obscenity.

"So that's how they think here," said Amanda.

I looked sideways and down at her.

"Every culture has its own fantasies," I said. "And
this culture's Hispanic, at least in heritage."

"Less than ten per cent of the Naharese population's Hispanic nowadays," she answered. "Besides,
this is a caricature of Hispanic attitudes."

She was right. Nahar had originally been colonized
by immigrants—Gallegos from the northwest of Spain
who had dreamed of large ranches in a large open
Territory. After the first wave, those who came to
settle here were of anything but Hispanic ancestry,
but still they had adopted the language and ways
they found there.

The original ranchers had become enormously
rich—for though Ceta was a sparsely populated planet,
it was food-poor. The later arrivals swelled the cities
of Nahar, and stayed poor—very poor.

"I hope the people I'm to talk to are going to have
more than ten per cent of ordinary sense," Amanda
said. "This picture makes me wonder if they don't
prefer fantasy. If that's the way it is at Gebel
Nahar . . ."

She left the sentence unfinished, shook her head,
and then smiled at me. The smile lit up her face. It
was something different, an inward lighting deeper
and greater than those words usually indicate. I had
only met her for the first time, three days earlier,
and Else was all I had ever or would ever want; but
now I could see what people had meant on the
Dorsai, when they had said she inherited her great-
great-grandmother's abilities to both command others and make them love her.

"No message for us?" she said.

"No—" I began. But then I turned, for out of the corner of my eye I had seen someone approaching us.

The man striding toward us on long legs was a Dorsai. He was big. Not the size of the Graeme twins, Ian and Kensie, who commanded at Gebel Nahar on the Naharese contract; but close to that size and noticeably larger than I was. He wore a Naharese army bandmaster's uniform, with warrant officer tabs at the collar; and he was blond-haired, lean-faced, and no more than in his early twenties. I recognized him as the third son of a neighbor from my own canton of High Island, on the Dorsai. His name was Michael de Sandoval, and little had been heard of him for six years.

"Sir—Ma'm," he said, stopping in front of us. "Sorry to keep you waiting. There was a problem getting transport."

"Michael," I said. "Have you met Amanda Morgan?"

"No, I haven't." He turned to her. "An honor to meet you ma'm. I suppose you're tired of having everyone say they recognize you from your great-great-grandmother's pictures?"

"Never tire of it," said Amanda cheerfully; and gave him her hand. "But you already know Corunna?"

"The El Man family are High Island neighbors," said Michael. "If you'll come along with me, please? I've already got your luggage in the bus."

"Bus?" I said, as we followed him toward one of the window-wall exits from the terminal.

"The band bus for Third Regiment. It was all I could get."

We emerged on to a small parking pad and Michael de Sandoval led us to a thirty-passenger bus. Inside was only an Exotic in a dark blue robe, white hair and a strangely ageless face, seated in the lounge area at the front of the bus. He stood up as we came in.

"Padma, Outbond to Ceta," said Michael. "Sir, may I introduce Amanda Morgan, Contracts Adjuster, and Corunna El Man, Senior Ship Captain, both from the Dorsai? Captain El Man just brought the Adjuster in by courier."

"Of course, I know about their coming," said Padma.

He did not offer a hand to either of us, nor rise. But, like many of the advanced Exotics I have known, he did not seem to need to. There was a warmth and peace about him that the rest of us were immediately caught up in, and any behavior on his part seemed natural and expected.

We sat down together, Michael ducked into the control compartment, and a moment later, with a soft vibration, the bus lifted from the parking pad.

"It's an honor to meet you, Outbond," said Amanda. "But it's even more of an honor to have you meet us."

Padma smiled slightly.

"I'm afraid I didn't come just to meet you," he said to her. "I had a call to make, and the phones at Gebel Nahar are not as private as I liked. When I heard Michael was coming to get you, I rode along to use the phones in the terminal here."

I could see Amanda signalling me to leave her alone with him. It showed in the way she sat and the angle at which she held her head.

"Excuse me," I told them. "I think I'll go have a word with Michael."

I got up and went forward through the door into the control section, closing it behind me. Michael sat relaxed, one hand on the control rod; and I sat down myself in the copilot's seat.

"How are things at home, sir?" he asked, without turning his head from the sky ahead of us.

"I've only been back this once since you have left,

yourself," I said. "But it hasn't changed much. My
father died last year."

"I'm sorry to hear that."

"Your father and mother are well—and I hear your
brothers are all right, out among the stars," I said.
"But, of course, you know that."

"No," he said, still watching the sky ahead. "I
haven't heard for quite a while."

A silence threatened.

"How did you happen to end up here?" I asked. It
was almost a ritual question between Dorsais away
from home.

"I heard about Nahar. I thought I'd take a look at
it."

"Did you know it was as fake Hispanic as it is?"

"Not fake," he said. "Something . . . but not that.
You know the situation here?"

"No. That's Amanda's job," I said. "I'm just a
driver on this trip. Why don't you fill me in?"

"You must know some of it already," he said, "and
Ian or Kensie Graeme will be telling you the rest.
But in any case El Conde, the titular ruler of Nahar,
is only a figurehead. His father was set up with that
title by the first Naharese immigrants. They had a
dream of starting their own hereditary aristocracy
here, but that never really worked. Still, on paper,
the Conde's the hereditary sovereign and Commander-
in-Chief. But the army's always been drawn from the
poor of Nahar and they hate the rich first-immigrants.
Now there's a revolution brewing."

"I see," I said. "So the Graeme's contract here is
with a government which may be out of power tomorrow. Amanda's got a problem."

"It's everyone's problem," Michael said. "The only
reason the army hasn't declared itself for the revolutionaries is because its parts don't work together too
well. Coming from the outside, the way you have,
the ridiculousness of the locals' attitudes may be

what catches your notice first. But actually those attitudes are all the non-rich have, here, outside of a bare existence—this business of the flags, the uniforms, the music, the duels over one wrong glance and the idea of dying for your regiment—or being ready to go at the throat of any other regiment at the drop of a hat."

"But," I said, "what you're describing isn't any practical, working sort of military force."

"No. That's why Kensie and Ian were contracted in here, to turn the local army into something like an actual defense force. The other principalities around Nahar all have their eyes on the ranchlands, here. Given a normal situation, the Graemes'd already be making progress—you know Ian's reputation for training troops. But the common soldiers here think of the Graemes as tools of the ranchers. The truth is, I think Kensie and Ian'd be wise to take their loss on the contract and get out."

"If accepting loss and leaving was all there was to it, someone like Amanda wouldn't be needed here," I said. "How about you? What's your position here? You're Dorsai too."

"Am I?" he said to the windshield, in a low voice.

I had at last touched on what had been going unspoken between us. There was a name for individuals like Michael, back home. They were called "lost Dorsai." The name was not used for those who had chosen to do something other than a military vocation. It was reserved for those of Dorsai heritage who seemed to have chosen their life work, whatever it was, and then—suddenly and without explanation—abandoned it. In Michael's case, as I knew, he had graduated from the Academy with honors; but after graduation he had abruptly withdrawn his name from assignment and left the planet, with no explanation.

"I'm Bandmaster of the third Naharese Regiment," he said, now. "My regiment likes me. The local

people don't class me with the rest of you, generally—"
he smiled a little sadly, again, "except that I don't
get challenged to duels."

"I see—" I said.

The door to the control compartment opened and
Amanda stepped in.

"Well, Corunna," she said, "how about giving me
a chance to talk with Michael?"

She smiled past me at him; and he smiled back.
Her very presence, with all it implied of home, was
plainly warming to him.

"Go ahead," I said, getting up. "I'll go say a word
to the Outbond."

"He's worth talking to," Amanda spoke after me as
I went.

I stepped out, and rejoined Padma. He was looking out the window, down at the plains area that lay
between the city and the small mountain from which
Gebel Nahar took its name. Around and beyond that
mountain—for the fort-like residence that was Gebel
Nahar faced east—the actual, open grazing land of
the cattle plains began. Our bus was designed to fly
at about tree-top level, but right now we were about
three hundred meters up. As I stepped out Padma
took his attention from the window.

"Michael's been telling me that a revolution seems
to be brewing here in Nahar," I said to him. "That
wouldn't be what brings someone like you to Gebel
Nahar?"

His hazel eyes were suddenly amused.

"I thought Amanda was the one with the questions," he said.

He sat in perfectly relaxed stillness, his hands
loosely together in the lap of his robe, light brown
against the dark blue. His face was calm and unreadable. "It's part of the overall pattern of events on this
world."

"Just this world?"

He smiled back at me.

"Of course," he said gently, "our Exotic science of ontogenetics deals with the interaction of all known human and natural forces, on all the inhabited worlds. But the situation here in Nahar, and specifically the situation at Gebel Nahar, is primarily a result of local, Cetan forces."

"International planetary politics."

"Yes," he said.

"Which ones are backing the revolutionaries?"

He gazed out the window for a moment without speaking. It was a presumptuous thought on my part to imagine that my strange geas, that made people want to tell me private things, would work on an Exotic. But for a moment I had had the familiar feeling that he was about to open up to me.

"Actually," he said, "all of the five think they have a hand in it on the side of the revolutionaries. But bad as Nahar is, now, it would be a shambles after a successful revolution, with everybody fighting everybody else for different goals. The other principalities all look for a situation in which they can move in and gain. But you're quite right. International politics is always at work, and it's never simple."

"What's really fueling this situation, then?"

"William," Padma looked directly at me and for the first time I felt the remarkable effect of his hazel eyes. His face held such a calmness that all his expression seemed to be concentrated in those eyes.

"William?" I asked.

"William of Ceta."

"That's right," I said, remembering. "He owns this world, doesn't he?"

"It's not really correct to say he owns it," Padma said. "He controls after a fashion, but only by manipulating the outside conditions such as those the ranchers here have to deal with."

"So he's behind the revolution?"

"Yes."

It was plainly William's involvement that had brought Padma to this backwater section of the planet. The Exotic science of ontogenetics, which was essentially a study of how humans interacted, both as individuals and societies, was something they took very seriously; and William, as one of the movers and shakers of our time would always have his machinations closely watched by them.

"Well, it's nothing to do with us, at any rate," I said, "except as it affects the Graeme's contract."

"I wouldn't be so sure," he said. "William hires a good many mercenaries, directly and indirectly. It would benefit him if events here could lower the Dorsai reputation and market value."

"I see—" I began; and broke off as the hull of the bus rang suddenly—as if to a sharp blow.

"Down!" I said, pulling Padma to the floor of the vehicle.

"What was it?" he asked after a moment, but without moving.

"Solid projectile slug. Probably from a heavy hand weapon," I told him. "We've been shot at. Stay down, if you please, Outbond."

I got up myself, staying low, and went into the control compartment. Amanda and Michael both looked around at me, their faces alert.

"Who's out to get us?" I asked Michael.

He shook his head.

"Here in Nahar," he said, "it could be anybody. The revolutionaries, or simply someone who doesn't like the Dorsai; or someone who doesn't like Exotics—or me. It could be someone drunk, drugged, or just in a macho mood."

"—who also has a military hand weapon."

"There's that," Michael said. "But everyone in Nahar is armed; and most of them, legitimately or not, own military weapons. Anyway, we're almost down."

I looked out. The interlocked mass of buildings that was Gebel Nahar was sprawled halfway down from the top of the small mountain. In the tropical sunlight, it looked like a resort hotel. The only difference was that each terrace terminated in a wall, and the lowest of the walls were solid fortifications, with heavy weapons.

"What's the other side like?" I asked.

"Mountaineering cliff—there's heavy weapon emplacements cut out of the rock there, too, and reached by tunnels going clear through the mountain," Michael answered. "The ranchers spared no expense. They and their families might all have to hole up here, one day."

But a few moments later we were on the poured concrete surface of a vehicle pool. The parking area was abnormally silent.

"I don't know what's happened—" said Michael.

A voice shouting brought our heads around. A moment later a soldier wearing an energy sidearm, but dressed in the green and red Naharese army uniform with band tabs, burst into sight and slid to a halt, panting before us.

"Sir—" he wheezed, it the local dialect of archaic Spanish.

We waited for him to get his breath; after a second, he tried again.

"They've deserted, sir!" he said to Michael, trying to pull himself to attention. "They've gone—all the regiments, everybody!"

"When?" asked Michael.

"Two hours past. It was all planned. Certainly, it was planned! In each group, at the same time, a man stood up. He said that now was the time to desert, to show the *ricones* where the army stood. They all marched out, with their flags, their guns, everything. Look!"

He turned and pointed outwards. It was possible to see, from this as from any of the other levels, straight out for miles over the plains. Looking now, we saw tiny, occasional twinkles of reflected sunlight, seemingly right on the horizon.

"They are camped out there."

"Everyone's gone?" Michael's words in Spanish brought the soldier's eyes back to him.

"All but us. The soldiers of your band, sir. We are the Conde's Elite Guard, now."

"Where are the two Dorsai Commanders?"

"In their offices, sir."

"I'll have to go to them right away," said Michael to the rest of us. "Outbond, will you wait in your quarters, or will you come along with us?"

"I'll come," said Padma.

The five of us went across the parking area, between the crowded vehicles and into a maze of corridors. Through these we found our way finally to a large suit of offices, where the outward wall of each room was all window. We found Kensie and Ian Graeme together in one of the inner offices, standing talking before a massive desk large enough to serve as a conference table for a half-dozen people.

They turned as we came in—and once again I was hit by the curious illusion that I usually experienced on meeting these two.

In my own mind I had always laid it to the fact that in spite of their size—and either one is nearly a head taller than I am—they are so evenly proportioned physically that from a distance it is easy to take them for not much more than ordinary height. Then, having unconsciously underestimated them, you or someone else whose size you know approaches them; and it is that individual who seems to shrink as he, she, or you get close. If it is you, you are directly aware of the change. But if it is someone else, you can still seem to shrink, along with that other person. To feel yourself become smaller that way is a strange sensation, even if it is entirely subjective.

In this case, the measuring element turned out to be Amanda, who ran into the two brothers the minute we entered the room. Her homestead, Fal Morgan, was the one closest to the Graeme home of Foralie and the three of them had grown up together. She was not a small woman, but by the time she had reached them and was hugging Kensie, she seemed to have become not only tiny, but fragile; and suddenly—again, as it always does—the room seemed to orient itself about the two Graemes.

I followed her and held out my hand to the first one I reached, who was Ian.

"Corunna!" he said. His large hand wrapped around mine. His face—so different, yet so like, to his twin brother's—looked down into mine. Only it was not a physical difference, for all its powerful effect on the eye. Literally, it was that Ian was lightless, and all the bright element that might have been in him was instead in his brother, so that Kensie radiated double the human normal amount of sunny warmth. Dark and light. Night and day. Brother and brother.

And yet, there was a closeness between them of a kind that I have never seen in any other two human beings.

"Do you go back right away?" Ian was asking me. "Or will you be staying to take Amanda?"

"I can stay," I said. "Can I be of use here?"

"Yes," Ian said. "You and I should talk. Just a minute, though—"

He turned to greet Amanda in his turn and tell Michael to check and see if the Conde was available for a visit. Michael went out with the soldier who had met us at the vehicle pool. It seemed that Michael and his bandsmen, plus a handful of servants and the Conde himself, added up to the total present population of Gebel Nahar, outside of those in this room. The ramparts were designed to be defended by a handful of people, if necessary; but we had barely more than a handful in the forty members of the regimental band Michael had led and they were evidently untrained in anything but marching.

We left Kensie with Amanda and Padma. Ian led me into an adjoining office, waved me to a chair, and took one himself.

His arms lay relaxed upon the arms of the chair, his massive hands loosely curved about the ends of those chair arms. There was, as there always had been, something utterly lonely but utterly invincible about Ian. Most non-Dorsais seem to draw a noticeable comfort from having a Dorsai around in times of physical danger, as if they assumed that any one of us would know the right thing to do and so do it. It may sound fanciful, but I have to say that in somewhat the same way as the non-Dorsai reacted to the Dorsai, so did most of the Dorsai I've known always react to Ian.

"It'll take them two days to settle in out there," Ian said now, nodding at the window wall, beyond which lay the nearly invisible encampments on the plain. "After that, they'll either have to move against us, or they'll start fighting among themselves. That means we can expect to be overrun in two days."

"Unless what?" I asked. He looked back at me.

"There's always an unless," I said.

"Unless Amanda can find us an honorable way out of the situation," he said. "As it now stands, there doesn't seem to be any way out. Our only hope is that she can find something in the contract or the situation that the rest of us have overlooked."

"Isn't there anything you think she might be able to use?" I asked.

"No," he said. "It's a hope against hope. An honor problem."

"What makes it so sensitive that you need an Adjuster from home?" I asked.

"William. You know him, of course. But how much do you know about the situation in Nahar?"

I repeated what I had picked up from Michael and Padma.

"Nothing else?" he asked.

"I haven't had time to find out anything else."

"William . . ." he said. "It's my fault we're into this, rather than Kensie's. I'm the strategist, he's the tactician on this contract. The large picture was my job, and I didn't look far enough."

"If there were things the Naharese government didn't tell you, then there's your out, right there."

"Oh, the contract's challengeable, all right," Ian said. He smiled. I know there are those who like to believe that he never smiles; and that notion is nonsense. But his smile is like all the rest of him. "It isn't the information they held back that's trapped us, it's this matter of honor. Not just our personal honor—the reputation and honor of all Dorsai. They've got us in a position where whether we stay and die or go and live, it'll tarnish the planetary reputation."

I frowned at him.

"How can they do that?"

"Partly," said Ian, "because William's an extremely able strategist himself. Partly, because it didn't occur to me or Kensie that we were getting into a three-party rather than a two-party agreement."

"I don't follow you."

"The type of country the original settlers tried to set up here," he said "was something that could only exist under uncrowded, near-pioneering conditions. After that, the semi-feudal notion of open plains and larger individual holdings of land got to be impractical, on the international level of this world. Of course, the first settlers, those Gallegos from Galicia in northwest Spain, saw that coming from the start. That was why they built this place we're setting in."

His smile came again.

"But that was back when they were only trying to delay the inevitable," he said. "Sometime in more recent years they evidently decided to come to terms with it."

"Bargain with the neighbor countries?"

"Bargain with the rest of Ceta," he said. "Which is William—for all practical purposes."

"There again, if they had an agreement with William that they didn't tell you about," I said, "you've every excuse to void the contract."

"Their deal with William isn't a written, or even a spoken contract," Ian answered. "What the ranchers did was let him know that he could have the control he wanted here in Nahar if he'd meet their terms."

"And what did they want in exchange?"

"A guarantee that their life style and this pocket culture they'd developed would be maintained and protected."

He looked under his dark brows at me.

"I see," I said. "How did they think William could do that?"

"They didn't know. But they didn't worry about it. They just let the fact be known to William that if they got what they wanted they'd stop fighting his attempts to control Nahar directly. That's why there's no other contract we can cite as an excuse to break this one."

"It sounds like William. If I know him," I said, "he'd even enjoy engineering whatever situation was needed to keep this country fifty years behind the times. But you still haven't explained this business of your being trapped here, not by the contract, but by the general honor of the Dorsai."

Ian nodded.

"William's taken care of both things," he said. "His plan was for the Naharese to hire Dorsai to make their army a working unit. Then his revolutionary agents would cause a revolt of that army. Then he could step in with his own non-Dorsai officers to control the situation and bring order back to Nahar."

"I see," I said.

"He then would mediate the matter," Ian went on, "the revolutionary people would be handed some limited say in the government—under his control, of course—and the ranchers would give up their absolute authority but little of anything else."

"So," I said, thoughtfully, "what he's after is to show that his military people can to things Dorsai can't?"

"That's it," said Ian. "We command the price we do now only because military experts like ourselves are in limited supply. If they want Dorsai results—military situations dealt with at either no cost or a minimum cost, in life and materiel—they have to hire Dorsai. That's as it stands now. But if it looks like others can do the same job as well or better, our price has to go down, and our world will begin to starve."

"It'd take some years for the Dorsai to starve. In that time we could live down the results of this, maybe."

"But it goes farther than that. William isn't the first to dream of being able to hire all the Dorsai and use them as a personal force to dominate the other worlds. We've never considered allowing that yet. But if William can depress our price below what we need to keep the Dorsai free and independent, then he can offer us survival wages, available from him alone, and we'll have no choice but to accept."

"Then you've got no choice, yourself," I said. "You've got to break this contract, no matter what it costs."

"I'm afraid not," he answered. "The cost looks right now to be the one we can't afford to pay. You'll understand when you see El Conde—"

The door opened and Amanda herself looked in.

"It seems some local people calling themselves the Governors have just arrived—" Her tone was humorous, but every line of her body spoke of serious concern. "Evidently, I'm supposed to go and talk with them right away. Are you coming, Ian?"

"Kensie is all you'll need," Ian said. "We've trained them to realize that they don't necessarily get both of us on deck every time they whistle. You'll find it's just another step in the dance, anyway—there's nothing to be done with them."

"All right," she said, and went out.

"Sure you don't want to be there?" I asked him.

"No need." He got up. "Come along, then. It's important you understand the situation here thoroughly. If Kensie and myself should both be knocked out, Amanda would only have you to help her handle things. I wanted you to meet the Conde de Nahar. I've been waiting to hear from Michael as to whether the old man's receiving, right now, but we won't wait any longer. Let's go see how the old gentleman is."

He led the way out of the room. We left the suite of offices and began to travel the corridors of Gebel Nahar once more. Twice we took lift tubes and once we rode a motorized strip down one long corridor; but at the end Ian pushed open a door and we stepped into what was obviously the orderly room fronting a barracks section.

The soldier bandsman seated behind the desk there came to his feet immediately at the sight of us.

"Sirs!" he said, in Spanish.

"I ordered Mr. de Sandoval to find out for me if the Conde would receive Captain El Man here, and myself," Ian said in the same language. "Do you know where the Bandmaster is now?"

"No, sir. He has not come back. Sir—it is not always possible to contact the Conde quickly—"

"I'm aware of that," said Ian. "Rest easy. Mr. de Sandoval's due back here shortly, then?"

"Yes, sir. Any minute now. Would the sirs care to wait in the Bandmaster's office?"

"Yes," said Ian.

The orderly turned to usher us through a farther entrance into a larger room, very orderly and with a clean desk, filing cabinets and with its walls hung with musical instruments.

Most of these were ones I had never seen before. There was one that looked like an early Scottish bagpipe. It had only a single drone, some seventy centimeters long, and a chanter about half that length. Another was obviously a keyed bugle of some sort, but with most of its central body length wrapped with red cord ending in dependent tassels. I moved about the walls, examining each as I came to it, while Ian took a chair and watched me. I came back at length to the deprived bagpipe.

"Can you play this?" I asked Ian.

"I'm not a piper," said Ian. "I can blow a bit, of course—but I've never played anything but regular highland pipes. You'd better ask Michael if you want a demonstration. Apparently, he plays everything— and plays it well."

I turned away from the walls and took a seat, myself.

"What do you think?" asked Ian. I was gazing around the office.

I looked back at him and saw his gaze curiously upon me.

"It's . . . strange," I said.

And the room was strange. Just as there are subtle characteristics by which one born to the Dorsai will recognize another, so there are small signals about the office of anyone on military duty and from that world. So, Michael de Sandoval's office was unmistakably the office of a Dorsai. But, at the same time, it owned a strange difference from any other Dorsai's office.

"He's got these musical instruments displayed as if they were fighting tools," I said, "and no weapons visible."

Ian nodded. If Michael had chosen to hang a banner from one of the walls testifying to the fact that he would absolutely refuse to lay his hands upon a weapon, he could not have announced himself more plainly to Ian and myself.

"It seems to be a strong point with him," I said. "I wonder what happened?"

"His business, of course," said Ian.

"Yes," I said.

But the discovery hit me hard—because suddenly I identified what I had felt in young Michael from the first moment I had met him, here on Ceta. It was pain, a deep and abiding pain; and you cannot have known someone since he was in childhood and not be moved by that sort of pain.

The orderly stuck his head into the room.

"Sirs," he said, "the Bandmaster comes."

"Thank you," said Ian.

A moment later, Michael came in. "Sorry to keep you waiting—" he began.

"Perfectly all right," Ian said. "The Conde made you wait?"

"Yes sir."

"Well, is he available now?"

"Yes sir. You're both most welcome."

"Good." Ian stood up and so did I. "Amanda Morgan is seeing the Governors, at the moment. You might keep yourself available for her."

"I'll be right here," said Michael. "Sir—I wanted

to apologize for my orderly's making excuses about my not being here when you came—my men have been told not to—"

"It's all right, Michael," said Ian. "You'd be an unusual Dorsai if they didn't try to protect you."

"Still—" said Michael.

"Still," said Ian, "I know they've trained only as bandsmen. They may be line troops at the moment— all the line troops we've got to hold this place with— but I'm not expecting miracles."

"Well," said Michael. "Thank you, Commander."

We went out. Once more Ian led me through a maze of corridors and lifts.

"How many of his bandsmen decided to stay with him when the regiments moved out?" I asked as we went.

"All of them," said Ian.

"And no one else stayed?"

Ian looked at me with a glint of humor.

"You have to remember," he said, "Michael did graduate from the Academy, after all."

A final short distance down a wide corridor brought us to a massive pair of double doors. Ian touched a visitor's button on the right-hand door and spoke to an annunciator panel in Spanish.

"Commander Ian Graeme and Captain El Man are here with permission to see the Conde."

There was the pause of a moment and then one of the doors opened to show us another of Michael's bandsmen.

"Be pleased to come in, sirs," he said.

"Thank you," Ian said as we walked past. "Where's the Conde's majordomo?"

"He's gone, sir. Also the other servants."

"I see."

The room we had just been let into was a wide foyer filled with enormous and magnificently-kept furniture but lacking windows. The bandsman led us through two more rooms like it, into a third, finally window-walled room. A stick-thin old man dressed in black was standing with the help of a silver-headed cane, before the center of the window area.

The soldier slipped out of the room. Ian led me to the old man.

"El Conde," he said Spanish, "may I introduce Captain Corunna El Man? Captain, you have the honor of meeting El Conde de Nahar, Macias Francisco Ramón Manuel Valentin y Compostela y Abente."

"You are welcome, Captain El Man," said the Conde. He spoke a more correct, if more archaic, Spanish than that of the other Naharese I had so far met; and his voice was the thin remnant of what once must have been a remarkable bass. "We will sit down now, if you please. If my age produces a weakness, it is that it is wearisome to stand for any length of time."

We settled ourselves in heavy, overstuffed chairs with massively padded arms—more like thrones than chairs.

"Captain El Man," said Ian, "has brought Amanda Morgan here to discuss the present situation with the Governors. She's talking to them now."

"I have not met . . ." the Conde hesitated over her name, "Amanda Morgan."

"She is one of our experts."

"I would like to meet her."

"She's looking forward to meeting you."

"Possibly this evening? I would have liked to have had all of you to dinner, but my servants have gone."

"I just learned that," said Ian.

"They may go," said the Conde. "They will not be allowed to return. Nor will the regiments who have deserted their duty be allowed to return to my armed forces."

"With the Conde's indulgence," said Ian, "we don't

yet know all their reasons for leaving. Perhaps some leniency is justified."

"I can think of none." The Conde's back was as erect as a flagstaff and his dark eyes did not waver. "But, if you think so, I can reserve judgment momentarily."

"We'd appreciate that," Ian said.

"You are very lenient." The Conde looked at me. His voice took on an unexpected timbre. "Captain, has the Commander here told you? Those deserters out there—" he flicked a finger toward the window and the plains beyond, "under the instigation of people calling themselves revolutionaries, have threatened to take over Gebel Nahar. If they dare to come here, I and what few loyal servants remain will resist. To the death!"

"The Governors—" Ian began.

"The Governors have nothing to say in the matter!" the Conde turned fiercely on him. "Once, their fathers and grandfathers chose my father to be El Conde. I inherited that title and while I live, I will be El Conde. I will remain, I will fight—alone if need be—as long as I am able. But I will retreat, never! I will compromise, *never!*"

He continued to talk for some minutes; but although his words changed, the message of them remained the same. He would not give an inch to anyone who wished to change the governmental system in Nahar. He would never yield, in spite of reason or the overwhelming odds against him.

After a while he ran down. He apologized graciously for his emotion, but not for his attitude; and after a few minutes more of meaninglessly polite conversation on the history of Gebel Nahar itself, let us leave.

"So you see part of our problem," said Ian to me when we were alone again, walking back to his offices. "We can't just abandon him."

We went a little distance together in silence.

"Part of that problem," I said, "seems to lie in the difference between our idea of honor, and theirs. Did you ever read Calderon's poem about the Mayor of Zalemea?"

"I don't think so. Calderon?"

"Pedro Calderon de la Barca, seventeenth century Spanish poet. He wrote a poem called *El Alcalde de Zalamea.*"

I gave him the lines of which he had reminded me.

> *Al Rey la hacienda y la vida*
> *Se ha de dar; pero el honor*
> *Es patrimonio del alma*
> *Y el alma soló es de Dios.*

" '—*Fortune and life we owe to the King*,' " murmured Ian, " '*but honor is patrimony of the soul and the soul belongs to God alone.*' I see what you mean."

I started to say something, then decided it was too much effort. I was aware of Ian glancing sideways at me as we went.

"When did you eat last?" he asked.

"I don't remember," I said. "But I don't particularly need food right now."

"You need sleep, then," said Ian, "I'm not surprised, after the way you made it here from the Dorsai."

"Yes," I said.

Now that I had admitted to tiredness, it was an effort even to think. For those who have never navigated between the stars, it is easy to forget the implications of the fact that danger increases rapidly with the distance moved in a single shift—beyond a certain safe amount of light-years. For three days I had had no more than catnaps between periods of calculation. I was numb with a fatigue I had held at bay until this moment with the body adrenalin.

The bandsman supplied by Ian showed me at last

to my suite. It consisted of three window-walled rooms, each with a door in it to let me out onto a small balcony running the length of this particular level. The balcony was divided into areas for each suite by tall plants in pots at each division point.

I checked balcony and suit, locked the doors, and slept.

It was sometime after dark when I awoke, suddenly, to the sound of the call chime at the front door of my suite.

I reached over and keyed on the annunciator circuit.

"Yes?" I said. "Who is it?"

"Michael de Sandoval," said Michael's voice, "can I come in?"

I touched the stud that unlocked the corridor door in the adjoining sitting room. It swung open, letting in a knife-blade sharp swath of light I could see through the doorway to my bedroom. I was on my feet and moving to meet him in the sitting room as the door closed behind him.

"What is it?" I asked.

"The ventilating system's gone out on this level," he said; and I realized that the air in the suit was now perfectly motionless—motionless and beginning to be a little warm and stuffy.

"I wanted to check the quarters of everyone on this level," Michael said. "I'd suggest I open the door to the balcony for you, sir."

"Thanks," I said. "What was the situation with the servants? Were they revolutionary sympathizers, too?"

"Not necessarily." He unlocked the door and propped it open to the night air, which came coolly and sweetly through the aperture. "They just didn't want their throats cut along with the Conde's, when the army stormed its way back in here."

"I see," I said.

"Yes." He came back to me in the center of the sitting room.

"What time is it?" I asked. "I've been sleeping as if I was under drugs."

"A little before midnight."

I sat down in one of the chairs of the unlighted sitting room. The glow of the soft exterior lights spaced at ten meter intervals along the balcony came dimly through the window wall.

"Sit for a moment," I said. "Tell me. How did Amanda do with the Governors?"

I barely saw the shrug of his shoulders in the gloom.

"There was nothing much to be done with them," he said. "They wanted reassurances that Ian and Kensie could handle the situation. Effectively, it was all choreographed."

"They've left, then?"

"That's right. They asked for guarantees for the safety of the Conde. Both Ian and Kensie told them that there was no such thing as a guarantee; but we'd protect the Conde, of course, with every means at our disposal. Then they left."

"It sounds," I said, "as if Amanda could have saved her time and effort."

"No. She said she wanted to get the feel of them," he leaned forward. "You know, she's something to write home about. She says there's no question that there's a way out—it's just that finding it in the next twenty-four to thirty-six hours is asking a lot."

"I see," I said. "Is there anything I can do? Would you like me to spell you on the duty officer bit?"

"You're to rest, Ian says. He'll need you tomorrow. I'm getting along fine with my duties." He moved toward the front door of the suite. "Good night."

"Good night," I said.

He went out, the knife of light from the corridor briefly cutting across the carpeting of my sitting room again and vanishing as the door latched behind him.

I stayed where I was, enjoying the night breeze through the propped-open door. I may have dozed. At any rate I came to, suddenly, to the sound of voices from the balcony. Not from my portion of the balcony, but from the portion next to it, beyond my bedroom window to the left.

". . . yes," a voice was saying. Ian had been in my mind; and for a second I thought I was hearing him speak. But it was Kensie.

"I don't know . . ." It was Amanda's voice answering, a troubled voice.

"Time goes by quickly," Kensie said. "Look at us. It was just yesterday we were in school together."

"I know," she said, "you're talking about it being time to settle down. But maybe I never will."

"How sure are you of that?"

"Not sure, of course." Her voice changed as if she had moved some little distance from him.

"Then you could take the idea of settling down under consideration."

"No," she said. "I know I don't want to do that." Her voice changed again, as if she had turned and come back to him. "Maybe I'm ghost-ridden, Kensie. Maybe it's the old spirit of the first Amanda that's ruling out the ordinary things for me."

"She married—three times."

"But her husbands weren't important to her, that way. She really belonged to everyone, not just to her husbands and children. Don't you understand? I think that's the way it's going to have to be for me, too."

He said nothing. After a long moment she spoke again, and her voice was lowered, and drastically altered.

"Kensie! Is it that important?"

His voice was lightly humorous, but the words came a fraction more slowly than they had before.

"It seems to be."

"But it's something we both just fell into, as children. It was just an assumption on both our parts. Since then, we've grown up. You've changed. I've changed."

"Yes."

"You don't need me. Kensie, you don't need *me*—" her voice was soft. "Everybody loves you."

"Could I trade?" The humorous tone persisted. "Everybody for you?"

"Kensie, don't!"

"You ask a lot," he said; and now the humor was gone, but there was still nothing in the way he spoke that reproached her. "I'd probably find it easier to stop breathing."

There was another silence.

"Why can't you see? I don't have any choice," she said. "We're both what we are, and stuck with what we are."

"Yes," he said.

The silence, this time, lasted. But they did not move. My ear was not sensitized. They had been standing apart, and they stayed standing apart.

"Yes," he said again, finally—and this time it was a long, slow *yes*, a tired *yes*. "Life moves. And all of us move with it, whether we like it or not."

She moved to him, now.

"You're exhausted," she said. "Get some rest. Things'll look different in the daylight."

"That sometimes happens." The humor was back, but there was effort behind it. "Not that I believe it, in this case."

They went back inside.

I sat where I was, wide awake. There had been no way for me to get up and get away from their conversation without letting them know I was there. I still had the ugly feeling that I had been intruding where I should not have been.

There was no point in moving now. I sat where I was, so concerned with my own feelings that I did not pay close attention to the sounds around me. A small noise in my own entrance to the balcony area alerted me; and I looked up to see a dark silhouette in the doorway.

"You heard," Amanda's voice said.

"Yes," I told her. "I happened to be sitting here when you came out on the balcony. There was no chance to shut the door or move."

"It's all right," she came in. "No, don't turn on the light."

I dropped the hand I had lifted toward the control studs in the arm of my chair. With the illumination from the balcony behind her, she could see me better than I could see her. She sat down in the chair Michael had occupied a short while before.

"I told myself I'd step over and see if you were sleeping," she said. "Ian has a lot of work for you tomorrow. But I think I was really hoping to find you awake."

"I don't want to intrude," I said.

"If I reach out and haul you in by the scruff of the neck, are you intruding? I'm the one who's thinking of intruding—of intruding my problems on you."

"That's not necessarily an intrusion," I said.

"I hoped you'd feel that way," she said. "I need to have all my mind on what I'm doing here and personal matters have ended up getting in the way."

She paused.

"You don't really mind people spilling all over you?"

"No," I said.

"I thought so. I had the feeling you wouldn't. Do you think of Else much?"

"When other things aren't on my mind."

"I wish I'd known her."

"She was someone to know."

"Yes. Knowing someone else is what makes the difference. The trouble is, often we don't know. Or we don't know until too late." She paused. "I suppose you think, after what you heard just now, that I'm talking about Kensie?"

"Aren't you?"

"No. Kensie and Ian—the Graemes are so close to us Morgans that we might as well all be related. You don't usually fall in love with a relative when you're young. The kind of person you imagine falling in love with is someone strange and exciting—someone from fifty light years away."

"I don't know about that," I said. "Else was a neighbor and I think I grew up being in love with her."

"I'm sorry." Her silhouette shifted a little in the darkness. "I'm really just talking about myself. When I was younger, I just assumed I'd wind up with Kensie, that I'd have to have something wrong with me not to want someone like him."

"And you've got something wrong with you?" I said.

"Yes," she said. "That's it. I grew up, that's the trouble."

"Everybody does."

"I don't mean I grew up physically. I mean, I matured. We live a long time, we Morgans, and I suppose we're slower growing up than most. Did you ever have a wild animal for a pet as a child?"

"Several," I said.

"Then you've run into what I'm talking about. While it's young, it's cuddly and tame; but when it grows up, the day comes when it bites or slashes at you without warning. People talk about that being part of their wild nature. But it isn't. Humans change the same way. You grow up. Then the day comes when someone tries to play with you and you aren't in a playing mood—and you react with *'Back off! What I want is just as important as what you want!'*

And all at once, the time of your being young and cuddly is over, forever."

"Of course," I said. "That happens to all of us."

"But to us—to us Dorsai—it happens too late!" she said. "That's the cruel part of it. Or rather, we start life too early. By the age of seventeen we have to be out and working like an adult, either at home or on some other world. We're pitchforked into adulthood. There's never any time to take stock, to realize what it's going to turn us into. We don't realize we aren't cubs any more until one day we slash or bite someone without warning; and then we know we've changed. But it's too late then for us to adjust to the change in the other person because we've already been trapped by our own change."

She stopped. I sat, waiting. From my experience with this sort of thing since Else died, I knew that I no longer needed to talk. She would carry the conversation, herself.

"No, it wasn't Kensie I was talking about when I first came in here and said the trouble is you don't know someone else until too late. It's Ian."

"Ian?" I echoed.

"Yes," she said. "When I was young, I didn't understand Ian. I do now. Then, I thought he was simply solid all the way through, like a piece of wood. But he's not. Everything you can see in Kensie is there in Ian, only there's no light to see it by. Now I know. And now it's too late."

"To late?" I said. "He's not married, is he?"

"Married? Not yet. But you didn't know? Look at the picture on his desk. Her name's Leah. She's on Earth. He met her there, four years ago. But that's not what I mean. I mean—it's too late for me. I've got the curse of the first Amanda. I'm born to belong to a lot of people, first; and to any single person, second. As much as I'd give for Ian, that equation would sooner or later put even him in second place for me. I can't do that to him.

"Maybe Ian'd be willing to agree to those terms."

She did not answer for a second. Then I heard a slow intake of breath from the the darker darkness that was her.

"Would you suggest something like that to Ian if our positions were reversed?"

"I didn't suggest it," I said. "I mentioned it."

Another pause.

"You're right," she said. "I know what I want and what I'm afraid of in myself, and it seems to me so obvious I keep thinking everyone else must know too."

She stood up.

"Thank you, Corunna," she said.

"I've done nothing," I said.

"Thank you, anyway. Good night. Sleep if you can."

She stepped out through the door; and through the window wall I watched her, very erect, pass to my left until she walked out of my sight beyond the sitting room wall.

I went back to bed, not really expecting to fall asleep again easily. But I dropped off and slept like a dead man.

When I woke it was morning and my bedside phone was chiming. I flicked it on and Michael looked at me out of the screen.

"I'm sending a man up with maps of the interior of Gebel Nahar," he said, "so you can find your way around. Breakfast's available in the General Staff Lounge, if you're ready."

"Thanks," I told him.

I got up and was ready when his bandsman arrived; and the bandsman showed me to the General Staff Lounge. Ian was the only other there and he was just finishing his meal.

"Sit down," he said.

I sat.

"I'm assuming we'll be defending this place in twenty-four hours or so," he said. "I'd like you to familiarize yourself with its defenses, particularly at the first line of walls and its weapons, so that you can either direct the men working them, or take over the general defense."

"What have you got in mind for a general defense?" I asked.

"We've got just about enough of Michael's troops to man that first wall and have a handful in reserve," he said. "Most of them have never touched anything but a handweapon in their lives, but we've got to use them to fight with the emplaced energy weapons against foot attack up the slope. I'd like you to drill them on the weapons. Get breakfast in you; and I'll tell you how I expect the regiments to attack and what we might do when they try it."

He went on talking while my food came and I ate. Boiled down, his expectations were of a series of infantry wave attacks up the slope until the first wall was overrun. He planned a defense of the first wall until the last safe moment, then destruction of the emplaced weapons, and a quick retreat to the second wall with its weapons—and so, step by step, retreating up the terraces. It was essentially the sort of defense that Gebel Nahar had been designed for by its builders.

The problem would be in getting absolutely green troops like the Naharese bandsmen to retreat cool-headedly. If they could not, then the first wave over the ramparts could reduce their numbers to the point where there would not be enough of them to make any worthwhile defense of the second terrace, to say nothing of the third, the fourth, and so on, and still have men left for a final stand within the top three levels.

Given an equal number of veteran, properly trained troops, to say nothing of Dorsai-trained ones, we might even have held Gebel Nahar in that fashion and inflicted enough casualties to eventually make them pull back. But the most we could hope to do with what we had was inflict a maximum of damage while losing.

I finished eating and got up to go.

"Where's Amanda?" I asked.

"She's working with Padma," Ian said.

"I didn't know Exotics took sides."

"He's not." Ian said. "He's just making—his knowledge available. That's standard Exotic practice as you know as well as I do. He and Amanda are still hunting some political angle."

"What do you think their chances are?"

Ian shook his head.

"But," he said, shuffling together the papers he had spread out before him on the lounge table, "of course, where they're looking is a far ways out, beyond the areas of strategy I know. We can hope."

He got up, holding his papers and went out; I to Michael's office, he to his own.

Michael was not in his office. The orderly directed me to the first wall; and I found him there, already drilling his men on the emplaced weapons. I worked with them for most of the morning and then we stopped, because his untrained troops were exhausted and beginning to make mistakes simply out of fatigue.

Michael sent them to lunch. He and I went back to his office and had sandwiches and coffee brought in by his orderly.

"What about this?" I asked, after we were done, getting up and going to the wall where the archaic-looking bagpipe hung. "I asked Ian about it, but he said he'd only played highland pipes; and that if I wanted a demonstration, to ask you."

Michael looked up from his seat behind his desk.

"That's a *gaita gallega*," he said. "Or, to be correct, it's a local imitation of the gaita gallega you can still find back on Earth. It's a perfectly playable instrument to anyone who's familiar with the highland pipes. Ian could have played it."

"He seemed to think you could play it better," I said.

"Well . . ." Michael grinned again. "Perhaps, a bit. Do you really want to hear it?" he asked.

"Yes, I would."

He took it down from the wall.

"We'll have to step outside," he said.

We went back out on to the first terrace. He swung the pipe up in his arms, the long single drone resting on his left shoulder and pointing up into the air behind him. He took the mouthpiece between his lips and laid his fingers across the holes of the chanter. Then he blew up the bag and began to play.

Michael played something Scottish and standard—*The Flowers of the Forest*, I think—pacing slowly up and down. Then, abruptly he swung around and stepped out, playing something entirely different.

I wish there were words in me to describe it. It was anything but Scottish. It was hispanic, right down to its backbones—a wild, barbaric, musically ornate challenge that heated the blood in my veins.

He finished at last with a sort of dying wail as he swung the deflating bag down from his shoulder. He looked drawn and old.

"What was that?" I demanded.

"It's got a polite name for polite company," he said. "But nobody uses it. The Naharese call it *Su Madre*."

"*Your Mother*?" I echoed. Then, of course, it hit me. The Spanish language has a number of elaborate and poetically insulting curses to throw at your enemy about his ancestry; and the words *su madre* are found in most of them.

"Yes," said Michael. "It's what you play when you're daring the enemy to come out and fight. It accuses him of being less than a man in all the senses of that phrase—and the Naharese love it."

He sat down on the rampart suddenly, like someone very tired and discouraged.

"And they like me," he said. "My bandsmen, my regiment—they like me."

"Usually," I said, "men like their Dorsai officers."

"That's not what I mean." He was still staring at the wall. "I've made no secret here of the fact I won't touch a weapon. They've all known it from the day I signed on."

"I see," I said. "So that's it."

He looked up at me, abruptly.

"Do you know how they react to cowards—as they consider them—in this splinter culture? They show their manhood by knocking them around here. But they don't touch me. They don't even challenge me to duels, as I said."

"That don't believe you," I said.

"That's it." His face was almost savage. "Why not?"

"Because you only *say* you won't use a weapon," I told him bluntly. "In body language and every other language you speak, you broadcast just the opposite information—that you're so good none of them who'd challenge you would stand a chance. You could not only defeat someone like that, you could make him look foolish. The message is in the very way you walk and talk. How else could it be?"

"That's not true!" he got suddenly to his feet, holding the gaita. "I live what I believe in—"

He stopped.

"Maybe we'd better get back to work," I said.

"No!" The word burst out of him. "I want to tell someone. I want someone to . . ."

He broke off. He had been about to say "someone to understand . . ." but I could not help him. There is something in me that tells me when to speak and when not to.

And now I was being held silent.

He struggled with himself for a few seconds, and then calm seemed to flow over him.

"No," he said, as if talking to himself, "what people think doesn't matter. But we're not likely to live through this and I want to know how you react."

He looked at me.

"I've got to know how they'd take it, back home," he said, "if I could explain it to them. And your family is like mine, from the same canton, the same neighborhood, the same sort of ancestry . . ."

"Did it occur to you you might not owe anyone an explanation?" I said. "When your parents raised you, they only paid back the debt they owed their parents for raising them. If you've any obligation it's to the Dorsai in general, to bring in interstellar exchange credits. And you've done that by becoming bandmaster here. Anything beyond that's your own private business."

It was quite true. The vital currency between worlds was not wealth, but work credits. The inhabited worlds trade special skills, packaged in human individuals; and the exchange credits earned by a Dorsai on Newton enables the Dorsai to hire a geophysicist from Newton—or a physician from Kultis. Michael had been earning such credits ever since he had come here. True, he might have earned these at a higher rate if he had chosen work as a mercenary combat officer; but the credits he did earn as bandmaster more than justified the expense of his education and training.

"I'm not talking about that—" he began.

"No," I said, "you're talking about a point of obligation and honor not very different from what the Naharese use."

He stood for a second, absorbing that.

"You're telling me," he said "you don't want to listen."

"Now," I said, "you really are talking like a Naharese."

"Yes," he said, suddenly weary. "Would you sit down?"

He gestured to the rampart and sat down himself.

"Do you know I'm a happy man?" he demanded. "I really am. I've got everything I could want. I've got a military job I like. I'm in touch with all the things that I grew up thinking made the kind of life one of my family ought to have. I'm better at what I do than anyone else they can find—and I've got my other love, music, as my main duty. My men like me.

I nodded, watching him.

"But then there's this other part . . ." His hands closed on the gaita's bag, and there was a faint sound from the drone.

"Your refusal to fight?"

"Yes." He got up and began to pace, holding the instrument, talking jerkily. "This feeling against hurting anything . . . I've had it as long as I've had the other—all the dreams I made up as a boy from the stories I heard. When I was young it didn't matter that the feeling and the dreams hit head on. It just always happened that, in my visions, the battles I won were always bloodless. No one ever got hurt. I didn't worry about any conflict, then. It was something that would take care of itself later. But what was in me didn't change. It was there with me all the time, not changing."

"No normal person likes the actual fighting and killing," I said. "What sets our people off by ourselves is that often we *can* win without having dead bodies piled all over the place. Our way justifies itself by saving employers money; but also it gets us away from the essential brutality of combat and keeps us human. Remember what Cletus says about that? He hated killing just as much."

"But he could do it when he had to," Michael looked at me with a face drawn tight. "So can you. Or Ian. Or Kensie."

That was true, of course. I could not deny it.

"You see," said Michael, "that's the difference between life and being at the Academy. In life, sooner or later, you get to the killing part. When I graduated and faced going out as a fighting officer, I finally had to decide. And I did. I won't hurt anyone—even to save my own life, I think. But at the same time I'm bred and born a soldier. I don't want any other life, I can't conceive of any other; and I love it."

"He broke off, and stood, staring out at the flashes of light from the camp of the deserted regiments.

"Well, there it is," he said.

"Yes," I said.

He turned to look at me.

"Will you tell my family that?" he asked. "If you should get home and I don't?"

"All right," I said. "But we're not dead, yet."

He grinned, unexpectedly—a sad grin.

"I know," he said. "It's just that I've had this on my conscience for a long time. You don't mind?"

"Of course not."

He hefted the gaita in his hands.

"My men will be back out here in about fifteen minutes," he said. "I can carry on the drilling myself, if you've got other things you want to do."

I looked at him a little narrowly.

"What you're trying to tell me," I said, "is that they'll learn faster if I'm not around."

"Something like that." He laughed. "They're used to me; but you make them self-conscious."

"Whatever works," I said. "I'll go and see what else Ian can find for me to do."

I turned and went to the door that would let me back into the interior of Gebel Nahar.

"Thank you again," he called after me. I waved at him and went inside.

I found my way back to Ian's office. He was not there, so I went looking, and found Kensie with his desk covered with large scale printouts of terrain maps.

"Ian?" he said. "No, I don't know. But he ought to be back soon. I'll have some work for you tonight. I want to mine the approach slope. Michael's bandsmen can do the actual work; but you and I are going to need to go out first and make a sweep to pick up any observers the regiments have sent. Then, later, before dawn I'd like to do a scout of their camp and get some hard ideas as to how many of them there are, what they have to attack with, and so on . . ."

"Fine," I said. "I'm slept up. Call me when you want."

"You could try asking Amanda if she knows where Ian is."

Amanda and Padma were in a conference room two doors down from Kensie's office, seated at one end of a table covered with text printouts and an activated display screen. Amanda was studying the screen and they looked up as I came in. But while Padma's eyes were sharp, Amanda's were abstract.

"I'll come," Padma said to me before I could speak.

He got up and came to me, stepping into the outside room and shutting the door behind him.

"I'm trying to find Ian."

"I don't know where he'd be just now," said Padma.

I nodded toward the door he had just shut.

"It's getting rather late, isn't it," I asked, "for Amanda to hope to turn up some sort of legal solution?"

"Not necessarily." Next to the window wall of the outer office were several armchairs. "Why don't we sit down there? If he comes in from the corridor, he's got to go through this office, and if he comes out on the terrace of this level, we can see him through the window."

We went over and took chairs.

"It's not exact, actually, to say that there's a legal way of handling this situation that Amanda's looking for.

"You might get a better word picture if you said what Amanda is searching for is a *social* solution to the situation."

"I see," I said. "This morning Ian talked about Amanda saying that there always was a solution, but the problem here was to find it in so short a time. Did I hear that correctly?"

"There's always any number of solutions," Padma said. "The problem is to find the one you'd prefer. Once they happen, of course, they become history—"

He smiled at me.

"—and history, so far, is something we can't change. But changing what's about to happen simply requires getting to the base of the forces involved in time. What takes time is identifying the forces, finding what pressures are possible and where to apply them."

"And we don't have time."

"No," he said. "In fact, you don't."

I looked squarely at him.

"In that case, shouldn't you be thinking of leaving, yourself?" I said. "Aren't you too valuable to get your throat cut by some battle-drunk soldier?"

"I'd like to think so," he said. "But we think the value of studying people as closely as possible at times like this is important enough to take priority over everything else."

"People? You can't mean us who are here. Who then? William?" I said. "The Conde? Someone in the revolutionary camp?"

Padma shook his head.

"All of you, one way or another, have a hand in shaping history. But who shapes it largely, and who only a little is something I can't tell you. The science of ontogenetics isn't that sure. As to whom I may be studying, I study everyone."

It was a gentle, but impenetrable, shield he set up.

"Maybe you can explain how Amanda or you go about looking for a solution?" I said.

"It's a matter of looking for the base of the existing forces at work—"

"The ranchers—and William?"

He nodded.

"Particularly William—since he's the prime mover. To get results, William or anyone else had to set up a structure of cause and effect, operating through individuals. For anyone else to control the forces already set to work, it's necessary to find where that structure is vulnerable to cross-pressures and arrange for those to operate—again through individuals."

"And Amanda hasn't found a weak point yet?"

"Of course she has. Several." He frowned at me, but with a touch of humor. "But none that can be implemented between now and sometime tomorrow, if the regiments attack Gebel Nahar then."

I had a strange sensation. As if a gate was slowly but inexorably being closed in my face.

"It seems to me," I said, "the easiest thing to change would be the position of the Conde. If he'd just agree to come to terms with the regiments, the whole thing would collapse."

"Obvious solutions are usually not the easiest," Padma said. "Stop and think. Do you really think the Conde would change his mind?"

"No. You're right," I said. "He's a Naharese. More than that, he's honestly an hispanic. *El honor* forbids that he yield to soldiers threatening to destroy him."

"But tell me," said Padma, watching me. "Even if

el honor was satisfied, would he want to treat with the rebels?"

I shook my head.

"No," I said. "You're right again. This is the great moment of his life, the chance for him to substantiate that paper title of his, to make it real. This way he can prove to himself he's a real aristocrat. He'd give his life—in fact, he can hardly wait to give his life—to prove that."

There was a little silence.

"So you see," said Padma. "And in what other ways can you see a solution being found?"

"Ian and Kensie could void the contract. But they won't. No responsible officer from our world would risk giving the Dorsai the sort of bad name that could give, and neither of those two brothers would abandon the Conde as long as he insisted on fighting."

"What others ways, then?"

"I can't think of any," I said. "I'm out of suggestions—which is probably why I was never considered for anything like Amanda's job, in the first place."

"As a matter of fact, there are a number of other possible solutions," Padma said softly. "There's the possibility of bringing counter economic pressure upon William. There's also the possibility of bringing social and economic pressure upon the ranchers; and there's the possibility of disrupting the control of the revolutionaries who've come in from outside Nahar to run this rebellion. But none of these solutions can very easily be made to work in the short time we've got."

"In fact, there's no solution that can be made to work in time," I said.

Padma shook his head.

"No. If we could stop the clock at this second and take the equivalent of some months to study the situation, we'd undoubtedly find not only one, but several solutions. What's lacking isn't time to act, since that's merely something specified for the solution. What's lacking is time in which to find the solution that will work in the time there is to act."

"So you mean," I said, "that we're to sit here tomorrow and face the attack of six thousand line soldiers, all the time knowing there's a way in which that attack doesn't have to happen, if only we had the sense to find it?"

"The sense—and the time," said Padma. "But you're right."

The door I had sensed closing had just closed. It was unbelievable. I am Dorsai. The words *"Abandon hope . . ."* have no emotional reality for me. But there was no shadow of a doubt that this was what Padma was telling me.

PART TWO

"I see," I said. "Well, I find I don't accept it that easily."

"No." Padma's gaze was level and cooling upon me. "Neither does Amanda. Neither does Ian or Kensie. Nor, I suspect, even Michael. But then, you're all Dorsai."

I said nothing.

"In any case," Padma went on. "None of you are being called on to merely accept it. Amanda's still at work. So is Ian, so are all the rest of you. I didn't mean to sneer at the reflexes of your culture. I envy you—a great many people envy you—that inability to give in. My point is that the fact we know there's an answer makes no difference."

"True enough," I said—and at that moment we were interrupted.

"Padma?" It was the general officer annunciator speaking from the walls around us with Amanda's voice.

Padma got to his feet.

"I've got to go," he said.

He went out. I sat where I was, held by that odd little melancholy that had caught me up at moments all through my life. It is not a serious thing, just a touch of loneliness and sadness at the fact that life is measured; and there are only so many things that can be accomplished, try how you may.

Ian's return woke me out of it.

I got up.

"Corunna!" he said, and led the way into his private office. "How's the training going?"

"As you'd expect," I said. "I left Michael alone with them, at his suggestion. He thinks they might learn faster without my presence to distract them."

"Possible," said Ian.

He stepped to the window wall and looked out.

"They don't seem to be doing badly," he said.

He was still on his feet, of course, and I was standing next to his desk. I looked at it now, and found the cube holding the image Amanda had talked about. The woman pictured there was obviously not Dorsai, but there was something not unlike our people about her. She was strong-boned and dark-haired, the hair sweeping down to her shoulders, longer than most Dorsais out in the field would have worn it, but not long according to the styles of Earth.

I looked back at Ian. His face was turned toward the wall beyond which Amanda would be working with Padma at this moment. I noticed a tiredness about him. Not that it showed anywhere specifically in the lines on his face. He was, as always, like a mountain of granite, untouchable. But the way he stood spoke of a fatigue—perhaps one of the spirit rather than of the body.

"I just heard about Leah," I nodded at the image cube.

He turned.

"Leah? Oh, yes." His own eyes went to the cube and away again. "Yes, she's Earth. I'll be going to get her after this is over. We'll be married in two months."

"That soon?" I grinned at him. "I hadn't even heard you'd fallen in love."

"Love?" he echoed. His eyes were still on me, but their attention had gone away again. "No, it was years ago . . ."

His attention focused, suddenly. He was back with me. "Sit down," he said. "Have you talked to Kensie?"

"Just a little while ago."

"He's got a couple of runs outside the walls he'd like your hand with, tonight after dark's well settled in."

"He told me about them," I said. "A sweep of the slope in front to clear it before laying mines, and a scout of the regimental camp before tomorrow."

"That's right," Ian said.

"Do you have any solid figures on how many they'll have?"

"Regimental rolls," said Ian, "give us over five thousand of all ranks. Fifty-two hundred and some. But something like this invariably attracts a number of Naharese who scent the chance for personal glory. Then there's perhaps seven or eight hundred honest revolutionaries in Nahar, plus a hundred or so agents provocateurs from outside."

"In something like this, we can discount the civilians?"

Ian nodded.

"How many of the actual soldiers'll have had any actual combat experience?" I asked.

"Combat experience here," Ian said, "means a border clash with the armed forces of the surrounding principalities. Maybe one in ten of the line soldiers has had that. On the other hand, every Naharese male has dreamed of a moment like this."

"So they'll all come on hard with the first attack," I said.

"That's as I see it," said Ian, "and Kensie agrees. I'm glad to hear it's your thought, too. If we can throw them back even once, some won't come again. And so on. They won't lose heart as a group, but each setback will take the heart out of some, and we'll work them finally down to the hard core that's serious about being willing to die, if only they can reach us."

"Yes," I said, "how many do you think?"

"That's the problem," said Ian, calmly. "At the very least, there's going to be one in fifty we'll have to kill to stop. Even if half of those are already out of it by the time we get down to it, that's sixty left; and we've got to figure thirty percent casualties ourselves— Man to man, on the attackers making it over the walls, the bandsmen that're left will be lucky to take care of an equal number of attackers. Padma, of course, doesn't exist in our defensive table. That leaves you, me, Kensie, Michael, and Amanda to handle about thirty bodies. Are you in condition?"

I grinned.

"That's good," said Ian. "I forgot to figure that scar-face of yours. Be sure to smile like that when they come at you. It ought to slow them down for a couple of seconds at least, and we'll need all the help we can get."

I laughed.

"If Michael doesn't want you, how about working with Kensie?"

"Fine," I said.

Kensie looked up from his printouts when he saw me again.

"Find him?" he asked.

"Yes. He suggested you could use me."

"I can. Join me."

We worked together the rest of the afternoon.

What Kensie needed to know was what the ground was like meter by meter from the front walls on out over perhaps a couple of hundred meters of plain beyond. Given that knowledge, it would be possible to make reasonable estimates as to how a foot attack might develop, how many attackers we might be likely to have on a front, and on which parts of that front they might be expected to fall behind their fellows during a rush.

The Naharese terrain maps had never been made with such detailed information in mind. Kensie had spent most of the day before taking pictures of three-meter square segments of the ground, using the watch cameras built into the ramparts. With these pictures as reference, we now proceeded to make notes on blown up versions of the clumsy Naharese maps.

It took us the rest of the afternoon. We knocked off, with the job done, finally, about the dinner hour.

We found no one else at dinner but Ian. Michael was still teaching his bandsmen to be fighting troops; and Amanda was still with Padma.

"You'd both probably better get an hour of sleep," Ian said. "We might be able to pick up an hour or two more of rest just before dawn, but there's no counting on it."

"Yes," said Kensie. "You might sleep some, yourself."

Brother looked at brother. They knew each other so well that neither bothered to discuss the matter further. It had been discussed silently in that one momentary exchange of glances, and now they were concerned with other things.

As it turned out, I got a full three hours of sleep. It was just after ten o'clock when Kensie and I came out from Gebel Nahar. Michael led us, with our faces and hands blackened, along a passage that would let us out into the night a good fifty meters beyond the wall.

"How did you know about this?" I asked. "If there's more secret ways like this, and the regiments know about them—"

"There aren't and they don't," said Michael. "This is a private secret of the Conde's, His father had it built thirty-eight years ago. Our Conde told me about it when he heard the regiments had deserted."

I nodded. There was plainly a sympathy and a friendship between Michael and the old Conde that I had not had time to ask about. Perhaps it had come of their each being the only one of their kind in Gebel Nahar.

We reached the end of the passage and a short ladder leading up to a circular metal hatch. Michael turned out the light and we were suddenly in absolute darkness. I heard him cranking something well-oiled. Above us the hatch lifted to show starlit sky.

"Go ahead," Michael whispered. "Keep your heads down. The bushes that hide this spot have thorns."

We went up; I led, as being the most expendable. I heard Kensie come up and the hatch closed behind us. Michael was to open it again in two hours and fourteen minutes.

Kensie touched my shoulder. I looked and saw his hand held up, silhouetted against the stars. He made the hand signal for *move out*, and disappeared. I turned away to move off in the opposite direction, staying close to the ground.

I worked to the right as Kensie was working left. It was all sand, gravel and low brush, most with thorns or burrs. The night wind blew, cooling me under a sky where no clouds hid the stars.

The light of a moon would have been welcome, but Ceta has none. After fifteen minutes I came to the first of nine positions in my area that we had marked as possible locations for watchers from the enemy camp. Picking such positions is simple reasoning. Anyone but the best trained of observers, given the job of watching something like the Gebel Nahar, from which no action is really expected to develop, finds the hours long; and with the animal instinct in him he drifts automatically to the most comfortable or sheltered location from which to do his watching.

But there was no one at the first of the positions I came to. I moved on.

It was just about this time that I began to be aware of a change in the way I was feeling. The exercise, the adjustment of my body to the darkness and the night temperature, had begun to have their effects. I was no longer physically self-conscious. Instead, I was beginning to enjoy the action.

Old habits and reflexes had awakened in me. I flowed over the ground, now, not an intruder in the night of Nahar, but part of it. There was an excitement to it, a feeling of naturalness and rightness in my quiet search through this dim-lit land. I felt not only at home there, but as if in some measure I owned the night. The wind, the scents, the sounds I heard, all entered into me; and I recognized suddenly that I had moved completely beyond an awareness of myself as a physical body separate from what surrounded me. I was now pure observer, with the keen involvement that a wild animal feels in the world he moved through.

Then a sense of duty came and hauled me back to my obligations. I finished my sweep. There were no observers at all, either at any of the likely positions Kensie and I had picked out or anywhere else in the area I had covered. Unbelievable as it seemed from a military standpoint, the regiments had not bothered to keep even a token watch on us.

I returned to the location of the tunnel-end, and met Kensie there. His hand-signal showed that he had also found his area deserted. There was no reason why Michael's men should not be moved out as soon as possible and put to work laying the mines.

Michael opened the hatch at the scheduled time and we went down the ladder by feel in the darkness. With the hatch once more closed overhead, the light came on again.

"What did you find?" Michael asked, as we stood squinting in the glare.

"Nothing," said Kensie. "It seems they're ignoring us. You've got the mines ready to go?"

"Yes," said Michael. "If it's safe out there, do you want to send the men out by one of the regular gates? I promised the Conde to keep the secret of this tunnel."

"Absolutely," said Kensie. "In any case, the less people who know about this sort of way in and out of a place like Gebel Nahar, the better. Let's go back inside and get things organized."

We went. Back in Kensie's office, we were joined by Amanda. We sat around in a circle and Kensie and I reported on what we had found.

"I haven't waked the men yet," said Michael, when we were done. "They needed all the sleep they can get. I'll call the orderly and wake them now. We can be at work in half an hour; and except for my rotating them in by groups for food and rest breaks, we can work straight through the night. We ought to have all the mines placed by a little before dawn."

"Good," said Ian.

I sat watching him, and the others. My sensations, outside of having become one with the night, had left my senses keyed to an abnormally sharp pitch.

They were all deadly tired—each in his or her own way, very tired, with a personal, inner exhaustion that had finally been exposed by the physical tiredness to which the present situation had brought all of them except me. It seemed that what physical tired-

ness had accomplished had been to strip away the
polite covering that before had hidden the private
exhaustion; and it was now plain on every one of
them.

". . . Then there's no reason for the rest of us to
waste any more time," Ian was saying. "Amanda, you
and I'd better dress and equip for that scout of their
camp. Knife and sidearm, only."

His words brought me suddenly out of my separate awareness.

"You and Amanda?" I said. "I thought it was Kensie
and I, Michael and Amanda who were going to take a
look at the camp?"

"It was," said Ian. "One of the Governors who
came in to talk to us yesterday is on his way in by
personal aircraft. He wants to talk to Kensie again,
privately—he won't talk to anyone else."

"Some kind of a deal in the offing?"

"Possibly," said Kensie. "We can't count on it,
though, so we go ahead. On the other hand we can't
ignore the chance. So I'll stay and Ian will go."

"We could do it with three," I said.

"Not as well as it could be done by four," said Ian.
"That's a good sized camp to get into and look over
in a hurry. If anyone but Dorsai could be trusted to
get in and out without being seen, I'd be glad to take
half a dozen more. It's not like most military camps,
where there's a single overall headquarters area. We're
going to have to check the headquarters of each
regiment; and there're six of them."

I nodded.

"You'd better get something to eat, Corunna," Ian
went on. "We could be out until dawn."

It was good advice. When I came back from eating, the other three were already in Ian's office. On
his right thigh Michael was wearing a knife—which
was after all, more tool than weapon—but no side-
arms, and I noticed Ian did not object. With her

hands and face blacked, wearing the black stocking cap, overalls and boots, Amanda looked taller and more square-shouldered.

"All right," said Ian, "we'll go by field experience. I'll take two of the six regiments—the two in the center. Michael, because he's more recently from his Academy training and because he knows these people, will take two regiments—the two on the left wing that includes the far left one that's his own Third Regiment. You'll take the Second Regiment, Corunna, and Amanda will take the Fourth."

"It's unlucky you and Michael can't take regiments adjoining each other." I said. "That'd give you a chance to work together. You might need that with two regiments each to cover."

"Ian needs to see the Fifth Regiment for himself, if possible," Michael said. "That's the Guard Regiment, the one with the best arms. My regiment is a traditional enemy of the Guard Regiment, so the two have deliberately been separated as far as possible— that's why the Guards are in the middle and my Third's on the wing."

"Anything else? Then we should go," said Ian.

We went out by the same tunnel, leaving the hatch propped a little open against our return. Once out we spread apart at ten meter intervals and began to jog toward the lights of the regimental camp, in the distance.

We were an hour coming up on it. We began to hear it some distance off. It did not sound like a military camp on the eve of battle half so much as it did a large open-air party.

The camp was laid out in a crescent. The center of each regimental area was made up of the usual beehive-shaped buildings of blown bubble-plastic that could be erected so easily on the spot. Behind and between these were tents of all types and sizes.

There was steady traffic between these tents and the plastic buildings.

We stopped a hundred meters out, opposite the center of the crescent and checked off.

"All back here in forty minutes," Ian said.

We checked chronometers and split up, going in. My target, the Second Regiment, was between Ian's two regiments and Michael's two; and it was a section that had few tents, these seeming to cluster most thickly either toward the center of the camp or out on both wings. I slipped between the first line of buildings, moving from shadow to shadow.

It was foolishly easy. Effectively, the people moving between the buildings and among the tents had neither eyes nor ears for what was not directly under their nose. Getting about unseen under such conditions boils down simply to the fact that you move quietly—which means moving all of you in a single rhythm, including your breathing; and that, when you stop, you become utterly still—which means relaxing completely in whatever bodily position you have stopped in.

Breathing is the key to both, of course, as we learn back home in childhood games even before school age. Move in rhythm and stop utterly, and you can sometimes stand in plain sight without being observed.

A quick circuit of my area told me all we needed to know about this particular regiment. Most of the soldiers were between late twenties and early forties, in age. Under other conditions this might have meant a force of veterans. In this case, it indicated the opposite, time-servers who liked the uniform, the relatively easy work, and the authority. I found a few field energy weapons—light, three-man pieces that were not only out-of-date, but impractical in open territory, like that before Gebel Nahar. The heavier weapons on the ramparts would be able to take out such as these almost as soon as the rebels could try

to put them into action, and long before they could
do any real damage to the heavy defensive walls.

The hand weapons varied from the best of newer
energy guns, cone rifles and needle guns—in the
hands of the soldiers—to ancient and modern hunting tools and slug-throwing sport pieces—carried by
those in civilian clothing. Civilian and military hand
weapons alike, however, had one thing in common
that surprised me, in the light of everything else I
saw—they were clean, well-cared for, and handled
with respect.

I decided I had found out as much as necessary
about this part of the camp. I headed back to the first
row of plastic structures and the darkness of the
plains beyond, having to detour slightly to avoid a
drunken brawl that had spilled out of one of the
buildings into the space between it and the next.

It was on this detour that I became conscious of
someone quietly moving parallel to me. Since it was
on the side given to Michael to investigate, I guessed
it was he. I went to look, and found him.

I've got something to show you, he hand signalled
me. *Are you done, here?*

Yes, I told him.

Come on, then.

He led me to one of the larger plastic buildings in
the territory of the second regiment. The curving
sides of the structures are not difficult to climb quietly. He led me to the top and a small hole torn
there.

I looked in and saw six men with the collar rabs of
Regimental Commanders at a table, apparently having sometime since finished a meal. Their conversation was just below comprehension level. I could
hear their words, but not understand them.

But I could watch the way they spoke and tell how
they were reacting to each other. There were a great
many tensions around that table. There was no open

argument, but they looked at each other in ways next
to open challenges and the rumble of their voices
bristled with the electricity of controlled angers.

I felt my shoulder tapped, and took my attention
from the hole. It took a few seconds to adjust to the
darkness, but when I did, I could see Michael again
talking with his hands.

*Look at the youngest Commander—the one with
the very black mustache. That's the Commander of
my regiment.*

I looked, and lifted my gaze briefly to nod.

*Now look across the table and as far down from
him as possible. You see the somewhat heavy Commander with the gray sideburns and the lips that
almost pout?*

I looked, raised my head and nodded again.

*That's the Commander of the Guard Regiment. He
and my Commander are beginning to wear on each
other. If not, they'd be seated side by side and pretending friendship. It's almost as tense with the ju-
nior officers, if you know the signs to look for. Can
you guess what's triggered it off?*

No, I told him, *but I suppose you do.*

*I've been watching for some time. They had the
maps out earlier. The position of each regiment in
the line of battle, tomorrow. They've agreed, but no
one's happy with the decision.*

I nodded.

*I wanted you to see it for yourself. They're all
ready to go at each other's throats. Maybe Amanda
can find something in that she can use. I brought
you here because I was hoping you'll support me in
suggesting she come and see this for herself.*

I nodded again. The brittle emotions below had
been obvious, even to me, the moment I had first
looked through the hole.

We slipped quietly back down the curve of the
building to the ground and moved out together to-

ward the rendezvous point. Ian and Amanda were already there; and we stood together, looking back at the activity in the encampment as we compared notes.

"I called Captain El Man to look at something I'd found," Michael said. "In my alternate area, there was a meeting going on between the regimental commanders—"

The sound of a shot from someone's antique explosive firearm cut him short. We all turned toward the encampment; and saw a lean figure wearing a white shirt brilliantly reflective in the lights, running toward us, while a gang of men poured out of one of the tents, stared about, and then started in pursuit.

The one they chased was running directly for us, in his obvious desire to get away from the camp. It was obvious that, with his eyes still dilated from the lights of the camp, and staring at black-dressed figures like ours, he was completely unable to see us.

We dropped flat into the sparse grass of the plain. But he still came straight for us. Another shot sounded.

The fugitive had all the open Naharese plain into which to run. He came toward us instead as if drawn on a cable. We lay still. Unless he actually stepped on one of us, there was a chance he could run right through us and not know we were there.

He did not step on one of us, but he did trip over Michael, stagger on a step, check, and glance down to see what had interrupted his flight. He looked directly at Amanda, and stopped, staring down in astonishment. A second later, he had started to swing around to face his pursuers, his mouth open to shout.

He was obviously about to betray our presence, and Amanda did exactly the correct thing—even if it produced the least desirable results. She uncoiled from the ground like a spring released from tension, one fist taking the fugitive in the adam's apple to cut off his cry and the other going into him just under the breastbone to take the wind out of him and put

him down without killing him. But the incredible
bad luck of the moment was still with us.

As she took the man down, another shot sounded
from the pursuers, clearly aimed at the now-stationary
target of the fugitive—and Amanda went down with
him.

She was up again in a second.

"Fine—I'm fine," she said. "Let's go!"

We went, off into the darkness at the same trot at
which we had come. Until we were aware of specific
pursuit there was no point in burning our reserves of
energy. We moved steadily back toward Gebel Nahar,
while the pursuers reached the fugitive, surrounded
him, got him on his feet and talking.

By that time we could see them flashing around
the lights some had been carrying, searching for us.
But we were well away and drawing farther off every
second. No pursuit developed.

"Too bad," said Ian, as the sound and lights of the
camp dwindled behind us. "But no great harm done.
What happened to you, 'Manda?"

She did not answer. Instead, she went down again,
stumbling and dropping abruptly. In a second we
were all back around her.

She was plainly having trouble breathing.

"Sorry . . ." she whispered.

Ian was already cutting away the clothing over her
left shoulder.

"Not much blood," he said.

The tone of his voice said he was angry with her.
So was I. It was entirely possible that she might have
killed herself by trying to run with a wound that
should not have been excited by that kind of treatment. She had acted instinctively to hide the fact
that she had been hit, so that the rest of us would
not hesitate in getting away. It was not hard to
understand the impulse that had made her do it—
but she should not have.

"Corunna," said Ian, "this is more in your line."

He was right. As a captain, I was the closest thing to a physician aboard my ship. I moved in and checked the wound as best I could. In the faint starlight it showed as a small patch of darkness against a pale patch of exposed flesh. I felt it with my fingers and put my cheek down against it.

"Small caliber slug," I said. Ian breathed out harshly. He had already deduced that much. "Not a sucking wound. High up, just below the collarbone. No immediate pneumothorax, but the chest cavity'll be filling with blood. Are you very short of breath, Amanda? Don't talk, just nod or shake your head."

She nodded.

"How do you feel. Dizzy? Faint?"

She nodded again. Her skin was clammy to my touch.

"Going into shock," I said.

I put my ear to her chest again.

"Right," I said. "The lung on this side's not filling with air. She can't run. We'll need to carry her."

"I'll do that," said Ian. He was still angry, but trying to control it. "How fast do we have to get her back, do you think?"

"Her condition ought to stay the same for a couple of hours," I said. "Looks like no large blood vessels were hit; and the smaller vessels tend to be self-sealing. But the pleural cavity on this side's been filling up with blood and she's collapsed a lung. That's why she's having trouble breathing. No blood around her mouth, so it probably didn't nick an airway going through . . ."

I felt around behind her shoulder.

"It didn't go through. If there're MASH med-mech units back at Gebel Nahar and we get her back in the next two hours, she should be all right—if we carry her."

Ian scooped her into his arms. He stood up.

"Head down," I said.

"Right," he answered and put her over one shoulder in a fireman's carry. "No, wait—we'll need some padding."

Michael and I took our our jerseys and made a pad for his other shoulder. He transferred her to that shoulder, with her head hanging down his back. I sympathized with her. Even with the padding, it was not a comfortable way to travel; and her wound and shortness of breath would make it a great deal worse.

"Try it at a slow walk, first," I said.

"I'll try it. Be we can't go slow walk all the way," said Ian. "It's nearly three klicks from where we are now."

He was right, of course. To walk her back over three kilometers would take too long. We started off, and he gradually increased his pace until we were moving smoothly but briskly.

"How are you?" he asked her, over his shoulder.

"She nodded," I reported, from my position behind him.

"Good," he said, and began to jog.

We travelled. She did not speak; and, as far as I could tell, she did not lose consciousness once on that long, jolting ride. Ian forged ahead, like something made of gears and shafts rather than ordinary flesh, his gaze on the lights of Gebel Nahar, far off across the plain.

There is something that happens under those conditions where the choice is either to count the seconds, or disregard time altogether. In the end we all—and I think Amanda, too—went off a little way from ordinary time, and did not come back to it until we were at the entrance to the Conde's secret tunnel, leading back under the walls of Gebel Nahar.

By the time I got Amanda laid out in the medical section she looked very bad indeed and was only semi-conscious. Luckily, the medical section had everything necessary. I was able to find a portable unit that could be rigged for bed rest—vaccum pump, power unit, drainage bag. It was a matter of inserting a tube between Amanda's lung and chest wall—and this I left to the med-mech—so that the unit could exhaust the blood from the pleural space into which it had drained.

It was also necessary to rig a unit to supply her with reconstituted whole blood while this draining process was going on. I finally got her fixed up and left her to rest—she was in no shape to do much else.

I went off to the offices to find Ian and Kensie with my report on Amanda's treatment and my estimate of her condition.

"She shouldn't do anything for the next few days, I take it," said Ian when I was done.

"That's right," I said.

"There ought to be some way we could get her out of here, to safety and a regular hospital," said Kensie.

"How?" I asked. "It's almost dawn. The Naharese would zero in on any vehicle that tried to leave, by ground or air."

Kensie nodded soberly.

"They should be starting to move now," said Ian, "if this dawn was to be the attack moment."

He turned to the window, and Kensie and I turned with him. Dawn was just breaking.

"After all their parties last night, they may not get going until noon," I said.

"I don't think they'll be that late," said Ian, absently. He had taken me seriously. "At any rate, it gives us a little more time. Are you going to have to stay with Amanda?"

"I'll want to look in on her from time to time—in fact, I'm going back down now," I said. "I just came up to tell you how she is. But in between visits, I can be useful."

"Good," said Ian. "As soon as you've had another look at her, why don't you go see if you can help Michael? He's been saying he's got his doubts about those bandsmen of his."

"All right." I went out.

When I got back to the medical section, Amanda was asleep. I was going to leave, when she woke and recognized me.

"Corunna," she said, "how am I?"

"You're fine," I said. "All you need now is to get a lot of sleep and do a good job of healing."

Her head moved restlessly on the pillow.

"Better if that slug had been more on target."

I looked down at her.

"According to what I've heard about you," I said, "you of all people ought to know that when you're in a hospital bed it's not the best time in the world to be worrying over things."

She started to speak, interrupted herself to cough, and was silent for a little time until the pain of the tube, rubbing inside her with the disturbance of her coughing, subsided.

"No," she said. "I can't *want* to die. But the situation's impossible; and every way out of it is impossible, for all three of us. Just like our situation here in Gebel Nahar."

"Kensie and Ian are able to make up their own minds."

"It's not a matter of making up minds. It's a matter of impossibilities."

"Well," I said, "is there anything you can do about that?"

"I ought to be able to."

"Ought to, maybe, but can you?"

She breathed shallowly. Slowly she shook her head.

"Then let it go. Leave it alone," I said. "I'll be back to check on you from time to time. Wait and see what develops."

"How can I wait?" she said. "I'm afraid of myself.
Afraid I might throw everything overboard and do
what I want most—and so ruin everyone."

"You won't do that."

"I might."

"You're exhausted," I told her. "You're in pain.
Stop trying to think. I'll be back in an hour or two to
check on you. Until then, rest!"

I went out, in search of Michael and found him in
the supply section. He was going from supply bin to
supply bin, checking the contents of each and testing
the automated delivery system of each to make sure
it was working.

The overhead lights were very bright, and their
illumination reflected off solid concrete walls painted
a utilitarian, flat white. I watched his face as he
worked. There was no doubt about it. He looked
much more tired, much leaner, and older than he had
appeared to me only a few days before when he had
met Amanda and me at the spaceport terminal of
Nahar City. But the work he had been doing and
what he had gone through could not alone have cut
him down so visibly, at his age.

He finished checking the last of the delivery systems and the last of the bins. He turned away.

"Ian tells me you're concerned over your bandsmen," I said.

His mouth thinned and straightened.

"Yes," he said. There was a little pause, and then
he added: "You can't blame them. If they'd been real
soldier types they would have been in one of the line
companies. There's security, but no chance for promotion in a band."

"On the other hand," I said, "they stayed."

"Well . . ." He sat down a little heavily on a short
stack of boxes and waved me to another, "so far it
hasn't cost them anything but some hard work. And
they've been paid off in excitement. Excitement—

drama—is what most Naharese live for; and die for, for that matter, if the drama is big enough."

"You don't think they'll fight when the time comes?"

"I don't know." His face was bleak again. "I only know I can't blame them—I can't, of all people—if they don't."

"Your attitude's a matter of conviction."

"Maybe theirs is, too. You never know enough to make a real comparison."

"True," I said. "But I still think that if they don't fight, it'll be for somewhat lesser reasons than yours."

He shook his head slowly.

"Maybe I'm wrong, all wrong." His tone was almost bitter. "But I can't get outside myself to look at it. I only know I'm afraid."

"Afraid?" I looked at him. "Of fighting?"

"I wish it was of fighting," he laughed, briefly. "No, what I'm afraid of is that I don't have the will *not* to fight. I'm afraid at the last moment it'll all come back, those early dreams and all the training; and I'll find myself killing, even though I'll know it won't make any difference in the end and that the Naharese will take Gebel Nahar, anyway."

"I don't think it'd be Gebel Nahar you'd be fighting for," I said slowly. "I think it'd be out of a natural, normal instinct to stay alive yourself as long as you can—or to help protect those who are fighting alongside you."

"Yes," he said. His nostrils flared as he drew in an unhappy breath. "The rest of you. That's what I won't be able to stand. It's too deep in me. I might be able to let myself be killed. But can I stand there when they start to kill someone else—like Amanda, and she already wounded?"

He and I walked back to his offices in silence. When we arrived, there was a message for me, to call Ian. I did.

"The Naharese still haven't started to move," he

said. "They're so unprofessional I'm beginning to think we can get Padma, at least, away from here. He can take one of the small vehicles and fly out to Nahar City. My guess is that once they see he's an Exotic, they'll simply wave him on."

"It could be," I said.

"I'd like you to go and put that point to him," said Ian. "He seems to want to stay, but he may listen if you make him see that by staying here, he simply increases the load of responsibility on the rest of us. I'd like to order him out but I don't have the authority."

"All right," I said. "I'll go talk to him right now. Where is he?"

"In his quarters."

I found Padma's suite and spoke to him.

"I see," he said. "Did Ian or Kensie ask you to talk to me, or is this the result of an impulse of your own?"

"Ian asked me," I said. "The Naharese are delaying their attack. Once they see you're an Exotic—"

His smile interrupted me.

"I have my duty, too. In this instance, it's to gather information for Mara and Kultis." His smile broadened. "Also, there's the matter of my own temperament. Watching a situation like the one here is fascinating. I wouldn't leave if I could. In short, I'm as chained here as the rest of you."

I shook my head at him.

"It's a fine argument," I said. "But, if you'll forgive me, a little hard to believe."

"In what way?"

"I'm sorry," I told him, "but I don't seem to be able to give any real faith to the idea that you're being held here by patterns that are essentially the same as mine, for instance."

"Not the same," he said. "Equivalent. The fact other can't match you Dorsai in your own area doesn't mean others don't have equal areas in which equal commitments apply."

"With identical results?"

"With comparable results—could I ask you to sit down?" Padma said mildly. "I'm getting a stiff neck looking up at you."

I sat down facing him.

"For example," he said. "In the Dorsai ethic, you and the others here have something that directly justifies your natural human hunger to do things for great purposes. The Naharese here have no equivalent ethic; but they feel the hunger just the same. So they invent their own customs, their *leto de muerte* concepts. But can you Dorsais, of all people, deny that their concepts can lead them to as true a heroism, or as true a keeping of faith as your ethnic leads you to?"

"Of course I can't deny it," I said. "But the Dorsai can at least be counted on to perform as expected. Can the Naharese? You sound a little like Michael when you get on the subject of these people. All right, stay if you want. I think I'd better leave now, before you talk me into going out and offering to surrender before they even get here."

He laughed. I left.

It was time again for me to check Amanda. I went to the medical section. But she was honestly asleep now. Apparently she had been able to put her personal concerns aside enough so that she could exercise a little of the basic physiological control we are all taught from birth. I left her sleeping.

It was a shock to see the sun as high in the sky as it was, when I emerged once more, on to the first terrace. The sky was almost perfectly clear and there was a small, steady breeze. The day would be hot. Ian and Kensie were each at one end of the terrace, looking through watch cameras at the Naharese front.

Michael, the only other person in sight, was also at a watch camera. I went to him.

"They're on the move," he said, stepping back from the watch camera. I looked into its rectangular viewing screen, bright with the daylight scene it showed. He was right. The regiments had finally formed for the attack and were now coming toward us at the pace of a slow walk.

I could see their flags spaced along the front of the crescent formation and whipping in the breeze. The Guard regiment was still in the center and Michael's Third Regiment on the right wing. Behind the wings I could see the darker swarms that were the volunteers and the revolutionaries.

The attacking force had already covered a third of the distance to us. I stepped away from the screen and all at once the front I looked at became a thin line with little bright flashes of reflected sunlight and touches of color, still distant.

"Another thirty or forty minutes," said Michael.

I looked at him. The clear daylight showed him pale and wire-tense. He looked as if he had been whittled down—nothing but nerves were left. He was not wearing weapons.

The rifles woke me to something I had noted but not focused upon. The bays with the fixed weapons were empty.

"Where's your bandsmen?" I asked Michael.

He gazed at me.

"They've gone," he said.

"Gone?"

"Decamped. Deserted, if you want to use that word."

I stared at him.

"You mean they've joined—"

"No, no." He broke in on me. "They haven't gone over to the enemy. They just decided to save their own skins. I told you—you remember, I told you they might. You can't blame them. They're not Dorsai; and staying here meant death."

"If Gebel Nahar is overrun," I said.

"Can you believe it won't be?"

"It's become hard to," I said, "now that there's just us. But there's always a chance as long as anyone's left to fight. At Baunpore, I saw men and women firing from hospital beds, when the North Freilanders broke in."

I should not have said it. I saw the shadow cross his eyes and knew he had taken my reference to Baunpore personally, as if I had been comparing his present weaponless state with the last efforts of the defenders I had seen then.

"That's a general observation only—" I began.

"It's not what you accuse me of, it's what I accuse myself of," he said in a low voice looking at the regiments.

There was nothing more I could say. We both knew that without his forty men we could not even make a pretense of holding the first terrace. There were just too few of us, and too many of them, to stop them from coming over the top.

"They're probably hiding just out beyond the walls," he said. "If we do manage to hold out for a day or two, there's a slight chance they might trickle back—"

He broke off, staring past me. I turned and saw Amanda.

How she had managed it by herself, I do not know. But she had gotten up and strapped the portable drainage unit on to her. It was not heavy, or much bigger than a thick book; and it was designed for wearing by an ambulatory patient; but it must have been hell for her to rig it by herself with that tube rubbing inside her at every deep breath.

Now she was here, looking as if she might collapse at any time, but on her feet with the unit slung from her right shoulder and strapped to her right side.

She had a sidearm clipped to her left thigh, over the cloth of the hospital gown; and the gown itself was ripped up the center so that she could walk in it.

"What the hell are you doing?" I said. "Get back to bed!"

"Corunna—" she gave me the most level and unyielding stare I had ever encountered. "Don't give me orders. I rank you."

I blinked at her. It was true I had been asked to be her driver for the trip here, and in a sense that put me under her orders. But for her to presume to tell a Captain of a full flight of fighting ships, with an edge of half a dozen years in seniority and experience that in a combat situation like this she ranked him—it was raving nonsense. I opened my mouth to explode—and found myself breaking into laughter, instead. The situation was too ridiculous.

But, obviously she was out here on the terrace to stay; and obviously, I was not going to make any real issue of it under the circumstances. We both understood what was going on. Which did not change the fact that she should not have been on her feet. Like Ian out on the plain, and in spite of having been forced to see the humorous side of it, I was still angry with her.

"Next time you're wounded, better hope I'm not your medico," I told her. "What can you do up here, anyway?"

"I can be with the rest of you," she said.

I closed my mouth again. There was no arguing with that answer. Out of the corner of my eyes I saw Kensie and Ian approaching. They looked down at her but said nothing, and we all turned to look again out across the plain.

We stood together, the four of us, looking at the slow, ponderous advance upon us. All my life I had been plagued by an awareness of the ridiculous. What mad god had decided that an army should march against a handful—and that the handful should not only stand to be marched upon, but should prepare to fight back? But then the sense of the ridiculousness passed.

With that, I passed into the final stage that always came on me before battle. It was as if I stepped down into a place of private quiet. What was coming would come, and I would meet it when it came. I was aware of Kensie, Ian, Michael and Amanda standing around me, and aware that they were experiencing much the same feelings. Something like telepathy flowed between us, binding us together. In all my life's experience there has been nothing like that feeling of unity, and I have noticed that those who have once felt it never forget it. It is as it is, as it always has been, and we who are there at that moment are together. Against that togetherness, odds do not matter.

There was a faint scuff of a foot on the terrace floor, and Michael was gone. I looked at the others, and the thought was unspoken between us. He had gone to put on his weapons. We turned and saw the Naharese now close enough so that they were recognizable as individual figures. They were almost close enough for their approach to be heard.

We moved forward to the parapet of the terraces and stood watching. The day-breeze, strengthening, blew in our faces. There was time now to appreciate the sunlight, the not-yet-hot temperature of the day and the moving air. Another few hundred meters and they would be within the range of our emplaced weapons. Until then, there was nothing urgent to be done.

The door opened behind us. I turned, but it was not Michael. It was Padma, supporting El Conde, who was coming out to help us with the help of a silver-headed walking stick. Padma helped him out to the parapet, and for a second he ignored us,

looking instead at the oncoming troops. Then he
turned to us.

"Gentlemen and lady," he said in Spanish, "I will
join you."

"We're honored," Ian answered him in the same
tongue. "Would you care to sit down?"

"Thank you, no. I will stand. You may go about
your duties."

He leaned on the cane, watching across the parapet. We stepped back away from him, and Padma
spoke in a low voice.

"I'm sure he won't be in the way," Padma said.
"But he wanted to be here, and there was no one but
me left to help him."

"It's all right," said Kensie. "But what about you?"

"I'd like to stay, too," said Padma.

Ian nodded. A harsh sound came from the throat
of the count, and we looked at him. He was rigid as
some ancient dry spearshaft, staring out at the approaching soldiers, his face carved with the lines of
fury and scorn.

"What is it?" Amanda asked.

I had been as baffled as the rest. Then a faint
sound came to my ear. The regiments were at last
close enough to be heard; and what we were hearing
were their bugle calls as faint snatches of melody on
the breeze. We could barely hear it, but I recognized it, as El Conde already had.

"They're playing the *te guello*," I said. "Announcing '*no quarter*'."

The *te guello* is a promise to cut the throat of
anyone opposing. Amanda's eyebrows rose.

"For us?" she said. "What good do they think
that'll do?"

"They may think Michael's bandsmen are still with
us," I said. "But probably they're doing it just because it's always done."

The others listened for a second. The *te guello* is

an effectively chilling piece of music; but, as Amanda had implied, it was a little beside the point to play it to Dorsai.

"Where's Michael?" she asked now.

I looked around. It was a good question. If he had indeed gone for weapons, he should have been back out on the terrace sometime since. But there was no sign of him.

"I don't know," I said.

"They've stopped their portable weapons," Kensie said, "and they're setting them up to fire. Completely out of effective range, against walls like this."

"We'd probably be better down behind the armor of our own emplacements, " said Ian. "They can't hurt the walls but they might get lucky and hurt some of us."

He turned to El Conde.

"If you'd care to step down into one of the weapons emplacements, sir—" he said.

El Conde shook his head.

Ian nodded. He looked at Padma.

"Of course," said Padma. "I'll come in with one of you—unless I can be useful in some other way?"

"No," said Ian. A shouting from the approaching soldiers turned him and the rest of us at once more toward the plain.

The front line of the attackers had broke into a run toward us. They were only a hundred meters or so now from the foot of the slope leading to the walls of Gebel Nahar. Whether it had been decided that they should attack from that distance, or—more likely—someone had been carried away and started forward early, did not matter. The attack had begun.

For a moment, this development had given us a temporary respite. With their own soldiers flooding out ahead, it would be difficult for those behind to fire at Gebel Nahar without killing their own men. It was the sort of small happening that can sometimes

be turned to an advantage—but, as I stared out at
the plain, I had no idea of what we might do that
would make any real difference to the battle's outcome.

"Look!" called Amanda.

The shouting of the soldiers had stopped, suddenly. The front line of the attackers was trying to
slow down against the pressure of those behind. The
attack was halting as more and more of them checked
and stared at the slope.

What was happening there was that the lid of El
Conde's private exit from Gebel Nahar was rising. To
the Naharese military it must have looked as if some
secret weapon was about to unveil itself on the slope—
and it would have been this that had caused them to
have sudden doubts and dig in their heels. They
were still two or three hundred meters from the
tunnel, and the first line of attackers, trapped by
those behind them, were sitting ducks for whatever
field-class weapon might elevate itself through this
unexpected opening and zero in on them.

But of course no such weapon came out. Instead,
what emerged was a head wearing a regimental cap,
with what looked like a stick tilted back by its right
ear . . . and slowly, up on to the level of the ground,
and out to face them all came Michael.

He was without weapons. But he was dressed in
his full parade regimentals as band officer; and the
gaita gallega was resting in his arms. He stepped on
to the slope and began to march down it toward the
Naharese.

The silence was deadly; and into that silence, striking up, came the sound of the *gaita gallega*. Clear
and strong it came to us; and clearly it reached as
well to the now-silent and motionless ranks of the
Naharese. He was playing *Su Madre.*

He went forward at a march step, shoulders level,
the instrument held securely in his arms; and his
playing went before him, throwing its challenge di-

rectly into their faces. A single figure marching against three thousand.

From where I stood, I had a slight angle on him; and with the magnification of the watch camera, I could get just a glimpse of his face from the side and behind. He looked peaceful and intent. He marched as if on parade, with the intentness of a good musician in performance, and all the time *Su Madre* was calling and mocking at the armed regiments before him.

I touched the camera to make it give me a closeup look at the men in the Naharese force. They stood as if paralyzed. They were saying nothing, doing nothing, only watching Michael come toward them as if he meant to march right through them. All along their front, they were stopped and watching.

But their inaction was something that could not last. As I watched, they began to stir. Michael was between us and them, and the incredible voice of the bagpipe came almost loudly to our ears. But rising behind this, we now began to hear a sound like the growl of some enormous beast.

I looked in the screen. The regiments were still not advancing, but none of the figures I now saw as I panned down the front were standing frozen with shock. In the middle of the crescent formation, the soldiers of the Guard Regiment, who held a feud with Michael's Third, were shaking weapons at him.

All alone the line, the front boiled. They had all seen that Michael was unarmed. For a few moments this held them in check. They threatened, but did not fire. But I could feel the fury building in them.

I wanted to shout at Michael to turn and come back. He had broken the momentum of their attack and thrown them into confusion. With troops like these they would not take up their advance where they had halted it. Their senior officers would pull them back and reform them. A breathing space had been gained. It could be some hours before they would be able to mount a second attack; and in that time internal tensions or any number of developments might help us further. Michael still had them between his thumb and forefinger. If he turned his back on them now, their inaction might well hold until he was back in safety.

But there was no way I could reach him and he went steadily forward, scorning them with his music, taunting them for attacking in their numbers an opponent so much less than themselves.

Still the Naharese soldiery only shook their weapons and shouted insults at him; but now, in by the Third Regiment there were uniformed figures beginning to wave Michael back. I moved the view of the screen further along that wing and saw civilians from the following swarm of volunteers and revolutionaries, who were shoving their way to the front, kneeling down and putting weapons to their shoulder.

The Third Regiment soldiers were pushing these others back and jerking their weapons away. Fights had begun to break out; but on that wing those who wished to fire on Michael were being held back. It was plain the Third Regiment was torn now between the attack on Gebel Nahar and its impulse to protect their former bandmaster in his act of outrageous bravery. Still, I saw in the screen one civilian with a starved and furious face, who had literally to be held on the ground by three of the Third Regiment before he could be stopped from firing.

A sudden suspicion passed through me. I swung the screen's view to the opposite wing, also, the soldiers were trying to check those who attempted to shoot Michael. But here, the effort to prevent that firing was scattered and ineffective.

I saw a number of weapons of all types leveled at Michael. No sound could reach me, but it was clear that death was finally in the air around Michael.

I switched the view back to him. For a moment he continued to march as if some invisible armor was protecting him. Then he stumbled, caught himself, went forward, and fell.

For a second time—for a moment only—the voice of the attackers stopped, cut off as if a multitude of invisible hands had been clapped over the mouths of those there. I lifted the view on the screen from the fallen shape of Michael and saw soldiers and civilians alike standing motionless, staring at him, as if they could not believe that he had at last been brought down.

Then, on the wing opposite to the Third Regiment, the civilians firing began to dance and wave their weapons in the air—and suddenly the whole formation seemed to collapse inward, as the soldiers of the Third Regiment charged across at the rejoicing civilians, and the Guard Regiment swirled out to oppose them. The fighting spread as individual attacked individual. In a moment they were all embroiled. A wild mob without direction or purpose except to kill whoever was closest, took the place of the military formation that had existed only five minutes before.

As the fighting became general, the tight mass of bodies spread out like butter melting; and the struggle extended over a larger and larger area, until at last it covered even the place where Michael had fallen. Amanda turned away from the parapet and I caught her as she staggered. I held her upright and she leaned heavily against me.

"I have to lie down, I guess," she murmured.

I led her towards the door and the bed that was waiting for her. Ian, Kensie and Padma followed, leaving only El Conde, leaning on his silver headed stick and staring at what was taking place on the plain, his face lighted with the fierce satisfaction of a hawk perched above the body of its kill.

It was twilight before all the fighting had ceased; and, with the dark, there began to be heard the small sounds of the annunciator chimes at the main gate. One by one Michael's bandsmen began to slip back to us in Gebel Nahar. With their return, Ian, Kensie and I were able to stop taking turns at standing watch, as we had up until then. But it was not until after midnight that we felt it was safe to leave long enough to go out and recover Michael's body.

Amanda insisted on going with us. There was no reason to argue against her coming with us and a good deal of reason in favor of it. She was responding very well to the drainage unit and a further eight hours of sleep had rebuilt her strength to a remarkable degree. Also, she was the one who had suggested we take Michael's body back to the Dorsai for burial.

The cost of travel between the worlds was such that few individuals could afford it; and few Dorsai who died in the course of their duties off-planet had their bodies returned for internment in native soil. But we had adequate space to carry Michael's body with us in the courier vessel; and it was Amanda's point that Michael had solved the problem by his action—something for which the Dorsai world in general owed him a debt. Both Padma and El Conde had agreed, after what had happened today, that the Naharese would not be brought back to the idea of revolution again for some time. William's machinations had fallen through. Ian and Kensie could now either make it their choice to stay and execute their contract, or legitimately withdrew from it for the reason that they had been faced with situations beyond their control.

In the end, all of us except Padma went out to look for Michael's body, leaving the returned bandsmen to stand duty. It was full night by the time we emerged once more on to the plain through the secret exit.

"El Conde will have to have another of these made for him," said Kensie, as we came out under the star-brilliant sky. "This one is more a national monument than a secret, now."

The night was like the one before, when Kensie and I had made our sweep in search of observers from the other side. But this time we were looking only for the dead; and that was all we found.

During the afternoon all the merely wounded had been taken away by their friends; but there were bodies to be seen as we moved out to the spot where we had seen Michael go down, but not many of them. It had been possible to mark the location exactly using the surveying equipment built into the watch cameras. But the bodies were not many. The fighting had been more a weaponed brawl than a battle. Which did not alter the fact that those who had died were dead. They would not come to life again, any more than Michael would. A small night breeze touched our faces from time to time as we walked. It was too soon after the fighting for the odors of death to have taken possession of the battlefield. For the present moment under the stars the scene we saw, including the dead bodies, had all the neatness and antiseptic quality of a stage setting.

We came to the place where Michael's body should have been, but it was gone. Ian switched on a pocket lamp; and he, with Kensie, squatted to examine the ground. I waited with Amanda. Ian and Kensie were the experienced field officers, with Hunter Team practice. I could spend several hours looking to see what they would take in at a glance.

After a few minutes they stood up again and Ian switched off the lamp. There were a few seconds while our eyes readjusted, and then the plain became real around us once more, replacing the black wall of darkness that the lamplight had instantly created.

"He was here, all right," Kensie said. "Evidently quite a crowd came to carry his body off someplace else. It'll be easy enough to follow the way they went."

We followed the trail of scuffed earth and broken vegetation left by the footwear of those who had carried away Michael's body. The track they had left was plain enough so that I myself had no trouble picking it out, even by starlight, as we went along at a walk. It led further away from Gebel Nahar, toward where the center of the Naharese formation had been when the general fighting broke out; and as we went, bodies became more numerous. Eventually, at a spot which must have been close to where the Guard Regiment had stood, we found Michael.

The mound on which his body lay was visible as a dark mass in the starlight, well before we reached it. But it was only when Ian switched on his pocket lamp again that we saw its true identity and purpose. It was a pile nearly a meter in height and a good two meters long and broad. Most of what made it up was clothes; but there were many other things mixed in with the cloth items—belts and ornamental chains, ancient weapons, so old that they must have been heirlooms, bits of personal jewelry, even shoes and boots.

But, as I say, the greater part of what made it up was clothing—in particular uniform jackets or shirts, although a fair number of detached sleeves or collars bearing insignia of rank had evidently been deliberately torn off by their owners and added as separate items.

On top of all this, lying on his back with his dead face turned toward the stars, was Michael. I did not need an interpretation of what I was seeing here, after my earlier look at the painting in the Nahar

City Spaceport Terminal. Michael lay not with a
sword, but with the *gaita gallega* held to his chest;
and beneath him was the *leto de muerte*—the real
leto de muerte, made up of everything that those
who had seen him there that day, and who had
fought for and against him after it was too late,
considered the most valuable thing they could give
from what was in their possession at the time.

Each had given the best he could, to build up a
bed of state for the dead hero—a bed of triumph,
actually, for in winning here Michael had won everything, according to their rules and their ways. After
the supreme victory of his courage, as they saw it,
there was nothing left for them but the offering of
tribute; their possessions or their lives.

We stood, we three, looking at it all in silence.
Finally, Kensie spoke.

"Do you still want to take him home?"

"No," said Amanda. The word was almost a sigh
from her, and she stood looking at the dead Michael.
"No. This is his home, now."

We went back to Gebel Nahar, leaving the corpse
of Michael with his honor guard of the other dead
around him.

The next day Amanda and I left Gebel Nahar to
return to the Dorsai. Kensie and Ian had decided to
complete their contract; and it looked as if they
should be able to do so without difficulty. With
dawn, individual soldiers of the regiments had begun
pouring back into Gebel Nahar, asking to be accepted once more into their duties. They were eager
to please, and for Naharese, remarkably subdued.

Padma was also leaving. He rode into the spaceport with us, as did Kensie and Ian, who had come
along to see us off. In the terminal, we stopped to
look once more at the *leto de muerte* painting.

"Now I understand," said Amanda, after a moment. She turned from the painting and lightly

touched both Ian and Kensie who were standing on either side of her.

"We'll be back, she said, and led the two of them off.

I was left with Padma.

"Understand?" I said to him. "The *leto de muerte* concept?"

"No," said Padma, softly. "I think she meant that now she understands what Michael came to understand, and how it applies to her. How it applies to everyone, including me and you."

I felt coldness on the back of my neck.

"To me?" I said.

"You have lost part of your protection, the armor of your sorrow and loss," he answered. "To a certain extent, when you let yourself become concerned with Michael's problem, you let someone else in to touch you again."

I looked at him, a little grimly.

"You think so?" I put the matter aside. "I've got to get out and start the checkover on the ship. Why don't you come along? When Amanda and the others come back and don't find us here, they'll know where to look."

Padma shook his head.

"I'm afraid I'd better say goodbye now," he replied. "There are other urgencies that have demanded my attention for some time and I've put them aside for this. Now, it's time to pay them some attention. So I'll say goodby now; and you can give my farewells to the others."

"Goodby, then," I said.

As when we had met, he did not offer me his hand; but the warmth of him struck through to me; and for the first time I faced the possibility that perhaps he was right. That Michael, or he, or Amanda—or perhaps the whole affair—had either worn thin a spot, or chipped off a piece, of that shell that had closed around me when I watched them kill Else.

"Perhaps we'll run into each other again," I said.

"With people like ourselves," he said, "it's very likely."

He smiled once more, turned and went.

I crossed the terminal to the Security Section, identified myself and went out to the courier ship. It was no more than half an hour's work to run the checkover—these special vessels are practically self-monitoring. When I finished the others had still not yet appeared. I was about to go in search of them when Amanda pulled herself through the open entrance port and closed it behind her.

"Where's Kensie and Ian?" I asked.

"They were paged. The Board of Governors showed up at Gebel Nahar, without warning. They both had to hurry back for a full-dress confrontation. I told them I'd say goodby to you for them."

"All right. Padma sends his farewells by me to the rest of you."

She laughed and sat down in the copilot's seat beside me.

"I'll have to write Ian and Kensie to pass Padma's on," she said. "Are we ready to lift?"

"As soon as we're cleared for it. That port sealed?"

She nodded. I reached out to the instrument bank before, keyed Traffic Control and asked to be put in sequence for liftoff. Then I gave my attention to the matter of warming the bird to life.

Thirty-five minutes later we lifted, and another ten minutes after that saw us safely clear of the atmosphere. I headed out for the legally requisite number of planetary diameters before making the first phase shift. Then, finally, with mind and hands free, I was able to turn my attention again to Amanda.

She was lost in thought, gazing deep into the pinpoint fires of the visible stars in the navigation

screen above the instrument bank. I watched her
without speaking for a moment, thinking again that
Padma had possibly been right. Earlier, even when
she had spoken to me in the dark of my room of how
she felt about Ian, I had touched nothing of her. But
now, I could feel the life in her as she sat beside me.

She must have sensed my eyes on her, because
she roused from her private consultation with the
stars and looked over.

"Something on your mind?" she asked.

"No," I said. "Or rather, yes. I didn't really follow
your thinking, back in the terminal when we were
looking at the painting and you said that now you
understood."

"You didn't?" She watched me for a fraction of a
second. "I meant that now I understood what Michael had."

"Padma said he thought you'd meant you understood how it applied to you—and to everyone."

She did not answer for a second.

"You're wondering about me—and Ian and Kensie,"
she said.

"It's not important what I wonder," I said.

"Yes, it is. After all, I dumped the whole matter in
your lap in the first place, without warning. It's
going to be all right. They'll finish up their contract
here and then Ian will go to Earth for Leah. They'll
be married and she'll settle in Foralie."

"And Kensie?"

"Kensie." She smiled sadly. "Kensie'll go in . . . in
his own way."

"And you?"

"I'll go mine." She looked at me very much as
Padma had looked at me, as we stood below the
painting. "That's what I meant when I said I'd understood. In the end the only way is to be what you
are and do what you must. If you do that, everything
works. Michael found that out."

"And threw his life away putting it into practice."

"No," she said, swiftly. "He threw nothing away. There were only two things he wanted. One was to be the Dorsai he was born to be and the other was never to use a weapon; and it seemed he could have either one but not the other. Only, he was true to both and it worked. In the end, he was Dorsai and unarmed—and by being both he stopped an army."

Her eyes held me so powerfully that I could not look away.

"He went his way and found his life," she said, "and my answer is to go mine. Ian, his, Kensie, his; and—"

She broke off so abruptly I knew what she had been about to say.

"Give me time," I said; and the words came a little more thickly than I had expected. "It's too soon yet. Still too soon since she died. But give me time, and maybe . . . maybe, even me."

Last Voyage

"What's up?" asked Barney Dohouse, the engineer, coming through the hatch and swinging up the three metal steps of the ladder to the control room. Both Jed Alant (the captain), and the young mate Tommy Ris were standing in front of the vision screen.

"We're being followed, Barney," said Jed, without turning around. "Come here and take a look."

The heavy old engineer swung himself forward to stand between the stocky, grizzled captain and the slim young mate. The screen was set on a hundred and eighty degrees rear—which meant it was viewing the segment of space directly behind them. Barney squinted at it. An untrained eye would have seen nothing among the multitude of star points that filled it like an infinite number of gleaming drops from the spatter-brush of an artist; but the engineer, watching closely, made out in the lower left corner of the screen a tiny dark shape that occulted point after glowing point in its progress toward the center of the screen.

The point seemed to crawl with snail-like slowness, but Barney frowned. "Coming up fast, isn't he? Who do you suppose he is?"

"There's no scheduled craft on that course," said Tommy Ris, his blue eyes serious under the carefully combed forelock of his brown hair.

"Uh," grunted Barney. "Think it's Pellies?"

"I'm afraid so," Jed sighed. "And us with passengers."

The three men fell silent, gazing at the screen. It was a reflection on their years of experience in the void that they thought of the passengers rather than themselves. Your true spaceman is a fatalist out of necessity, and as a natural result of having his nose constantly rubbed in the fact that—cosmically speaking—he is not the least bit important. With passengers, as they all three knew, the case was different. Passengers, by and large, are planet-dwellers, comfortably self-convinced of the necessity for their own survival and liable to kick and fuss when the man with the scythe comes along.

The *Tecoatepetl*—*Teakettle* to her friends and crew—had no business carrying passengers in the first place. She had been constructed originally to carry vital drugs and physiological necessities to the pioneer worlds, as soon as they were opened for self-supporting colonists. When the first belt of extra-solar worlds had been supplied, she was already a little outdated. Her atomic power plant and her separate drive section—like one end of a huge dumbell— balanced the control and payload section at the other end of a connecting section like a long tube. Powerful, but not too pretty, she was useful, but not so efficient, by the time sixty years had passed and the hair of her captain and engineer had greyed. As a result she had been downgraded to the carrying of occasional passenger loads—according to the standards of interstellar transportation, where human life is usually slightly less important than cargoes of key materials for worlds who lack them.

Old spaceships never die until something kills them, the demand for anything that will travel between the stars fantastically out-weighing the available carrying space. An operating spaceship is worth its weight in—spaceships. To human as well as alien; which was why the non-human ship from the Pleiades was swiftly overhauling them. Neither humans nor cargo could hold any possible interest for the insectivorous humanoids; but the ship itself was a prize.

"We're five hours from Arcturus Base," said Tommy, "and headed for it at this velocity he can't turn us. Wonder how he figures on getting us past our warships there without being shot up."

"Ask him," said Barney, showing his teeth in a grin.

"You mean—talk to him?" Tommy looked at the captain for permission.

"Why not?" said Jed. "No, wait; I'll do it. Key me in, Tommy."

The younger man seated himself at the transmission board and set himself to locating the distantly-approaching ship with a directional beam. Fifteen minutes later, a green light began to glow and wink like a cat's eye in front of him; and he grunted with satisfaction.

"All yours," he said to Jed. The captain moved over to stand in front of the screen as Tommy turned a dial and the stars faded to give an oddly off-key picture of a red-lighted control room. A tall, supple-looking member of the race inhabiting the Pleiades stars his short trunk-snout looking like a comic nose stuck in the middle of his elongated face, looked back at him.

"You speak human?" asked Jed.

"I speak it," answered the other. The voice strongly

resembled a human's except for a curious ringing quality, like a gong being struck in echo to the vowels. "You don't speak mine?"

"I haven't got the range," replied Jed. They stood looking at each other with curiosity, but without emotion, like professional antagonists.

"So," said Pellie. "It takes a trained voice, you." He was referring to the tonal changes in the language of his race, which covers several octaves, even for the expression of simple ideas. "Why you have called?"

"We were wondering," said Jed, "how you thought you could take our ship and carry it through the warfleet we're due to pass in five hours."

"You stay in ship, you," answered the other, "when we pass by fleet we let you leave ship by small boat."

"I bet," said Jed.

The Pleiadan did not shrug, but the tone of his voice conveyed the sense of it. "Your choice, you."

"I'll make you a deal," said Jed. "Let us out into the lifeboats now. None of us can turn at this velocity, so we'll all ride together up as far as the base. Once our small boats are safe under the guns of the fleet, you can chase the ship here and take it over without any trouble."

"Only one person you leave on ship blows it up," said the Pleiadan. "No. You stay. Say nothing to fleetships. We stay close in for one pip on screen Arcturus. After we pass, we let you go. You trust us."

"Well," said Jed. "You can't blame a man for trying." He waved to the Pellie, who repeated the gesture and cut the connection. "That's that," Jed went on, turning back to the other two humans, as Tommy thoughtfully returned the star-picture to the screen. The occulting shape that was the ship they had just been talking to was looming quite large now, indicating its closeness.

"D'you think there's any chance of him doing what he says?" Barney asked the Captain.

"No reason to, and plenty of reason not to," replied Jed. "That way he keeps the two lifeboats with the ship—they're valuable in their own right." This was true, as all three men knew. A lifeboat was nothing less than a spaceship in miniature—as long as you kept it away from large planetary bodies, whose gravity were too much for the simple, one-way-thrust engines.

"I suppose the passengers will have to be told," broke in Tommy. "They'll be seeing it on the lounge screen sooner or later. What do you say, Jed?"

"Let's not borrow trouble until we have to," frowned the captain. They were all thinking the same thing, imagining the passenger's reactions to an announcement of the true facts of the situation. Hysteria is a nasty thing for a man to witness just before his own death.

"I wish there was something the fleet could do," said Tommy a trifle wistfully. He knew the hopelessness of the situation as well as the two older men; but the youngness of him protested at such and early end to his life.

"If we blew ourselves up, they'd get *him*, eh, Jed?" said Barney.

"No doubt of it," said the captain. "But I can't with these passengers. If it was us . . .

There was the sudden suck of air, and the muted slam of the opening and closing of the bulkhead door between the control section and the passengers lounge above. Leni Hargen, the chief steward swung down the ladder, agile in spite of his ninety years, his small, wiry figure topped by a face like an ancient monkey's. He joined the circle.

"Got company have we, Jed?" he asked, his sharp voice echoing off the metal, equipment-jammed walls.

"A Pellie," Jed nodded. "The pay-load excited?"

"So-so," replied Leni. "It hasn't struck home yet. First thing they think of when they see another ship is that it's human, of course. 'Damned clever, these aliens, but you don't mean to say they can really do what we do'—that sort of attitude. No, they think it's human. And they want to know who their traveling companions are; sent me up to ask."

"I'll go talk to them," said Jed.

"Why talk?" said Leni. Living closest of them all to the passengers, he had the most contempt for them. "Won't do no good. Wait till the long-nose gets close, then touch off the fuel, and let everybody die happy."

Barney swore. "He's right, Jed. We don't have a prayer, none of us. And I want to go when the old girl goes."

He was talking about the *Teakettle*, and the captain winced. With the exception of Tommy and the assistant steward, the ship had been their life for over half a century. It was unthinkable to imagine an existence without her. The thought of Tommy made him glance at the young mate. "What d'you say, son?"

"I . . ." Tommy hesitated. Life was desperately important to him and at the same time he was afraid of sounding like a coward. "I'd like to wait," he said at last, shamefacedly.

"I'm glad to hear it," replied Jed, decisively. "Because that's what we're going to do. I know what you think of your charges, Leni; but so far as I'm concerned, human life rates over any ship—including this one. And as long as there's one wild chance to take, I've got to take it."

"What chance?" said Leni. "They promise to turn us loose?"

Jed nodded. "They did. And I'm going to have to go on the assumption that they will."

"They will like . . ."

"Steward!" said Jed; and Leni shut his mouth. "I'll go out and talk to the passengers. The rest of you wait here."

He turned and went up the ladder toward the lounge door in the face of their silence.

The hydraulically-operated door whooshed away from its air seal as he turned the handle, and sucked back into position after he had stepped through. He stood on the upper level of the lounge, looking down its length at the gay swirl of colorfully dressed passengers. For a moment he stood unnoticed, seeing the lounge as it had been in the days when it was the main hold and he was younger. Then "Oh, there's the captain!" cried someone; and they flocked around him, chattering questions. He held up his hand for silence.

"I have a very serious announcement to make," he said. "The ship you see pulling up on us is not human but Pleiadan. They are not particularly interested in humans, but they want this ship. So after we pass Arcturus Station, we may have to take to the lifeboats and abandon the ship to them—unless some other means of dealing with the situation occurs."

He stopped and waited, bracing himself for what he knew would follow: first the stunned silence; then the buzz of horrified talk amongst themselves; and finally the returning to him of their attention and their questions.

"Are you sure, Captain?"

"Look for yourself," Jed waved a hand at the screen at the far end of the lounge on which the ship was now quite noticeable. "And I've talked to their captain."

"What did he say?" they cried, a dozen voices at once.

"He gave me the terms I just passed on to you," said Jed.

A silence fell on them. Looking down into their faces, Jed read their expressions clearly. This threat was too fantastic; there must be someone who had blundered. The spaceship company? The captain?

They looked back up at him, and questions came fast.

"Why don't we speed up and run away from them?"

Patiently Jed explained that maximum acceleration for humans was no more than the maximum acceleration for Pellies; and that the "speed" of a ship depended on the length of time it had been undergoing acceleration.

"Can't we dodge them?"

A little cruelly, Jed described what even a fraction of a degree of sudden alteration of course would do to the people within the ship at this present velocity.

"The warships!" someone was clamoring, an elderly, professional looking man. "You can call them, Captain!"

"If they came to meet us," said Jed, "we'd pass at such relatively high velocities that they could do us no good. We can only continue on our present course, decelerating as we normally would, and hope to get safely away from the ship after we pass Arcturus station."

The mood of the crowd in the lounge began to change. Stark fear began to creep in, and an ugly note ran through it.

"It's up to you," said one woman, her face whitened and sharply harsh with unaccustomed desperation. "You do something!"

"Rest assured," Jed answered her, speaking to them all. "Whatever I and the crew can do, will be done. Meanwhile . . ." he caught the eye of Eli Pellew, the young assistant steward, standing at the back of the room, "The bar will be closed; and I'll expect all of you to remain as quiet as possible. Pellew, come up forward when you've closed the bar. That's all ladies and gentlemen."

He turned and went back through the door, the babble of voices behind him shut off suddenly by its closing. He re-descended the ladder to find the mate, engineer and steward in deep discussion, which broke off as he came in.

"What's this?" he said cheerfully. "Mutiny?"

"Council of war," said Barney. "It's your decision, but we thought . . ."

"Go ahead," said Jed. Sixty years of experience had taught him when to stand on his rights as captain, and when to fit in as one of the group.

"We've been talking a few things over," said Barney, "proceeding on the assumption—which most of us figure is a downright fact—that the Pellie hasn't any intention of letting us go, anyway."

"Go on."

"Well," said Barney. Almost exactly Jed's age and almost his equal in rank, the engineer slipped easily into the position of spokesman for the rest of the crew. "Following that line of thought, the conclusion is we've got nothing to lose. So to start out with, why not notify the Arcturus Base ships, anyway?"

"Because he just *might* keep that promise," said Jed. Behind them, the lounge door swished and banged. Pellew came down the steps, his collar and stewards jacket somewhat messed up.

"They're steaming up in there," he announced.

"Better go back and dog that door shut then," said Jed.

"I already did," replied Eli, his round young face under its blond hair rosy with excitement. "I locked the connecting door to the galley, too. They're shut in."

"Good job," approved Jed. "Hope it doesn't lead to panic, though. I may have to talk to them again. You were saying, Barney . . ."

"The point is," said the engineer, taking up his argument again, "we're like a walnut in its shell with the difference that they want the shell, not the meat inside it. They way to take a ship like this is with a boarding party cutting its way through the main lock. Bloody, but the least damaging to the ship itself. They won't want to fire on us; and if they try to put a boarding party aboard between here and Arcturus Base, we'll certainly message ahead and the warships'll have no reason for not opening fire on them. *But* if we simply message ahead and stay put, they'll just have to ride along and hope to use us for hostages when we reach the Base area."

"Sensible," said Jed, "provided they really don't mean to let us get away afterward."

"You know they don't, Jed," protested the engineer. "When did they ever let crew or passengers get away? It's not in their psychology— *I* think."

"They like to tidy up afterwards, that's true," said Jed. He thought for a minute. "All right; we'll call. *Then* what do you suggest?"

There was a moment's uncomfortable silence.

"At least we know *he* won't get away then," said old Leni. "The warships'll follow and take care of him."

Jed smiled a little sadly. "I thought as much." He glanced at Tommy. "Well, make a message off. How long should it take to reach the Base?"

"About ten minutes."

"All right," Jed nodded. "Let me know if you

rouse any reaction from our friend behind us." He
looked at the stewards. "You two keep an eye on the
passengers; Barney, come along with me."

They had been shipmates and friends for a long
time. Barney turned and followed without a word as
the captain took the three steps of the down ladder
to the bulkhead door leading under the passenger
quarters; and led the way through.

They stepped into a narrow passageway that was
all metal, except for the rubbery plastic matting underfoot: the door sucked to behind them. Like all
sections of the ship sealed by the heavy doors, it was
soundproof to all other sections. But the light overhead was merely an occasional glimmer from spaced
tubes; and the passageway itself was so narrow that
there was barely room for two men to stand breast-to-
breast and talk.

Jed, therefore, did not talk here. Instead he led
the way back down the ship, ducking at the middle
where the lifeboat blisters—one on each side of the
ship—bulged down into the passage; and up three
more steps at the far end. Here another door waited
to be passed; when they had gone through it, they
found themselves in the central tube that ran connected the payload section of the ship with the drive
section where the atomics were located.

This passage was wider, being the full size of the
tube, and its circular shape apparent to the eye. Two
and a half meters in diameter was the tube, but its
walls were relatively thin and uninsulated—except
for a radiation protective coating between the two
skins of metal that made the tube. In spite of the ships
heating system, the "cold of space" seemed to seep
through. Jed led the way to the midpoint of the tube
where two small vision screens were set, one on
each side of the tube. These relayed the picture—
seen by antennae arms that extended like two huge

knitting needles jutting out on each side of the ship beyond the screens—and looked back to scan each its own side of the space-going vessel. The trouble-shooting screens. Jed gestured at them, to the identical dumbbell shape imaged on each.

"What do you see, Barney?"

The engineer looked at the screens and back at his captain, puzzled. "The ship," he said at last. "Why, what do you see?"

"A fifty-fifty chance."

At that moment, there was a sudden shock that shook the vessel from end to end and sent the two men staggering. Recovering first, the captain took two quick steps back to the screen. On the rear left could now be seen, beyond the bulge of the drive section, the distant forward half of the Pleiadan ship. On the drive section itself, was a black hole with outcurling ragged metal edges—was the mark of a hit by an explosive shell in space.

"So they don't want to fire on us," said Jed, turning to Barney grimly.

The engineer looked shaken. "The message to Arcturus Base must have made him mad." Suddenly he turned and began plunging back down the tunnel. "I've got to find out what damage they did!" he shouted back.

Jed nodded; turning on his heel, he hurried back toward the control room. He came up the ladder to find the young first mate and Leni facing each other. Tommy was white, but the eyes of the wizened little steward glowed black with rage.

"Ram them!" shouted the small man, spinning on Jed as he came up the three steps of the ladder in one jump.

"Leni," said Jed, coldly. "You're under arrest; get to your quarters and stay there."

The steward hesitated, his old face twisted and

violent. Suddenly, the expression of his features twisted and broke, leaving him looking simply ancient and pathetic. He choked on a sob and turned away, stumbling blindly toward the door on the level of the cabin floor, between the two stairways, that led to the captains and crew quarters under the upper level of the passenger lounge.

"Go with him," Jed instructed Eli Pellew, who was still at his station by the intercom screen, watching proceedings among the passengers. "Wait a second," he added, as the young second steward turned to go. "How've they been in there?"

"Noisy, but quiet now," answered the boy. "That shot we took seems to have quieted them. They're praying, some of them."

Jed nodded, and Eli dived through the door leading back to crew's quarters. The captain turned back to Tommy. "Have you touched anything since we were fired on?"

"No sir," said Tommy. "I had my hands full, keeping Leni off the controls. But we're tumbling end-over-end."

"Good. We won't touch anything. Make him wonder whether he did as any vital damage, or not. Any answer from Arcturus?"

"Just before you came back," answered the mate. "They acknowledged and said they were standing by to receive or follow us."

"Also good, I've got a gamble in mind; but it's among the three of us—you, Barney, and me; and he's back looking at the drive section. There's nothing more to be done here. I don't want to answer the Pellie if he calls us anyway; keep him guessing. Come on with me back and we'll talk with Barney."

A curious look in the younger man's eyes warned Jed he was talking with an unusual excitement. Mentally reproving himself, he turned on his heel and led the way back down below the passenger section and through the full length of the tube back to the drive section. They stepped through a further door into one vast chamber honeycombed with equipment and to be traversed only by a network of ladders and catwalks.

"Barney!" Jed yelled.

"Yo!" came a distant answer and shortly the engineer came into view whisking his heavy old bulk up and down ladders with the agility of long practise. He came forward at a level about two meters over their head and dropped hand over hand down a ladder to stand at last in front of them.

"How was it?" asked the captain.

"Not bad, thank the Lord," said Barney, wiping his face. There was a black smudge of resealing material on his forehead. "It was back of the fuel bins and the whole section sealed off automatically."

"Barney . . ." said Jed.

"Yes?" The engineer had found a cleaner-cloth in his pocket and was scrubbing at the black gunk below his receded hairline.

"You remember we were looking at the ship and I said I thought I saw a fifty-fifty chance?"

"That's right." The hand holding the cloth dropped suddenly to Barney's side and he looked at his captain with alert interest.

"Well, tell me something," said Jed. "We haven't used power since before the Pellie showed up. That means the tubes have all been closed, haven't they?"

"Of course," said the engineer, indignantly. "They're always closed immediately after firing; you know that."

"And with the tubes closed, our back end looks just like our front, doesn't it?"

"Why, sure," said Barney, "but I still don't see what good that does us."

"When we're all in one piece, it doesn't," replied

Jed. "But suppose, just as we hit the Arcturus Base area, we break in the middle of our connecting tube and our two halves go in opposite directions? What's the Pellie to do then? He can run down one section only at the cost of getting separated from the other; and by that time the warships'll be up. So if we cut the ship in half, it gives us an even chance of being the section he doesn't chase."

His words left the two other men in a stunned silence for several seconds. Tommy was the first to recover. His eyes lit up at the possibility and he wheeled on the engineer. "That's terrific—isn't it Barney? We can fool him! Isn't that a fine idea?"

To the younger man's surprise, the engineer did not take fire from his enthusiasm. In fact, he pursed his heavy lips, doubtfully. "I don't know," he said slowly. "We'd have to think it over."

Jed was watching his old friend and shipmate with hard, bright eyes. "All right, cut it out, Barney."

The engineer raised innocent, wondering eyes to the captain. "Cut it out?" he echoed. "I don't know what you mean, Jed."

"You know damn well what I mean." said Jed. "I already had to put Leni under arrest in his quarters, with Eli as guard over him, because of the same attitude you're taking. She's a fine old ship, Barney, and I love her, too—more than anything else I can think of. But get this straight. The passenger's lives come first and ours too. Then the *Teakettle. Is that clear?*"

The last three words came out like the crack of a whip. Barney dropped his head, and Tommy was astonished to see the glint of tears in the old man's eyes. "I don't know what I'll do without her," he mumbled.

"Nor I," answered Jed, more gently now. "But what must be, must, Barney. We can't become self-

ish because our remaining years are short. Now . . .
how are we going to cut the tube?"

"Explosive?" suggested Tommy. "Have we got any?"

"Not a gram," said Jed, grimly.

Barney spoke up. "There's cutting torches back in
the drive section."

Jed bit his lower lip. "I don't like that notion too
well," he said, slowly. "It means we'd have to work
in suits, because we'd loose air from the tube with
the first hole made. And then, they'd see us busy at
it and have time to think of some counter-move."

"The metal's thin," said Tommy. "If we pried off
the inside plates with a crowbar, and chiseled out
the insulation, a metal saw should do the work."

"Fine," said Barney. "Only we don't have a metal
saw."

"I thought every drive section had metal saws
among its tools," Tommy said.

"Do you think I carry a machine shop? Torches
were all I ever needed."

The old man was still upset. Jed, who had been
thinking, spoke up. "We've got signal flares, haven't
we, Tom?"

"Yes sir," answered Tommy. The emergency equipment was his responsibility.

"Isn't the powder in them hot enough to melt
through the outer skin of the tube here?"

"By God, yes," said Tommy. "It's got a thermite
base; this stuff'd boil like water."

"Then that's it," said Jed. "Go bring us as much as
you've got." Tommy started off at a run down the
tube.

Jed turned to the engineer, who was leaning, his
face sagging, against the curve of the wall. "Don't
take it so hard, you old idiot!" he said, in a fierce,
soft voice. "Chances are the Pellie'll give up when he

sees us split. Then it's just a matter of running the two halves down and sticking them together again."

Barney pushed himself away from the wall and shook his head. "We'll kill her; you know we will. We'll kill her." And he turned and moved heavily off in the direction of the drive section, passing through the door and leaving Jed alone.

The young mate seemed to take a long time returning and Jed had the chance to feel his age and the loneliness that was to come; before the payload-section door opened and Tommy backed through, pushing his way with his shoulders, his arms loaded down with the long metal tubes of the flares.

"Stack them here," said Jed, taking charge. "Now, how are we going to stick the powder to the wall?"

". . . Thought of everything," grunted Tommy. He settled his armload on the floor, and, reaching around behind him, unhooked two short crowbars from his belt. His bulging pockets produced several bottles of the pitch-like emergency sealer. "We pry off the inner skin, gouge out insulation to the outer skin, and seal the powder in with gunk."

"Good boy," approved Jed.

They set to work, captain and mate together. In the narrow space of the tube, back-to-back, they grunted and pried until a half-meter width of the inner metal pannelling had been removed. Then the sharp points of the crowbars came into action; they chipped and pounded at the heavy, brittle insulation until metal showed through beyond. A fine, searing dust rose form the fragmented insulation and hung in the passage. They coughed and choked but worked on.

"All done," said Tommy, finally. "Except for the control cables." He was referring to the thick metal conduits running between the control room and the drive section.

"Leave them—they'll burn, too," wheezed Jed. "Now help me with the powder."

Step by step they drew their circle around the tube; white, innocent-looking powder, held in by sticky blackness. Finally, they were done.

"Fuse?" said Jed.

"Here." Tommy pulled a coil of shining, slim wire from within his tunic. It was regulation electrical contact cable, spliced and fitted with an explosive cap. Jed took the end and wedged it into the gunk, pushing it through to the powder beneath. Then they moved back, paying it out as they went, along the tube, through the door, up the under passage and into the control room.

The two men collapsed on to seats before the equipment boards.

"Whew!" said Tommy, after a few moments. "That was a job!"

Jed nodded. He was feeling his age, and there was a sharp pain in his chest. After he had rested a few more minutes, he got up and began checking their position.

They were close to Arcturus Base Area, that imaginary globe of space which enclosed the waiting warfleet, whose duty is to guard the Arcturian planets. Jed set his viewer up to maximum range and probed the empty distances ahead. There was nothing on it, but the armed ships which might rescue them could not be too far away.

"I'll give them another fifteen minutes; then we'll split," said Jed, glancing at the younger man. Suddenly he was aware of the emptiness of the control room. "By heaven, Barney's still back in the drive section. Get him up front here!"

Tommy dived for the down stairs; and vanished through the door. Jed grimaced and glanced at the clock. He reached out to call ahead to the armed vessels, then remembered the shot that had been fired at them on the previous occasion and took his hand away. He checked the scanner.

There were a couple of pips tiny in the distance, too far to show on the screen.

The waiting seemed interminable. Finally Tommy reappeared, almost literally herding the old engineer before him.

"We aren't going to waste any more time," said Jed. "Take seats and strap yourself in." He leaned over and keyed in the intercom to the passenger lounge.

"Attention," he said. The view on the screen faded from the stars to the lounge's interior. Weary, hopeless and frightened people looked up at him without much reaction. "Will you please take seats and fasten yourself in them. We are about to attempt evasive action."

"What for?" said a tall man, standing greyfaced toward the back of the room. "You said before it was no use."

"We're almost up to the Arcturus Base Fleet," answered Jed. "It may do some good now. Will you strap yourself in, please?"

"Why should we strap ourselves in?" cried a little man who had been sitting with his head in his hands. He now raised it, his deep eyes wild. "Why did you lock the doors? What . . ."

"*Strap yourselves in! That's an order!*" thundered Jed suddenly, tried beyond all patience.

Stunned by the volume of the intercom amplifier, the passengers fell into their seats without further protest, stumbling over each other in their haste. Safety belts snapped: and when Jed could tell by looking at the screen that all were secured, he switched back to an outside view.

*   *   *

Ahead, the warships of the Base were being rapidly overhauled in spite of the fact that they were building up velocity in the same direction as the *Teakettle* and the Pleiadan at maximum bearable acceleration. The alien ship itself was hanging in close and directly behind the *Teakettle*, so that they too would show as long as possible as a single pip on the warship's screens. Now was the time to do whatever could be done.

Jed turned and threw a quick glance about the control room. Leni and young Eli Pellew had come out of the crew quarters and were strapped in side by side, in the observer seats. Tommy must have warned them. The young mate himself was strapped into the acceleration chair before the auxiliary screen; and on Jed's other side to his right, Barney sat belted to the chair before the direct drive controls. This was his proper post; and although there was nothing now for him to do there, Jed thought he understood the impulse that had pushed the old man to his accustomed place. Jed reached for the contact switch and lifted it. The cable trailed away from him on the floor, silver to the bottom of the door and disappeared beneath it.

Jed glanced once more about the control room. Tommy's face, to his left, was tense on the screen, watching the growing shapes of the warship, pale— but not so pale as the face of Eli Pellew behind him, who seemed drugged with shock. Beside Eli's young face, Leni's eyes glared up at him, black and bitter. On his right, Barney sat slumped before his board, his fingers resting laxily upon the controls, his face unreadable.

He seemed chained and bound to inertness by the depression within him. But as Jed turned his way and closed his fingers about the switch, from the corner of his eyes, he seemed to see the fingers of the old man flicker, once.

And almost in the same heartbeat, closed his own fingers, closing the switch.

The ship bucked once like an insane thing; as the superheated air in the tube exploded outward through the vaporized metal of the outer skin. The stars spun like a pinwheel on the screen; and into view swam the full length of the Pleiadan and the tumbling other half of the *Teakettle*. Fingers working on the direction finders, flickering but working on the self-contained emergency power stored in the controlroom itself, Jed kept the two images on the screen together.

As the warships swelled on the screen, the nose of the Pellie ship swung first in this direction, then in that, sniffing after the two fragments of what had been the *Teakettle*, like a hunting terrier after two scuttling mice. The warships were growing fast, and for the alien, death was certain. It fired once at the drive section; then, ominously, its nose swung toward the payload half. Nose-on on the screen it stood before them.

"Sweetheart . . ." whispered Barney. And at that moment, from the tattered half-tube attached to the fleeting drive section shot a sudden, long spurt of yellow flame, hurtling it further and faster . . .

. . . And the alien swung to follow it. For the first time, from its tubes came a flare of power—not a change of direction, but an additional thrust forward that, though diverging brought it up level and close to the burning tube and ball.

And its guns began to pound the fleeing drive section.

Behind Jed, Leni sobbed once. And Jed, looking over at Barney, saw the heavy old man press back in his seat, eyes wide, but with an imcomprehensible wildness on his face.

The warships were closing up now. Ranging shells

from their heavy guns began to search out the alien. But before they could strike home; Barney shouted like a berserker, his old voice cracking. The drive section opened up like a flower into a brilliant pure white blossom of flame whose lightest touch was extinction. And the alien ship flared like a burnt moth.

In the silence of the control room they sat and watched it burn. And when the fire had died; and the warships were far behind, but coming up fast now, Jed turned to the engineer. "Thanks, Barney," he said.

"Thank her," said Barney emptily. "All I did was to pull the damping rods."

They looked at each other across the little distance and the useless controls between; two old men understanding each other.

Jed turned away and flicked on the intercom. "Attention all passengers," he said. "You may unstrap now."

Call Him Lord

"He called and commanded me
—Therefore, I knew him;
But later on, failed me; and
—Therefore, I slew him!"

"Son of the Shield Bearer"

The sun could not fail in rising over the Kentucky hills, nor could Kyle Arnam in waking. There would be eleven hours and forty minutes of daylight. Kyle rose, dressed, and went out to saddle the gray gelding and the white stallion. He rode the stallion until the first fury was out of the arched and snowy neck; and then led both horses around to tether them outside the kitchen door. Then he went in to breakfast.

The message that had come a week before was beside his plate of bacon and eggs. Teena, his wife, was standing at the breadboard with her back to him. He sat down and began eating, rereading the letter as he ate.

". . . The Prince will be traveling incognito under one of his family titles, as Count Sirii North; and should not be addressed as 'Majesty'. *You will call him 'Lord'* . . ."

"Why does it have to be you?" Teena asked.

He looked up and saw how she stood with her back to him.

"Teena—" he said, sadly.

"Why?"

"My ancestors were bodyguards to his—back in the wars of conquest against the aliens. I've told you that," he said. "My forefathers saved the lives of his, many times when there was no warning—a Rak space-ship would suddenly appear out of nowhere to lock on, even to a flagship. And even an Emperor found himself fighting for his life, hand to hand."

"The aliens are all dead now, and the Emperor's got a hundred other worlds! Why can't his son take his Grand Tour on them? Why does he have to come here to Earth—and you?"

"There's only one Earth."

"And only one you, I suppose?"

He sighed internally and gave up. He had been raised by his father and his uncle after his mother died, and in an argument with Teena he always felt helpless. He got up from the table and went to her, putting his hands on her and gently trying to turn her about. But she resisted.

He sighed inside himself again and turned away to the weapons cabinet. He took out a loaded slug pistol, fitted it into the stubby holster it matched, and clipped the holster to his belt at the left of the buckle, where the hang of his leather jacket would hide it. Then he selected a dark-handled knife with a six-inch blade and bent over to slip it into the sheath inside his boot top. He dropped the cuff of his trouser leg back over the boot top and stood up.

"He's got no right to be here," said Teena fiercely

to the breadboard. "Tourists are supposed to be kept
to the museum areas and the tourist lodges."

"He's not a tourist. You know that," answered
Kyle, patiently. "He's the Emperor's oldest son and
his great-grandmother was from Earth. His wife will
be, too. Every fourth generation the Imperial line
has to marry back into Earth stock. That's the law—
still." He put on his leather jacket, sealing it closed
only at the bottom to hide the slug-gun holster, half
turned to the door—then paused.

"Teena?" he asked.

She did not answer.

"Teena!" he repeated. He stepped to her, put his
hands on her shoulders and tried to turn her to face
him. Again, she resisted, but this time he was having
none of it.

He was not a big man, being of middle height,
round-faced, with sloping and unremarkable-looking,
if thick, shoulders. But his strength was not ordinary. He could bring the white stallion to its knees
with one fist wound in its mane—and no other man
had ever been able to do that. He turned her easily
to look at him.

"Now, listen to me—" he began. But, before he
could finish, all the stiffness went out of her and she
clung to him, trembling.

"He'll get you into trouble—I know he will!" she
choked, muffledly into his chest. "Kyle, don't go!
There's no law making you go!"

He stroked the soft hair of her head, his throat stiff
and dry. There was nothing he could say to her.
What she was asking was impossible. Ever since the
sun had first risen on men and women together,
wives had clung to their husbands at times like this,
begging for what could not be. And always the men
had held them, as Kyle was holding her now—as if
understanding could somehow be pressed from one

body into the other—and saying nothing, because
there was nothing that could be said.

So, Kyle held her for a few moments longer, and
then reached behind him to unlock her intertwined
fingers at his back, and loosen her arms around him.
Then, he went. Looking back through the kitchen
window as he rode off on the stallion, leading the
gray horse, he saw her standing just where he had
left her. Not even crying, but standing with her arms
hanging down, her head down, not moving.

He rode away through the forest of the Kentucky
hillside. It took him more than two hours to reach
the lodge. As he rode down the valleyside toward it,
he saw a tall, bearded man, wearing the robes they
wore on some of the Younger Worlds, standing at
the gateway to the interior courtyard of the rustic,
wooded lodge.

When he got close, he saw that the beard was
graying and the man was biting his lips. Above a
straight, thin nose, the eyes were bloodshot and
circled beneath as if from worry or lack of sleep.

"He's in the courtyard," said the gray-bearded
man as Kyle rode up. "I'm Montlaven, his tutor.
He's ready to go." The darkened eyes looked almost
pleadingly up at Kyle.

"Stand clear of the stallion's head," said Kyle.
"And take me in to him."

"Not that horse, for him—" said Montlaven, looking distrustfully at the stallion, as he backed away.

"No," said Kyle. "He'll ride the gelding."

"He'll want the white."

"He can't ride the white," said Kyle. "Even if I let
him, he couldn't ride this stallion. I'm the only one
who can ride him. Take me in."

The tutor turned and led the way into the grassy
courtyard, surrounding a swimming pool and looked
down upon, on three sides, by the windows of the

lodge. In a lounging chair by the pool sat a tall young
man in his late teens, with a mane of blond hair, a
pair of stuffed saddlebags on the grass beside him.
He stood up as Kyle and the tutor came toward him.

"Majesty," said the tutor, as they stopped, "this is
Kyle Arnam, your bodyguard for the three days here."

"Good morning, Bodyguard . . . Kyle, I mean."
The Prince smiled mischievously. "Light, then. And
I'll mount."

"You ride the gelding, Lord," said Kyle.

The Prince stared at him, tilted back his handsome
head, and laughed.

"I can ride, man!" he said. "I ride well."

"Not this horse, Lord," said Kyle, dispassionately.
"No one rides this horse, but me."

The eyes flashed wide, the laugh faded—then
returned.

"What can I do?" The wide shoulders shrugged. "I
give in—always I give in. Well, almost always." He
grinned up at Kyle, his lips thinned, but frank. "All
right."

He turned to the gelding—and with a sudden leap
was in the saddle. The gelding snorted and plunged
at the shock; then steadied as the young man's long
fingers tightened expertly on the reins and the fingers of the other hand patted a gray neck. The Prince
raised his eyebrows, looking over at Kyle, but Kyle
sat stolidly.

"I take it you're armed, good Kyle?" the Prince
said slyly. "You'll protect me against the natives if
they run wild?"

"Your life is in my hands, Lord," said Kyle. He
unsealed the leather jacket at the bottom and let it
fall open to show the slug pistol in its holster for a
moment. Then he resealed the jacket again at the
bottom.

"Will—" The tutor put his hand on the young
man's knee. "Don't be reckless, boy. This is Earth

and the people here don't have rank and custom like
we do. Think before you—"

"Oh, cut it out, Monty!" snapped the Prince. "I'll
be just as incognito, just as humble, as archaic and
independent as the rest of them. You think I've no
memory! Anyway, it's only for three days or so until
my Imperial father joins me. Now, let me go!"

He jerked away, turned to lean forward in the
saddle, and abruptly put the gelding into a bolt for
the gate. He disappeared through it, and Kyle drew
hard on the stallion's reins as the big white horse
danced and tried to follow.

"Give me his saddlebags," said Kyle.

The tutor bent and passed them up. Kyle made
them fast on top of his own, across the stallion's
withers. Looking down, he saw there were tears in
the bearded man's eyes.

"He's a fine boy. You'll see. You'll know he is!"
Montlaven's face, upturned, was mutely pleading.

"I know he comes from a fine family," said Kyle,
slowly. "I'll do my best for him." And he rode off out
of the gateway after the gelding.

When he came out of the gate, the Prince was
nowhere in sight. But it was simple enough for Kyle
to follow, by dinted brown earth and crushed grass,
the marks of the gelding's path. This brought him at
last through some pines to a grassy open slope where
the Prince sat looking skyward through a singlelens
box.

When Kyle came up, the Prince lowered the instrument and, without a word, passed it over. Kyle
put it to his eye and looked skyward. There was the
whir of the tracking unit and one of Earth's three
orbiting power stations swam into the field of vision
of the lens.

"Give it back," said the Prince.

"I couldn't get a look at it earlier," went on the
young man as Kyle handed the lens to him. "And I

wanted to. It's a rather expensive present, you know—it and the other two like it—from our Imperial treasury. Just to keep your planet from drifting into another ice age. And what do we get for it?"

"Earth, Lord," answered Kyle. "As it was before men went out to the stars."

"Oh, the museum areas could be maintained with one station and a half-million caretakers," said the Prince. "It's the other two stations and you billion or so free-loaders I'm talking about. I'll have to look into it when I'm Emperor. Shall we ride?"

"If you wish, Lord." Kyle picked up the reins of the stallion and the two horses with their riders moved off across the slope.

". . . And one more thing," said the Prince, as they entered the farther belt of pine trees. "I don't want you to be misled—I'm really very fond of old Monty, back there. It's just that I wasn't really planning to come here at all—*Look at me, Bodyguard!*"

Kyle turned to see the blue eyes that ran in the Imperial family blazing at him. Then, unexpectedly, they softened. The Prince laughed.

"You don't scare easily, do you, Bodyguard . . . Kyle, I mean?" he said. "I think I like you after all. But look at me when I talk."

"Yes, Lord."

"That's my good Kyle. Now, I was explaining to you that I'd never actually planned to come here on my Grand Tour at all. I didn't see any point in visiting this dusty old museum world of yours with people still trying to live like they lived in the Dark Ages. But—my Imperial father talked me into it."

"Your father, Lord?" asked Kyle.

"Yes, he bribed me, you might say," said the Prince thoughtfully. "He was supposed to meet me here for these three days. Now, he's messaged there's been a slight delay—but that doesn't matter. The point is, he belongs to the school of old men who still

think your Earth is something precious and vital.
Now, I happen to like and admire my father, Kyle.
You approve of that?"

"Yes, Lord."

"I thought you would. Yes, he's the one man in
the human race I look up to. And to please him, I'm
making this Earth trip. And to please him—only to
please *him*, Kyle—I'm going to be an easy Prince for
you to conduct around to your natural wonders and
watering spots and whatever. Now, you understand
me—and how this trip is going to go. Don't you?"
He stared at Kyle.

"I understand," said Kyle.

"That's fine," said the Prince, smiling once more.
"So now you can start telling me all about these trees
and birds and animals so that I can memorize their
names and please my father when he shows up.
What are those little birds I've been seeing under
the trees—brown on top and whitish underneath?
Like that one—there!"

"That's a Veery, Lord," said Kyle. "A bird of the
deep woods and silent places. Listen—" He reached
out a hand to the gelding's bridle and brought both
horses to a halt. In the sudden silence, off to their
right they could hear a silver bird-voice, rising and
falling, in a descending series of crescendos and di-
minuendos, that softened at last into silence. For a
moment after the song was ended the Prince sat
staring at Kyle, then seemed to shake himself back to
life.

"Interesting," he said. He lifted the reins Kyle had
let go and the horses moved forward again. "Tell me
more."

For more than three hours, as the sun rose toward
noon, they rode through the wooded hills, with Kyle
identifying bird and animal, insect, tree and rock.
And for three hours the Prince listened—his atten-

tion flashing and momentary, but intense. But when the sun was overhead that intensity flagged.

"That's enough," he said. "Aren't we going to stop for lunch? Kyle, aren't there any towns around here?"

"Yes, Lord," said Kyle. "We've passed several."

"Several?" The Prince stared at him. "Why haven't we come into one before now? Where are you taking me?"

"Nowhere, Lord," said Kyle. "You lead the way. I only follow."

"I?" said the Prince. For the first time he seemed to become aware that he had been keeping the gelding's head always in advance of the stallion. "Of course. But now it's time to eat."

"Yes, Lord," said Kyle. "This way."

He turned the stallion's head down the slope of the hill they were crossing and the Prince turned the gelding after him.

"And now listen," said the Prince, as he caught up. "Tell me I've got it all right." And to Kyle's astonishment, he began to repeat, almost word for word, everything that Kyle had said. "Is it all there? Everything you told me?"

"Perfectly, Lord," said Kyle. The Prince looked slyly at him.

"Could you do that, Kyle?"

"Yes," said Kyle. "But these are things I've known all my life."

"You see?" The Prince smiled. "That's the difference between us, good Kyle. You spend your life learning something—I spend a few hours and I know as much about it as you do."

"Not as much, Lord," said Kyle, slowly.

The Prince blinked at him, then jerked his hand dismissingly, and half-angrily, as if he were throwing something aside.

"What little else there is probably doesn't count," he said.

They rode down the slope and through a winding valley and came out at a small village. As they rode clear of the surrounding trees a sound of music came to their ears.

"What's that?" The Prince stood up in his stirrups. "Why, there's dancing going on, over there."

"A beer garden, Lord. And it's Saturday—a holiday here."

"Good. We'll go there to eat."

They rode around to the beer garden and found tables back away from the dance floor. A pretty, young waitress came and they ordered, the Prince smiling sunnily at her until she smiled back—then hurried off as if in mild confusion. The Prince ate hungrily when the food came and drank a stein and a half of brown beer, while Kyle ate more lightly and drank coffee.

"That's better," said the Prince, sitting back at last. "I had an appetite . . . Look there, Kyle! Look, there are five, six . . . seven drifter platforms parked over there. Then you don't all ride horses?"

"No," said Kyle. "It's as each man wishes."

"But if you have drifter platforms, why not other civilized things?"

"Some things fit, some don't, Lord," answered Kyle. The Prince laughed.

"You mean you try to make civilization fit this old-fashioned life of yours, here?" he said. "Isn't that the wrong way around—" He broke off. "What's that they're playing now? I like that. I'll bet I could do that dance." He stood up. "In fact, I think I will."

He paused, looking down at Kyle.

"Aren't you going to warn me against it?" he asked.

"No, Lord," said Kyle. "What you do is your own affair."

The young man turned away abruptly. The waitress who had served them was passing, only a few tables away. The Prince went after her and caught up with her by the dance floor railing. Kyle could see the girl protesting—but the Prince hung over her, looking down from his tall height, smiling. Shortly, she had taken off her apron and was out on the dance floor with him, showing him the steps of the dance. It was a polka.

The Prince learned with fantastic quickness. Soon, he was swinging the waitress around with the rest of the dancers, his foot stamping on the turns, his white teeth gleaming. Finally the number ended and the members of the band put down their instruments and began to leave the stand.

The Prince, with the girl trying to hold him back, walked over to the band leader. Kyle got up quickly from his table and started toward the floor.

The band leader was shaking his head. He turned abruptly and slowly walked away. The Prince started after him, but the girl took hold of his arm, saying something urgent to him.

He brushed her aside and she stumbled a little. A busboy among the tables on the far side of the dance floor, not much older than the Prince and nearly as tall, put down his tray and vaulted the railing onto the polished hardwood. He came up behind the Prince and took hold of his arm, swinging him around.

". . . Can't do that here," Kyle heard him say, as Kyle came up. The Prince struck out like a panther— like a trained boxer—with three quick lefts in succession into the face of the busboy, the Prince's shoulder bobbing, the weight of his body in behind each blow.

The busboy went down. Kyle, reaching the Prince, herded him away through a side gap in the railing. The young man's face was white with rage. People were swarming onto the dance floor.

"Who was that? What's his name?" demanded the

Prince, between his teeth. "He put his hand on me!
Did you see that? *He put his hand on me!*"

"You knocked him out," said Kyle. "What more do
you want?"

"He manhandled me—*me!*" snapped the Prince.
"I want to find out who he is!" He caught hold of the
bar to which the horses were tied, refusing to be
pushed farther. "He'll learn to lay hands on a future
Emperor!"

"No one will tell you his name," said Kyle. And
the cold note in his voice finally seemed to reach
through to the Prince and sober him. He stared at
Kyle.

"Including you?" he demanded at last.

"Including me, Lord," said Kyle.

The Prince stared a moment longer, then swung
away. He turned, jerked loose the reins of the gelding and swung into the saddle. He rode off. Kyle
mounted and followed.

They rode in silence into the forest. After a while,
the Prince spoke without turning his head.

"And you call yourself a bodyguard," he said, finally.

"Your life is in my hands, Lord," said Kyle. The
Prince turned a grim face to look at him.

"Only my life?" said the Prince. "As long as they
don't kill me, they can do what they want? Is that
what you mean?"

Kyle met his gaze steadily.

"Pretty much so, Lord," he said.

The Prince spoke with an ugly note in his voice.

"I don't think I like you, after all, Kyle," he said.
"I don't think I like you at all."

"I'm not here with you to be liked, Lord," said
Kyle.

"Perhaps not," said the Prince, thickly. "But I
know *your* name!"

They rode on in continued silence for perhaps
another half hour. But then gradually the angry hunch

went out of the young man's shoulders and the tight-
ness out of his jaw. After a while he began to sing to
himself, a song in a language Kyle did not know; and
as he sang, his cheerfulness seemed to return. Shortly,
he spoke to Kyle, as if there had never been anything but pleasant moments between them.

Mammoth Cave was close and the Prince asked to
visit it. They went there and spent some time going
through the cave. After that they rode their horses
up along the left bank of the Green River. The
Prince seemed to have forgotten all about the incident at the beer garden and be out to charm everyone they met. As the sun was at last westering toward
the dinner hour, they came finally to a small hamlet
back from the river, with a roadside inn mirrored in
an artificial lake beside it, and guarded by oak and
pine trees behind.

"This looks good," said the Prince. "We'll stay
overnight here, Kyle."

"If you wish, Lord," said Kyle.

They halted, and Kyle took the horses around to
the stable, then entered the inn to find the Prince
already in the small bar off the dining room, drinking
beer and charming the waitress. This waitress was
younger than the one at the beer garden had been; a
little girl with soft, loose hair and round brown eyes
that showed their delight in the attention of the tall,
good-looking, young man.

"Yes," said the Prince to Kyle, looking out of
corners of the Imperial blue eyes at him, after the
waitress had gone to get Kyle his coffee. "This is the
very place."

"The very place?" said Kyle.

"For me to get to know the people better—what
did you think, good Kyle?" said the Prince and laughed
at him. "I'll observe the people here and you can
explain them—won't that be good?"

Kyle gazed at him, thoughtfully.

"I'll tell you whatever I can, Lord," he said.

They drank—the Prince his beer, and Kyle his coffee—and went in a little later to the dining room for dinner. The Prince, as he had promised at the bar, was full of questions about what he saw—and what he did not see.

". . . But why go on living in the past, all of you here?" he asked Kyle. "A museum world is one thing. But a museum people—" he broke off to smile and speak to the little, soft-haired waitress, who had somehow been diverted from the bar to wait upon their dining-room table.

"Not a museum people, Lord," said Kyle. "A living people. The only way to keep a race and a culture preserved is to keep it alive. So we go on in our own way, here on Earth, as a living example for the Younger Worlds to check themselves against."

"Fascinating . . ." murmured the Prince; but his eyes had wandered off to follow the waitress, who was glowing and looking back at him from across the now-busy dining room.

"Not fascinating. Necessary, Lord," said Kyle. But he did not believe the younger man had heard him.

After dinner, they moved back to the bar. And the Prince, after questioning Kyle a little longer, moved up to continue his researches among the other people standing at the bar. Kyle watched for a little while. Then, feeling it was safe to do so, slipped out to have another look at the horses and to ask the innkeeper to arrange a saddle lunch put up for them the next day.

When he returned, the Prince was not to be seen.

Kyle sat down at a table to wait; but the Prince did not return. A cold, hard knot of uneasiness began to grow below Kyle's breastbone. A sudden pang of alarm sent him swiftly back out to check the horses. But they were cropping peacefully in their stalls.

The stallion whickered, low-voiced, as Kyle looked in on him, and turned his white head to look back at Kyle.

"Easy, boy," said Kyle and returned to the inn to find the innkeeper.

But the innkeeper had no idea where the Prince might have gone.

". . . If the horses aren't taken, he's not far," the innkeeper said. "There's no trouble he can get into around here. Maybe he went for a walk in the woods. I'll leave word for the night staff to keep an eye out for him when he comes in. Where'll you be?"

"In the bar until it closes—then, my room," said Kyle.

He went back to the bar to wait, and took a booth near an open window. Time went by and gradually the number of other customers began to dwindle. Above the ranked bottles, the bar clock showed nearly midnight. Suddenly, through the window, Kyle heard a distant scream of equine fury from the stables.

He got up and went out quickly. In the darkness outside, he ran to the stables and burst in. There in the feeble illumination of the stable's night lighting, he saw the Prince, pale-faced, clumsily saddling the gelding in the center aisle between the stalls. The door to the stallion's stall was open. The Prince looked away as Kyle came in.

Kyle took three swift steps to the open door and looked in. The stallion was still tied, but his ears were back, his eyes rolling, and a saddle lay tumbled and dropped on the stable floor beside him.

"Saddle up," said the Prince thickly from the aisle. "We're leaving." Kyle turned to look at him.

"We've got rooms at the inn here," he said.

"Never mind. We're riding. I need to clear my head." The young man got the gelding's cinch tight, dropped the stirrups and swung heavily up into the saddle. Without waiting for Kyle, he rode out of the stable into the night.

"So, boy . . ." said Kyle soothingly to the stallion. Hastily he untied the big white horse, saddled him, and set out after the Prince. In the darkness, there was no way of ground-tracking the gelding; but he leaned forward and blew into the ear of the stallion. The surprised horse neighed in protest and the whinny of the gelding came back from the darkness of the slope up ahead and over to Kyle's right. He rode in that direction.

He caught the Prince on the crown of the hill. The young man was walking the gelding, reins loose, and singing under his breath—the same song in an unknown language he had sung earlier. But, now as he saw Kyle, he grinned loosely and began to sing with more emphasis. For the first time Kyle caught the overtones of something mocking and lusty about the incomprehensible words. Understanding broke suddenly in him.

"The girl!" he said. "The little waitress. Where is she?"

The grin vanished from the Prince's face, then came slowly back again. The grin laughed at Kyle.

"Why, where d'you think?" The words slurred on the Prince's tongue and Kyle, riding close, smelled the beer heavy on the young man's breath. "In her room, sleeping and happy. Honored . . . though she doesn't know it . . . by an Emperor's son. And expecting to find me there in the morning. But I won't be. Will we, good Kyle?"

"Why did you do it, Lord?" asked Kyle, quietly.

"Why?" The Prince peered at him, a little drunkenly in the moonlight. "Kyle, my father has four sons. I've got three younger brothers. But I'm the one who's going to be Emperor; and Emperors don't answer questions."

Kyle said nothing. The Prince peered at him. They rode on together for several minutes in silence.

"All right, I'll tell you why," said the Prince, more loudly, after a while as if the pause had been only momentary. "It's because you're not *my* bodyguard, Kyle. You see, I've seen through you. I know whose bodyguard you are. You're *theirs!*"

Kyle's jaw tightened. But the darkness hid his reaction.

"All right—" The Prince gestured loosely, disturbing his balance in the saddle. "That's all right. Have it your way. I don't mind. So, we'll play points. There was that lout at the beer garden who put his hands on me. But no one would tell me his name, you said. All right, you managed to bodyguard him. One point for you. But you didn't manage to bodyguard the girl at the inn back there. One point for me. Who's going to win, good Kyle?"

Kyle took a deep breath.

"Lord," he said, "some day it'll be your duty to marry a woman from Earth—"

The Prince interrupted him with a laugh, and this time there was an ugly note in it.

"You flatter yourselves," he said. His voice thickened. "That's the trouble with you—all you Earth people—you flatter yourselves."

They rode on in silence. Kyle said nothing more, but kept the head of the stallion close to the shoulder of the gelding, watching the young man closely. For a little while the Prince seemed to doze. His head sank on his chest and he let the gelding wander. Then, after a while, his head began to come up again, his automatic horseman's fingers tightened on the reins, and he lifted his head to stare around in the moonlight.

"I want a drink," he said. His voice was no longer thick, but it was flat and uncheerful. "Take me where we can get some beer, Kyle."

Kyle took a deep breath.

"Yes, Lord," he said.

He turned the stallion's head to the right and the gelding followed. They went up over a hill and down to the edge of a lake. The dark water sparkled in the moonlight and the farther shore was lost in the night. Lights shone through the trees around the curve of the shore.

"There, Lord," said Kyle. "It's a fishing resort, with a bar."

They rode around the shore to it. It was a low, casual building, angled to face the shore; a dock ran out from it, to which fishing boats were tethered, bobbing slightly on the black water. Light gleamed through the windows as they hitched their horses and went to the door.

The barroom they stepped into was wide and bare. A long bar faced them with several planked fish on the wall behind it. Below the fish were three bartenders—the one in the center, middle-aged, and wearing an air of authority with his apron. The other two were young and muscular. The customers, mostly men, scattered at the square tables and standing at the bar wore rough working clothes, or equally casual vacationers' garb.

The Prince sat down at a table back from the bar and Kyle sat down with him. When the waitress came they ordered beer and coffee, and the Prince half-emptied his stein the moment it was brought to him. As soon as it was completely empty, he signaled the waitress again.

"Another," he said. This time, he smiled at the waitress when she brought his stein back. But she was a woman in her thirties, pleased but not over-whelmed by his attention. She smiled lightly back and moved off to return to the bar where she had been talking to two men her own age, one fairly tall, the other shorter, bullet-headed and fleshy.

The Prince drank. As he put his stein down, he seemed to become aware of Kyle, and turned to look at him.

"I suppose," said the Prince, "you think I'm drunk?"

"Not yet," said Kyle.

"No," said the Prince, "that's right. Not yet. But perhaps I'm going to be. And if I decide I am, who's going to stop me?"

"No one, Lord."

"That's right," the young man said. "That's right." He drank deliberately from his stein until it was empty, and then signaled the waitress for another. A spot of color was beginning to show over each of his high cheekbones. "When you're on a miserable little world with miserable little people . . . hello, Bright Eyes!" he interrupted himself as the waitress brought his beer. She laughed and went back to her friends. ". . . You have to amuse yourself any way you can," he wound up.

He laughed to himself.

"When I think how my father, and Monty—everybody—used to talk this planet up to me—" he glanced aside at Kyle. "Do you know at one time I was actually scared—well, not scared exactly, nothing scares me . . . say *concerned*—about maybe having to come here, some day?" He laughed again. "Concerned that I wouldn't measure up to you Earth people! Kyle, have you ever been to any of the Younger Worlds?"

"No," said Kyle.

"I thought not. Let me tell you, good Kyle, the worst of the people there are bigger, and better-looking and smarter, and everything than anyone I've seen here. And I, Kyle, I—the Emperor-to-be—am better than any of them. So, guess how all you here look to me?" He stared at Kyle, waiting.

"Well, answer me, good Kyle. Tell me the truth. That's an order."

"It's not up to you to judge, Lord," said Kyle.

"Not—? Not up to me?" The blue eyes blazed. "*I'm* going to be Emperor!"

"It's not up to any one man, Lord," said Kyle. "Emperor or not. An Emperor's needed, as the symbol that can hold a hundred worlds together. But the real need of the race is to survive. It took nearly a million years to evolve a survival-type intelligence here on Earth. And out on the newer worlds people are bound to change. If something gets lost out there, some necessary element lost out of the race, there needs to be a pool of original genetic material here to replace it."

The Prince's lips grew wide in a savage grin.

"Oh, good, Kyle—good!" he said. "Very good. Only, I've heard all that before. Only, I don't believe it. You see—I've seen you people, now. And you don't outclass us, out on the Younger Worlds. *We* outclass *you*. We've gone on and got better, while you stayed still. And you know it."

The young man laughed softly, almost in Kyle's face.

"All you've been afraid of, is that we'd find out. And I have." He laughed again. "I've had a look at you; and now I know. I'm bigger, better and braver than any man in this room—and you know why? Not just because I'm the son of the Emperor, but because it's born in me! Body, brains and everything else! I can do what I want here, and no one on this planet is good enough to stop me. Watch."

He stood up, suddenly.

"Now, I want that waitress to get drunk with me," he said. "And this time I'm telling you in advance. Are you going to try and stop me?"

Kyle looked up at him. Their eyes met.

"No, Lord," he said. "It's not my job to stop you."

The Prince laughed.

"I thought so," he said. He swung away and walked between the tables toward the bar and the waitress, still in conversation with the two men. The Prince came up to the bar on the far side of the waitress and ordered a new stein of beer from the middle-aged bartender. When it was given to him, he took it, turned around, and rested his elbows on the bar, leaning back against it. He spoke to the waitress, interrupting the taller of the two men.

"I've been wanting to talk to you," Kyle heard him say.

The waitress, a little surprised, looked around at him. She smiled, recognizing him—a little flattered by the directness of his approach, a little appreciative of his clean good looks, a little tolerant of his youth.

"You don't mind, do you?" said the Prince, looking past her to the bigger of the two men, the one who had just been talking. The other stared back, and their eyes met without shifting for several seconds. Abruptly, angrily, the man shrugged, and turned about with his back hunched against them.

"You see?" said the Prince, smiling back at the waitress. "He knows I'm the one you ought to be talking to, instead of—"

"All right, sonny. Just a minute."

It was the shorter, bullet-head man, interrupting. The Prince turned to look down at him with a fleeting expression of surprise. But the bullet-headed man was already turning to his taller friend and putting a hand on his arm.

"Come on back, Ben," the shorter man was saying. "The kid's a little drunk, is all." He turned back to the Prince. "You shove off now," he said. "Clara's with us."

The Prince stared at him blankly. The stare was so

fixed that the shorter man had started to turn away, back to his friend and the waitress, when the Prince seemed to wake.

"Just a minute—" he said, in his turn.

He reached out a hand to one of the fleshly shoulders below the bullet head. The man turned back, knocking the hand calmly away. Then, just as calmly, he picked up the Prince's full stein of beer from the bar and threw it in the young man's face.

"Get lost," he said, unexcitedly.

The Prince stood for a second, with the beer dripping from his face. Then, without even stopping to wipe his eyes clear, he threw the beautifully trained left hand he had demonstrated at the beer garden.

But the shorter man, as Kyle had known from the first moment of seeing him, was not like the busboy the Prince had decisioned so neatly. This man was thirty pounds heavier, fifteen years more experienced, and by build and nature a natural bar fighter. He had not stood there waiting to be hit, but had already ducked and gone forward to throw his thick arms around the Prince's body. The young man's punch bounced harmlessly off the round head, and both bodies hit the floor, rolling in among the chair and table legs.

Kyle was already more than halfway to the bar and the three bartenders were already leaping the wooden hurdle that walled them off. The taller friend of the bullet-headed man, hovering over the two bodies, his eyes glittering, had his boot drawn back ready to drive the point of it into the Prince's kidneys. Kyle's forearm took him economically like a bar of iron across the tanned throat.

He stumbled backwards choking. Kyle stood still, hands open and down, glancing at the middle-aged bartender.

"All right," said the bartender. "But don't do anything more." He turned to the two younger bartenders. "All right. Haul him off!"

The pair of younger, aproned men bent down and came up with the bullet-headed man expertly hand-locked between them. The man made one surging effort to break loose, and then stood still.

"Let me at him," he said.

"Not in here," said the older bartender. "Take it outside."

Between the tables, the Prince staggered unsteadily to his feet. His face was streaming blood from a cut on his forehead, but what could be seen of it was white as a drowning man's. His eyes went to Kyle, standing beside him; and he opened his mouth—but what came out sounded like something between a sob and a curse.

"All right," said the middle-aged bartender again. "Outside, both of you. Settle it out there."

The men in the room had packed around the little space by the bar. The Prince looked about and for the first time seemed to see the human wall hemming him in. His gaze wobbled to meet Kyle's.

"Outside . . . ?" he said, chokingly.

"You aren't staying in here," said the older bartender, answering for Kyle. "I saw it. You started the whole thing. Now, settle it any way you want—but you're both going outside. Now! Get moving!"

He pushed at the Prince, but the Prince resisted, clutching at Kyle's leather jacket with one hand.

"Kyle—"

"I'm sorry, Lord," said Kyle. "I can't help. It's your fight."

"Let's get out of here," said the bullet-headed man.

The Prince stared around at them as if they were some strange set of beings he had never known to exist before.

"No. . ." he said.

He let go of Kyle's jacket. Unexpectedly, his hand darted in towards Kyle's belly holster and came out holding the slug pistol.

"Stand back!" he said, his voice high-toned. "Don't try to touch me!"

His voice broke on the last words. There was a strange sound, half grunt, half moan, from the crowd; and it swayed back from him. Manager, bartenders—watchers—all but Kyle and the bullet-headed man drew back.

"You dirty slob . . ." said the bullet-headed man, distinctly. "I knew you didn't have the guts."

"Shut up!" The Prince's voice was high and cracking. "Shut up! Don't any of you try to come after me!"

He began backing away toward the front door of the bar. The room watched in silence, even Kyle standing still. As he backed, the Prince's back straightened. He hefted the gun in his hand. When he reached the door he paused to wipe the blood from his eyes with his left sleeve, and his smeared face looked with a first touch of regained arrogance at them.

"Swine!" he said.

He opened the door and backed out, closing it behind him. Kyle took one step that put him facing the bullet-headed man. Their eyes met and he could see the other recognizing the fighter in him, as he had earlier recognized it in the bullet-headed man.

"Don't come after us," said Kyle.

The bullet-headed man did not answer. But no answer was needed. He stood still.

Kyle turned, ran to the door, stood on one side of it and flicked it open. Nothing happened; and he slipped through, dodging to his right at once, out of line of any shot aimed at the opening door.

But no shot came. For a moment he was blind in the night darkness, then his eyes began to adjust. He went by sight, feel and memory toward the hitching rack. By the time he got there, he was beginning to see.

The Prince was untying the gelding and getting ready to mount.

"Lord," said Kyle.

The Prince let go of the saddle for a moment and turned to look over his shoulder at him.

"Get away from me," said the Prince, thickly.

"Lord," said Kyle, low-voiced and pleading, "you lost your head in there. Anyone might do that. But don't make it worse, now. Give me back the gun, Lord."

"Give you the gun?"

The young man stared at him—and then he laughed.

"Give *you* the gun?" he said again. "So you can let someone beat me up some more? So you can not-guard me with it?"

"Lord," said Kyle, "please. For your own sake—give me back the gun."

"Get out of here," said the Prince, thickly, turning back to mount the gelding. "Clear out before I put a slug in you."

Kyle drew a slow, sad breath. He stepped forward and tapped the Prince on the shoulder.

"Turn around, Lord," he said.

"I warned you—" shouted the Prince, turning.

He came around as Kyle stooped, and the slug pistol flashed in his hand from the light of the bar windows. Kyle, bent over, was lifting the cuff of his trouser leg and closing his fingers on the hilt of the knife in his boot sheath. He moved simply, skillfully, and with a speed nearly double that of the young man, striking up into the chest before him until the hand holding the knife jarred against the cloth covering flesh and bone.

It was a sudden, hard-driven, swiftly merciful blow. The blade struck upwards between the ribs lying open to an underhanded thrust, plunging deep into the heart. The Prince grunted with the impact driving the air from his lungs; and he was dead as Kyle caught his slumping body in leather-jacketed arms.

Kyle lifted the tall body across the saddle of the gelding and tied it there. He hunted on the dark ground for the fallen pistol and returned it to his holster. Then, he mounted the stallion and, leading the gelding with its burden, started the long ride back.

Dawn was graying the sky when at last he topped the hill overlooking the lodge where he had picked up the Prince almost twenty-four hours before. He rode down towards the courtyard gate.

A tall figure, indistinct in the pre-dawn light, was waiting inside the courtyard as Kyle came through the gate; and it came running to meet him as he rode toward it. It was the tutor, Montlaven, and he was weeping as he ran to the gelding and began to fumble at the cords that tied the body in place.

"I'm sorry . . ." Kyle heard himself saying; and was dully shocked by the deadness and remoteness of his voice. "There was no choice. You can read it all in my report tomorrow morning—"

He broke off. Another, even taller figure had appeared in the doorway of the lodge giving on the courtyard. As Kyle turned towards it, this second figure descended the few steps to the grass and came to him.

"Lord—" said Kyle. He looked down into features like those of the Prince, but older, under graying hair. This man did not weep like the tutor, but his face was set like iron.

"What happened, Kyle?" he said.

"Lord," said Kyle, "you'll have my report in the morning . . ."

"I want to know," said the tall man. Kyle's throat was dry and stiff. He swallowed but swallowing did not ease it.

"Lord," he said, "you have three other sons. One of them will make an Emperor to hold the worlds together."

"What did he do? Whom did he hurt? Tell me!" The tall man's voice cracked almost as his son's voice had cracked in the bar.

"Nothing. No one," said Kyle, stiff-throated. "He hit a boy not much older than himself. He drank too much. He may have got a girl in trouble. It was nothing he did to anyone else. It was only a fault against himself." He swallowed. "Wait until tomorrow, Lord, and read my report."

"*No!*" The tall man caught at Kyle's saddle horn with a grip that checked even the white stallion from moving. "Your family and mine have been tied together by this for three hundred years. What was the flaw in my son to make him fail his test, back here on Earth? *I want to know!*"

Kyle's throat ached and was dry as ashes.

"Lord," he answered, "he was a coward."

The hand dropped from his saddle horn as if struck down by a sudden strengthlessness. And the Emperor of a hundred worlds fell back like a beggar, spurned in the dust.

Kyle lifted his reins and rode out of the gate, into the forest away on the hillside. The dawn was breaking.

And Then There Was Peace

At nine hundred hours there were explosions off to the right at about seven hundred yards. At eleven hundred hours the slagger came by to pick up the casualties among the gadgets. Charlie saw the melting head at the end of its heavy beam going up and down like the front end of a hardworking chicken only about fifty yards west of his foxhole. Then it worked its way across the battlefield for about half an hour and, loaded down with melted forms of damaged robots, of all shapes and varieties, disappeared behind the low hill to the west, and left, of Charlie. It was a hot August day somewhere in or near Ohio, with a thunderstorm coming on. There was that yellow color in the air.

At twelve hundred hours the chow gadget came ticking over the redoubt behind the foxhole. It crawled into the foxhole, jumped up on the large table and opened itself out to reveal lunch. The menu this day was liver and onions, whole corn, whipped potato and raspberries.

"And no whipped cream," said Charlie.

"You haven't been doing your exercises," said the chow gadget in a fine soprano voice.

"I'm a front-line soldier," said Charlie. "I'm an infantryman in a foxhole overlooking ground zero. I'll be damned if I take exercises."

"In any case, there is no excuse for not shaving."

"I'll be damned if I shave."

"But why *not* shave? Wouldn't it be better than having that itchy, scratchy beard—"

"No," said Charlie. He went around back of the chow gadget and began to take its rear plate off.

"What are you doing to me?" said the chow gadget.

"You've got something stuck to you here," said Charlie. "Hold still." He surreptitiously took a second out to scratch at his four-day beard. "There's a war on, you know."

"I know that," said the chow gadget. "Of course."

"Infantry men like me are dying daily."

"Alas," said the chow gadget, in pure, simple tones.

"To say nothing," said Charlie, setting the rear plate to one side, "of the expenditure of your technical devices. Not that there's any comparison between human lives and the wastage of machines."

"Of course not."

"So how can any of you, no matter how elaborate your computational systems, understand—" Charlie broke off to poke among the innards of the chow machine.

"Do not damage me," it said.

"Not if I can help it," said Charlie. "—understand what it feels like to a man sitting here day after day, pushing an occasional button, never knowing the results of his button pushing, and living in a sort of glass-case comfort except for the possibility that he may just suddenly be dead—suddenly, like that, before he knows it." He broke off to probe again. "It's no life for a man."

"Terrible, terrible," said the chow gadget. "But there is still hope for improvement."

"Don't hold your breath," said Charlie. "There's—ah!" He interrupted himself, pulling a small piece of paper out of the chow gadget.

"Is there something the matter?" said the chow gadget.

"No," said Charlie. He stepped over to the observation window and glanced out. The slagger was making its return. It was already within about fifty yards of the foxhole. "Not a thing," said Charlie. "As a matter of fact, the war's over."

"How interesting," said the chow gadget.

"That's right," said Charlie. "Just let me read you this little billet-doux I got from Foxhole thirty-four. *Meet you back at the bar, Charlie. It's all over. Your hunch that we could get a message across was the clear quill. Answer came today the same way, through the international weather reports. They want to quit as well as we do. Peace is agreed on, and the gadgets—*" Charlie broke off to look at the chow gadget. "That's you, along with the rest of them."

"Quite right. Of course," said the chow gadget.

"*—have already accepted the information. We'll be out of here by sundown.* And that takes care of the war."

"It does indeed," said the chow gadget. "Hurrah! And farewell."

"Farewell?" said Charlie.

"You will be returning to civilian life," said the chow gadget. "I will be scrapped."

"That's right," said Charlie. "I remember the pre-programming for the big units. This war's to be the last, they were programmed. Well—" said Charlie. For a moment he hesitated. "What d'you know? I may end up missing you a little bit, after all."

He glanced out the window. The slagger was almost to the dugout.

"Well, well," he said. "Now that the time's come
. . . we did have quite a time together, three times a
day. No more string beans, huh?"

"I bet not," said the chow gadget with a little
laugh.

"No more caramel pudding."

"I guess so."

Just then the slagger halted outside, broke the
thick concrete roof off the dugout and laid it carefully
aside.

"Excuse me," it said, its cone-shaped melting head
nodding politely some fifteen feet above Charlie.
"The war's over."

"I know," said Charlie.

"Now there will be peace. There are orders that
all instruments of war are to be slagged and stockpiled for later peaceful uses." It had a fine baritone
voice. "Excuse me," it said, "but are you finished
with that chow gadget there?"

"You haven't touched a bite," said the chow gadget. "Would you like just a small spoonful of raspberries?"

"I don't think so," said Charlie, slowly. "No, I
don't think so."

"Then farewell," said the chow gadget. "I am now
expendable."

The melting head of the slagger dipped toward the
chow gadget. Charlie opened his mouth suddenly,
but before he could speak, there was a sort of invisible flare from the melting head and the chow gadget
became a sort of puddle of metal which the melting
head picked up magnetically and swung back to the
hopper behind it.

"Blast it!" said Charlie with feeling. "I could just
as well have put in a request to keep the darn thing
for a souvenir."

The heavy melting head bobbed apologetically back.

"I'm afraid that wouldn't be possible," it said. "The

order allows no exceptions. *All* military instruments are to be slagged and stockpiled."

"Well—" said Charlie. But it was just about then that he noticed the melting head was descending toward him.

Whatever Gods There Be

At 1420 hours of the eighth day on Mars, Major Robert L. (Doc) Greene was standing over a slide in a microscope in the tiny laboratory of Mars Ship Groundbreaker II. There was a hinged seat that could be pulled up and locked in position, to sit on; but Greene never used it. At the moment, he had been taking blood counts on the four of them that were left in the crew, when a high white and a low red blood cell count of one sample had caught his attention. He had proceeded to follow up the tentative diagnosis this suggested, as coldly as if the sample had been that of some complete stranger. But, suddenly, the scene in the field of the microscope had blurred. And for a moment he closed both eyes and rested his head lightly against the microscope. The metal eyepiece felt cool against his eyelid; and caused an after-image to blossom against the hooded retina—as of a volcanic redness welling outward against a blind-dark background. It was his own deep-held inner fury exploding against an intractible universe.

Caught up in this image and his own savage emotion, Greene did not hear Captain Edward Kronzy,
who just then clumped into the lab, still wearing his
suit, except for the helmet.

"Something wrong, Bob?" asked Kronzy. The youngest of the original six-officer crew, he was about
average height—as were all the astronauts—and his
reddish, cheerful complexion contrasted with the shock
of stiff black hair and scowling, thirty-eight year old
visage of Greene.

"Nothing," said Greene, harshly, straightening up
and slipping the slide out of the microscope into a
breast pocket. "What's the matter with you?"

"Nothing," said Kronzy, with a pale grin that only
made more marked the dark circles under his eyes.
"But Hal wants you outside to help jack up."

"All right," said Greene. He put the other three
slides back in their box; and led the way out of the
lab toward the airlock. In the pocket, the glass slide
pressed sharp-edged and unyielding against the skin
of his chest, beneath. It had given Greene no choice
but to diagnose a cancer of the blood—leukemia.

Ten minutes later, Greene and Kronzy joined the
two other survivors of Project Mars Landing outside
on the Martian surface.

These other two—Lt. Colonel Harold (Hal) Barth,
and Captain James Wallach—were some eighty-five
feet above the entrance of the airlock, on the floor of
the crater in which they had landed. Greene and
Kronzy came toiling up the rubbled slope of the pit
where the ship lay; and emerged onto the crater
floor just as Barth and Wallach finished hauling the
jack into position at the pit's edge.

Around them, the crater floor on this eighth day
resembled a junk yard. A winch had been set up
about ten feet back from the pit five days before; and
now oxygen tanks, plumbing fixtures, spare clothing,

and a host of other items were spread out fanwise from the edge where the most easily ascendible slope of the pit met the crater floor—at the moment brilliantly outlined by the sun of the late Martian 'afternoon'. A little off to one side of the junk were two welded metal crosses propped erect by rocks.

The crosses represented 1st Lieutenant Saul Moulton and Captain Luthern J. White, who were somewhere under the rock rubble beneath the ship in the pit.

"Over here, Bob," Greene heard in the earphones of his helmet. He looked and saw Barth beckoning with a thick-gloved hand. "We're going to try setting her up as if in a posthole."

Greene led Kronzy over to the spot. When he got close, he could see through the faceplates of their helmets that the features of the other two men, particularly the thin, handsome features of Barth, were shining with sweat. The eighteen-foot jack lay with its base end projecting over a hole ground out of solid rock.

"What's the plan?" said Greene.

Barth's lips puffed with a weary exhalation of breath before he answered. The face of the Expedition's captain was finedrawn with exhaustion; but, Greene noted with secret satisfaction, with no hint of defeat in it yet. Greene relaxed slightly, sweeping his own grim glance around the crater, over the hole, the discarded equipment and the three other men.

A man, he thought, could do worse than to have made it this far.

"One man to anchor. The rest to lift," Barth was answering him.

"And I'm the anchor?" asked Greene.

"You're the anchor," answered Barth.

Greene went to the base end of the jack and picked up a length of metal pipe that was lying ready

there. He shoved it into the hole and leaned his
weight on it, against the base of the jack.

"Now!" he called, harshly.

The men at the other end heaved. It was not so
much the jack's weight, under Mars' gravity, as the
labor of working in the clumsy suits. The far end of
the jack wavered, rose, slipped gratingly against
Greene's length of pipe—swayed to one side, lifted
again as the other three men moved hand under
hand along below it—and approached the vertical.

The base of the jack slipped suddenly partway into
the hole, stuck, and threatened to collapse Greene's
arms. His fingers were slippery in the gloves, he
smelled the stink of his own perspiration inside the
suit, and his feet skidded a little in the surface dust
and rock.

"Will it go?" cried Barth gaspingly in Greene's
earphones.

"Keep going!" snarled Greene, the universe dis-
solving into one of his white-hot rages—a passion in
which only he and the jack existed; and it must yield.
"Lift, damn you! Lift!"

The pipe vibrated and bent. The jack swayed—
rose—and plunged suddenly into the socket hole,
tearing the pipe from Greene's grasp. Greene, left
pushing against nothing, fell forward, then rolled
over on his back. Above him, twelve protruding feet
of the jack quivered soundlessly.

Greene got to his feet. He was wringing wet.
Barth's faceplate suddenly loomed before him.

"You all right?" Barth's voice asked in his earphones.

"All right?" said Greene. He stared; and burst
suddenly into loud raucous laughter, that scaled upward toward uncontrollability. He choked it off. Barth
was still staring at him. "No, I broke my neck from
the fall," said Greene roughly. "What'd you think?"

Barth nodded and stepped back. He looked up at the jack.

"That'll do," he said. "We'll get the winch cable from that to the ship's nose and jack her vertical with no sweat."

"Yeah," said Kronzy. He was standing looking down into the pit. "No sweat."

The other three turned and looked into the pit as well, down where the ship lay at a thirty degree angle against one of the pit's sides. It was a requiem moment for Moulton and White who lay buried there; and all the living men above felt it at the same time. Chance had made a choice among them—there was no more justice to it than that.

The ship had landed on what seemed a flat crater floor. Landed routinely, upright, and apparently solidly. Only, twenty hours later, as Moulton and White had been outside setting up the jack they had just assembled—the jack whose purpose was to correct the angle of the ship for takeoff—chance had taken its hand.

What caused it—Martian landslip, vibration over flawed rock, or the collapse of a bubble blown in the molten rock when the planet was young—would have to be for those who came after to figure out. All the four remaining men who were inside knew was that one moment all was well; and the next they were flung about like pellets in a rattle that a baby shakes. When they were able to get outside and check, they found the ship in a hundred foot deep pit, in which Moulton and White had vanished.

"Well," said Barth, "I guess we might as well knock off now, and eat. Then, Jimmy—" his face-plate turned toward Wallach, "you and Ed can come up here and get that cable attached while I go over the lists you all gave me of your equipment we can still strip from the ship; and I'll figure out if she's

light enough to lift on the undamaged tubes. And
Bob—you can get back to whatever you were doing."

"Yeah," said Greene. "Yeah, I'll do that."

After they had all eaten, Greene shut himself up
once more in the tiny lab to try to come to a decision. From a military point of view, it was his duty to
inform the commanding officer—Barth—of the diagnosis he had just made. But the peculiar relationship
existing between himself and Barth—

There was a knock on the door.

"Come on in!" said Greene.

Barth opened the door and stuck his head in.

"You're not busy."

"Matter of opinion," he said. "What is it?"

Barth came all the way in, shut the door behind
him, and leaned against the sink.

"You're looking pretty washed out, Bob," he said.

"We all are. Never mind me," said Greene. "What's
on your mind?"

"A number of things," said Barth. "I don't have to
tell you what it's like with the whole Space Program.
You know as well as I do."

"Thanks," said Greene.

The sarcasm in his voice was almost absent-minded.
Insofar as gratitude had a part in his makeup, he was
grateful to Barth for recognizing what few other people had—how much the work of the Space Program
had become a crusade to which his whole soul and
body was committed.

"We just can't afford not to succeed," Barth was
saying.

It was the difference between them, noted Greene.
Barth admitted the possibility of not succeeding. Nineteen years the two men had been close friends—
since high school. And nowadays, to many people,
Barth *was* the Space Program. Good-looking, brilliant, brave—and possessing that elusive quality which

makes for newsworthiness at public occasions and on the TV screens—Barth had been a shot in the arm to the Program these last six months.

And he had been needed. No doubt the Russian revelations of extensive undersea developments in the Black Sea area had something to do with it. Probably the lessening of world tensions lately had contributed. But it had taken place—one of those unexplainable shifts in public interest which have been the despair of promotion men since the breed was invented.

The world had lost much of its interest in spatial exploration.

No matter that population pressures continued to mount. No matter that natural resources depletion was accelerating, in spite of all attempt at control. Suddenly—space exploration had become old hat; taken for granted.

And those who had been against it from the beginning began to gnaw, unchecked, at the roots of the Program. So that men like Barth, to whom the Space Program had become a way of life, worried, seeing gradual strangulation as an alternative to progress. But men like Greene, to whom the Program had become life itself, hated, seeing *no* alternative.

"Who isn't succeeding?" said Greene.

"We lost Luthern and Saul," said Barth, glancing downward almost instinctively toward where the two officers must be buried. "We've got to get back."

"Sure. Sure," said Greene.

"I mean," said Barth, "we've got to get back, no matter what the cost. We've got to show them we could get a ship up here and get back again. You know, Bob—" he looked almost appealingly at Greene—"the trouble with a lot of people who're not in favor of the Project is they don't really believe in the moon or Mars of anyplace like it. I mean—the way they'd believe in Florida, or the South Pole.

They're sort of half-clinging to the notion it's just a sort of cut-out circle of silver paper up in the air, there, after all. But if we go and come back, they've *got to* believe!"

"Listen," said Greene. "Don't worry about people like that. They'll all be dead in forty years, anyway.—Is this all you wanted to talk to me about?"

"No. Yes—I guess," said Barth. He smiled tiredly at Greene. "You pick me up, Bob. I guess it's just a matter of doing what you have to."

"Do what you're going to do," said Greene with a shrug. "Why make a production out of it?"

"Yes." Barth straightened up. "You're right. Well, I'll get back to work. See you in a little while. We'll get together for a pow-wow as soon as Ed and Jimmy get back in from stringing that cable."

"Right," said Greene. He watched the slim back and square shoulders of Barth go out the door and slumped against the sink, himself, chewing savagely on a thumbnail. His instinct had been right, he thought; it was not the time to tell Barth about the diagnosis.

And not only that. Nineteen years had brought Greene to the point where he could, in almost a practical sense, read the other man's mind. He had just done so; and right now he was willing to bet that he had a new reason for worry.

Barth had something eating on him. Chewing his fingernail, Greene set to work to puzzle out just what that could be.

A fist hammered on the lab door. "Bob?"

"What?" said Greene, starting up out of his brown study. Some little time had gone by. He recognized his caller now. Kronzy.

"Hal wants us in the control cabin, right away."

"Okay. Be right there."

Greene waited until Kronzy's boot sounds had gone

away in the distance down the short corridor and up the ladder to the level overhead. Then he followed, more slowly.

He discovered the others already jammed in among the welter of instruments and controls that filled this central space of the ship.

"What's the occasion?" he asked, cramming himself in between the main control screen and an acceleration couch.

"Ways and means committee," said Barth, with a small smile. "I was waiting until we were all together before I said anything." He held up a sheet of paper. "I've just totalled up all the weight we can strip off the ship, using the lists of dispensable items each of you made up, and checked it against the thrust we can expect to get safely from the undamaged tubes. We're about fifteen hundred Earth pounds short. I made the decision to drop off the water tanks, the survival gear, and a few other items, which brings us down to being about five hundred pounds short."

He paused and laid down the paper on a hinge-up desk surface beside him.

"I'm asking for suggestions," he said.

Greene looked around the room with sudden fresh grimness. But he saw no comprehension yet, on the faces of the other two crew members.

"How about—" began Kronzy; then hesitated as the words broke off in the waiting silence of the others.

"Go on, Ed," said Barth.

"We're not short of fuel."

"That's right."

"Then why," said Kronzy, "can't we rig some sort of auxiliary burners—like the jato units you use to boost a plane off, you know?" He glanced at Greene and Wallach, then back at Barth. "We wouldn't have to care whether they burnt up or not—just as long as they lasted long enough to get us off."

"That's a good suggestion, Ed," said Barth, slowly. "The only hitch is, I looked into that possibility, myself. And it isn't possible. We'd need a machine shop. We'd need—it just isn't possible. It'd be easier to repair the damaged tubes."

"I suppose that isn't possible, either?" said Greene, sharply.

Barth looked over at him, then quickly looked away again.

"I wasn't serious," Barth said. "For that we'd need Cape Canaveral right here beside us.—And then, probably not."

He looked over at Wallach.

"Jimmy?" he said.

Wallach frowned.

"Hal," he said. "I don't know. I can think about it a bit. . . ."

"Maybe," said Barth, "that's what we all ought to do. Everybody go off by themselves and chew on the problem a bit." He turned around and seated himself at the desk surface. "I'm going to go over these figures again."

Slowly, they rose. Wallach went out, followed by Kronzy. Greene hesitated, looking at Barth, then he turned away and left the room.

Alone once more in the lab, Greene leaned against the sink again and thought. He did not, however, think of mass-to-weight ratios or clever ways of increasing the thrust of the rocket engines.

Instead, he thought of leukemia. And the fact that it was still a disease claiming its hundred per cent of fatalities. But also, he thought of Earth with its many-roomed hospitals; and the multitude of good men engaged in cancer research. Moreover, he thought of the old medical truism that while there is life, there is hope.

All this reminded him of Earth, itself. And his

thoughts veered off to a memory of how pleasant it had been, on occasion after working all the long night through, to step out through a door and find himself unexpectedly washed by the clean air of dawn. He thought of vacations he had never had, fishing he had never done, and the fact that he might have found a woman to love him if he had ever taken off enough time to look for her. He thought of good music—he had always loved good music. And he remembered that he had always intended someday to visit La Scala.

Then—hauling his mind back to duty with a jerk—he began to scowl and ponder the weak and strong points that he knew about in Barth's character. Not, this time, to anticipate what the man would say when they were all once more back in the control cabin. But for the purpose of circumventing and trapping Barth into a position where Barth would be fenced in by his own principles—the ultimate jiujitsu of human character manipulation. Greene growled and muttered to himself, in the privacy of the lab marking important points with his forefinger in the artificial and flatly odorous air.

He was still at it, when Kronzy banged at his door again and told him everybody else was already back in the control cabin.

When he got to the control cabin again, the rest were in almost the identical positions they had taken previously.

"Well?" said Barth, when Greene had found himself a niche of space. He looked about the room, at each in turn. "How about you, Jimmy?"

"The four acceleration couches we've still got in the ship—. With everything attached to them, they weigh better than two hundred apiece," said Wallach. "Get rid of two of them, and double up in the two left. That gets rid of four of our five hundred pounds. Taking off from Mars isn't as rough as taking off from Earth."

"I'm afraid it won't work," Kronzy commented.

"Why not?"

"Two to a couch, right?"

"Right."

"Well, look. They're made for one man. Just barely. You can cram two in by having both of them lying on their sides. That's all right for the two who're just passengers—but what about the man at the controls?" He nodded at Barth. "He's got to fly the ship. And how can he do that with half of what he needs to reach behind him, and the man next to him blocking off his reach at the other half?" Kronzy paused. "Besides, I'm telling you—half a couch isn't going to help hardly at all. You remember how the G's felt, taking off? And this time all that acceleration is going to be pressing against one set of ribs and a hipbone."

He stopped talking then.

"We'll have to think of something else. Any suggestions, Ed?" said Barth.

"Oh." Kronzy took a deep breath. "Toss out my position taking equipment. All the radio equipment, too. Shoot for Earth blind, deaf and dumb; and leave it up to them down there to find us and bring us home."

"How much weight would that save?" asked Wallach.

"A hundred and fifty pounds—about."

"A hundred and fifty! Where'd you figure the rest to come from?"

"I didn't know," said Kronzy, wearily. "It was all I could figure to toss, beyond what we've already planned to throw out. I was hoping you other guys could come up with the rest."

He looked at Barth.

"Well, it's a good possibility, Ed," said Barth. He turned his face to Greene. "How about you, Bob?"

"Get out and push!" said Greene. "My equip-

ment's figured to go right down to the last gram.
There isn't any more. You want my suggestion—we
can all dehydrate ourselves about eight to ten pounds
per man between now and takeoff. That's it."

"That's a good idea, too," said Barth. "Every pound
counts." He looked haggard around the eyes, Greene
noticed. It had the effect of making him seem older
than he had half an hour before during their talk in
the lab; but Greene knew this to be an illusion.

"Thank you," Barth went on. "I knew you'd all try
hard. I'd been hoping you'd come up with some
things I had overlooked myself. More important than
any of us getting back, of course, is getting the ship
back. Proving something like this will work, to the
people who don't believe in it."

Greene coughed roughly; and roughly cleared his
throat.

"—We can get rid of one acceleration couch as Ed
suggests," Barth continued. "We can dehydrate ourselves as Bob suggested, too; just to be on the safe
side. That's close to two hundred and fifty pounds
reduction. Plus a hundred and fifty for the naviga-
tional and radio equipment. There's three hundred
and ninety to four hundred. Add one man with his
equipment and we're over the hump with a safe
eighty to a hundred pound margin."

He had added the final item so quietly that for a
minute it did not register on those around him.

—Then, abruptly, it did.

"A man?" said Kronzy.

There was a second moment of silence—but this
was like the fractionary interval of no sound in which
the crowd in the grandstand suddenly realizes that
the stunt flyer in the small plane is not coming out of
his spin.

"I think," said Barth, speaking suddenly and loudly
in the stillness, "that, as I say, the important thing is
getting the ship back down. We've got to convince

those people that write letters to the newspapers that something like this is possible. So the job can go on."

They were still silent, looking at him.

"It's our duty, I believe," said Barth, "to the Space Project. And to the people back there; and to ourselves. I think it's something that has to be done."

He looked at each of them in turn.

"Now Hal—wait!" burst out Wallach, as Barth's eyes came on him. "That's going a little overboard, isn't it? I mean—we can figure out something!"

"Can we?" Barth shook his head. "Jimmy—. There just isn't any more. If they shoot you for not paying your bills, then it doesn't help to have a million dollars, if your debts add up to a million dollars and five cents. You know that. If the string doesn't reach, it doesn't reach. Everything we can get rid of on this ship won't be enough. Not if we want her to fly."

Wallach opened his mouth again; and then shut it. Kronzy looked down at his boots. Greene's glance went savagely across the room to Barth.

"Well," said Kronzy. He looked up. Kronzy, too, Greene thought, now looked older. "What do we do—draw straws?"

"No," Barth said. "I'm in command here. I'll pick the man."

"*Pick* the man!" burst out Wallach, staring. "You—"

"Shut up, Jimmy!" said Kronzy. He was looking hard at Barth. "Just what did you have in mind, Hal?" he said, slowly.

"That's all." Barth straightened up in his corner of the control room. "The rest is my responsibility. The rest of you get back to work tearing out the disposable stuff still in the ship—"

"I think," said Kronzy, quietly and stubbornly, "we ought to draw straws."

"You—" said Wallach. He had been staring at

Barth ever since Kronzy had told him to shut up. "*You'd* be the one, Hal?"

"That's all," said Barth, again. "Gentlemen, this matter is not open for discussion."

"The hell," replied Kronzy, "you say. You may be paper CO of this bunch; but we are just not about to play Captain-go-down-with-his-ship. We all weigh between a hundred-sixty and a hundred and eighty pounds and that makes us equal in the sight of mathematics. Now, we're going to draw straws; and if you won't draw, Hal, we'll draw one for you; and if you won't abide by the draw, we'll strap you in the other acceleration couch and one of us can fly the ship out of here. Right, Jimmy? Bob?"

He glared around at the other two. Wallach opened his mouth, hesitated, then spoke.

"Yes," he said. "I guess that's right."

Kronzy stared at him suddenly. Wallach looked away.

"Just a minute," said Barth.

They looked at him. He was holding a small, black, automatic pistol.

"I'm sorry," Barth said. "But I am in command. And I intend to stay in command, even if I have to cripple every one of you, strip the ship and strap you into couches myself." He looked over at Greene. "Bob. *You'll* be sensible, won't you?"

Greene exploded suddenly into harsh laughter. He laughed so hard he had to blink tears out of his eyes before he could get himself under control.

"Sensible!" he said. "Sure, I'll be sensible. And look after myself at the same time—even if it does take some of the glory out of it." He grinned almost maliciously at Barth. "Much as I hate to rob anybody else of the spotlight—it just so happens one of us can stay behind here until rescued and live to tell his grandchildren about it."

They were all looking at him.

"Sure," said Greene. "There'll be more ships coming, won't there? In fact, they'll have no choice in the matter, if they got a man up here waiting to be rescued."

"How?" said Kronzy.

"Ever hear of suspended animation?" Greene turned to the younger man. "Deep freeze. Out there in permanent shadow we've got just about the best damn deep freeze that ever was invented. The man who stays behind just takes a little nap until saved. In fact, from his point of view, he'll barely close his eyes before they'll be waking him up; probably back on Earth."

"You mean this?" said Barth.

"Of course, I mean it!"

Barth looked at Kronzy.

"Well, Ed," he said. "I guess that takes care of your objections."

"Hold on a minute!" Greene said. "I hope you don't think still you're going to be the one to stay. This is my idea; and I've got first pick at it.—Besides, done up in suits the way we are outside there, I couldn't work it on anybody else. Whoever gets frozen has got to know what to do by himself; and I'm the only one who fits the bill." His eyes swept over all of them. "So that's the choice."

Barth frowned just slightly.

"Why didn't you mention this before, Bob?" he said.

"Didn't think of it—until you came up with your notion of leaving one man behind. And then it dawned on me. It's simple—for anyone who knows how."

Barth slowly put the little gun away in a pocket of his coveralls.

"I'm not sure still, I—" he began slowly.

"Why don't you drop it?" blazed Greene in sudden fury. "You think you're the only one who'd like to play hero? I've got news for you. I've given the Project everything I've got for a number of years now; but I'm the sort of man who gets forgotten easily. You can bet your boots I won't be forgotten when they have to come all the way from Earth to save me. It's my deal; and you're not going to cut me out of it. And what—" he thrust his chin at Barth— "are you going to do if I simply refuse to freeze anybody but myself? Shoot me?"

Barth shook his head slowly, his eyes shadowed with pain.

Rocket signal rifle held athwart behind him and legs spread, piratically, Greene stood where the men taking off in the rockets could see him in the single control screen that was left in the ship. Below, red light blossomed suddenly down in the pit. The surface trembled under Greene's feet and the noise of the engines reached him by conduction through the rocks and soles of his boots.

The rocket took off.

Greene waved after it. And then wondered why he had done so. Bravado? But there was no one around to witness bravado now. The other three were on their way to Earth—and they would make it. Greene walked over and shut off the equipment they had set up to record the takeoff. The surrounding area looked more like a junkyard than ever. He reached clumsy gloved fingers into an outside pocket of his suit and withdrew the glass slide. With one booted heel he ground it into the rock.

The first thing they would do with the others would be to give them thorough physical checks, after hauling them out of the south Atlantic. And when that happened, Barth's leukemia would immediately be discovered. In fact, it was a yet-to-be-solved mystery why it had not shown up during

routine medical tests before this. After that—well,
while there was life, there was hope.

At any rate, live or die, Barth, the natural identifi-
cation figure for those watching the Project, would
hold the spotlight of public attention for another six
months at least. And if he held it from a hospital
bed, so much the better. Greene would pass and be
forgotten between two bites of breakfast toast. But
Barth—that was something else again.

The Project would be hard to starve to death with
Barth dying slowly and uncomplaining before the
eyes of taxpayers.

Greene dropped the silly signal rifle. The rocket
flame was out of sight now. He felt with gloved
hands at the heat control unit under the thick covering of his suit and clumsily crushed it. He felt it give
and break. It was amazing, he thought, the readiness
of the laity to expect miracles from the medical pro-
fession. Anyone with half a brain should have guessed
that something which normally required the person-
nel and physical resources of a hospital, could not be
managed alone, without equipment, and on the naked surface of Mars.

Barth would undoubtedly have guessed it—if he
had not been blinded by Greene's wholly unfair im-
plication that Barth was a glory-hunter. Of course, in
the upper part of his mind, Barth must know it was
not true; but he was too good a man not to doubt
himself momentarily when accused. After that, he
had been unable to wholly trust his own reasons for
insisting on being the one to stay behind.

He'll forgive me, thought Greene. He'll forgive
me, afterwards, when he figures it all out.

He shook off his sadness that had come with the
thought. Barth had been his only friend. All his life,
Greene's harsh, sardonic exterior had kept people at
a distance. Only Barth had realized that under
Greene's sarcasms and jibes he was as much a fool

with stars in his eyes as the worst of them. Well, thank heaven he had kept his weakness decently hidden.

He started to lie down, then changed his mind. It was probably the most effective position for what time remained; but it went against his grain that the men who came after him should find him flat on his back in this junkyard.

Greene began hauling equipment together until he had a sort of low seat. But when he had it all constructed, this, too was unsatisfactory.

Finally he built it a little higher. The suit was very stiff, anyway. In the end, he needed only a little propping for his back and arms. He was turned in the direction in which the Earth would rise over the Martian horizon; and, although the upper half of him was still in sunlight, long shadows of utter blackness were pooling about his feet.

Definitely, the lower parts of his suit were cooling now. It occurred to him that possibly he would freeze by sections in this position. No matter, it was a relatively painless death.—Forgive me, he thought in Barth's direction, lost among the darkness of space and the light of the stars.—It would have been a quicker, easier end for you this way, I know. But you and I both were always blank checks to be filled out on demand and paid into the account of Man's future. It was only then that we could have had any claim to lives of our own.

As Greene had now, in these final seconds.

He pressed back against the equipment he had built up. It held him solidly. This little, harmless pleasure he gave his own grim soul. Up here in the airlessness of Mars' bare surface, nothing could topple him over now.

When the crew of the next ship came searching, they would find what was left of him still on his feet.

Minotaur

When Jake Lundberg finally broke his way through the inner door of the airlock into the *Prosper Prince*, he found himself in pitch darkness.

"*That's* not going to work," he said, and went back along the line of the small magnetic grapple that held the two ships together and into his own *Molly B*.

The *Molly B.*, a range scout, while large enough and comfortable enough by the ordinary standards of a Government trouble-shooter, was at the moment looking rather minnowlike and feeling rather cramped, at the end of the fragile little line that was all that was required to keep the two vessels together in the absence of gravity. For the *Prosper Prince* had been a full-scale survey ship, with its own labs and shops and a crew of nine.

"What could happen to nine trained men twelve light-years from the nearest star?" said Jake, who was used to talking out loud for the benefit of the little throat microphone that connected him with the recorder on the *Molly B.*, no matter how far he might wander from her. "You tell me."

Molly B. made no effort to tell him. She was agreeable but dumb, in the literal sense of that word.

"Now I'm getting self-powered lights which I'll carry over and string out along the corridor to the control room there as I go," Jake added, for the recorder, as he dug into a supply locker. "Don't get lonely now, Molly."

He went back out and along the line into the *Prosper Prince* once more, moving a little awkwardly, for if the lights he was carrying weighed nothing, in the absence of gravity, they made a pretty full armload.

Through the airlock into the *Prosper Prince* proper, Jake encountered a small amount of weight. About one-half G. Which meant that although the lights were not functioning, the ship he was in was not completely dead. The air, however, though his helmet counter showed it as good, smelled musty when he flipped the helmet back. Whatever else was operating, the circulating fans were off.

Loaded, with his lights on, Jake headed down the main corridor in what he knew must be the route to the control area forward. Every forty feet or so, or at each bend in the corridor, he stopped to set one of the lights in place against the corridor wall. The magnetic base of each light stuck firmly, and its lens, with a theoretical thousand years of power self-contained behind it, began to flood the corridor with light as soon as it made contact with the wall. The main corridor, Jake noted as he went along, was comparable to the air in the ship. It looked all right, but it gave evidence of having been unused for some time.

A hundred yards down the corridor and up an emergency ladder (the lift tube was, of course, not working) and along the corridor above for another

twenty yards brought Jake to the door of the main
control center of the ship. He stepped inside, fixed
one of his lights to a handy wall and put down the
rest of his load while he looked the situation over.

The control center—except for the faintly musty
odor of the air and the slight film of dust—might
have been abandoned just a moment or so before.
All the equipment was in workable-looking shape.
The one exception was the coffee and water taps in a
little alcove off the plotting board. These had been
battered into the wall from which they protruded, as
if by a sledge-hammer.

"Now what do you think of that?" said Jake, and
proceeded to detail the situation for the benefit of
the recorder back on the *Molly B*. He could imagine
one of the think-boys back at Earth Headquarters,
six months from now, pausing as this part of the tape
was played back, and scratching his head.

"Don't let it get you down, Pete," he said. Jake
called all the think-boys Pete. Headquarters had sent
him several stiff memos about it. He paid no attention. He had to risk his neck as an occasional part of
his job. They didn't. If they didn't like the way he
made his reports, they knew exactly what they could
do about it.

Jake moved over to the log desk, passing the main
screen as he did so. The screen was dead, its silvery
surface reflecting a picture of the control room and
himself. He paused to inspect the two V-shaped
inroads of scalp into his hairline. Yes, they were
definitely going back. There was no use blinking the
fact. And that was no good. All right, perhaps, for
some skinny intellectual type to have a high forehead, but a broad, square-jawed character like
himself—he just looked half-shorn. He'd probably
better see about repilation, next trip home to Earth.

"—or else a good hair tonic," he said out loud.
"Make a note of that, Pete."

The logbook was also turned off. But when he flipped the switch, it lit up in proper shape. He ran the tape back to the last entry.

June 34, 2462: Still on twelfth jump between Runyon's World and Ceta. Biochemist Walter Latham, slight case of hives. Taking infra-red treatments. Acid condition of soil in grass plantation tank of air-freshener room corrected. The coffee continues to have a burned taste. No evidence of spoilage, but suggest Quartermaster look into this on return to Earth. Today was the nineteenth anniversary of the launching of this ship, and the event was duly celebrated by the crew and staff at a dinner at which an original poem written in honor of the occasion by Engineer's Assistant Rory Katchuk was recited and, by unanimous vote of the whole crew, ordered to be written into the ship's log. It is as follows:

> *Oh, Prosper Prince*
> *You made me wince,*
> *Right from the start,*
> *And ever since.*

Some more of the corridor lights have been smashed about the ship. If this is one of the elaborate practical jokes that sometimes crops up on long voyages, it is in bad taste, and the man responsible, when found, will be severely dealt with. This applies also to whoever is responsible for the sobbing noise.

Jake raised bushy eyebrows upward into the growingly naked scalp he had just been examining. He read off the entry in the log for Pete's benefit.

"Sobbing noise?" he echoed. "Now, that's a new one. Let's look a little farther back."

He spun the tape back at random and stopped it. He read off the entry before him out loud.

"*April 29, 2462: Due to lift from Runyon's World tomorrow. All reports complete and planet looks good.*

The Prosper Prince may well congratulate herself on having discovered and tested a prime colonizable world. Breathable atmosphere, benign temperature range, flora and fauna. Largest native life-form encountered, the creatures we have named Goopers. These are very similar to the Earthly baboon in appearance, but have marked internal differences, and large, apparently atrophied glands for which no purpose can be discerned, on the underside of their forearms. It is difficult to figure why these creatures do not overrun the planet, since they are entirely herbivorous and seem to have no natural enemies. Perhaps their racial fear of entering the forests or any shadowy or enclosed place acts as a process of natural selection. (See Jeffers-Bradley report #297, log inclusion Jan. 3, 2462.)"

Jake spun the log back to January the third of that year and discovered the report inclusion.

"We found the forest to consist of vegetation similar to our hardwood forests—oaklike trees with many small branches and twigs, but no leaves. The twigs, however, are so numerous and thick that sunlight is cut to a minimum; there is almost no ground-cover or small vegetation between the trees but a sort of moss, and no animal life to be seen, except an occasional firefly kind of insect. Phosphorescence noticeable in darker spots coating tree trunks and even the ground, due to a fungoid life-form which excretes a zinc-sulphate phosphor."

Jake spun the log ahead to April 29th and finished reading the entry there.

"A possible clue may lie in the fact that these creatures avoid the streaks of zinc-sulphate phosphors which make their appearance mysteriously at night even in the open meadows. At any rate, this is a puzzle for later investigation, if the planet is opened for colonization."

Jake shut off the log, thoughtfully.

"Well, Pete," he said, "what do you think of that? They lifted for home on April 30th. By July they were posted overdue. I was sent out to look for them July 10th and it's only taken me 40 days to find them. They're right where they should be if they'd just quit jumping on the 12th jump. No sign of trouble—except those coffee and water taps over there. But no sign of anybody aboard either. You don't suppose they just all decided to walk right out of the airlock?"

There was no answer to that question, of course, so Jake shook his head, gathered up his armload of lights and went on exploring and distributing illumination about the *Prosper Prince*.

He found the ship in good shape, but empty. The control section was empty, the officer's quarters were empty, the recreation areas were empty, and the men's quarters were empty.

Going down one level, he found himself in the section reserved for the labs and shops—and it was here that he reached the end of his supply of lights. Taking the last one and hand-activating it, he proceeded, carrying it like a searchlamp before him, and began to work back aft toward the greenery, where the grass plantation tank that renewed the oxygen supply in the ship had its existence, with the water reservoir, and the drive units.

When he stepped through the door into the greenery, at first sight it looked as a greenery should. It was a large, almost empty-seeming room with the equivalent of two city lots planted in a very tall grass which looked totally undisturbed. But at one end, where the ventilating system was, the fan housing had been completely wrecked and the fan inside it smashed.

"Aha!" said Jake to his mike. "Somebody decided

to dispose of the ventilating system, Pete. Suppose we just take a closer look at that." He moved forward toward the fan housing.

But before he could reach it, noise exploded upon his eardrums. It was distant but thunderous noise, coming from the front end of the ship, a racket like a gang of medieval smiths working on armor.

Jake spun about and burst out of the room. He ran back up the corridor. As he neared the noise, it echoed and reechoed through the metal walls about him.

He scrambled up the ladder to the mid-level of the ship and just as he reached the top, the noise stopped. He stopped, too. In the new and sudden silence, he could hear his own heart pounding.

He stood listening: then he went forward again. He moved down the mid-level corridor, the one he had first entered on coming into the ship. But he saw nothing amiss until he rounded the curve to the point where the airlock pierced the inner and outer skins of the vessel. The massive latch handle, which dogged shut the inner door to the lock, had been battered completely off.

For a long moment, Jake said nothing. Then he cleared his throat, but not noisily.

"Are you still there, Pete?" he half-whispered. There was no answer, of course, but the sound of his own voice shocked a little common sense back into him.

He looked up and down the corridor. The lights still burned, undisturbed.

"Pete," he said fervently, "there's something aboard here and it doesn't love me."

He looked again at the door. Damaged as it was, there was no hope of his opening it—not, at least, without tools. For a second he felt a completely irrational flash of rage. There was the *Molly B.* out there, a few feet from him, with the very tools he needed to break through to get to her. And for lack of the tools, he could not do so.

He suddenly reminded himself there should be tools aboard this ship as well. It was only a matter of finding them. He turned about and headed once more toward the control room. In there, there should be a master chart of the vessel and a list of the supplies and equipment she would have been carrying.

Back in the control room, Jake found his normal good spirits recovering. After all, he considered, it was only a matter of taking the time to locate tools on board this ship. Then he could break open the door and slap a tow-line from the *Molly B.* onto this ship and haul her to Earth, where whatever was aboard could be captured by properly armed and protected men. He even whistled a bit as he thought of it.

His whistling ended abruptly a few moments later. He had located the design chart, the equipment list and the arms locker. The arms locker, however, was locked. And Jake had discovered that the combination to it was missing from the papers in his hand.

"Oh-oh," said Jake. "I don't like this, Pete. I don't like it at all."

He reached for the locker door nonetheless—and abruptly he felt a crawling sensation on the back of his neck. He whirled about. But the control room was empty. The entrance to it was empty. And as far as he could see, down the corridor beyond it, that too was empty.

"Nerves," he told himself and Pete, out loud. "Nerves."

Suddenly, the light halfway down the corridor and out of sight of the doorway, from where Jake was then standing, went out. And there was a tinkling smash in the darkness.

Jake froze. And then the hair on the back of his neck began to rise. For, eerily, from the darkened

corridor, there came to his ears the sound of a sobbing. A sobbing like that of a soul whose last hope
had been stolen and lost forever.

Jake backed up against the drive control. His hand,
groping instinctively behind him for some sort of
weapon, closed about the short metal length of the
captain's wireless microphone. He grabbed it up in
one hand, an eight-inch club weighing maybe four
pounds.

And the sobbing stopped. It stopped as short as if
the sobber had had his breath choked off. Still bris-
tling, Jake circled quietly about the room and approached the door, sidling along the wall. As he
passed the wall of the control room he detached the
lamp he had put against the wall there; and, hand-
activating it to keep on burning, he carried it with
him. When he reached the doorway, he swung suddenly into it and flashed its beam down the full long
corridor.

The corridor was absolutely empty.

Jake stood there in baffled frustration. Then he
turned and went back to the arms locker. He tried to
batter it open, using the captain's microphone. He
managed to bend the microphone, but he did not
manage to open the door.

"Pete," he said softly putting the bent microphone
down, "this is a heck of a situation. You heard that
banging before, and you heard the sobbing this time.
Tell me, Pete, what sort of something would want to
make noises like that?"

He shook his head tensely and went back to the
list. On it, he located the section that dealt with
tools. The tools he would want, he discovered, were
down in the tool shop on the lower level again, back
by the greenery. Jake whistled tunelessly through
his teeth as he read this little item of information.

"It *would* be out there!" he said. "Well, Pete, here

we go down to the bottom level of the ship again. Down to the tool room to get ourselves a cutter torch and pry bar."

He took the lamp from the control room wall and placed it so it would catch part of the corridor as well as the control room. Then, picking up the light he had been carrying as a hand lamp, he headed back for the bottom level. He went off down the corridor, and when he reached the point where the other light had been, he stopped.

The light that had been there was lying on the floor of the corridor. It had been thoroughly smashed.

Jake puzzled over the remains, found no answer, and continued on to the ladder, careful to keep the light ahead of him. A little farther on, however, he moved into the area of another light, which was shining brightly, intact. He hooked his own light onto his belt. Then he went on until he came to the ladder leading both up and down, and climbed down it to the lower level once more.

He went along the lower level corridor to the greenery. He paused warily to glance in, but the room was empty. He continued on to where the corridor ended in a door. Opening this door, he stepped through into the tool shop of the ship. He was in a moderately sized square room, about twice the size of an ordinary earthside kitchen. A number of power tools stood around the wall and magnetic racks were fitted with hand tools.

He selected a portable torch flame cutter and a spring-operated pry bar. Then he came back out of the tool room into the lower level corridor. He started his walk back up the corridor toward the ladder. As he went he found himself wishing that he had been able to bring a second load of lights before he had been made a prisoner aboard this vessel. The lamp at his belt flung a brilliant glare before him. It was more than adequate to the subjects it illuminated.

Nevertheless, darkness followed; and shadows jumped and slid along the walls as he walked. He had just reached the foot of the ladder when a sound reached his ears.

It was the sound of a light somewhere distant in the ship, smashing.

He stopped with his hands on the ladder. He found himself straining his ears to listen. But there was no other sound. He climbed up the ladder, went down the corridor a little way and came to the inner airlock door. He chose a spot along the corridor wall where the light would illuminate the door well, without shadows; and at this spot, some ten feet from him, he clamped the light to the wall and raised the torch to go to work on the door.

Once more, somewhere distant in the ship, a light smashed and tinkled.

Jake shut his jaw a little grimly and turned to the inner door of the airlock. The flame from the cutting torch in his hand splattered against the metal.

It was some moments before Jake realized that it was having little or no effect.

He stopped and checked, first the torch, then the door. The torch was in perfectly good shape. The door, however, carried in its lower right corner a little legend stamped into the metal. The legend consisted of a small "c" with a circle around it.

Jake straightened up, breathed deeply, and ran his thick fingers slowly through his close-cropped hair.

"Well, Pete," he said, his voice sounding odd in his own ears, "how do you like that? They *would* decide to make their airlock out of collapsed steel instead of something cuttable."

He glanced once more at the torch, hanging useless in his hand, and stuck the tool back into his belt. There was nothing that would get him through the collapsed steel of the airlock he faced now, he knew, but some of the special equipment he had on board the *Molly B*.

"O.K., Pete," he said softly. "Mohammed and the mountain, all over again. If I can't tow this ship home with the *Molly B.*, maybe I can tow the *Molly B*. home with this ship."

He turned away and headed up the corridor toward the control room.

Some time later, with the door to the control room closed and welded shut with the torch at his belt against interruption, Jake was busy overhauling the controls. As far as he could see, they were in excellent shape. He had nothing to do now but simply start the vessel moving and keep it at it.

However, handling a ship this size was not simple at all. It was not so much the question of driving as it was of figuring where to. The process by which an interstellar ship moved in space was by making large "shifts." These shifts instantly caused the vessel to cease to be at one particular point in time and space and caused it to be at another point in space. There was literally no effort to it.

The calculations required to tell the person running the ship where he was and where he would be once he shifted, though, were very complicated indeed. In this instance, it was further complicated by the fact that Jake had to stop and figure out all over again where he was. That information was on board the *Molly B*. But, since the *Molly B*. was out of reach, Jake theoretically had to go back to Earth and retrace his steps all the way out to this point. Of course he had the great calculators of the ship here to do it with. But still, it was a time-consuming job.

It took two hours to get the ship in working condition. It took three more hours to find out where he was. Nearly six hours had gone by since Jake had entered the ship; and when he was finally done, he found himself tired, hungry and thirsty. But the shifts were programmed that would take the ship to Earth.

He started the *Prosper Prince* toward its first shift point, and then cautiously he cut open the door to the control room and looked out down the corridor. He saw utter darkness. No lamp, no light was showing anywhere. Through his teeth he whistled two short bars of a tune. Then he took down one of the two lamps that yet remained in the control room, the one he had carried in his belt; and taking this with him, holding it before him, he lit it and walked down the corridor.

He saw nothing as he went, although the sounds of his own footfalls were loud in his ear. Halfway down the length of the ship, past the officers quarters, he came to the ship's galley. Closing this door, he made welds at its four corners and set about preparing himself something to eat and drink.

It was not that he expected his welds would secure the door against whatever had had strength enough to smash the water and coffee taps in the control room, or dismember the blower equipment in the greenery; but he hoped its having to break through the door would give him time to adopt a posture of defense. And the cutting torch in his hand would be a weapon of sorts.

He made himself a pretty fair meal out of dehydrated stores, and a pot of coffee. After he had eaten, he sat at the galley table, with one eye on the welded-shut door, drinking the coffee. The ship's logbook hadn't lied; the coffee did have a burned taste. He mentioned this to Pete in passing.

Then his mind switched off onto speculation as to what it might be that roamed the ship and had evidently disposed of its original crew. He had a long talk with Pete about the matter, exploring several likely possibilities, but coming back to the pretty

obvious conclusion that it must have been a life-form
common to the Runyon's World that had somehow
got on board.

"But how," Jake said, "something that large and
dangerous could get on a ship like this without being
seen or known about, I can't understand."

A sudden thought hit him. He cleaned up the
remains of his meal, cut open the door and went
back up to the control room. Sealing himself in there,
he went to check the ship's records once more.

This time, in a different record section, he found a
small list of livestock taken from the planet. This
ranged from sub-microscopic life-forms, strains of
the phosphorescent bacteria, and on up to one of the
Goopers mentioned in the log and in the report he
had read earlier. The record also told him where
these were to be found—in the ship's organic laboratory on the top level. Jake put the record away
thoughtfully.

He checked to see that the ship was properly
approaching the point for its first shift through no-
space, then took his torch and lamp, and unsealed
the control room. He went down the corridor and up
to the top level of the ship. A few doorways down
the corridor of the top level, he discovered the entrance to the ship's organic laboratory.

The door was ajar. He stepped inside without
touching it. The laboratory was a pretty large room,
three-quarters of which were given over to chemical
equipment and supplies, and one-quarter of which
was equipped with cages and containers. Jake saw at
a glance that all the cages and containers had been
broken open, except the largest of them—a cage
which might possibly have contained something the
size of an adult chimpanzee.

Almost against his will, Jake felt a slightly sickening shiver run down his spine. It occurred to him

that something had been in here with an appetite, and for the first time, he had a mental image of what might have happened to the original crew of the vessel.

He leaned over to examine the cage from which two bars had been wrenched out, in the light of his lamp which he had set against the wall just inside the door. He put his hands on two of the bars and felt them turn in his grasp. He took his hands away and stared. The bars appeared solid, but they had been twisted loose in their sockets. He twisted one again and it came neatly out in his hand, being loose at the top and broken off at the bottom. He put it back— and suddenly, without warning, there was a smashing sound; and he was plunged into total darkness.

Jake whirled, the torch which was in his hand coming up automatically. There was a sound of movement in the direction of the doorway. A strange and undefinable odor smote his nostrils. He sensed rather than saw a large body leaping at him and triggered the torch.

Its flame lashed out for a fractionary moment; then the torch was knocked from his hand. In that split second of light, he saw something hulking and vaguely manlike, but larger than any man had a right to be. Then he saw no more, because the torch was gone from his hand and automatically shut off. But a hideous howl rang through the room. There was a smashing noise from the direction of the doorway. Then the howl rose again, out in the corridor, and there was a sound of running. For a third time he heard the howl, distant half the ship's length from him, but hideous as ever. Then there was silence.

Down on hands and knees, with frantically searching fingers, Jake pawed about for the torch. He found it and pressed its trigger. By the lurid gleam of its flame he saw the light he had put against the wall lying smashed on the floor.

Jake drew in a shaky breath.

"Well, Pete," he whispered with a dry throat. "Here we are in the dark with just a cutting torch. And whatever it is isn't feeling too happy right about this moment." He got to his feet in the darkness. "I'll try to make it back to the control room," he said, "using the torch here to light me."

Cautiously, keeping the torch triggered, Jake moved out into the corridor. The flame it threw was not an effective light. It illuminated poorly and glared in his eyes at the same time. Half-blinded, and half-smothered in darkness, Jake found the ladder and fumbled his way down it to the main level. Still holding the torch, he headed back to the control room.

At that moment the first of the shifts hit him. He was conscious of the peculiar fleeting moment of nausea that marked one of the great jumps in space. It was disturbing, coming when his nerves were wire-tense, but it was also reassuring. The ship, he knew, was headed home.

He had paused when the shift hit him. Now, as he started forward again, the torch in his hand sputtered and went out. For a second, he stood paralyzed in the dark. Then the torch flamed on once more.

Instantly, he realized what was happening. The torch was nearing the end of its charge and it was the only weapon he had—and the tool room from which it had come was clear across the ship away from him.

Hastily, he shut it off. Blackness rushed in around him. Utter blackness. He strained his eyes in both directions up and down the main level corridor, but there was not the faintest glimmer of light. It came to him then that all the lights he had set up must have been found and smashed. He was alone, in the dark, with whatever was prowling the ship.

He reached out to touch the wall with his fingertips for guidance. And as he did so, he became aware for the first time of a faint glow. His eyes were adjusting to a level of illumination just barely above the level of darkness. He stood still, letting his vision continue to adjust.

Gradually there emerged the eeriness of long streaks of phosphorescence glowing on the walls of the ship. By their total shape, he was able to make out the directions and the dimensions of the corridor in both directions. His breath caught in his throat in relief.

"How do you like that?" he whispered. "Looks like Runyon's World can be useful, too."

He began to feel his way down the corridor toward the control room. He was, he estimated, about halfway there when an indescribable uneasiness caused him to hesitate. He halted. He stood stone still in the darkness, his eyes staring ahead.

Then he saw what instinct had warned him of— one of the streaks of phosphorescence down by the entrance to the control room was slowly being occluded by something large and black, thirty feet or so from him.

In sheer reflex his finger tightened on the trigger of the torch. Blue flame spurted blindingly from the torch's muzzle. And although the distance was far too great for the flame to have done any damage, the animal howl of hate and terror and pain he had heard before rang out.

Jake whirled about and ran stumblingly back the way he had come.

He paused, finally, and leaned against the wall to catch his breath. Looking back along the corridor he saw the streaks of phosphorescence clear and uneclipsed. The creature, whatever it was, must have fled in the opposite direction.

His mind racing, Jake reached out one finger and touched the streak of phosphorescence close behind him, realizing suddenly that as he had seen the monster obscuring the phosphorescence, so the monster had also seen him. A little of the shining stuff came away on his finger, which glowed ghostlike before him. A wild thought leaped and hammered in his brain.

He turned about once again with his back to the control room and began to work his way toward the clinic. He found the entrance to it and slipped inside. Easing the door closed behind him, he risked the fading power of the torch in one brief sputter of light. Immediately it was dark again, but as blackness washed in, his hand closed around the stem of the infrared lamp that had been used in treating the crewman with hives he had read about in the log. Lamp and torch in hand, he stepped back out into the corridor.

"The phosphorescence is something that works for *it*, Pete," he whispered. "let's see how it likes this!"

He switched on the lamp and began moving down the corridor. At one spot along its length he shut it off and paused to look back. What he saw then made him smile in the darkness with satisfaction.

Ten days later, a survey ship and the *Molly B.* were taken in tow just outside Earth's orbit. Aboard was found a very large baboonlike creature, somewhat burned about the upper arms or forelimbs but quite alive, although huddled in the welded-shut greenery, from which the creature had to be drugged before it could be removed. And a very much alive and self-possessed Jake.

"The thing is, Pete," explained Jake cheerfully later to Albin Rhinehart, a fat, hard-faced man who

was Director of the Investigatory Bureau, "the vege-
tarian Goopers the crew got acquainted with on the
planet were simply a pre-form, from which emerged
an occasional black sheep, possibly mutant variety,
which took to carnivorous ways and acted as a natural
control by preying on its own species. The mutants
grew much larger and normally hid out in the forest
areas. The forest areas that were lighted at night by
this fungoid which produced a marked zinc-sulphate
phosphorescence."

"But—" began Albin.

"Let me tell it my way, Pete," went on Jake,
perching on the corner of the desk and wiping his
forehead. His fingers explored his hairline for an
absent-minded second. "You don't happen to know
any good repilators, do you? . . . No, I didn't think
so. Well, to get on with it, these large, carnivorous,
mutant Goopers preyed on the vegetarians. Evidently
the crew of the ship took aboard one of the vegetar-
ian variety, not knowing he was also a mutant pre-
form. The change came about, or perhaps something
during the trip triggered it, and the Gooper grew
large and escaped. One night it started preying on
the crew in the darkness." Pete's face became grim.
"I found some of their bones, as well as some of the
bones of the lesser laboratory animals. These mutant
forms are evidently pretty intelligent."

"What makes you think that?" said Albin.

"Well," answered Jake, "judging from the reports
of smashed lights and sobbing noises, this one had been
out of his cage and back in again several times
before he ran wild. Otherwise there would have
been a report in the log to the effect that he had
broken out. Remember those two bars that looked all
right but were actually broken loose?"

"Then what did happen, do you think?" Albin
asked.

*   *   *

"I think," said Jake, "that the Gooper, following his instincts as well as his intelligence, went out first to spread phosphorescent fungus around the ship, then returned to his cage. Or he may have done it in several trips. Then one night, or at some particular time when most of the men were separated or asleep, it smashed all the lights, then hunted them down and killed them one by one. I found where one man had tried to hide in the ventilating blower, down in the greenery, and I suspect another must have been getting himself a cup of coffee when he was attacked."

"Biology reports the creature's eyes are particularly adapted to seeing under the conditions of this phosphorescence," commented Albin.

"It figures," said Jake. "It probably lived off the men it killed for a couple of weeks at least, and after that polished off the laboratory animals. But it was evidently pretty well starving by the time I came aboard, judging by all the loose skin about it."

"That fungoid phosphorescence is interesting," said Albin. "Evidently it fostered cultures in the forearm glands, which were active in the carnivorous beast, and which it distributed by rubbing the glands over surfaces it passed."

"A form of symbiosis, maybe," suggested Jake. He yawned and stretched.

"Well," said Albin, staring at him, "you seemed to have come out all right. How come the phosphorescence didn't help it get you?"

"That infra-red lamp I told you about, remember?" replied Jake, grinning.

Albin did not grin back. "I don't get it."

"Red light quenches phosphorescence. In the dark, the beast, for all its size, was more afraid of me than I was of it. It'd already had a taste of the cutting torch and it couldn't know I was about out of fuel. I herded it into the greenery and sealed it there." Jake cocked an eye at Albin. "But I'm surprised at you, not knowing that little fact about phosphorescence and red light, a man in your position. Maybe you ought to take a few night study courses, Pete."

"The name's not Pete," said Albin stiffly.

Enter A Pilgrim

In the square around the bronze statue of the
Cymbrian bull, the crowd was silent. The spring sky
over Aalborg, Denmark, was high and blue; and on
the weather-grayed red brick wall of the building
before them a man was dying upon the triple blades,
according to an alien law. The two invokers sat their
riding beasts, watching, less than two long paces
from where Shane Evert stood among the crowd of
humans on foot.

"My son," the older and bulkier of the two was
saying to the younger in the heavy Aalaag tongue,
plainly unaware that there was a human nearby who
could understand him, "as I've told you repeatedly,
no creature tames overnight. You've been warned
that when they travel in a family the male will defend his mate, the female and male defend their
young."

"But, my father," said the younger, "there was no
reason. I only struck the female aside with my power-
lance to keep her from being ridden down. It was a

321

consideration I intended not a discipline or an attack . . ."

Their words rumbled in Shane's ears and printed themselves in his mind. Like giants in human form, medieval and out of place, the two massive Aalaag loomed beside him, the clear sunlight shining on the green and silver metal of their armor and on the red, camel-like creatures that served them as riding animals. Their concern was with their conversation and the crowd of humans they supervised in this legal deathwatch. Only slightly did they pay attention to the man they had hung on the blades.

Mercifully, for himself as well as for the humans forced to witness his death, it happened that the Dane undergoing execution had been paralyzed by the Aalaag power-lance before he had been thrown upon the three sharp lengths of metal protruding from the wall twelve feet above the ground. The blades had pierced him while he was still unconscious; and he had passed immediately into shock. So that he was not now aware of his own dying; or of his wife, the woman for whom he had incurred the death penalty, who lay dead at the foot of the wall below him. Now he himself was almost dead. But while he was still alive all those in the square were required by Aalaag law to observe.

". . . Nonetheless," the alien father was replying, "the male misunderstood. And when cattle make errors, the master is responsible. You are responsible for the death of this one and his female—which had to be, to show that we are never in error, never to be attacked by those we have conquered. But the responsibility is yours."

Under the bright sun the metal on the alien pair glittered as ancient and primitive as the bronze statue of the bull or the blades projecting from the homely brick wall. But the watching humans would have learned long since not to be misled by appearances.

Tradition, and something like superstition among the religionless Aalaag, preserved the weapons and armor of a time already more than fifty thousand Earth years lost and gone in their history, on whatever world had given birth to these seven-foot conquerors of humanity. But their archaic dress and weaponry were only for show.

The real power of the two watching did not lie in their swords and power-lances; but in the little black-and-gold rods at their belts, in the jewels of the rings on their massive forefingers, and in the tiny, continually-moving orifice in the pommel of each saddle, looking eternally and restlessly left and right among the crowd.

". . . Then it is true. The fault is mine," said the Aalaag son submissively. "I have wasted good cattle."

"It is true good cattle have been wasted," answered his father, "innocent cattle who originally had no intent to challenge our law. And for that I will pay a fine, because I am your father and it is to my blame that you made an error. But you will pay me back five times over because your error goes deeper than mere waste of good cattle, alone."

"Deeper, my father?"

Shane kept his head utterly still within the concealing shadow of the hood to his pilgrim's cloak. The two could have no suspicion that one of the cattle of Lyt Ahn, Aalaag Governor Of All Earth, stood less than a lance-length from them, able to comprehend each word they spoke. But it would be wise not to attract their attention. An Aalaag father did not ordinarily reprimand his son in public, or in the hearing of any cattle not of his own household. The heavy voices rumbled on and the blood sang in Shane's ears.

"Much deeper, my son . . ."

The sight of the figure on the blades before him sickened Shane. He had tried to screen it from him with one of his own private imaginings—the image he had dreamed up of a human outlaw whom no Aalaag could catch or conquer. A human who went about the world anonymously, like Shane, in pilgrim robes; but, unlike Shane, exacting vengeance from the aliens for each wrong they did to a man, woman, or child. However, in the face of the bloody reality before Shane on the wall, fantasy had failed. Now, though, out of the corner of his right eye, he caught sight of something that momentarily blocked that reality from his mind, and sent a thrill of unreasonable triumph running through him.

Barely four meters or so, beyond and above both him and the riders on the two massive beasts, the sagging branch of an oak tree pushed its tip almost into the line of vision between Shane's eyes and the bladed man; and on the end of the branch, among the new green leaves of the year, was a small, cocoon-like shape, already broken. From it had just recently struggled the still-crumpled shape of a butterfly that did not yet know what its wings were for.

How it had managed to survive through the winter here was beyond guessing. Theoretically, the Aalaag had exterminated all insects in the towns and cities. But here it was: a butterfly of Earth being born even as a man of Earth was dying—a small life for a large. The utterly disproportionate feeling of triumph sang in Shane. Here was a life that had escaped the death sentence of the alien and would live in spite of the Aalaag—that is, if the two now watching on their great red mounts did not notice it as it waved its wings, drying them for flight.

They must not notice. Unobtrusively, lost in the crowd with his rough gray pilgrim's cloak and staff, undistinguished among the other drab humans, Shane drifted right, toward the aliens, until the branch-tip with its emerging butterfly stood squarely between him and the man on the wall.

It was superstition, magic . . . call it what you liked, it was the only help he could give the butterfly. The danger to the small life now beginning on the branch-tip should, under any cosmic justice, be insured by the larger life now ending for the man on the wall. The one should balance out the other. Shane fixed the nearer shape of the butterfly in his gaze so that it hid the further figure of the man on the blades. He bargained with fate. I will not blink, he told himself; and the butterfly will stay invisible to the Aalaag. They will see only the man . . .

Beside him, neither of the massive, metal-clad figures had noticed his moving. They were still talking.

". . . in battle," the father was saying, "each of us is equal to more than a thousand of such as these. We would be nothing if not that. But though one be superior to a thousand, it does not follow that the thousand is without force against the one. Expect nothing, therefore, and do not be disappointed. Though they are now ours, inside themselves the cattle remain what they were when we conquered them. Beasts, as yet untamed to proper love of us. Do you understand me now?"

"No, my father."

There was a burning in Shane's throat; and his eyes blurred, so that he could hardly see the butterfly, clinging tightly to its branch and yielding at last to the instinctive urge to dry its folded, damp wings at their full expanse. The wings spread, orange, brown and black—like an omen, it was that species of sub-Arctic butterfly called a Pilgrim—just as Shane himself was called a Pilgrim because of the hooded robe he wore. The day three years gone by at the University of Kansas rose in his mind. He remembered standing in the student union, among the mass of other students and faculty, listening to the broadcast that announced the Earth had been conquered, even before any of them had fully been able to grasp that

beings from a further world had landed amongst
them. He had not felt anything then except excitement, mixed perhaps with a not unpleasant appre-
hension.

"Someone's going to have to interpret for us to
those aliens," he had told his friends, cheerfully.
"Language specialists like me—we'll be busy."

But it had not been to the aliens; it had been for
the aliens, for the Aalaag themselves, that interpre-
ting had needed to be done—and he was not, Shane
told himself, the stuff of which underground resistance fighters were made. Only . . . in the last two
years . . . Almost directly over him, the voice of the
elder Aalaag rumbled on.

". . . To conquer is nothing," the older Aalaag was
saying. "Anyone with power can conquer. We rule—
which is a greater art. We rule because eventually
we change the very nature of our cattle."

"Change?" echoed the younger.

"Alter," said the older. "Over their generations we
teach them to love us. We tame them into good
kine. Beasts still, but broken to obedience. To this
end we leave them their own laws, their religions,
their customs. Only one thing we do not tolerate—
the concept of defiance against our will. And in time
they tame to this."

"But—always, my father?"

"Always, I say!" Restlessly, the father's huge riding animal shifted its weight on its hooves, crowding Shane a few inches sideways. He moved. But he
kept his eyes on the butterfly. "When we first arrive,
some fight us—and die. Later, some like this one on
the wall here rebel—and likewise die. Only we know
that it is the heart of the beast that must at last be
broken. So we teach them first the superiority of our
weapons, then of our bodies and minds; finally, that
of our law. At last, with nothing of their own left to
cling to, their beast-hearts crack; and they follow us

unthinkingly, blindly loving and trusting like new-
born pups behind their dam, no longer able to dream
of opposition to our will."

"And all is well?"

"All is well for my son, his son, and his son's son,"
said the father. "But until that good moment when
the hearts of the cattle break, each small flicker of
the flame of rebellion that erupts delays the coming
of their final and utter love for us. Inadvertently
here, you allowed that flame to flicker to life once
more."

"I was in error. In the future I will avoid such
mistakes."

"I shall expect no less," said the father. "And now,
the man is dead. Let us go on."

They set their riding beasts in motion and moved
off. Around them, the crowd of humans sighed with
the release of tension. Up on the triple blades, the
victim now hung motionless. His eyes stared, as he
hung there without twitch or sound. The butterfly's
drying wings waved slowly between the dead face
and Shane's. Without warning, the insect lifted like a
colorful shadow and fluttered away, rising into the
dazzle of the sunlight above the square until it was
lost to the sight of Shane. A feeling of victory exploded in him. Subtract one man, he thought, half-
crazily. Add, one butterfly—one small Pilgrim to
defy the Aalaag.

About him, the crowd was dispersing. The butterfly was gone. His feverish elation over its escape
cooled and he looked about the square. The Aalaag
father and son were more than halfway across it,
heading toward a further exiting street. One of the
few clouds in the sky moved across the face of the
sun, graying and dimming the light in the square.
Shane felt the coolness of a little breeze on his hands
and face. Around him now, the square was almost
empty. In a few seconds he would be alone with the

dead man and the empty cocoon that had given up the butterfly.

He looked once more at the dead man. The face was still, but the light breeze stirred some ends of long blond hair that were hanging down.

Shane shivered in the abrupt chill from the breeze and the withdrawn sun-warmth. His spirits plunged, on a sickening elevator drop into self-doubt and fear. Now that it was all over, there was a shakiness inside him, and a nausea . . . he had seen too many of the aliens' executions these last two years. He dared not go back to Aalaag Headquarters feeling as he did now.

He would have to inform Lyt Ahn of the incident which had delayed him in his courier duties; and in no way while telling it must he betray his natural feelings at what he had seen. The Aalaag expected their personal cattle to be like themselves— Spartan, unyielding, above taking notice of pain in themselves or others. Any one of the human cattle who allowed his emotions to become visible would be "sick," in Aalaag terms. It would reflect on the character of an Aalaag master—even if he was Governor Of All Earth—if he permitted his household to contain unhealthy cattle.

Shane could end up on the blades himself, for all that Lyt Ahn had always seemed to like him personally. He would have to get his feelings under control, and time for that was short. At best, he could steal perhaps half an hour more from his schedule in addition to what had already been spent watching the execution—and in those thirty minutes he must manage to pull himself together. He turned away, down a street behind him leading from the square, following the last of the dispersing crowd.

The street had been an avenue of small shops once, interspersed with an occasional larger store or business establishment. Physically, it had not changed.

The sidewalks and the street pavement were free of cracks and litter. The windows of the stores were whole, even if the display areas behind the glass were mainly empty of goods. The Aalaag did not tolerate dirt or rubble. They had wiped out with equal efficiency and impartiality the tenement areas of large cities, and the ruins of the Parthenon and Athens; but the level of living permitted to most of their human cattle was bone-bare minimal, even for those who were able to work long hours.

A block and a half from the square, Shane found and turned in at a doorway under the now-dark shape of what had once been the lighted neon sign of a bar. He entered a large gloomy room hardly changed from the past, except that the back shelf behind the bar itself was bare of the multitude of liquor bottles which it had been designed to hold. Only small amounts of distilled liquors were allowed to be made, nowadays. People drank the local wine, or beer.

Just now the place was crowded, with men for the most part. All of them silent after the episode in the square; and all of them drinking draft ale with swift, heavy gulps from the tall, thick-walled glasses they held in their hands. Shane worked his way down to the service area in the far corner where the bartender stood, loading trays with filled glasses for the single waitress to take to the tables and booths beyond the bar.

"One," he said.

A moment later, a full glass was placed in front of him. He paid, and leaned with his elbows on the bar, his head in his hands, staring into the depths of the brown liquid.

The memory of the dead man on the blades, with his hair stirring in the wind, came back to Shane. Surely, he thought, there must be some portent in the butterfly also being called a Pilgrim? He tried to put the image of the insect between himself and the

memory of the dead man, but here, away from the
blue sky and sunlight, the small shape would not
take form in his mind's eye. In desperation, Shane
reached again for his private mental comforter—the
fantasy of the man in a hooded robe who could defy
all Aalaag and pay them back for what they had
done. Almost he managed to evoke it. But the Avenger
image would not hold in his head. It kept being
pushed aside by the memory of the man on the
blades. . . .

"Undskylde!" said a voice in his ear. "Herre . . .
Herre!"

For a fraction of a second he heard the words only
as foreign noises. In the emotion of the moment, he
had slipped into thinking in English. Then the sounds
translated. He looked up, into the face of the bartender. Beyond, the bar was already half empty,
once more. Few people nowadays could spare more
than a few minutes from the constant work required
to keep themselves from going hungry—or, worse
yet, keep themselves from being forced out of their
jobs and into becoming legally exterminable vagabonds.

"Excuse me," said the bartender again; and this
time Shane's mind was back in Denmark with the
language. "Sir. But you're not drinking."

It was true. Before Shane the glass was still full.
Beyond it, the bartender's face was thin and curious,
watching him with the amoral curiosity of a ferret.

"I . . ." Shane checked himself. Almost he had
started explaining who he was—which would not be
safe. Few ordinary humans loved those of their own
kind who had become servants in some Aalaag
household.

"Disturbed by what you saw in the square, sir? It's
understandable," said the bartender. His green eyes
narrowed. He leaned closer and whispered. "Per-

haps something stronger than beer? How long since you've had some schnapps?"

The sense of danger snapped awake in Shane's mind. Aalborg had once been famous for its aquavit, but that was before the Aalaag came. The bartender must have spotted him as a stranger—someone possibly with money. Then suddenly he realized he did not care what the bartender had spotted, or where he had gotten a distilled liquor. It was what Shane needed right now—something explosive to counter the violence he had just witnessed.

"It'll cost you ten," murmured the bartender.

Ten monetary units was a day's wage for a skilled carpenter—though only a small fraction of Shane's pay for the same hours. The Aalaag rewarded their household cattle well. Too well, in the minds of most other humans. That was one of the reasons Shane moved around the world on his master's errands wearing the cheap and unremarkable robe of a Pilgrim.

"Yes," he said. He reached into the pouch at the cord about his waist and brought forth his money clip. The bartender drew in his breath with a little hiss.

"Sir," he said, "you don't want to flash a roll, even a roll like that, in here nowadays."

"Thanks. I . . ." Shane lowered the money clip below bartop level as he peeled off a bill. "Have one with me."

"Why, yes, sir," said the bartender. His eyes glinted, like the metal of the Cymbrian bull in the sunlight. "Since you can afford it . . ."

His thin hand reached across and swallowed the bill Shane offered him. He ducked below the counter level and came up holding two of the tall glasses, each roughly one-fifth full with a colorless liquid. Holding glasses between his body and Shane's so that they were shielded from the view of others in the bar, he passed one to Shane.

"Happier days," he said, tilted up his glass to empty it at a swallow. Shane imitated him; and the harsh oiliness of the liquor flamed in his throat, taking his breath away. As he had suspected, it was a raw, illegally distilled, high-proof liquid with nothing in common with the earlier aquavit but the name it shared. Even after he had downed it, it continued to cling to and sear the lining of his throat, like sooty fire.

Shane reached automatically for his untouched glass of beer to lave the internal burning. The bartender had already taken back their two liquor glasses and moved away down the bar to serve another customer. Shane swallowed gratefully. The thick-bodied ale was gentle as water after the rough-edged moonshine. A warmth began slowly to spread through his body. The hard corners of his mind rounded; and on the heels of that soothing, without effort this time, came his comforting, familiar daydream of the Avenger. The Avenger, he told himself, had been there unnoticed in the square during the executions, and by now he was lying in wait in a spot from which he could ambush the Aalaag father and son, and still escape before police could be called. A small black and golden rod, stolen from an Aalaag arsenal, was in his hand as he stood to one side of an open window, looking down a street up which two figures in green and silver armor were riding toward him . . .

"Another, sir?"

It was the bartender back again. Startled, Shane glanced at his ale glass and saw that it, too, was now empty. But another shot of that liquid dynamite? Or even another glass of the ale? He could risk neither. Just as in facing Lyt Ahn an hour or so from now he must be sure not to show any sign of emotion while reporting what he had been forced to witness in the square, so neither must he show the slightest sign of any drunkenness or dissipation. These, too, were

weaknesses not permitted servants of the alien, as
the alien did not permit them in himself.

"No," he said, "I've got to go."

"One drink did it for you?" the bartender inclined
his head. "You're lucky, sir. Some of us don't forget
that easily."

The touch of a sneer in the bitterness of the other's voice flicked at Shane's already overtight nerves.
A sudden sour fury boiled up in him. What did this
man know of what it was like to live with the Aalaag,
to be treated always with the indifferent affection
that was below contempt—the same sort of affection
a human might give a clever pet animal—and all the
while to witness scenes like those in the square, not
once or twice a year but weekly, perhaps daily?

"Listen—" he snapped; and checked himself. Almost, once more, he had nearly given away what he
was and what he did.

"Yes, sir?" said the bartender, after a moment of
watching him. "I'm listening."

Shane thought he read suspicion in the other's
voice. That reading might only be the echo of his
own inner upset, but he could not take a chance.

"Listen," he said again, dropping his voice, "why
do you think I wear this outfit?"

He indicated his Pilgrim robe.

"You took a vow." The bartender's voice was dry
now, remote.

"No. You don't understand . . ." The unaccustomed warmth of the drink in him triggered an inspiration. The image of the butterfly slid into—and
blended with—his image of the Avenger. "You think
it was just a bad accident, out there in the square
just now? Well, it wasn't. Not just accidental, I
mean—I shouldn't say anything."

"Not an accident?" The bartender frowned; but
when he spoke again, his voice, like Shane's was
lowered to a more cautious note.

"Of course, the man ending on the blades—it wasn't planned to finish that way," muttered Shane, leaning toward him. "The Pilgrim—" Shane broke off. "You don't know about the Pilgrim?"

"The Pilgrim? What Pilgrim?" The bartender's face came close. Now they were both almost whispering.

"If you don't know I shouldn't say—"

"You've said quite a lot already—"

Shane reached out and touched his six-foot staff of polished oak, leaning against the bar beside him.

"This is one of the symbols of the Pilgrim," he said. "There're others. You'll see his mark one of these days and you'll know that attack on the Aalaag in the square didn't just happen by accident. That's all I can tell you."

It was a good note to leave on. Shane picked up the staff, turned quickly and went out. It was not until the door to the bar closed behind him that he relaxed. For a moment he stood breathing the cooler air of the street, letting his head clear. His hands, he saw, were trembling.

As his head cleared, sanity returned. A cold dampness began to make itself felt on his forehead in the outside air. What had gotten into him? Risking everything just to show off to some unknown bartender? Fairy tales like the one he had just hinted at could find their way back to Aalaag ears—specifically to the ears of Lyt Ahn. If the aliens suspected he knew something about a human resistance movement, they would want to know a great deal more from him; in which case death on the triple blades might turn out to be something he would long for, not dread.

And yet, there had been a great feeling during the few seconds he had shared his fantasy with the bartender, almost as if it were something real. Almost as great a feeling as the triumph he had felt on seeing the butterfly survive. For a couple of moments he

had come alive, almost, as part of a world holding a
Pilgrim-Avenger who could defy the Aalaag. A Pilgrim who left his mark at the scene of each Aalaag
crime as a promise of retribution to come. The Pilgrim, who in the end would rouse the world to over-
throw its tyrant, alien murderers.

He turned about and began to walk hurriedly toward
the square again, and to the street beyond it that
would take him to the airport where the Aalaag
courier ship would pick him up. There was an empty
feeling in his stomach at the prospect of facing Lyt
Ahn, but at the same time his mind was seething. If
only he had been born with a more athletic body and
the insensitivity to danger that made a real resistance
fighter. The Aalaag thought they had exterminated
all cells of human resistance two years since. The
Pilgrim could be real. His role was a role any man
really knowledgeable about the aliens could play—if
he had absolutely no fear, no imagination to make
him dream nights of what the Aalaag would do to
him when, as they eventually must, they caught and
unmasked him. Unhappily, Shane was not such a
man. Even now he woke sweating from nightmares
in which the Aalaag had caught him in some small
sin, and he was about to be punished. Some men
and women, Shane among them, had a horror of
deliberately inflicted pain. . . . He shuddered, grimly,
fear and fury making an acid mix in his belly that
shut out awareness of his surroundings.

Almost, this cauldron of inner feelings brewed an
indifference to things around him that cost him his
life. That and the fact that he had, on leaving the
bar, instinctively pulled the hood of his robe up over
his head to hide his features; particularly from anyone who might later identify him as having been in a
place where a bartender had been told about someone called "the Pilgrim." He woke from his thoughts

only at the faint rasp of dirt-stiff rags scuffing on cement pavement behind him.

He checked and turned quickly. Not two meters behind, a man carrying a wooden knife and a wooden club studded with glass chips, his thin body wound thick with rags for armor, was creeping up on him.

Shane turned again, to run. But now, in the suddenly tomblike silence and emptiness of the street, two more such men, armed with clubs and stones, were coming out from between buildings on either side to block his way. He was caught between the one behind and the two ahead.

His mind was suddenly icy and brilliant. He had moved in one jump through a flash of fear into something beyond fright, into a feeling tight as a strung wire, like the reaction on nerves of a massive dose of stimulant. Automatically, the last two years of training took over. He flipped back his hood so that it could not block his peripheral vision, and grasped his staff with both hands a foot and a half apart in its middle, holding it up at the slant before him and turning so as to try to keep them all in sight at once.

The three paused.

Clearly, they were feeling they had made a mistake. Seeing him with the hood over his head, and his head down, they must have taken him for a so-called praying pilgrim; one of those who bore staff and cloak as a token of non-violent acceptance of the sinful state of the world which had brought all people under the alien yoke. They hesitated.

"All right, Pilgrim," said a tall man with reddish hair, one of the two who had come out in front of him, "throw us your pouch and you can go."

For a second, irony was like a bright metallic taste in Shane's mouth. The pouch at the cord around a pilgrim's waist contained most of what worldly goods he might own; but the three surrounding him now were "vagabonds"—Nonservs—individuals who either could not or would not hold the job assigned them by the aliens. Under the Aalaag rule, such outcasts had nothing to lose. Faced by three like this, almost any pilgrim, praying or not, would have given up his pouch. But Shane could not. In his pouch, besides his own possessions, were official papers of the Aalaag government that he was carrying to Lyt Ahn; and Lyt Ahn, warrior from birth and by tradition, would neither understand nor show mercy to a servant who failed to defend property he carried. Better the clubs and stones Shane faced now than the disappointment of Lyt Ahn.

"Come and get it," he said.

His voice sounded strange in his own ears. The staff he held seemed slight as a bamboo pole in his grasp. Now the vagabonds were moving in on him. It was necessary to break out of the ring they were forming around him and get his back to something so that he could face them all at the same time. . . There was a store front to his left just beyond the short, gray-haired vagabond moving in on him from that direction.

Shane feinted at the tall, reddish-haired man to his right, then leaped left. The short-bodied vagabond struck at him with a club as Shane came close, but the staff in Shane's hand brushed it aside and the staff's lower end slammed home, low down on the body of the vagabond. He went down without a sound and lay huddled up. Shane hurdled him, reached the storefront and turned about to face the other two.

As he turned, he saw something in the air and ducked automatically. A rock rang against the masonry at the edge of the glass store window, and glanced off. Shane took a step sideways to put the glass behind him on both sides.

The remaining two were by the curb, now, facing him, still spread out enough so that they blocked his

escape. The reddish-haired man was scowling a little, tossing another rock in his hand. But the expanse
of breakable glass behind Shane deterred him. A
dead or battered human was nothing, but broken
store windows meant an immediate automatic alarm
to the Aalaag police; and the Aalaag were not merciful in their elimination of Nonservs.

"Last chance," said the reddish-haired man. "Give
us the pouch—"

As he spoke, he and his companion launched a
simultaneous rush at Shane. Shane leaped to his left
to take the man on that side first, and get out away
from the window far enough to swing his stave freely.
He brought its top end down in an overhand blow
that parried the club-blow of the vagabond and struck
the man himself to the ground, where he sat clutching at an arm smashed between elbow and shoulder.

Shane pivoted to face the reddish-haired man, who
was now on tiptoes, stretched up with his own heavy
club swung back in both hands over his head for a
crushing down-blow.

Reflexively, Shane whirled up the bottom end of
his staff; and the tough, fire-hardened tip, traveling
at eye-blurring speed, smashed into the angle where
the other man's lower jaw and neck met.

The vagabond tumbled; and lay still in the street,
his head unnaturally sideways on his neck.

Shane whirled around, panting, staff ready. But
the man whose arm he had smashed was already
running off down the street in the direction from
which Shane had just come. The other two were still
down and showed no intention of getting up.

The street was still.

Shane stood, snorting in great gasps of air, leaning
on his staff. It was incredible. He had faced three
armed men—armed at least in the same sense that
he, himself was armed—and he had defeated them
all. He looked at the fallen bodies and could hardly

believe it. All his practice with the quarterstaff . . . it had been for defense; and he had hoped never to have to use it against even one opponent. Now, here had been three . . . and he had won.

He felt strangely warm, large and sure. Perhaps, it came to him suddenly, this was the way the Aalaag felt. If so, there could be worse feelings. It was something lung-filling and spine-straightening to know yourself a fighter and a conqueror. Perhaps it was just this feeling he had needed to have, to understand the Aalaag—he had needed to conquer, powerfully, against great odds as they did. . . .

He felt close to rejecting all the bitterness and hate that had been building in him the past two years. Perhaps might actually could make right. He went forward to examine the men he had downed.

They were both dead. Shane stood looking down at them. They had appeared thin enough, bundled in their rags, but it was not until he stood directly over them that he saw how bony and narrow they actually were. They were like claw-handed skeletons.

He stood, gazing down at the last one he had killed; and slowly the fresh warmth and pride within him began to leak out. He saw the stubbled sunken cheeks, the stringy neck, and the sharp angle of the jawbone jutting through the skin of the dead face against the concrete. These features jumped at his mind. The man must have been starving—literally starving. He looked at the other dead man and thought of the one who had run away. All of them must have been starving, for some days now.

With a rush, his sense of victory went out of him; and the sickening bile of bitterness rose once more in his throat. Here, he had been dreaming of himself as a warrior. A great hero—the slayer of two armed enemies. Only the weapons carried by those enemies had been sticks and stones, and the enemies themselves were half-dead men with barely the strength to use what they carried. Not Aalaag, not the powerfully-armed world conquerors challenged by his imaginary Pilgrim, but humans like himself reduced to near-animals by those who thought of these and Shane, in common, as "cattle."

The sickness flooded all through Shane. Something like a ticking time bomb in him exploded. He turned and ran for the square.

When he got there, it was still deserted. Breathing deeply, he slowed to a walk and went across it, toward the now-still body on the triple blades, and the other body at the foot of the wall. The fury was gone out of him now, and also the sickness. He felt empty, empty of everything—even of fear. It was a strange sensation to have fear missing—to have it all over with; all the sweats and nightmares of two years, all the trembling on the brink of the precipice of action.

He could not say exactly, even now, how he had finally come to step off that precipice at last. But it did not matter. Just as he knew that the fear was not gone for good. It would return. But that did not matter, either. Nothing mattered, even the end he must almost certainly come to now. The only thing that was important was that he had finally begun to act, to do something about a world he could no longer endure as it was.

Quite calmly he walked up to the wall below the blades holding the dead man. He glanced around to see if he was observed; but there was no sign of anyone either in the square or watching from the windows that overlooked it.

He reached into his pocket for the one piece of metal he was allowed to carry. It was the key to his personal living quarters in Lyt Ahn's residence, Denver-"warded" as all such keys had to be, so that they would not set off an alarm by disturbing the field which the Aalaag had set up over every city and

hamlet, to warn of unauthorized metal in the possessions of humans. With the tip of the key, Shane
scratched a rough figure on the wall below the body;
the Pilgrim and his staff.

The hard tip of the metal key bit easily through
the weathered surface of the brick to the original
light red color underneath. Shane turned away, putting the key back into his pouch. The shadows of late
afternoon had already begun to fall from the buildings to hide what he had done. And the bodies
would not be removed until sunrise—this by Aalaag
law. By the time the figure scratched on the brick
was first seen by one of the aliens he would be back
among the "cattle" of Lyt Ahn's household, indistinguishable among them.

Indistinguishable, but different, from now on—in
a way the Aalaag had yet to discover. He turned and
walked swiftly away down the street that would bring
him to the alien courier ship that was waiting for
him. The colorful flicker of a butterfly's wings—or
perhaps it was just the glint of a reflection off some
high window that seemed momentarily to wink with
color—caught the edge of his vision. Perhaps, the
thought came suddenly and warmly, it actually was
the butterfly he had seen emerge from its cocoon in
the square. It was good to feel that it might be the
same, small, free creature.

"Enter a Pilgrim," he whispered to it triumphantly.
"Fly, little brother. Fly!"

Armageddon

Yes, they are only deer.
Nervous instincts, fitted with hooves and horns,
That foolishly stamp among these Christian pines
Affixed like seals to the legal foolscap of winter;
And, illiterately facing the line of the snowplowed asphalt
Scrawled by a book-learned hand among these hills,
Cross to the redcapped men.

JOHN DALMAS

John Dalmas has just about done it all—parachute infantryman, army medic, stevedore, merchant seaman, log-
ger, smokejumper, administrative forester, farm worker,
creamery worker, technical writer, free-lance editor—and
his experience is reflected in his writing. His marvelous
sense of nature and wilderness combined with his high-
tech world view involves the reader with his very real
characters. For lovers of fast-paced action-adventures!

THE REGIMENT
The planet Kettle is so poor that it has only one re-
source: its fighting men. Each year three regiments are
sent forth into the galaxy. And once a regiment is
constituted, it never recruits again; as casualties mount
the regiment becomes a battalion . . . a company . . . a
platoon . . . a squad . . . and then there are none. But
after the last man of *this* regiment has flung himself into
battle, the Federation of Worlds will never be the same.

THE GENERAL'S PRESIDENT
The stock market crash of 1994 made the black Mon-
day of 1929 look like a minor market adjustment . . .
the rioters of the '90s made the Wobblies of the '30s
look like country-club Republicans . . . Soon the fabric
of society will be torn beyond repair. The Vice President resigns under a cloud of scandal— and when the
military hints that they may let the lynch mobs through
anyway, the President resigns as well. So the Generals
get to pick a President. But the man they choose turns
out to be more of a leader than they bargained for . . .

FANGLITH
Fanglith was a near-mythical world to which criminals and
misfits had been exiled long ago. The planet becomes all
too real to Larn and Deneen when they track their parents
there, and find themselves in the middle of the Age of
Chivalry on a world that will one day be known as Earth.

RETURN TO FANGLITH

The oppressive Empire of Human Worlds, temporarily foiled in *Fanglith*, has struck back and resubjugated its colony planets. Larn and Deneen must again flee their home. Their final object is to reach a rebel base—but first stop is Fanglith, the Empire's name for medieval Earth.

THE REALITY MATRIX

Is the existence we call life on Earth for real, or is it a game? Might Earth be an artificial construct designed by a group of higher beings—a group of which we are all members, and of which we are unaware, until death? Forget the crackpot theories, the psychics, the religions of the world—*everything* is an illusion, everything, that is, except the Reality Matrix! But self-appointed "Lords of Chaos" have placed a "chaos generator" in the matrix, and it is slowly destroying our world.

PLAYMASTERS (with Rod Martin)

The aliens want to use Earth as a playing field for their hobby and passion: war. But they are prohibited from using any technology not developed on the planet, and 20th-century armaments are too primitive for good sport. As a means of accelerating Earth to an appropriately sporting level, Cha, a galactic con artist, flimflams the Air Force Chief of Staff into founding a think-tank for the development of 22nd-century weapons.